YANKEE
AIR PIRATES

OTHER BOOKS BY DEEDS PUBLISHING

War Stories - Utah Beach to Pleiku

What Now, Lieutenant?

Operation Iraqi Freedom I: A Year in the Sunni Triangle

Wolfhound Reflections

My Son is Alive...

You Don't Know Jack... or Jerry

Broomsticks to Battlefields

The Decision

All Gave Some, Some Gave All

Unchained Eagle

Deeds Publishing Company
Marietta, GA
www.deedspublishing.com

YANKEE
AIR PIRATES

A NOVEL BY

C.K. McCUSKER

IN COLLABORATION WITH

COLONEL ROBERT G. CERTAIN, USAF, RET.

Deeds Publishing

www.deedspublishing.com

Yankee Air Pirates is a work of fiction, based in part on some events that actually occurred. However, with the four exceptions noted in the prologue, all individual characters in the novel are purely fictional and have no relation to any real persons either living or dead. That said, about 80% of the events described in Pirates actually happened.

Cover Design by Grace McCusker and Mark Babcock

Printed in the United States of America
Published by Deeds Publishing, Marietta, GA

First Edition, July 2010

Books are available in quantity for promotional or premium use. For information write Deeds Publishing, PO Box 682212, Marietta, GA 30068 or www.deedspublishing.com

ISBN 978-0-9826180-5-9

DEDICATED TO

My beloved wife of forty years, Priscilla, our three children, and my entire family who have brought love and great joy into my life.

And to

My comrades that gave their lives in service to our Nation. May God bless them and bring comfort to the families they left behind.

TABLE OF CONTENTS

FOREWORD

BY COLONEL ROBERT G. CERTAIN, USAF, RET.

In the winter of 1972, President Nixon ordered Operation Linebacker II, the most massive aerial bombing campaign since the end of World War II. In this successful effort to end the Vietnam War, B-52s were sent from Thailand and from the US island territory of Guam to attack Hanoi and Haiphong, North Vietnam, cities protected by more surface-to-air missiles than any other metropolitan complex outside of Moscow, Russia. Between December 18th and 29th, in over 1,000 sorties, the B-52s dropped nearly 20,000,000 pounds of bombs, creating enough destruction and noise to convince the communist government of North Vietnam to sue for peace.

Yankee Air Pirates tells the story of that campaign from the eyes of the 20-something-year-old men who flew the massive Stratofortress into the jaws of death and mostly lived to tell about it. In the eleven nights of bombing, fifteen of the huge planes were shot down - ten over the city of Hanoi, five others making it to safety before the crews ejected and were rescued. Of the sixty-one crewmembers that went down over Hanoi, thirty-two were captured and later repatriated, the other made the ultimate sacrifice. The hundreds of other men who flew through the SAM defenses returned to their bases for crew rest and regeneration, before facing it all over again.

Who were these crewdogs (as B-52 crew members referred to themselves)? Were they heroes? Were they serious men? Were they wise beyond their years? Were they rowdy, undisciplined, hard-drinking misfits? Yes, they were all of these, and more. Some were less than three years out of college and still carried the youthful exuberance and reckless abandon they had known in their fraternity houses. They were also patriots when patriotism was a bad word in American society. Most of all, they were eager to do everything they could to end the war and free the prisoners so everyone could go home to their wives, families, and friends.

Yankee Air Pirates will give you insight into how American warriors face the dangers and terror of combat and how they cope with their fears when they are off duty. As with other wars, these young aviators were professional, skilled, and very good at what they did. As with other wars, when they weren't fighting the enemy, they were relieving their tensions and anxieties in the best way they knew so they could return to the fight the next night. You will be left laughing, crying, and scratching your head as you read this book and step into the very souls of the air crews of the Strategic Air Command in the early 1970s.

Yankee Air Pirates will introduce you to colorful characters: Spike, the best bombardier in SAC (in his own mind, along with many of his peers); Bulldog, Spike's navigator, close friend, and by his own design, an ongoing personal irritant to Spike. D-Kid, a 24-year-old navigator who became the first BUFF crewmember to be shot down and captured; and a host of others who flew hard, played hard, and finally brought the war to an end.

Like the collection of doctors and support personnel in M*A*S*H*, the aircrews and support personnel based in the middle of the Pacific could be downright outrageous in their behavior and in their conversation – until their duties demanded their best. Then they rose to the occasion and more. There was an inner circle of crewdogs comprised of the best aviators and the biggest hellraisers. These young men would take risks that no one else would – both in combat and off-duty. They were the real Yankee Air Pirates. In the pages of Yankee Air Pirates you will move from the fraternity-house like atmosphere of off-duty life on Guam to the tension-filled flights over enemy territory to the terrors of life as a POW in Hanoi to the joy of survival, repatriation, and homecoming. In these pages you will get a sense of how American fighting men and women put their lives on the line for this nation and how they cope with what happens to them in combat by relieving their fears when the battle is done.

After you have laughed at their antics, cried over their deaths and imprisonments, and rejoiced over their victories and homecomings, you will realize that we have always entrusted the defense of this nation to very young people. For over two centuries, those 20-something men and women have not only done their best under the most adverse circumstances, they have also defended this nation against all enemies, foreign and domestic, just as they promised to do. You will definitely come to a greater appreciation of our new heroes in the global war on terror. They seek out and destroy terrorists and the enemies of freedom no matter where they try to hide, and like their comrades in previous wars, they remain a mixture of youth, patriotism, and wisdom.

Whatever you think of any of the wars this nation has fought, Yankee Air Pirates will make you proud to know the men and women who have fought those wars for the rest of us. You may even come to see the remarkable potential for leadership these older but wiser veterans bring home to your own family, place of worship, or workplace.

ACKNOWLEDGEMENTS

The most important acknowledgement must go to my good friend and collaborator on this work, Colonel Robert Certain. I had been working on Pirates for over two years, off and on, when I was introduced to Robert. Our collaboration began after we figured out our incredibly unique and coincidental backgrounds, and the work took off. With his daily assistance and encouragement, I wrote almost every night and on weekends. I finished the first draft of Pirates in three months, inserting a novelized version of Robert's true-life experience where I had earlier placed a composite character.

My special thanks also to Captain Paul Danner, USN, a great friend of over 20 years, who inspired me to finally put this work in writing. Paul was an F-14 (the "Top Gun" bird) aviator right out of flight school, which is an extraordinary accomplishment. You don't get to be the top fighter in the Navy right out of flight training unless you are a great "stick" (pilot). Paul remained in the Naval Reserves and rose to the rank of Captain, which included a combat tour in Iraq in 2005 as a Marine Colonel.

While Pirates was in editing, I found the real Spike portrayed in this work, almost 35 years after we flew our last mission together. He is still the Spike you will get to know and love in the pages that follow, and you will get more detail on the real Spike later in this work.

Finally, the task of finding the right publisher ensued. My original choice as publisher did not work out for many reasons, primarily because the principal was seriously ill and could not continue. Bob Certain's "Big Boss" (Bob is an Episcopal priest so you know who that is) intervened yet again and Bob introduced me to Bob Babcock and his family team: Jan Babcock (wife), and Mark Babcock (son), at Deeds Publishing in Atlanta. They are a great team and very expert at what they do. They are also absolutely delightful people to work with.

Bob and his team put the novel on a "fast track" and had it fully edited and ready for publication in less than ninety days, which I consider a remarkable accomplishment knowing what they started with.

"HE DECIDED TO LIVE FOREVER OR DIE IN THE ATTEMPT, AND HIS ONLY MISSION EACH TIME HE WENT UP WAS TO COME DOWN ALIVE."

Captain Yossarian in Joe Heller's Catch-22, 1942

"HE COMPLETELY AGREED WITH HIS IDOL YOSSARIAN AND VOWED TO REMAIN NOT DEAD AS LONG AS POSSIBLE."

Captain R.J. Graham in Yankee Air Pirates, 1972

CREWDOG GLOSSARY OF TERMS

AC   Aircraft Commander, Pilot

AIR MEDAL (Combat)   Medal for heroism in air combat

AIR PIRATES   The enemy's derogatory term for us

AMF   Adios, motherfucker

APU   Auxiliary Power Unit: provides power for pre-flight before engine start

ARC LIGHT   B-52 operations in South East Asia

ARTICLE 15   A written reprimand that goes into your personnel record. Can ruin a career.

ATAs   Airfields That Aren't: Aircraft carriers

BAHT BUS   A highly decorated Toyota pick-up truck used for public transportation in Thailand

BASE OPS (OPS)   The heart of the air base, mission briefings, de-briefs

BBs   Black Boxes, analog computers inside a B-52

BAI-LAO-CHING-CHING   Hurry-hurry-go like fucking wind (Thai slang)

BINGO   Out of fuel, nearly out of fuel

BRAKE RELEASE   The actual beginning of take-off

BROWN BAR   Second Lieutenant- rank is denoted by a gold (brown) bar

BX   Base exchange, the on base store (non-food)

CAT	Clear Air Turbulence, or; a catapult that launches aircraft off of an aircraft carrier
CHAFF	Aluminum foil ejected from an aircraft to confuse attacking missiles
CHEESE RUN	Mission with some risk, i.e. milk turned "hard"
CHUP	Sir in Thai, pronounced "cup"
CINC PACAF	Commander-in Chief, Pacific Air Forces
CINC SAC	Commander-in Chief, Strategic Air Command
CLEAN	1. The aircraft is fully configured for flight after take-off (gear and flaps up); or, 2. After bomb release, the bomb bay/racks are empty. (see "Hangers'")
COA	Confirmed Operating Area. The active SAM coverage. The bombers are in range.
COMMISSARY	The on base supermarket
CONUS	Continental United States
DEAD	The best derogatory term for the enemy
DFC	Distinguished Flying Cross, the third highest award for heroism in air combat
DOWN AND LOCKED	Refers to the landing gear being in position to land. The gear could be down, but if not locked it could collapse on landing.
ECM	Electronic counter measures, designed to jam enemy radar, missile uplink
EM	Enlisted men. Airman through Chief Master Sergeant
EWS	Early warning station, an outpost to detect an enemy attack, usually remote and cold

FAC	Forward Air Controller, controls mission with radar on the ground, or airborne in aircraft
FAST BURNERS	Fighter aircraft, no more than two engines, can break the speed of sound
FIGJAM	Fuck I'm Good, Just Ask Me
FIREBALLED	A direct hit by an enemy missile resulting in an immediate explosion of the aircraft
FOB	Fuel On Board the aircraft
Gs	The weight of gravity, i.e. 3Gs = three times the weight of gravity
GAS BOTTLE	A Tanker; "Tank," refuels other aircraft in the air, a converted 707
GOB	Gas onboard the aircraft
GOOK	common derogatory term for the enemy
GOT	Gulf of Tonkin
HAIRBALL MISSION	Extremely dangerous mission. Very high threat level.
HANGER	An unreleased bomb that should have released. Can be very dangerous, since it might go off while landing.
IC	Intercom. Internal radio on a B-52
IR	Heat seeking missiles
JARS	U.S. Marines
KAMA	A Kamikaze, a Japanese suicide plane. The plane would intentionally crash into its target
LA-LA-LAND	Laos

LINEBACKER II	B-52 operations in South East Asia from 18 Dec to 29 Dec 72
MAC	Military Airlift Command, cargo planes, trash haulers
MESS DRESS	Formal tuxedo-like military uniform
MILK RUN	Safe mission, no threat coverage
MOH	Medal of Honor, the highest award for heroism in combat
NCO	Non-commissioned officer, Sergeant through Chief Master Sergeant
NKP	Nakom Phnom Royal Thai Airbase in northern Thailand
NVAF	North Vietnamese Air Force
PAF	Probably A Faggot
PCS	Permanent Change of Station, move to a new base
PFB	Post flight briefing
PORT	Left
PTOB	Pre-Takeoff Briefing
PUNCH	Eject from an aircraft
RD	Rapid Decompression, an aircraft loses pressurization at altitude
RECON	Reconnaissance
REMF	Pronounced "Rem-F," rear echelon motherfuckers
REVETMENT	Parking place for aircraft surrounded by large reinforced walls to protect against attack

RTB	Return to (air) Base
S and L	Straight and level flight
SAC	Strategic Air Command
SAM	Surface To Air Missile
SAR	Search and Rescue
SAWADEE	Goodbye, See ya later, in Thai
SHITBURNERS	Surface to ground missiles
SKY KING	Code name for Headquarters of the Strategic Air Command
SLAM THE SLOPES	1.Bomb the gooks; or, 2. Bomb a ski resort
SLOPES	Another derogatory term for the enemy
SO CHI	South China Sea
SOL	Shit Out of Luck
STARBOARD	Right
TAC	Tactical Air Command
TAS	True Air Speed: speed through the air
TDY	Temporary Duty
TF-BUNDY	Totally Fucked, But Not Dead Yet
TO	Take-Off
TOG	The Other Guy
TOT	Time Over Target, Bomb release
TOUCH	Touchdown. The wheels actually contact the runway on landing from the mission. The "Touch" time is the official end of the mission.

TRIPLE "A"	Anti-Aircraft fire
U-T	U-Tapao Royal Air Base, 200 miles SE of Bangkok
VOQ	Visiting Officers Quarters, an on base hotel
WHEELS IN THE WELL	Another term for take-off. The landing gear is brought up inside the fuselage.
WHITE BAR	First lieutenant-rank is denoted by a silver (white) bar
WHUP-WHUP	A Helicopter. Name derived from the sound of the blades in flight
WILCO	Understand and will comply with request
"Z"	De-militarized Zone, divides North and South Vietnam
ZIPS	Yet another derogatory term for the enemy

CHAPTER I:
A DAY AT THE BEACH, ALMOST

U-TAPAO ROYAL AIR NAVAL BASE, THAILAND
APRIL 1968

Major Spike Wilson, USAF, got off the crew bus that had just parked in front of the B-52 that he would fly tonight. He was about 5' 10" with slick black hair and a pencil thin mustache just above his lip. He had dark, beady eyes that were very close together (and seemed to stare right through you when he wanted them to) and a unique smile that was as thin as his mustache... most of the time. It was referred to as the "Spike smile," and its display could be interpreted many ways. He was in a rare foul mood.

The mood was a result of the night's target. The mission plan for tonight meant that they would fly north, which meant surface-to-air missiles. The missiles were designed by the Russians to do one thing: *shoot down B-52s.* He was not pleased with the SAMs and with the other side of the bomb team, his navigator, because both could get you killed.

Spike was an expert at his craft and had little patience with those that weren't experts at theirs. He was a "Mustang" meaning that he had been commissioned as an officer and had become a "rated" officer after successfully completing flight training and being awarded the coveted "wings" without a college degree. Getting commissioned and becoming an aviator *without* a college degree was almost impossible in the early 1960's, but Spike had always overcome impossibilities through sheer determination and unknown skills that always seemed to work.

With his crewdog buddies (other B-52 aviators), he was very closed about his personal life prior to the honor of flying for the United States Air Force.

The B-52 was the largest bomber ever built. The Russians had a larger bomber, the code name was the M4 "Bison," but it had a slight fault. It didn't fly. If it did, it would crash. So Spike disqualified it as competition. He wondered why USAF's Tactical Air Command kept building fighter interceptors to defend our shores against attack from Russian bombers that could only float over. Shit, the Navy could take care of those.

In reality, he knew why they kept building fighters. Flying those things was second only to sex... plus they got *paid* to do it. The bastards. He was rated navigator/bombardier and not pilot for only two reasons. His eyesight was not 20/20, and he was too smart. During both WWII and Korea, the smartest guys (as determined by entrance exams) were always sent to navigator training. Spike's thoughts were repetitive on the subject…

But if they got to fly fastburners (fighters) and he flew bombers, were they really that dumb? Yeah… he could fly fighters as well, but the B-52 was just fucking awesome looking. It scared people that saw it parked on the ramp, let alone flying. It was the ultimate flying intimidator. Besides, the B-52 was a navigator's aircraft. The pilot's job was to drive them to work. The offensive team (two navigators) blew the crap out of the target and got a ride home. Their 'chauffeurs' were generally nice guys and did a good job of avoiding potholes (SAMs) when necessary… like tonight.

The SAM thought brought Spike back. He turned toward his navigator, his eyes penetrating, with a hint of a snarl: "Nav, so help me… if you screw up the timing and checklists on this strike, I will personally kick your ass either back here or on the ground up North just before the gooks shoot us. The rest of the crews in this three ship rely on us as lead. They'll beat the shit out of you, too."

Lt. Terry Litmon was Spike's Nav. His call sign was "Lemon" because he was one. Most navigators assigned to B-52s were smart, dedicated, and good at their craft. Lemon was the exception. No one could understand how Lemon had made it through flight training, let alone gotten a B-52 assignment.

"I am prepared today, sir. I assure you that everything will go as planned."

"That's what I'm afraid of. I'm not sure we ever use the same plan."

Spike already knew that he would have to do both the Nav's job and his own tonight. Spike Wilson is a B-52 D "Radar Navigator," which was the new politically sensitive term for a bombardier. Spike, however, would never use or accept the term "Radar Navigator." Radar Navigators were pimps. He was a bombardier. He was known throughout SAC as the "best of the best" in the cockpit, especially in combat situations. On the ground, he was known as the best of the best as well… at raising hell, partying, business acumen, women, and (as a result of the former) juggling ex-wives who never seemed fully "ex."

The pilot was walking toward the aircraft with Spike: "Now c'mon, Spike. Nav was only nine minutes late Thursday, and we lost our SAM cover and nearly got blown out of the sky. Give him a break, man. He missed, but so did they." He was getting drilled by the pilot because his Nav sucked. Just like he would drill the pilot if the co-pilot sucked. The crew of Spike's bomber consisted of Spike, two Pilots, a navigator, an electronics warfare officer [EW], and a gunner. They boarded the aircraft quickly through the bottom hatch below the cockpits. The

Co (Co-pilot) did the exterior walk around. It was very hot, but much hotter inside.

The pilot said: "Hey, Chief! Why can't you get the damn A/C started ten minutes before our pre-flight so we don't swim! This is not the Navy, Chief!"

The Crew Chief was in charge of maintenance for the aircraft. "Sorry, sir. I will have it on next time."

It was started immediately and lasted for almost a full minute. As a result, they would sweat completely through their flight suits and then freeze once they got to altitude at FL350 (35,000 feet) in twenty minutes because the heat in the cockpit didn't "quite" work in any B-52.

The pilot was pissed. "Chief, you were playing Bocchi ball with Stubby on the back of the tarmac when we got here. Dammit, next time have the bird ready for pre-flight! Now, get the APU going. We have to get out of here."

Each member of the crew completed his checklists except for the Nav who was carefully studying sections that didn't apply. Spike completed his for him.

Spike, glaring at the Nav who was still studying the wrong checklist: "Pilot, offense is ready to taxi."

Pilot, chuckling: "You did both your checklist and the Nav's that fast? You never cease to amaze me, Spike."

"Hey, do me a favor, and you two guys upstairs circle the wagons, OK? Then you can have a true circle jerk." Spike's temper was on edge, which was unusual.

"You're right, but at least we'll have a wagon. Chief, pull the chocks and pins, and give me the count. Charlie Tower, Bronze One is ready to taxi." Charlie Tower controlled all the aircraft on the ground.

"Bronze Two ready, Charlie."

"Bronze Three."

The three enormous aircraft, carrying one hundred and eight 500 pound bombs each, taxied to the runway and launched one minute apart without any mechanical incident, which was highly unusual. The target tonight was a rail marshalling yard just on the outskirts of Vinh, which was the largest city in the southern part of the North. It was also the first city in the north with SAM site COAs (Confirmed Operating Area). If the rail yards were taken out, it would slow down the supply of munitions to Viet Cong and the NVA in the south by a few weeks. The zips would repair it over time, but then Spike or another bombardier would blow it up again.

Spike thought that was their *real* job: breaking things, *again*. It was the "agains" that would get you killed. The zips would figure out how to hit you, given enough chances.

The Major didn't like this shit at all. He had already flown over a hundred missions out of U-Tapao and been shot at by SAMs eleven times. In the last sixty days they were flying almost all their missions to the north, and that meant they were getting almost continuous exposure to SAMs. The NVA troops that manned the SAM sites were getting better with experience. They had hit two B-52s in the last thirty days, but none had gone down. The more of these missions they flew, again, the greater the odds became that a shooter would get lucky.

Bronze cell took off and flew northeast for one hour and fifty-one minutes until they reached the beginning of the bomb run over Vinh.

Lemon: "Crew, we're IP inbound. We will enter a COA in 45 seconds. Heads up."

Spike: "Confirm the target in the crosshairs, Nav. Bomb, run checklist. C'Mon, Nav, get with the program."

Lemon wasn't there, as usual.

Lemon: "Roger, radar. Bomb run checklist."

"Lemon, how many times have I told you never to call me radar? Now move it on the checklist, or I'll have the whole damn sequence done before you get through half of it."

"Don't call me a Lemon, Spike. I was number two in my class in flight training."

Spike was moving furiously, flipping switches and adjusting dials. "That proves you are not only a Lemon, but dumb. You're single, with an entire city full of beautiful women because of the University being right there, and you finish number two in your class. The only way you could have done that, since you are sure as shit no genius, is to study your ass off in lieu of drinking and broads. That proves my point... bomb run checklist complete. You're fired."

Lemon was cautiously defensive in his reply. "You can't fire me. Only the Squadron Commander can make a crew change."

Spike, now pissed off: "Pilot, Bombs, center the PDI... I just fired the Nav because it's impossible to fix dumb."

"Roger, Bombs, PDI centered. Nav fired due to dumb."

"I AM NOT DUMB!"

No one listened even though he yelled over the IC.

The pilot centered the Pilot Directional Indicator and turned control of the aircraft over to the bombardier who flew the aircraft by moving a joystick. Spike was a perfectionist and flew directly to the target.

Spike: "Bombs away in 15... 10... 5... Bombs away! We're clean."

Navigator: "Turn right heading one-one-zero. Start climb to flight level three six zero [36,000 feet]. Max the airspeed. We need to get out of here."

Pilot: "Roger that, former Nav. One-one-zero. Three six zero. At the firewall."

EW, nervously: "I have a threat radar, crew."

Threat radar meant a SAM site, or sites, were searching for the flight of the three B-52s. If they located one of the bombers, they would "lock on" and fire a SAM that would track an electronic uplink to the bomber at three times the speed of sound.

EW, his voice terrified: "I HAVE UPLINK!"

Spike: "Shit, E-dub! Jam it! Pilot, take evasive!"

The EW tried to break the uplink electronically. He had seconds to do it. He didn't.

There was a bright flash of light, and the aircraft jolted violently.

Pilot: "Red Crown, Red Crown. Bronze One has been hit! I repeat, Bronze One has been hit by a SAM!"

Red Crown is an airborne and seaborne command post. "Roger, Bronze One. Can you make it feet wet? [over water]"

Co-pilot: "SHIT! THE OUTBOARD STARBOARD POD IS GONE!"

The engines on a B-52 are all arrayed in pairs. There are four pairs of engines, eight in all. The pair on the far end of the right wing had been blown off by the SAM.

Pilot: "Crew, we're OK. Calm down, Co. This wonderbird can fly on four engines if need be, and you guys know that. Give me FOB [Fuel On Board]."

Co-pilot: "FIRE WARNING ON FIVE AND SIX!"

Pilot, his voice irritated: "GODAMMIT, calm down! Shut them down!"

"Red Crown, Bronze One has fire and all starboard engines shut down. Correct that. Five and six shut down, seven and eight are gone."

Red Crown: "Roger, Bronze One. Give intentions. Souls on board and fuel on board. Your nearest airfield is Udorn. I repeat Udorn."

Bronze Two, the bomber in trail behind One, came up on Guard frequency, which everyone can hear since it's not secure: "Bronze One, Bronze Two. Is your crew alright? We see a lot of flames. It looks like you took a direct hit by that SAM."

"Crew's OK, Two. *Almost* a direct hit, or I wouldn't be talking to you. We're under control for now."

Red Crown angrily came on Guard: "ALL AIRCRAFT STAY OFF GUARD UNLESS YOU HAVE AN EMERGENCY! I HAVE AN AIRCRAFT IN TROUBLE! REPEAT. STAY OFF GUARD!"

Co-pilot: "Pilot, we only have 6000 pounds of fuel left."

"That's better, kid. Only controlled hysteria is allowed."

Spike jumped in: "Pilot, we are 17 clicks at 105 from kilo."

He was giving the aircraft's position to expedite rescue if they ejected. He was also doing Lemon's job.

"Red Crown, Bronze One. We are almost bingo [out of fuel]. We're one seven at one zero five from kilo. Six souls on board. We're going to 10,000 ft. and leaving for a swim. Will advise."

The Pilot nosed the aircraft over into a fairly steep dive.

"Roger, Bronze One. You have no choice. SAR [Search and Rescue] is en route. Good luck and God's speed."

"Roger, Red Crown. Bronze One appreciates the SAR in the air."

Co-Pilot, in a calm, almost resigned tone: "Now we have a fire warning on four. Not that it makes any difference."

"That was much, much better, Co. OK, crew, we're getting out of here. Stand-by light and horn."

"Red Crown, we're going wet now."

The pilot didn't wait for a response. He reached up and flipped the cover on the ejection light and horn and flipped the switch. Bright red lights went on throughout the cockpit, and a loud buzzer sounded. The Gunner fired the explosive bolts that that held the guns and his radar onto the plane and bailed out manually from the tail, and then the ejections began with the navigator, followed by the other crewmembers, with the pilot going last. He checked his pins, rotated two handles on either side of the seat, and squeezed the levers on the handles. The hatch above him exploded off the aircraft, and he rocketed into the night.

Spike ejected just before the pilot, second from last. His hatch blew, and he ejected downward like the navigator had. The force of the ejection shocked him. He hit a wall of wind that was going over 400 miles an hour, and it was freezing cold. His chute deployed almost immediately, yanking him up and swinging him like the pendulum in a grandfather clock. He remembered to pull the releases on the risers, and the swinging settled down.

Spike thought to himself: *This is bullshit. I've spent twelve years practicing to kill or be killed, and they almost won this round. I have to be nuts to do this. Christ! Pay attention… you're over water… deploy the raft… check the beeper… roger, on… its getting warmer… check the…"*

Suddenly he was under water, but it wasn't nearly the shock he went through when he ejected. He popped to the surface quickly, buoyed by the survival vest that he had activated instinctively. He snapped the releases on his harness to get rid of his chute. The sea was fairly calm, and the moon allowed some visibility. He grabbed the lanyard and pulled the raft to within reach. It took two attempts, but he finally pulled himself into the one-man raft. He rolled over on his back and laid his head back onto the edge of the raft… *Shit, where's my helmet!?*

A light flash passed over him. *"What the hell? That was quick. They must have had a Navy boat in the area."* He started to search for his strobe light to signal the boat when he heard the "whup-whup" of a chopper.

The light passed over him again, but this time it stopped after passing him and slowly started to move back toward him. Spike suddenly realized that it could not be our Navy. It had to be a North Vietnamese patrol boat!

Shit! This raft is a yellow cork floating in the black sea! Get out fast! He rolled out of the raft and reached for the standard issue switchblade in the leg of his flight suit, opened it, and cut the lanyard that tethered the raft to him. He shoved the raft as hard as he could and then swam as fast as he could away from it. The light made another pass near him and then stopped on the yellow cork bobbing in the sea. An automatic weapon opened up and shredded the raft only thirty yards away as he continued swimming. Training kept him from panic, but if the SAR didn't get there soon, the boat would find him, and if the raft was an example, they would clearly kill him rather than take him prisoner.

The enemy boat had made a fatal mistake. The SAR team saw both the searchlight and the gunfire at the raft.

SAR consisted of one or more rescue choppers as well as fixed wing aircraft that dealt with other threats to the downed aircrew member. The USAF, or Navy fighter, bird on sight used the boat's searchlight to get a visual ID.

The bright flash and missile contrail were probably the last things the enemy saw. The boat exploded in a huge eruption that seemed to be only a few hundred yards away from Spike. He felt the concussion of it almost immediately.

Spike smiled his "Spike" smile to himself as he bobbed around in his life vest in the South China Sea. He would probably live through this now, but as much as he tried to set it aside, he was still terrified.

The noise of the chopper became louder, and the searchlight was scanning the water close by. Suddenly it was over him, and the light blinded him. A loudspeaker blared, "STAY WHERE YOU ARE! WE WILL COME TO YOU!"

The speaker call almost caused him to laugh out loud, but he wasn't sure if it would be a laugh or a scream. Plus, water was splashing over his mouth as the life vest barely held him above the light swells.

Stay where? I am where! You guys are there! C'mon, guys, get me out of this Naval environment! I traditionally fly rather than float!

The thought was instantaneous, but he again didn't find it funny. He gave a thumbs up and sighed in relief. He had survived his first shootdown and had not become dead due to missiles and bullets.

I gotta get a new job. Besides, I'm approaching the pinnacle of my mediocre career anyway. Maybe I marry some Thai princess and just do nothing but get laid and count money. Then spend it. Then get laid, count more, spend more. Pretty safe and simple. Run out of money? Raise taxes. Peasants get pissed and start revolt. Wife finds out about girlfriends and runs to King. He is pissed about revolt and a little bit about the Princess. He decides throwing me in a pit of cobras is a good idea. No princess. No getting laid. No money. No counting. No spending. Now cobras. Something is wrong with this checklist. Abort! Abort!

Spike left his nightmare checklist when the Navy para-rescue diver hit the water very close to him after jumping from the chopper. The crew lowered a "horse collar" harness, which they grounded in the ocean, and the diver helped him into the harness. He was hauled rapidly to the chopper door and wrapped in a blanket by the medic on board.

Spike was back at U-Tapao less than eight hours after being checked out by the flight surgeon on the carrier that picked him up. He flew his next combat mission just over 36 hours after his return. B-52 "crewdogs," as they called themselves, were in short supply. The entire crew of six had been rescued successfully, but the fired Nav had broken his hip on ejection, so he was grounded indefinitely. Spike thought it was a highly convenient break. He needed a navigator that knew how to navigate. He also needed a new Princess and a revised checklist. He realized he had very nearly been killed. That thought had always been pushed back as a distant possibility.

Not any more.

CHAPTER II:
DO YOU FEEL A DRAFT?

THE DRAFT, 1968

At the *same* moment that the chopper searchlight was shining on Spike Wilson in the South China Sea, a serious conversation was taking place thousands of miles away at the University of Arizona between two friends. One of them was destined to become one of Spike's closest friends, bonded through the trials of war, but he had no idea that could, or would, ever happen.

R.J. Graham was walking to a class with his good friend Bob "Ruts" Rothman. Ruts was a handsome, big, Jewish kid from Chicago who was a ZBT, which was the best Jewish fraternity at the U of A. Graham was a Phi Delt: "The Goyim House," so their friendship crossed any religious glass barriers. In fact, when they first met and Ruts called the Phi Delt's the "goyim house," Graham agreed that his fraternity had the best looking guys on the campus.

Ruts, snickering: "That's not what it means, putz."

Graham, smiling: "It does in English, prick."

"Oh really? Then what does Jew mean in English?"

Graham couldn't miss the opportunity.

"Not goyim, of course."

Their friendship was born from laughter.

Graham was just over six feet with sandy blond hair and quite good looking, but he didn't know it, since he could find multiple flaws in the mirror while shaving. He did know that he had blue eyes that captivated women because they had told him so. His major was business, but getting laid was far more important than academics. Consequently, he had decided to major in girls early in his freshman year. He was getting A's in his major but B's and C's in his business major because going to class often interfered with getting laid.

Graham was unusually serious: "We have big problems coming, and you know it. The only way we can beat it is to plan ahead."

Graham was expressing a concern that both of them harbored, but unlike the kids up north, they ignored it most of the time. They turned down the walkway leading to the Business building.

Ruts: "Yeah, I know… the damn draft. When I graduate, I bet my board will send my induction notice by courier to the ceremony. They are bound and determined to kill off as many young Jewish males as possible. That's why I have to find a bride on the quick man. That's about the only way to avoid certain death."

"Don't worry about it. The war will end soon. I hear there's too much political heat on the White House. They'll cave. But if they don't, you have to have a plan. If I get drafted, I'll just join the Air Force and fly things."

"You better get real, RJ. I checked into that stuff. Even a goyim can't get in the Air Force, Coast Guard, or even the Navy for months, even years, because everybody our age is trying to avoid becoming dead."

Graham was only half listening; his thoughts had shifted to women, as usual.

"Bullshit, Ruts. I'll find a way to get in the Air Force. Like I said, you need to plan ahead."

"'Find a way' isn't a very good plan, RJ. I told you that it's impossible right now man. The draft is going to grab your ass the minute your board finds out you are out of school."

"Then they won't find out I'm out of school. I'll go to graduate school or maybe law school and actually learn something. By the time I get out, the war will be over."

Ruts was amused: "You? Graduate school? Law school? Now you really are kidding yourself. You're a very smart guy, but you can't coast through that stuff like undergrad, man. You actually have to go to class, and you actually have to study. That would interfere with getting laid. What are you going to do? Study by putting your law book on her tits? No way, man. You'll flunk out at light speed and be up to your ass in rice paddies in a few months. You better get a better plan, man."

They were standing outside the business building, and two girls had already interrupted their conversation to say hi to RJ. He had just broken up with his girlfriend of two years, Ginny, for about the fourth time. He couldn't remember. She was arguably the best looking girl on campus with a killer body. He missed her, but he had to get over it. She had given him his pin back and said she was absolutely done this time. He was pretty sure that she was serious because she had heard that he was "kinda" seeing another girl, or girls, when the opportunity arose. She was right, and she knew she was. He loved Ginny, but the U of A was loaded with gorgeous women, and word of his break-up was obviously now out.

Graham ignored Ruts good advice. "Bullshit. I'll get into graduate school or fly planes. That's my plan, and it'll work."

Ruts laughed. " RJ, the only thing that'll work is your M-16 when it's wet and full of rice. At least you better hope it does. Man, you're tellin' me I need a plan, and yours sucks. You have to get a real plan that will work."

Graham was distracted by some cleavage passing by but was listening. He turned back to his friend.

"Oh yeah? Well what's your plan, buddy? Mine sucks? Then what's yours?"

Ruts almost sneered: "I have already learned the complete lyrics to 'Oh Canada'. When they deliver my draft notice to graduation, I'll be on a plane to any place there that's reasonably warm and is not French. How's Connecticut? It may be a good place to hide. How's the weather? Chicago is killing me."

Graham looked at his friend with an expression of surprise. "Southern Connecticut? You're kidding. It's the divorce capital of the U.S. And the weather?" Graham paused. "The summer is lush and green when it is a wet season. It was *breathtaking,* primarily because my asthma would kick in due to the heavy damp air.

"But then, the Fall comes, the leaves change, and it is truly beautiful. The leaves float to the ground and create a leaf blanket six inches deep... on my golf course making finding a slightly errant drive virtually impossible which results in a lost ball and a two stroke penalty."

Graham paused again, gathering the right picture in his mind.

"But then, the first snow arrived, silently and beautifully coating the landscape while I slept. My dad would awaken me at 6AM so I could dig his car out of the garage and clear a path in the driveway. But I was rewarded with a two minute hot shower until the hot water ran out because everyone had showered before me. I remember not having any feeling in my hands as I dressed for school."

Ruts, sneering: "You know nothing about *real* cold and *real* snow."

Graham ignored his friend: "But then, after an eternity of cold and snow, spring arrives and the gentle spring showers freeze at night and coat the roads and the phone lines break under the weight. So then, I couldn't call my girlfriend when

I was a senior to say the roads were impassable due to ice so I couldn't pick her up for school. Her neighbor kid had a 4WD Jeep and drove her to school. The little shit had been waiting for the spring ice. On the way to school, she decided that he wasn't that bad and I hadn't even called, so she decided to dump me and go out with him. Besides, he had a Jeep."

Ruts grinned. "You should have beaten him with an icicle."

Graham went on after a moment. "No. She wasn't that great, but that should answer your question. The only positive is that the Jews are divorcing just as fast as Christians, so you may be able to find a young, great looking, rich, Jewish divorcee and hide under her bed until the war ends. You might consider it because your plan sucks worse than mine. Jews can't get into Canada unless they speak French."

Ruts laughed out loud. "Oh yeah? Then vous le vous fuck you, goyim. I'll be Italian for the border crossing. I'm not staying in Chicago or Connecticut. The draft will find me. They may even take you hostage to find me."

Graham laughed with him. "Italian? That's a plan. All you need is a passport that says 'Roberto Rothmarino, non-Jew.' They'll probably turn you over to the American draft police that are stationed at the border."

"Draft police? Bullshit."

Graham put his hand on his friend's shoulder and looked him in the eye. "No, I'm serious, and they're all Italian Americans so they can spot a fake in a heartbeat. I got to go over to the Pi Phi house. I'll meet you at the Bayhorse for a beer at four."

Ruts knew it. "If you keep skipping classes, you'll be in a rice bowl even sooner. But get it all while you can. See ya at four."

They shook hands, and Graham started walking. The draft wouldn't get him. Besides, he didn't give a shit if he got killed anymore. He really missed Ginny, but she was history, and it was time to open a new chapter in his life, especially if it was going to be short due to rice in his gun. Linda Tate, a very beautiful Pi Phi that he had always wanted to date had broken up with her boyfriend. He headed to the Pi Phi house on a desperate hunch.

The Pi Phi house wasn't far off the campus. He was amazed to find that Linda *was* there, and even more amazingly, she seemed happy to see him.

On Spring Break and in the following weeks, they dated constantly, and she wanted to get really serious. But he couldn't deal with it. *Nothing serious again. Not for a long time.*

GRADUATION AND THE REAL WORLD

Graham graduated with no honors, as was the family tradition. When he received his grades for the final semester, he noted that he had received a "D" in experimental psychology. He and Ruts had signed up for it, but had decided to drop it, only they never did. Neither one of them even knew where the class was held. They didn't have the textbook either. No point in wasting dad's beer money on books that you will never read about stuff you don't want to know. Knowing stuff that means nothing to you clutters the mind. But, Graham thought that it was a great class given the effort required, and wondered what it was about.

Up north, the campus protests over the war had persisted. Graham didn't understand why kids would protest. Maybe their schools were too cold, and they were ugly with no tan, so they couldn't get laid and protested to keep warm. Poor white kids in the wrong schools. They were beyond the capability of influencing the political machine that was grinding out a prolonged conflict that had no end in sight. There was no outcome that could be claimed a victory by either side. He'd heard that the press was siding with the protesters, but he wasn't sure since he never watched the news. A fraternity brother had shot out the tubes of both sets at the house two months ago. Ironically, he had done it because he was protesting the news. No newspapers were delivered anymore to the Phi Delt house because it was too dangerous. Not as dangerous as pizza, but dangerous.

School was over for now. He needed to take the LSAT and get back in before Draft Board #19 in Bridgeport found out that he could now be legally killed. He opened the front door at the red brick colonial house that looked out of place in the desert. The door had been painted black in the spring when a brother who was a Marine Lieutenant was killed at a place called Hue. He was 23. He'd only been over there about three months. *"I better get my ass in law school."*

Pluto was sitting on the one remaining sofa in the living room reading a paper he must have bought or stolen. Pluto was an old roommate and a very bright and happy guy.

He was already in law school. That was happy.

He looked up as Graham walked in and smiled his quirky smile: "There's a surprise waiting for you in your room, RJ."

"Who? The draft board?"

"No. Far more enjoyable but far more dangerous."

Graham knew that Pluto would play mind games, and he wasn't in the mood. He headed upstairs to his "suite," called such only because it wasn't completely destroyed and was private. He opened the door and stared momentarily in disbelief.

It was his ex-girlfriend Ginny. She was the Homecoming Queen and remarkably beautiful. When he walked in, she was on his bed with a sheet over herself. She said nothing at all, smiled, and took the sheet away.

She was naked.

It was a great afternoon and night, but she made it clear before she left early in the morning that they were still broken up. Graham didn't care.

He'd won.

TIME TO GO HOME, SO YOU HAVE A PLACE TO LEAVE

It was getting hot in Tucson as the summer approached and the money was running out, so Graham decided to head back to Connecticut and take the LSAT there. Besides, it would add to the chain of addresses that his draft board would have to go through to find him. Linda had called and begged him to spend the summer with her parents and her at their house on Lake Tahoe, but he decided that situation would become awkward and possibly "dangerous."

Ruts headed back to Skokie immediately after graduation and met a "nice" girl at his father's club. They were engaged in two weeks, and the wedding was set for August. Within days of the ring going on Leslie Green's finger, the Government announced that married men were no longer exempt from the draft, and now only men with children would carry an exemption. Ruts decided to call off the engagement in a tearful encounter with his fiancée given there was no longer any motivation to continue. Upon learning of his son's action with his law partner's daughter, Ruts' father went berserk and threw him out of the house. But with the promise of some financial support that his father would never know about, Ruts' mother sent him West. He hated Skokie. It was cold six months a year and full of Jews the other six. He had a place to stay for free in California and his father's pet car.

In early July, he headed south on the Interstate right after his father left for work knowing he would have at least an eight hour jump before the prick found out his 1964 Austin Healy 3000 and his son were gone. Ruts knew that his dad wouldn't be too upset by his departure, but the car leaving would really piss him off. He pulled off the Interstate at the McDonald's oasis off the Kennedy just south of O'Hare and bought maps and a highlighter to plan his trip. After picking up a cooler and some Bud at the Circle K in case it got hot… or cold, he set out for the "Promised Land." He was delighted to find that a national map made the trip to Lake Tahoe look fairly simple.

RJ didn't deserve a nice girl like Linda. Besides, RJ would be drafted and in Vietnam before the end of the year. My board will never find me. They'll be looking for Rothman, not Ross. Bob Ross sounded nice and neutral.

WESTPORT, CONNECTICUT

Graham got a job as a market research analyst in Westport through one of his father's contacts. He was dating two girls in Westport, and an American Airline stew in New York. The stew was fantastic but gone all the time, so he started dating her roommate when she was on a trip. The arrangement approached sexual heaven. He had decided that he would never again have only one girlfriend. Maybe forever.

One afternoon he came back after lunch, and there was a note on his desk to call his mother. As usual, the phone rang forever before his mother picked up: "Mom. You called. What's up?"

"You got a letter from draft board number 19. Do you want me to open it?"

"No, mom. I know what it is. Just put it in my room, and I'll read it when I get home. Thanks, I love you. See you later."

Graham hung up. He realized he was actually shaking. *Shit…I'm screwed. I better get my plan going… and go to church.*

He drove straight to the Air Force recruiting station in Norwalk. There was a big guy with *lots* of stripes on his arm sitting at a desk facing the door. He didn't look up when Graham walked in.

"Have a seat right there, young man," he said, pointing to a chair in front of his desk. "You're lucky that everyone has gone, so you don't have to wait around to find out that there is no way in hell that you can get into the United States Air Force for at least six months, and to accomplish that you need to be a near genius. Forget it. You don't have six months before you'll be wrapped in green, in the jung, sweating your ass off, and getting shot at. Sorry that's just the way it is."

"So this is a waste of time is what you're saying."

"Roger that, kid, unless you are qualified to fly. That means you must have a college degree and pass the test that no one passes. The Air Force desperately needs aviators, but the test writers think the Air Force is too crowded with aviators."

"I have my degree. Can I take the test?"

"Sure kid. Just fill out all these forms in order and return them to me tomorrow morning. It will take you most of the night, but the test is Saturday morning in Bridgeport, and you don't have time to wait for the next test. You'll be in basic by then. Bring proof of your degree when you return this paperwork."

Graham took the packet from the recruiter. It was like a small novel. "Thank you, sir. I'll have it back tomorrow."

That Saturday, Graham took the test in a room with a hundred other guys. As he went through the exam, Graham realized the truth. *Shit. The Sergeant was right. No one could pass this test. I am screwed.*

In three weeks, he got home from work on Friday night and there was a letter from the *Department of Defense, United States Air Force* on his bed. He dreaded opening it. It was his last hope. He noticed that the envelope was a little thick for a "Dear Kid, You're Dead" letter. He ripped it open and everything spilled on the floor. He picked it up and read through the heading to the body quickly.

*"**Congratulations**…you have been selected for the United States Air Force Flight Training Program…**Report for induction physical**…attend **Officer Candidate School Class** 69-03…Lackland AFB, Texas…"*

Graham was stunned. *I can't believe this! I may not get killed after all! Thank you, Lord!* He had no idea how he had passed the test. It had to be a mistake, but he'd take it.

He partied the entire weekend. It was a blur of joy, fueled by beer and relief.

CHAPTER III:
COME FLY WITH US, IF YOU CAN

OCS

Two months later, Graham reported for duty in Bridgeport and was bused with the other lucky kids to the Hartford Airport for a commercial flight to San Antonio. Since he was going to attend OCS, he was given a packet with all the other kids' orders enclosed and told to ensure that there was no drinking on the flight to basic. *Yeah right.* The flight was uneventful until they landed and taxied to the gate. He looked out the window and there was a large group of really tough looking guys in *Smokey the Bear* hats waiting outside. He went down the stairs.

"GET IN FORMATION MAGGOT! STAND UP STRAIGHT YOU GOD DAMN HIPPIE PUKE!"

"YOU SHOULD HAVE GOTTEN A HAIRCUT BEFORE YOU CAME DOWN HERE SCUMBALL! NOW WE WILL SHAVE THAT THING YOU CLAIM TO BE A HEAD SO SHORT YOUR COMMIE CRAP HAIR WILL BE AFRAID TO GROW BACK!"

It went on like that for about ten minutes, much to the amusement of the other passengers. Graham just stood to the side near the stairs and waited. When things settled down, he walked over to one of the DIs: "Sir, I was told to deliver these orders upon landing."

The sergeant stared at Graham: "OCS no doubt. Don't call me 'sir,' son. I'm a non-commissioned officer. You will learn that quickly. You are one lucky man to make it through the test that no one can pass. I assume your specialty will be as an aviator. Either that or you're a doctor."

"Yes. Flight training after OCS, sir…excuse me…sergeant."

"Get on that bus over there, and sit in the second row."

"Yes, sergeant." Graham decided right then that this wouldn't be bad at all. *No sir. Piece of cake. Give orders and fly stuff. Hell of a deal.* In an hour, they were herded off the bus and into the building, except for Graham and one other guy. They were held back and taken to the front of the room. The other guy was a big guy, about six four and a little fat. Graham introduced himself: "Hi. I'm R.J. Graham. Are you here for OCS?"

"Yeah… Mike Butchermein. Nice to meet you. I'm sure as shit happy that we aren't with those other guys."

"No shit, man. They are in for some tough times."

From behind they heard a deep resonant voice: "So are you, boys. In fact, they will have a much better time for the next sixteen weeks than you will."

They both turned around as he was speaking and saw a tough looking, leathery, old guy with more stripes on his sleeve than they had ever seen. The sergeant went on: "I'm Chief Master Sergeant Perkins, NCO of Squadron One at Officer Candidate School. You gentlemen must be Mr. Graham and Mr. Botcerman … Bochermen…" Butchermein gave him the right pronunciation.

"Yes, gentlemen. You are lucky to have passed the test that can't be passed, but on the other hand you were assigned to us. Squadron One. Now I consider that an honor. You will not. We are known as the Medina Marines. Medina for the location of the school. Marines because we are tougher than any other squadron by far. When the other squadrons are done with PT, they run a mile. We run three. The other squadrons get up at 0500. We get up at 0400, and we run for an hour. You'll be in the best shape in your life - if you make it through."

Squadron One lived up to its reputation. Graham and the others did end up in the best shape they had ever been in, and they grew to have pride in being tougher than any other squadrons.

Graham and Butch, as he was called, made some serious dough betting with other squadrons on inter-squadron sports since they never lost. Butch was a great basketball player and Graham was good at baseball and flag football.

The other squadrons respected SQ One, but there was not much envy. They were not really there to be "Marines." Almost all were there to be aviators, and they were in good shape too. Not as good as the poor bastards at SQ One, but "good enough." What they didn't realize, or appreciate, was that the great condition the "Marines" were in would save some of their lives when they were forced to evade capture after being shot down. That was the only reason that the SQ One Commander was so insistent on the physical conditioning. He *had* been shot down in 1966 and had been chased through the jungle for five days before he was rescued by a chopper that had pulled him out even though they were under fire. If he hadn't been in great shape, he never would have evaded for five days. He would be dead, or perhaps worse, a POW. His young officers would be ready. It was his duty and a key responsibility.

The day finally came that the young men got their commissions. Graduation was all pomp and circumstance. All Squadrons "Passed-in Review" marching before a reviewing stand of senior officers that included a couple of Generals. Many of their families came in to see the graduation and seemed to be bursting with pride. Squadron One led the parade - not because they were "One" by designation but because they were first in academics and first in *every* inter-squadron sport.

As would be expected, the timing was perfect when the two star General finally said, "Gentlemen, congratulations!" Four fighters in perfect formation flew directly over the parade ground at low level, literally vibrating the stands.

"You are now officers in the United States Air Force! May God Bless and Guard you in your coming endeavors. You are dismissed!

The band broke out with the "Air Force" song as the cadet wheel hats flew high into the air. Everybody started congratulating each other. They were filled with pride and a sense of real accomplishment, as they should have been. The men from SQ One felt especially proud since they had made it through the "Marines" and proven to be the best both academically and physically.

Graham grabbed Butch, "C'mon, I'll buy you a beer at the OFFICER'S Club!"

As they walked through the only exit from the parade ground, Sergeant Perkins was waiting for them. Tradition was that the first enlisted man that saluted the new officers got a silver dollar in return. Perkins was saluting and smiling as he grabbed his reward. Tradition also said that not giving the sergeant his dollar was very, very bad luck.

Graham and Butch gave the sergeant the silver dollar. Graham "accidently" gave him two since he felt it was pretty cheap life insurance.

He turned to Butch at his side, smiling widely: "Well Butch, 'off we go into the wild blue yonder,' buddy. We just have to avoid getting dead too soon."

One of them would not.

FLIGHT TRAINING

Navigator flight training was conducted at Mather AFB in Sacramento, California. The University of California, Sacramento was there, and SFO, with hundreds of stewardesses going in and out each day, was a couple of hours away. Graham and Butch could forget about all the regimented crap and concentrate on women. Flight training would be secondary. In fact, Graham wondered if he had to go to class… the good ol' days would be back right after graduation from Stalag Squadron One.

When RJ and Butch got to training, it was a continuing party, even better than college. The parties where constant when they weren't flying, and studying interfered with parties. But they were both good in the air, which made up for academic grades that were barely acceptable. They didn't really care. If they graduated too soon, they would get killed if they got the wrong assignment. If they washed out, they would get a "not get dead" assignment. There was no rush. But the attitude and lifestyle started to catch up with them. Toward the end of the training they ran into an unanticipated bump in the road to avoiding being dead too soon.

FAT JACK

Butchermein and Graham were waiting outside Lieutenant Colonel Gregory ["Fat Jack"] Gross' office to get their ass chewed. Colonel Gross was the Squadron Commander of the 3535th Navigator Training Squadron. Gross had seen them before - many times. They were in the final weeks of flight training and were scheduled to graduate and get their Wings in late November. But they didn't want to graduate. If they graduated they were liable to get assigned to some damn suicide mission like airborne Forward Air Controller [FAC] and get their asses shot off somewhere in the Central Highlands of Vietnam. No sir. Not for them. The last guy that had washed out got assigned as the Assistant Club Officer at Hickam Air Force Base in Hawaii. It was truly unbelievable. Learn restaurant management in Hawaii for the duration, courtesy of the United States Air Force. There *had* to be more jobs like that.

Graham, whispering: "Butch. You just keep your mouth shut this time. Don't defend our screw-ups. It sounds like we want a tenth chance or whatever it would be. Let's wash out with dignity."

"Yeah. I'm ready this time. You handle it even though you screwed it up last time. I won't say shit this time."

Fat Jack yelled from his desk, behind a closed door, "ENTER GENTLEMEN!"

It was Gross playing hard ass. They were used to it, so it didn't work anymore. They walked in, came to attention, and saluted in front of his desk. "Be seated, lieutenants, but close the damn door first!" Butch closed the door, and they sat down and pretended to listen intently.

Fat Jack was almost growling at them. "I am on to you guys. I know what you are trying to do. You guys are trying to wash out because you think you can draw an assignment like Lt. Pulaski got at Hickam. I know this because I looked up your records. Graham, you had a 3.2 GPA at Arizona and were on your way to some shitbird law school before your draft board said 'no way.' You beat out a hundred other guys that would have killed to get into flight training which means you must have found a way to cheat. Know what that means, Lieutenant?"

"No, sir."

"Shut up! That was rhetorical! It means that you can improvise. Improvising is important in a combat situation. You'll find that out.

"And good old Lieutenant Butchermein. Your record is about the same, but the grades weren't as good since you played basketball day and night. But like Graham, your actual flying is good. You guys have flunked the weather exam twice. Three strikes and you're out, which I'm sure you are very aware of. I know that the weather exam is one of the toughest exams, but everybody else has passed it but you two monkeys. Now why would I call you fine young officers monkeys? Because if you don't pass the weather exam tomorrow, they will be your neighbors. If you two wash out, you will be immediately transferred to Project English. Now I know that may sound good, but believe me it isn't. Project English is a choice assignment where you get to teach English to the tribesmen in the Central Highlands of Vietnam. ALONE! You are taken in by Air Force Special Forces and dropped off with your supplies. You set up school and begin teaching classes in English to these tribesmen, if you can find them. These natives are theoretically our allies, at least sometimes. Every few weeks you get re-supplied and you get one, or maybe two, R&Rs in your 13 month tour. Sounds great, right!? Now this assignment does have some degree of risk in that there are VC *and* NVA all over the place, but the tribesmen are supposed to protect you from these bad guys and USAF HQ planning is *almost* sure that they will. And, as an added thing to contemplate, there is no O'Club, women, booze, or decent quarters. You will live in a tent. Now I expect you will be motivated to skip the Club and go back to quarters and study your sorry asses off! This is not bullshit! It has already been approved by Wing. It's *done* if you're *done*! Any questions, gentlemen?"

Graham wasn't going to the damn jungle for a year. He had joined the Air Force because snakes and leeches didn't fly. "No, sir! You have made our options perfectly clear, and I assure you, sir, that we are not motivated to wash out of the program, sir! "

Gross: "You are so full of shit, Lieutenant, that it boggles the mind."

Butch: "Yes, sir. We have really tried to pass the weather exam and studied long hours. We will study all night if necessary to provide our best effort."

"Don't bullshit me, Lieutenants. The only studying that you guys have done is at the O'Club or at the sororities at the University. You guys are now up shit creek. You are DISMISSED!"

They both came to attention, saluted, did an about face, and walked out of his office. Once outside, Butch went ballistic. "Great plan, RJ! Great fucking plan! You are going to get both of us killed! How are we going to study for the damn weather exam!? I don't even know where the books are! Jesus Christ! We are dead meat!"

"Shut up, Butch. I didn't pull a gun on you to get into this program. Relax. We'll pass the weather exam with flying colors. No sweat. Then we'll get some trash hauler assignment flying rum to Ramstein."

"Oh yeah, right. We don't have the books because you tossed them. It's the hardest written exam in flight school, and we have to know the shit by 0900 tomorrow. How the hell are we going to do that?" They were walking toward the Weather Squadron building. A classmate, Bob Foster, was walking toward them. Bob was a really good guy and a friend. He was smart and near the top of the class, even though he often partied with them. They stopped him.

Graham: "Bob, do you still have the weather book?"

"Hell no. I threw it out as soon as I passed that miserable exam. Why?"

"Because we still haven't passed and don't have the books to study for it. On top of that, we're wheels in the well [take-off] at 0900 tomorrow."

"I'd say you're both screwed if you don't come up with something quickly. You can never learn all the crap in that book in a day."

Graham: "Bob's right. We can't learn it in time. We don't need to know all the shit, so we don't need to study. We need to know what's *on* the test to pass the test. Simple."

Butch was about to explode. "Simple. SIMPLE! HOW THE HELL ARE WE GOING TO DO THAT! You're crazy. We have nineteen hours to learn this shit, and you say we will only need to know what's on the test. How are we going to do that?"

"Steal the test of course. Jesus, Butch. How'd you get through college?"

Bob, departing: "I think you just came up with your only option. Good luck guys."

They turned into the walkway leading to the weather building. "RJ, you can't just walk in and say 'excuse me, could you please direct me to the weather exam that we're taking tomorrow? We'd like to borrow it for a while.'"

Graham stopped on the walkway. "Listen, Butch. This will be a piece of cake. Weather Squadrons aren't used to conniving thieves like Universities are, so security will be very loose. We go in to see Donna, and I tell her that Colonel Berka would like to see Sergeant Calloway right away. Then we leave so Calloway doesn't see us. He'll race over to Wing because he's scared shitless of Berka. It will take him at least thirty minutes round trip even if he finds out Berka's not there right away, which he won't. We then go right back in, and I ask Donna if I can use the restroom, while you chit chat and charm her like I know you can. I go to Calloway's office, pull the master test and the answer key from his files, and copy all the answers. I replace everything, walk out, and chitchat with Donna. In fact, you ask her out when I'm in the restroom. If that doesn't work, I'll ask her out after you take the test answers out the door, and maybe she'll turn me down too. "

"Yeah? What if she says yes? You can't go out with her. You're engaged. Priscilla would kill you."

Graham was engaged to the prettiest girl at The University in his very biased opinion. Her father was also an Air Force Colonel. "Priscilla wouldn't give a shit if it kept me from teaching English to the savages for a year."

The plan worked.

"You amaze me, RJ. How did you know that would work? It worked perfectly. I even got a date with Donna."

"Good work, Butch. She's got great tits. It worked because they didn't anticipate it. Anticipation is everything. It's thirteen fifteen; let's go to the Club early so we can get out of there before Fat Jack shows up."

Many from their Flight Class were already at the Club. The consensus was that Graham and Butch could not possibly pass the weather test. With the test answers in pocket, Butch and Graham took on all bettors. These guys were fish.

C.K. McCUSKER

THE RANCH

At 1715 they headed for the Ranch in order to avoid Gross. The Ranch was a complex of three bedroom homes built on base for junior officer's families. They had been taken over and destroyed by Lieutenants in flight training due to the high demand for Navigators.

When they walked in there was the smell of something burning. Uh-oh. If one more of the houses burned down, they were going to put them all in tents on the back of the base.

Graham: "Butch, check the bedrooms. I'll go this way."

Graham turned left into the kitchen and saw the problem immediately. Their third roommate, Dennis "Trash Pile" Gorman was asleep, or more likely passed out, on the floor. His back was leaning against the oven door which was apparently on high. He had a nylon ski jacket on which was smoking from the oven heat. Graham grabbed a pitcher, filled it at the sink and poured water on the coat and Trash Pile. He woke up quickly. "Shit!" He tried to get up, but his jacket was melted to the oven door.

"Trash. Take the jacket off. You're stuck buddy."

He pulled his arms free and stood up cautiously. "Damn! That was my new jacket for Tahoe." He went to the sink, got a spatula from breakfast, and started to scrape his jacket off the oven. It took awhile, but it came off. He checked the oven and smoke billowed out. His pizza was black.

Trash Pile was a human garbage disposal that never turned on the switch. His room was almost impassable. Butch and Trash were opposites. Trash was short and wiry. Butch was tall, mostly as a result of his waist, and heavyset. Butch was almost maniacal about neat and clean. They regularly beat the shit out each other. It was close right now.

Butch: "Trash, you little shit. You could have burned the house down, let alone burn yourself up. You are an idiot! Get the hell out of here. I have to clean the damn kitchen… and stay out of the living room too! Get out!"

Trash didn't argue this time, primarily because he was just sober enough not to attack Butch in the mood that he was in. He took his jacket, now useless, and headed for his room. Trash had graduated two weeks before and was waiting to go to Survival School. He didn't go home on leave to visit his family like most guys did. They weren't sure he had a family. He just stayed on base and rode his motorcycle through the back acreage during the day and drank too much with his strange buddies in the afternoon after class and on into the evening.

Despite appearances, Trash had graduated number two in his class and picked up an RF-4, a fighter that did recon in SEA, which was a rare assignment. No one got fastburners out of flight school. Trash was strange and a drunk, but he was also brilliant. He had a photographic memory and could read any text at an incredible rate. He had the third highest academic record in the Squadron's history.

Vic Tennamen, a classmate and buddy, came through the open front door. "What did Trash do now? Torch the joint? Ya'll should glue him to his bed when you leave for class.'

Graham. "He nearly trashed himself. Look at the oven door."

"Christ almighty. What happened?"

Graham explained. Butch threw them out of the kitchen. They grabbed a beer and went into the living room.

"You and Butch out? I know ya'll saw Fat Jack today, and you were close."

Graham explained that situation, and Vic laughed. "Great plan, RJ. You boys would have been screwed if ya'll hadn't gone back to basics. Remember not to finish the test too quickly, or Calloway will be on to your scam."

Vic was also engaged, so he and Graham worked together to avoid their prior lives. They had both majored in girls in college and found themselves uncomfortable with only one model at times. Vic was particularly worried about Graham who always had a wandering eye.

"You going to see Priscilla tonight?"

"No, she has class. I need to figure out how to get all the answers to the test in and out without Calloway seeing them. I forgot how we did it at school....cuff I think, but that won't work with a uniform."

"Easy. Encode A, B, C, D into dots and then put them on your flight boots in the right order. You wear flight suits to the test and tell Calloway you have a make-up flight right after the test."

"You are a larcenous genius, Vic."

C.K. McCUSKER

THE TEST

Butch and Graham showed up for the test at 0855. Calloway was waiting with a smile. "You, sirs, have had a hard time with the first two. Don't concern yourselves though. This one is much harder."

What a dick.

Calloway handed out tests. They had it made. Graham planned to finish the test in half the time just to piss Calloway off. They both started the test, and Graham sailed through the first twenty questions. Then Graham noticed one question that he knew the answer to…it was a "B," but his answer key said "C." Uh-oh. Shit! He went back to the beginning and looked for other questions that he knew or had a good idea about. Definitely the wrong test…they were screwed. *Teach English to savages until death do them part.*

Graham whispered: "Butch. Butch. Wrong test!"

He looked like he was going to kill Graham. He was. They were both in deep shit. The only thing they could do was actually take the test. Graham was about halfway through the test with about 10 minutes left to go. He decided to race to the end, answer every question that he knew, or maybe knew, and then "dartboard" the rest. Calloway came into the room and walked up behind Graham. He was marking an answer when Calloway coughed. He moved to "D," and he heard a quiet "Uh-huh." Saved! He flipped to the first page, started over, and took the whole test in about ten minutes with Calloway standing over his shoulder. The Sergeant then moved back to Butch and went through the same routine. Calloway scored the tests immediately. Graham got an 84. Butch got an 88.

Calloway, quietly, before they left: "You gentlemen are some lucky bastards. My CO got a call from Gross last night who had just received a call from Berka, wherever the hell he is. The instructions were clear. You would pass. Period. I am sworn to secrecy, and so are you gentlemen. Shit, you guys must have pictures of Berka. Well…enjoy your tours. The only thing you *really* need to know about weather is stay out of thunderstorms." They shook his hand and left quickly. Graham had no idea why Berka had such an interest in them, but it had saved their ass.

"RJ, you don't want to know what I was going to do to you after we flunked that test. It *started* with a severe beating and got worse from there."

"Get bent, Butch. If Berka didn't like us, we'd be dodging poison darts in sixty days, so bite me."

PICK-A-DICK

About seventy-five percent of their class graduated. It was a very cool ceremony, complete with multiple flyovers. When they marched off the field at the conclusion wearing Wings on their chests, they were both proud and thankful that they hadn't washed out. Still, in the back of their minds they now had an obligation to try to avoid getting killed in the next four years. Now they anxiously waited "Pick-A-Dick" day when the aircraft assignments came down. The aircraft were picked in order of class rank so they would be in the bottom third. Butch had started a rumor that one of the best assignments was being a FAC in the hopes that some morons ahead of them would suck up whatever slots came down. They had no idea what the aircraft choices would be, but it beat teaching Savage English 101.

When Pick-A-Dick came, there was a big surprise: five B-52 assignments. The B-52 was a strategic bomber that was the cornerstone of the Strategic Air Command. It was a Navigator's aircraft. They would go in the top ten. It was one of the best assignments a Nav could get, next to fast burners [fighters]. On top of that, if you were assigned a B-52 you had to go through Navigator Bombardier Training (NBT) which was at Mather for an additional six months. After NBT, you had to go to B-52 flight training at Castle AFB in Central California for another three months. It worked out very well from a "stall until the war is over" standpoint. They went over to the Ops desk and filled out the paperwork on their "wish" list by aircraft and airbase. Graham listed all five B-52 assignments with Fairchild AFB in Spokane, Washington as his first choice, followed by Homestead AFB in Florida, and Loring AFB in Maine. Graham wanted to stay in the West, but the chances were slim. He turned in his wish list and knew he was screwed. *FAC you buddy.* They left Ops to celebrate at the Club,

"Well, Butch, what did you put down on your wish list? FACs I'm sure were at the top." It was bad luck to reveal your wish list.

"Shit yes, buddy. I figured since we've been together since OCS, we might as well get killed together. All FACs and the Gun Ships. They all go low and slow. Plus they are poorly armored, so the small arms shit goes right through them. Wouldn't miss that opportunity. Shit no … hey look …"

Colonel Berka, the Wing CO, was walking toward them. They saluted as he approached; Berka returned the salute and stopped them: "Lieutenants Graham and Butchermein, congratulations, gentlemen. I knew you would make it in spite of yourselves. You guys aren't the first through here to major in booze and broads and turn out to be pretty good aviators after all."

Graham: "Thank you, sir."

"Well, you guys just fill out your wish lists?"

Both: "Yes, sir."

"I won't ask you what you selected since we all know what that means, but I'm sure that you gentlemen will get some appropriate assignments. You have shown yourselves as pretty good aviators. That, to me, is of primary importance. I don't really care about weather exams. That's why we have weather officers. Class work is fine, but can the guy fly? We are aviators, gentlemen. Good luck. You'll get to fly what is best for you and the United States Air Force." They saluted, and the Colonel went into Ops.

"You know what, Butch - remember when Duke said that the majority of the selection process was rigged, so we should forget the wish lists anyway?"

"Yeah, that's when he said the senior staff meets secretly like a football draft and assigns most of the important birds based on the flight instructor's evals. I don't believe it for a minute. Look at Trashpile. He graduated high, wanted the RF, and got it. No, they go by class rank, man. And that means FAC you and FAC me. Better put, go FAC yourself."

"If you listened to Berka carefully… he already knows where we are going. Think about what he said, Butch. His last sentence was a dead giveaway."

"I wasn't listening that carefully. I thought it was the usual congrats shit, which it was. He was just chitchatting with the peon Lieutenants, man. That's all. Don't read shit into it. You're dreaming."

"He said, 'you'll get what is best for you and USAF.' Now how the hell can he say that if this thing is a so-called random draw based on class rank and our choice? I'm telling you he knows, and he told us he knows."

"Listen. We both know what we put down, and we both know that we are dreaming. Cram it, man, and get real. I'll buy."

Bob Foster joined them on the way into the Club. "I hear you guys passed the weather exam through some act of God. You guys might take up all the FAC jobs. Thanks a lot."

Butch jumped on Bob's comment. "Did we tell you you're buying, dickhead? Buying and lying rhyme. C'mon."

They ordered the usual. The Club was jammed with their classmates. Everybody was drinking too much and lying to each other. No one was saying what they really selected, so Graham started a count on a bar napkin. Vic came in and said one of his closest college buddies was a FAC and loved it. Got laid in Thailand all the time on R&R by beautiful Eurasian whores; only got shot at occasionally; he was stationed at Da Nang, et cetera. Graham gave up the count. The lies were overwhelming.

THE DAY THEY GET THE BIRD

1400 hrs Base Ops…

There was a line all the way out on the sidewalk. The front door had been locked when the assignments came in, so the entire Class was outside. It was raining. No one gave a shit. The doors opened at 1400 exactly, and the line started to move. The next four years of everyone's life, and in some cases their lives themselves, rested on what the paper inside the envelope said.·

When RJ and Butch got close to the door, they saw guys coming out with varying expressions and comments.

"I got a 130 [trash hauler] to Germany, man!"

"135 to Dyess! [gas passer to Texas]"

"I haven't heard any B-52s, man. Anybody that got one would be smiling and cheering. You're screwed for sure and so am I for being around your bad luck."

"Eat me, RJ. I ain't heard any 'I got my FAC to Deadsville' either. They are waiting for you and me."

Bob walked out smiling. Graham grabbed him by the arm: "OK, Lieutenant Foster. You're not smiling like a Cheshire cat because you got the big hose. Tell us what you got, or we'll dye your hair to a normal color." Bob had bright red hair, and he took constant shit about it. He didn't mind at all. He knew his classmates only gave shit to guys they liked.

"I got a B52 G to Blytheville in Arkansas, boys. So you guys can kiss my ass, or my red head, at sundown when you get your OV-10s to the Shooting Gallery." Graham and Butch congratulated him, and they meant it. He got a really choice assignment. The little shit… that meant that there were only four left. Inside there were three lines divided alphabetically: A to J, K to R, and S to Z. The first line was the longest. Graham intentionally got in the wrong line because it was the shortest.

Graham got to the table: "Graham, ma'am. R.J. Graham."

"You're in the wrong line, Lieutenant; this is the K to R line."

He put on his very best "but, mom, can't you help me just this once" look. The Eyes. It worked as it almost always did.

"But you waited so long. Laverne... Laverne, do you have Lieutenant Graham's envelope?"

Smiling his very best smile and using The Eyes again: "Thank you very, very much." On the way out to the sidewalk some of his classmates had noticed the stunt.

"Nice move, prick."

"Why the rush to get a FAC, RJ?"

"You're an asshole, RJ. Wish I'd thought of it."

He got out of the way, tore open the envelope, and scanned down:

Department of the Air Force ... Roswell J. Graham ... is hereby ordered to report ... to the ... 325th Bomb Squadron, 92nd Bomb Wing, 15th Air Force assigned as Navigator, AFSC 1 ... B-52G no later than 1600 hours on 2 June 70 ...

Thank you, Colonel Berka and Thank you, God...

Butch was astounded to find he had gotten a B-52 to Homestead AFB in Florida. RJ, Bob, and Butch all met at the Club which was jammed as expected. Everybody was drinking to the fact that they had been assigned their first choice, which was complete bullshit. It turned out that three of the guys in the top 20% got OV10s. They didn't show up at the Club.

RJ: "Well, guys, I told you so. Carm was right. The only guy standing here that should have gotten a BUFF if it wasn't rigged is Bob. Butch and I should have been lead rabbits in the Mekong Delta Shooting Gallery."

Bob, quizzically and slightly blasted: "You know guys, I still don't know how you passed the weather exam. I know that you went in to heist the answers, but I heard a couple of days later that Calloway was used to that, so he intentionally left the wrong exam with the wrong answers to trap us. You must have gotten lucky."

Butch, looking over at Graham and scowling behind Bob's back: "Yeah, we did luck out. We really lucked out."

Graham, snarling back at Butch behind Bob's shoulders briefly: "Yeah, but we all made it for whatever reason. Let's celebrate our fortune, and let's celebrate something else that you guys don't know about yet."

Bob: "Such as?"

"I'm getting married."

Bob: "You have got to be kidding. We never believed you would actually take yourself off the market. I'm stunned."

Butch, staring intently: "I never thought you'd go through with it either. I figured that as soon as you got done here and didn't need the Colonel's daughter anymore that it was bye-bye time."

"Well both you guys are wrong, and I would like to have you guys participate in my wedding. Butch, I would like you to be my Best Man. We'll be married as soon as we are all done with advanced flight training."

Bob jumped off the stool. "Wow! Double congratulations, man! Fantastic! Sure, I would be honored to do that."

Butch smiled his big full faced smile. He hugged his adopted brother as tears ran down his face: "You bet I'll be there. I'm honored to be your Best Man. Thanks, RJ. God Bless. You are a very lucky man."

The three completed Nav Bomb Training without much difficulty. They finished first, second, and fourth in class standing since RJ and Butch were no longer trying to flunk out. Bob finished first, so RJ and Butch tortured him for being a kiss ass. There next assignments were Survival School and then B-52 training at Castle AFB in Merced, CA, but first came RJ and Priscilla's wedding.

THE WEDDING

19 Dec 70

RJ had done what he usually did in finding the woman that would be his wife today. He stole her from another man. He had been blessed with good looks and penetrating blue eyes that many women found irresistible. Today that would all end. Today he would exchange vows with the most beautiful, charming, and intelligent woman he had ever met. He had met her very briefly at a party on base sponsored by the Cadets for the DGs at the University. When they first met, he couldn't continue the conversation because he had another date and had to leave for SFO. All the way to the City, he couldn't get her out of his mind. But he spent the weekend in the City with an American stew and she convinced him that his bachelor program was well worth the trade offs. Nothing serious. He had sworn to himself that he wouldn't get "serious" again until he was thirty. That way he wouldn't have to pass up "One time, Non-reoccurring Sexual Opportunities" or "ONSO's" as his classmates called them. He also wouldn't get emotionally damaged again nor would he damage any other girl. If he even thought things were getting serious, he moved on immediately. He forgot that rule three weeks later when he met Priscilla again. She was dating a Cadet that was absolutely crazy about her. Tough shit, buddy. All's fair in love and war. RJ attacked. He had never lost a battle yet.

Ten months later. ONSO's had ended. In fact they had ended for RJ ten months earlier. He awoke to Butch's boisterous voice. Butch was his best friend and would be his Best Man today. "Hey, RJ! Wake up! The wedding's been postponed on account of you have been re-assigned to Project English! Gross finally caught up with you because Berka got promoted."

RJ opened his eyes slowly and looked at the clock. 0809. "Get out, Butch. Get out now or I get up and kick you in the nuts instantly. So get out now and save your manhood, if you have one… wait… what time am I getting married? "

"Used to be 1400, RJ. But they tore the tent down and packed it so you could take it with you to the Central Highlands."

RJ rolled over, not smiling yet. "I wasn't getting married in a tent, dickbreath. You screwed up your bullshit."

"Oh yes you are. In the Central Highlands, that is if Priscilla wants to go there… and then if she can get there."

Graham had enough. He bolted out of bed toward Butch's voice. He was tackled hard and forcefully put back on the bed. Butch wasn't alone. The lights went on in the heavily curtained room. His entire wedding party was there. Vic, Bob, Trashpile, everybody.

RJ: "You are all fired. Get out."

Vic: "We ain't fired, RJ. But y'all is retired as of about 1430 ah estimate, when you will say 'Ah do.' No more ONSOs. Now take this so ya don't change your mind, boy." It was a shot glass full of some sort of booze. It was way too early *and* this was his wedding day.

RJ: "No way, you dicks. We have to WALK, not stumble down the aisle. Go home." There was a simultaneous "drink it" from the wedding party. He did.

He could tell immediately that it was Wild Turkey. It went off like a firecracker in his empty stomach. Vic produced the bottle, and they all had another shot and then another. Fortunately, there were nine of them so the bottle emptied quickly.

Six hours passed quickly in spite of the "Turkey Breakfast" as they coined it. They all found themselves in the anteroom of The Trinity Cathedral in downtown Sacramento, a beautiful old church that was famous for its elegance and architecture. They were all dressed in "Mess Dress" uniforms, the Air Force equivalent of a tuxedo. RJ hated them because they were the worst design of all the services. The Navy had the coolest, and the Marines were next, followed by the Army. He and his guys looked like a wait staff. Finally, at 1403, the processional started. Graham stood at the altar while his groomsmen escorted the bridesmaids down the aisle. *Boy those bridesmaids look terrific! Now there are some ONSOs that I didn't know. Priscilla did a good job of hiding them...* He was teasing himself and trying to control his emotions... *knock it off... this is your wedding day, and you are in God's House!* All those thoughts left the "confirmed bachelor's" mind when Priscilla and the Colonel turned into the aisle in the back of the church. *Absolutely spectacular! I have never ever seen a woman that beautiful. I am one lucky man. Thank you, Dear Lord in Your House.*

They took their vows and both managed to hold their emotions pretty well. The exit processional started and everything went as planned. Due to Sacramento being Priscilla's "home town" to the extent that an "Air Force Brat" can have a hometown, the Church was very full. Priscilla Graham was on Cloud Nine. RJ was on Ten. The newlyweds exited out the front of the Cathedral under the traditional crossed sabers held over their heads by the groomsmen. The last man holding the saber over the newlyweds' heads was the Best Man. Right after he helped his bride into the limo, RJ turned back to the groomsmen and looked straight at Butch. There were tears in his eyes, as well as RJ's. Graham slowly brought his right hand to the brim of his hat and saluted him. Almost as slowly, Butch brought the saber to the brim of his hat in a straight vertical, returning the salute.

The man that RJ had stolen Priscilla from was his Best Man.

There was no animosity from Butch. Priscilla was remarkably pretty and Butch had asked RJ to take her to her sister's coming out party because he was out of town that weekend. He had made a stupid error in judgment. He didn't blame RJ. She was a wonderful woman.

Right after Butch left town, Priscilla called and said that the coming out party had been cancelled but asked if they could go anyway. RJ gladly agreed because she was gorgeous and charming. She had a great figure and long strawberry blond hair. She laughed at his good jokes and frowned cutely at the bad ones. After the very first date, RJ knew he was toast. She was the one.

Forget the never serious routine. You don't have a choice this time.

What RJ found out much later, and Butch would never know, was that there never was a coming out party. Priscilla invented it knowing Butch had to go out of town. Butch had always been a means to an end. Her plan had always been RJ, but a little teasing and rivalry would probably seem "different" from the other girls that chased after this lieutenant. She would make herself a "prize" to be won.

Her plan clearly worked. RJ won the prize.

SURVIVAL SCHOOL

January, 1971

Graham and Butch had heard about Survival School but hadn't thought much about it until they realized that, with B-52 assignments, they had to go to it. Combat aviators had to go through it to teach them how to survive a shootdown and how to survive as a POW. It was two weeks of hell. In fact, they had heard that it was like hell week at the fraternity, but ten times worse. Passing Survival School was mandatory. If you didn't get through it, you lost your Wings. About twenty percent didn't get through it. The home of the school was ironically what would be Graham's home base, but the school had its own property which was all highly classified. No one knew where it was.

The School was divided into four phases: classroom instruction for four days, a simulated "shootdown" and attempted egress to escape, capture and imprisonment in an exact replica of a POW camp for a week, and "escape" and then evasion from the "enemy" for three days in the woods of northeast Washington.

Graham and Butch attended the classes and "sort of" listened as usual. They were both going to B-52 "G" models whose primary assignment was nuclear alert, so their chances of seeing combat were low. Besides, no one had ever shot down a B-52, except the older "D" models. They had been told in the classroom that everything was simulated and made as rough as possible without violating AFRs up to and including some physical abuse.

Lastly they were put on a point system. They would accumulate "points" for things that they did *wrong*. If they did something that would get them killed in a real POW situation they would get maxed on points and *start all over again* from the beginning. If they got maxed on points twice, they were washed out. Minor infractions resulted in fewer points than major infractions. No one wanted to start over, or worse, lose their Wings.

On the night of the fourth day, they were taken offsite and were dressed as instructed in flight suits and combat boots. They were dumped off in a field and told that they had just been shot down and they were to egress in "that" direction for five miles. If they made the entire five miles without capture, the school was over, and they would be graduated. What they didn't know was that no one ever had made the five miles.

It was sleeting.

Graham: "I'll tell you what I'm going to do. I'm going to that perimeter road over there, and I'm going to use the Squadron One conditioning and run the damn five miles and set myself free, man. None of these dipshit guards they must have out here can keep up with me. You should try the same on the other side of the field, Butch."

Butch: "Great idea. That way at least one of us should avoid capture. Let's get going."

They both took off running. Graham had gone about a half mile and was getting very cold and wet, but he hadn't seen anyone and was making good time. Then he ran into something that felt like a brick wall and knocked the wind out of him. He had been nailed. He lay on the ground in pain and unable to breathe when his eyes focused on a guy in a foreign uniform standing over him. He spoke in accented English: "You have just been shot to death, Lieutenant. You get to start over."

Graham was pushed into the back of a jeep-like vehicle and driven to what turned out to be the starting point. The sleet had begun to accumulate. Butch was already there. "Another brilliant idea, R.J. I'm dead. You must be the same."

"Yeah. If we try it again they might not expect it."

"You're right. They probably wouldn't think we could possibly be that stupid."

A Master Sergeant appeared from the dark: "Gentlemen, academic situation, you have already been "killed" once. If you listened in class you would know that if you get killed again you are out and goodbye Wings. Now I suggest that you get on your bellies and crawl as you should do given the threat environment that we are simulating which you would also have known had you listened in class."

Graham and Butch followed the instructor's suggestion and crawled over frozen and wet terrain for what seemed like an hour. Graham was getting so cold and wet that he thought he would get frostbite. Suddenly, from behind, he sensed a figure and there was a gun barrel pressed against his head. In the same kind of accented English: "Get up slow, and put your hands behind your head, you Yankee pig."

Graham complied with relief and started walking with the gun pressed in his back, hard at times. He was ushered into a dimly lit room after a short walk and saw Butch's tall outline in the light: "Hey, Butch."

He was slammed up against the wall. "Shut up, Yankee pig! You die!"

He was shoved into a closet the size of a coffin. He could barely turn at all, let alone sit down. He was left there for hours. He was freezing and tired when he was yanked out roughly and taken to a room for interrogation. It was intense and long, and he was still cold in a wet flight suit. They asked dozens of questions that he knew he shouldn't answer and didn't, but he was starting to shake from the cold. The interrogators were pros and obviously very well trained.

But so am I. Squadron One did me a great favor by teaching me I could do much more than I ever thought I could. They gave me the courage and motivation to put my head down and just do what is necessary for me... and my crew... to survive. The bad times won't last forever.

Finally, Graham sensed that the interrogation was wrapping up.

Interrogator: "Where is your home base?"

"RJ Graham, Lieutenant, United States Air Force."

"Shut your mouth, Yankee Pig!"

"Where is your home base?"

No answer.

"Answer, Pig!"

"You told me to shut my mouth."

"Home base NOW!"

"Disneyland."

"That bullshit! Give home base or we kill you, pig!"

"Fuck You Air Force Base, Home of the Flying Fucks."

A Master Sergeant in USAF uniform entered the room: "OK, gentlemen, academic situation. Lieutenant, you would have gotten yourself severely beaten for your last response. Given the conditions that you would be in, that would probably mean that you would die. The idea is to resist as we have taught you - not to get yourself killed. That's ten more points and you're on the verge of washing out, so follow your training."

Graham's mind was racing. *This sucked. Hell week was better, a lot better. Maybe a Club Officer job had opened up.* At dawn, Graham was given new clothing and escorted to a compound where other classmates were milling around by oil drums with fires inside. He was shoved rather violently into the compound by the guard and fell down. The guard was really good at being a prick. When the other prisoners saw Graham on the ground, they rushed over to try to carefully intervene.

The guard yelled, "If you cause any more trouble or tell more lies, you will be executed!" He flipped around his AK and slammed the butt on the ground next to Graham's head. Graham knew that the butt would have not missed in a real situation. He got the point.

The guard flipped his rifle back and pointed it toward the other prisoners. "You get back, or I shoot! I shoot all of you!"

They inched back a little and then held their ground. The guard seemed disgusted and furious but he suddenly turned and returned to the building. Graham was still on the freezing wet ground, his new dry "pajamas," which were similar to the clothes the real POWs wore, were now soaked. He was a bit stunned,

"Shit! That guy is either a real gook they imported for the role or he should be in Hollywood."

Bob Foster stepped forward and helped RJ up. "C'mon, RJ, you need to get warm or at least try to."

Bob was almost RJ's height but seemed much lighter. He had bright red hair and the light, freckled complexion that normally goes with red hair. He had an engaging smile that could, and did, disarm opponents in an argument or a debate. He had joined the Air Force through the Reserve Officer Training Corps (ROTC) at Emory University, which meant he really wanted to be in the Air Force *and* he had planned it. He was also a native of Georgia so he spoke in a dialect that Graham, the "Connecticut Yankee" as Bob often called him, barely understood. Despite the drawbacks of ROTC, planning ahead, and speaking in foreign tongues, RJ really respected and liked the guy. He and Butch had decided to convert him from almost a model officer to one of *them* and he was coming along. With a few beers as inspiration, they called him Howdy Doody at times, which Bob ignored with a smile.

RJ got a quick lesson in camaraderie with Bob's gesture. He felt the others cared for him, and he cared a great deal now for them. Survival School was teaching things that could never be taught in a classroom.

Bob led him in close to the fire and shared a cigarette. "Warm up, RJ. We heard that you and Butch got killed trying to run your way out. One strike, buddy. You are the acquisition officer by the way. I don't know what we need yet, but stick around. Dave Miller is commander. I'm the dep."

There was already a command structure in place, and they hadn't been there 24 hours. Somebody listened in class. One of the key things that they had learned in training was that the enemy did everything that they could to break down the command structure. If the structure broke down, it was far easier to demoralize the prisoners and get them to break down. The camp was a patchwork design of other POW camps from WWII, Korea, and Vietnam. Great care had been taken to make every detail as realistic as possible. There were Quonset huts with straw mats on the floor, but there was no heat. There were two burning oil drums in the dirt yard for heat, but there were about sixty "POWs" so they had to take turns getting warm.

Graham saw Butch over near the fence and walked over: "How you doing, Butch? Did you get interrogated?"

"I'm doing bad, thanks to you. I don't know why I listen to your cockamamie ideas. That 'run for the roses' escape plan was fucked, man. They put me in a closet that was smaller than a coffin. I damn near froze to death. No more big ideas."

"You could have said no and crawled if you wanted. Don't blame me for your decision to go along with a really bad idea. I have lots of really bad ideas. Want a new one?"

"Shit no I don't."

"What's your assignment?"

"I'm one of the escape officers. We're having a meeting at 0800 behind the Quonset over there."

One way that they could end their ordeal was to get a man out of the camp successfully.

Graham, excited: "Hey, when I was in the closet, I thought of a way that we could get a guy out fast rather than try to dig through this frozen shit. It would work, man."

"I told you I didn't want any more of your screwed up ideas."

"No, Butch, listen. Foster was a gymnast in college, and he is one of the lightest guys here. We get some sort of blanket or something like that and use it like a trampoline to toss him over the fence. Bob Damon was a tackle or guard at Illinois and you are one large, strong guy too. So what we do is have you two guys hold the blanket, and Bob runs up on to it just as you guys pull it up and he vaults over the fence and is gone in seconds."

"That is typical RJ. The guards would see what was going on and we'd get nowhere. I have to go to my meeting." The sun came out for about an hour, but the clouds came back, and it started snowing by noon. More interrogations were taking place, but they left Graham alone. He suspected that they didn't want him to wash out because navigators were in short supply. But hell, everybody was in short supply.

He ran into Butch by the fire barrel: "So what great plan did you guys come up with?"

"I can't tell anybody. There may be plants in here posing as POWs. There are a lot of guys we don't know very well."

Dave Miller came up and interrupted the conversation: "Graham, as acquisition officer, we need you to find a blanket. We need it right away. Meet us in an hour behind that Quonset."

He was pointing to the one at the far end of the camp, which Graham thought would be the place that every class had tried their escape since the beginning of the school. "Got it. I'll see what I can do. But why not try the jump from a place that they wouldn't expect it?"

Miller: "Like where?"

"Like the front gate, either on the left or the right."

"That is so stupid that it might actually work. We'll move the attempt to 1900 when it's dark, and I'll get the right people there. You show up with the blanket."

Miller walked away and Graham turned back to Butch. "You dirtbag, you stole my brilliant plan and took all the credit."

"Nobody had any plan. Everybody was too cold and couldn't think. The only thing they came up with was dig. But we have nothing to dig with, and the ground is frozen. So I gave them your cockamamie plan, and they said let's try it."

Graham spent the next several hours trying to get a blanket. There weren't any. One of the main "tortures" that they used was to keep everybody cold in the winter. He checked the straw mats, but they were old and brittle. They wouldn't work, even if doubled up. He showed up at the gate at just before 1900. Graham walked up to Miller. "There are no blankets. What we need to do is just have Butch and Bob *throw* Bob over the fence. If they locked hands and Bob took a running start he might get enough leverage to make it. Basically, we don't have a choice."

Miller: "Agreed. Let's go." Miller wandered in and out of the assembled people who appeared to be just shooting the shit in small groups and passed the final plan to them. Just before 1930, Foster appeared from the dark.

Foster, whispering to Miller and the others: "You know what, guys? I wasn't a gymnast in college. I don't know who volunteered my ass, but I do know I can't do any vaults or shit. So how do I get over?

Butch, grinning: "Simple. You're light, so we'll just throw your ass over the fence and hope you don't break your neck when you land. Remember not to." Butch and Damon turned and locked hands low. Foster walked briskly, put one foot on the joined hands, and jumped. He cleared the fence by a foot and landed on his feet on the other side. The instant he landed the spotlights went on him, and the guards with machine guns surrounded him.

The guards had been waiting for them. There was a "plant" among prisoners working for the enemy. Bob was dragged back through the front gate and taken to the "box." The box was a three by four foot box on the ground outside of the commandant's quarters that had a trap door lid and a floor made of large rocks. It was about a foot in height and had just enough room to cram a person inside if he laid in the fetal position. The guards forced him into the box, closed the lid, and locked it. It began to snow harder. Damon and Butch were taken inside for some closet time.

Shortly after midnight, the Commandant had all the POWs assembled in front of his quarters. Damon and Butch joined them. The Commandant, known only as "Boris," came out on the porch of his quarters and addressed the prisoners for about ten minutes, berating them as Yankee Dogs, criminals, and spies. He was good. He had a Russian accent, and he was very stern. Boris had been a prisoner of the Germans during the War and escaped twice. He was a naturalized citizen and an Air Force Colonel.

When he concluded his speech, a guard walked up to the box and kicked it: "Number twenty three!"

All "POWs" were given numbers when they were first interrogated. No names or rank were ever used by the guards as a further attempt to break down the command structure.

There wasn't an answer from the "box." Foster had been in the box for almost four hours. He was a tough little kid, but he'd been lying on the cold rocks and unable to move for a long time.

The guard kicked the box again: "Number twenty three!"

No answer.

One of the things that the school could not do was seriously injure a student. There was obvious concern as the guard kicked the box two more times and there wasn't any answer or sound at all.

Boris had been observing. "Open the box."

The guard did as he was ordered, unlocked it and pulled the door open. Foster was in a fetal position but turned his head and smiled at the guard.

The guard was furious: "Number twenty three, why didn't you answer!"

"I couldn't hear you. I was in the other room takin' a shit."

The guard lost it. The entire camp broke up. Even the Commandant was laughing.

The camp portion of the school was completed at 0600 the morning of the box incident. Butch, RJ, and Bob completed the rest of the school without much incident or difficulty aside from RJ not drinking enough water on the evasion trek and having to be hospitalized when they got back. Bob became a local hero for his response to the guard.

All three went to Castle AFB in Merced, California to train in B-52s and get qualified for crew duty. They graduated in May and left to report to their respective bases: Butch to Homestead AFB in Florida, Graham to Fairchild, and Bob to Blytheville, AFB in Arkansas.

What they didn't realize when they left Castle was that they were now official *crewdogs.*

CHAPTER IV:
CREWDOGS THAT WOULD BE PIRATES

FAIRCHILD AFB, SPOKANE, WASHINGTON

June, 1971

Graham reported for duty on 2 June. After a meeting with the Squadron Commander, Lt. Colonel Leonard Weinwiller, who welcomed him to the squadron and warned him to stay away from the Club and all the bad examples that hung out there, he was ushered around by a Master Sergeant to pick up his gear and flight suits. He was scheduled to meet his new crew at 0800 the following morning. He took the afternoon off and helped Priscilla with the unpacking. He had been assigned a three bedroom house in the junior officers housing area. Not a bad deal considering that housing was tough to get. It was tiny but more than adequate for just the two of them and Priscilla was happy with it. As the daughter of an Air Force Colonel, she had been raised on airbases in Germany and all over the U.S. Consequently, unlike many other junior officers' wives, she needed no acclimation to military life. She was twenty-two years old, beautiful, very bright, and quite charming. Graham surmised that her charm was a result of having to make new friends so many times as a child as she was uprooted and moved from base to base. She had certainly charmed him, so much so that he had fallen in love and broken all of his self-imposed rules.

Even if she hadn't been an "Air Force brat," as the children of USAF fathers were called, there would be no difference in her feelings for her new home because she didn't care where they lived as long as they were together. She had married the love of her life, and RJ had a "nuclear'" assignment, so he wouldn't have to go to that awful war. He had promised her that he wouldn't have to go.

At about 1600, RJ decided that he needed to head for the Club to see if he could meet any "bad examples" that might be there.

Walking into the living room, he grabbed Priscilla and pulled her close. "I have to go over to the club and meet some guys that I don't know yet. It's a mandatory formation, and I'll be back in a couple of hours."

She kissed him and smiled. "My ass it's mandatory, Lieutenant. You're talking to an Air Force girl remember? It's probably top secret but not mandatory."

Graham promptly slid has hand down her back and grabbed her butt. "Don't bring your gorgeous ass up or I'll miss my top secret mandatory formation and get assigned to Project English." He kissed her hard and nearly reconsidered but instead promised his princess dinner in town when he got back.

The Club was similar to the club at Mather. Dark on dark and smelling like years of beer and smoke. Graham went to the bar and looked around. There were two Majors in uniform sitting at the bar and four guys in civvies sitting at a low table in the corner. Graham went to the bar and got a beer. He noticed that the guys in the corner were playing some sort of dice game and decided to go over and quietly observe. He quickly picked up on the fact that whatever the game was it was pretty high stakes… at least for Air Force officers.

After about five minutes, one of the players confronted him. "You want to play, buddy, or just stand there and pretend you're playing?"

The man speaking to him had close-set dark eyes, black hair, and a thin mustache. He smiled after he completed his invitation. For some reason, Graham felt immediately at ease.

"No. I'm new on base and have no idea what you are playing. Besides, it looks like I can't afford it."

"You only can't afford it if you lose. Sit down. I'm Spike Wilson." He stuck out his hand, and Graham shook it.

"Spike, I'm RJ Graham, good to meet you."

"These bums that are taking my money… Walt Goldstein, callsign Wildman; Pat Duggen, callsign Sluggo; and Jack Wells, callsign Blackjack, for obvious reasons."

They all stood and shook hands. Wildman was a good looking man with a dark tan, blond hair, and a smile that never seemed to leave his face. Sluggo was about 5' 7" but seemed well built. The only way to describe his build was "thick." He wasn't fat, just thick. He had long brown hair and moved with confidence. Blackjack was tall, maybe 6'3." He was also black and his real first name was Jack. That made a pretty easy callsign. Graham sensed he was welcome by everybody except Blackjack who was standoffish and seemed cautious.

Spike: "What the hell does RJ stand for? Your mother couldn't think of a real name?"

"It's the initials for my real name which sucks, so I stick with those."

"Whatever. For now your new name is Jeep. That's a kinder name than what you really are which is FNG."

Graham foolishly asked for clarification. "What's a FNG?"

"Only a Fucking New Guy would ask that question. Sit down, Jeep."

"How did you know I was new on base?"

"Because you are my new navigator. I'm the bomber on E-05, which is your new crew. You'll meet all of us tomorrow morning. It's a very good sign that you showed up at the Club after just getting on base and reporting. I have no doubt Lennie told you to stay away from here." He grinned. "We might get along, Jeep."

Sluggo: "Understand that's very rare. Almost no one gets along with that asshole."

Spike: "That's by choice, you dwarf midget puke. Why don't you roll? Jeep, you just watch for a while. I don't want my new Nav to get fleeced his first day on base. Sluggo and Wildman are bomber drivers; Blackjack is a Nav. The drivers come in regularly and donate to the navigators."

Sluggo: "The point is five. You playing, Spike, or just chattering at your unfortunate new Nav?"

"I'm in. Now listen up, Jeep, I'm only going to tell you once how to play 4-5-6. All players ante up $20. Assume 5 players like we have here, so the pot equals $100. Roll three dice each to determine who is shooter. High count wins the dice: 666 wins, or 655, etc. Then the shooter comes out: He can bet any portion of the pot: $20, $50, $60 or all of it: $100. To win you have to do the following:

"If the shooter rolls a 456 he automatically wins whatever he bet and starts over. He keeps the dice and no one else rolls. If the shooter rolls a pair and a 6, called a "point" he automatically wins whatever he bet but the other shooters get to shoot. If the shooter rolls "trips" i.e. 444, 555, etc. he automatically wins whatever he bet but the other shooters get to shoot. Except for 111. He loses. If the shooter rolls trip 6s: 666 he automatically wins whatever he bet and he gets the dice after the roll unless someone rolls 456. Then they get the dice. If another shooter rolls 666, the dice stay with the current shooter. See how simple it is?

"Now losing, which the knuckle draggers specialize in. If the shooter rolls a 123 he automatically loses whatever he bet, and owes the pot double what he bet. He also loses the dice and passes them right. If the shooter rolls a "pair and a point," and the point is "1" he automatically loses whatever he bet, but the other shooters get to roll. If the shooter rolls a 111 he automatically loses whatever he bet, but the other shooters get to roll. The "point" is everything. So… the shooter rolls a 4. Next guy, 5: he wins. Next guy 3: he loses. Next guy, 4: tie. He starts over. What happens most commonly is the point rides and guys either win or lose.

"However, the dice holder may say 'all of it'… say $400. 456 takes it all. 666, 446, 336, etc. will probably take it all, but the other guys get to shoot. If there's a tie: nothing happens, and the dice stay with the current shooter. If the shooter rolls a 123, he automatically loses whatever he bet and passes the dice right. It's really a simple game and very fast. You can win, or lose, a small fortune in no time. You got that, Jeep?"

Graham: "Oh sure. Very simple."

Spike: "Good. Then you're in. Put in twenty."

Graham was a good gambler in college.

He lost $300 in fifteen minutes.

He had the money because it was his part of his moving allowance. Priscilla would kill him. He decided to play conservatively and watched to pick up on the nuances of the game. When the game broke up because everybody but Spike had to go home to their wives, Graham had won $460 in his first 4-5-6 game so he was $160 up. Not bad for a brown bar. He loved it.

Spike: "Jeep, you're setting a bad example for navigators. You're supposed to come in and lose a couple of times to the drivers so they get comfortable that we're as dumb as they are. Then we clean their clocks."

Wildman: "Screw you, Spike. I bought my boat with the dough you donated playing."

"Yeah, but I sank it, so what good did it do you?"

"He did, Jeep. Your new bomber hit a jetty going full throttle out at Fourth of July Lake. Don't ever loan him your boat. He'll wreck it on purpose."

"Bullshit. You drank that swill all day in the sun and passed out, or I wouldn't have been driving. If you had been awake, you would have wrecked your own boat."

Graham looked across the table at his new bomber. He sensed that he would learn a great deal more from Spike than how to play 4-5-6 in the months that lay ahead. He had gotten lucky.

CREW FAI-E05

Graham's crew were all in the mission planning room at 0800. The crew designator FAI-E05 stood for Fairchild Experienced crew number five. It was about the middle of the pack in the Squadron. The crew did not fit with Spike and Graham. Graham was introduced to the crew he would come to know very well in the coming months:

JOE BOB CARTER

Joe Bob was Major Dickie Carter's call sign. He was a Major and the pilot. Joe Bob was very unusual for a call sign, but it was fitting. He hated it. Joe Bob was the redneck's redneck. How in the hell he ever made Major defied logic and cast great doubt on the United States Air Force promotion system.

Joe Bob was a west Texas load. People say that his "Daddy is a big man too," which is west Texas for fat. He weighed at least 230 and was maybe 5' 9". He had the largest flight suit he could get and he could *barely* zip it up. He had close cropped red hair that came to a point in the middle of his forehead, a round fleshy face, and eyes that were so far apart that they almost reached his ears. When he smiled, which was almost never, he looked like he was growling at you. He had a very distinct Texas accent that irritated the hell out of most people, especially other Texans.

Joe Bob's *most* distinctive physical attribute was his neck. It was the same diameter as his head, so when you met him it appeared as though there was just a large boil protruding from his shoulders. But the topper was the back of his neck. The back of Joe Bob's neck was bright red.

Always.

It was fitting since he was a genuine walking definition of a redneck. Joe Bob had been trained from an early age by his west Texas parents, Eileen and Leon, to hate all ethnic diversities, women ('cep fer fuckin'), Yankees, Midwesterners (especially Oklahomans), and basically all people that didn't live in west Texas (and at least half of those that lived in West Texas were hated as well).

Joe Bob listened to his parents and grew up to be a world class bigot. Somehow he managed to acquire a reasonable amount of twisted intelligence that allowed him to complete pilot training. Spike marveled at how this could have occurred, then realized that he went into the USAF in the late 50's when no one was entering the military.

When the crew was first assembled, Joe Bob tried to be dictatorial and "commanding." His words and actions were completely wasted on Spike and would be on Graham as well. In fact, no one paid attention to him except the Nosepick [Electronic Warfare Officer]. He was a major kiss ass and re-born Christian before anyone knew that they could be re-born. His name was Don "Thump" (as in Bible) Darden, and Spike had a very low opinion of him. He couldn't do his job worth a shit, and he "preached" to the point that he pissed the others off.

So Joe Bob had one friend out of a crew of six (really five in his mind since "Guns" didn't exist). He gave orders that no one listened to and would launch into ethnic cleansing speeches whenever he got drunk.

ROLLER SEEPS

SSgt. Ron "Roller" Seeps was a B-52 gunner... and accomplished international polygamist. Roller was a thin, wiry guy with permanently dirty brown hair, close-set half open eyes, and an engaging slightly bucktoothed smile (save only the dark brown front tooth).

Roller got his nickname, which was short for rollercoaster, through his movement up and down the enlisted ranks. Prior to his mandatory assignment as a B-52 gunner, Roller had attempted to embark upon several other USAF specialties. No one could recall all of them, but most had been selected for the potential work ethic (little to none) and for the intellectual prowess required (none). He had been a gate guard when he was busted down to E-1 for the first time, when he had to be awakened at the gate by a two star's driver. He moved on to an assignment in Germany where he got married to a nice 200 pound Nazi blond ("Eva") who was much stronger than Roller and incredibly mean spirited. In spite of that, Roller settled down and worked his way up from E-1 to E-3 working as a "landscape specialist" at the base golf course. Roller loved this assignment because most of the work was done by somebody else.

Returning from Germany as an E-2, he went on to more assignments and was later transferred to SAC. No one could figure out how he got into SAC, but after a short stint with the sky cops he was sent to gunnery school. He was not given a choice of assignment. He would be a B-52 gunner. He was delighted! Once he found out that no B-52 had ever been attacked in the air by anything – ever – *and* he got to sit alone in the tail on long flights and sleep, he determined that this was the greatest job he could ever have. In addition, there were long TDY's [temporary duty's] that got him away from Fraulein Eva who had bulked up since coming to the States.

Roller got assigned to Fairchild and their crew because Joe Bob never paid any attention to enlisted people and generally didn't speak to them. As a result, Joe Bob didn't even review his personnel file, nor did he even know his name. He called all gunners "guns" when he spoke to them at all, which was rare.

THE CO

The co-pilot, Bart Matthews, was completely non-descript. He was just there. He flew in the right seat upstairs and almost no one ever said anything to him except in the course of flying the mission. Spike thought he was an alien spy from another planet.

Everybody had some sort of personality, except Bart.

THE INTRODUCTIONS

Joe Bob: "I want ya'll to welcome our new Nav, Lt. R.J. Graham. He finished well in his class at Castle and brings fresh spirit to the crew."

Spike: "We already met last night at the Club, Dickie. He cleaned our clocks at 4-5-6. He's got talent."

Joe Bob was pissed: "You mean you already ruint our brand new Nav!? You and those crim'nels you hang out with! Goddammit, Spike, you ruint the last one, and you cain't even wait a day to ruint this one! Nav, you stay the hell away from Spike and his crim'nel friends!"

"Now Dickie, how can he stay away from me if we have to fly together? And those criminals that I hang out with are the two best pilots in the Squadron and one of the best Navs. He can learn a lot from those fine young officers."

"They ain't the best pilots in the Squadron, me an' Leeper are, and don't you fergit that, boy! And Nav, you keep away from them! That's an order!"

Spike leaned forward and stared at Joe Bob. "Dickie, the last time you called me 'boy,' I knocked you on your fat ass, which I'm about to do again. You and Leeper couldn't come close to Sluggo and Wildman if you were real birds with real wings. You both suck, so don't kid yourselves. Why do you think they both drive StanBoard crews as Captains, while you are driving an 'E' as a Major? It's not that you're a loser, Dickie; you're just not my kind of winner."

C.K. McCUSKER

Thump: "You can't speak to the aircraft commander in that tone, Major Wilson. It is not respectful."

"Shut the hell up, kiss ass. You are not allowed to speak to me. Remember?"

Joe Bob, in a pathetic effort to command: "Enough of this shit! This ain't no way to welcome our new Nav! He'll think his new crew is all fucked up and request his self a crew change like the last kid did! Now ya'll shut up! We got an ORI readiness mission comin' up on Wednesday an' I want to ace it to keep Lizard off my back! That means you, Spike! No more shit in the weeds!"

THE LIZARD

Colonel Dick "Lizard" Roberson was the 92nd Bomb Wing Commander. He got his nickname from his penchant for licking his lips, and his tongue would dart in and out while speaking whenever he got nervous.

He was always nervous.

Lizard lived in a world of Operational Readiness Inspections: the ORI. It was a large threatening cloud that hung over his head all the time. ORI's were SAC's way of seeing if your Wing was capable of wiping out a large portion of an assigned continent should the need arise. The ORI team would show up completely unannounced to the point of total secrecy and seal the Base. They would then go to the Command Post and initiate a simulated war order. *Everything* had to go perfectly or the Wing CO could kiss any chance for a star goodbye. Everybody had to fly a simulated ORI every month, and Lizard would personally review the results of each mission. If *anything* went wrong, Lizard would jump down the AC's throat and make life miserable for him until he flew a flawless simulation the next month. The problem was that a B-52 crew was just that, a crew. Joe Bob could fly a perfect mission, but if Spike threw a couple of simulated bombs out in the weeds the mission failed, and Joe Bob was in for another month of misery.

Spike always threw a couple of bombs in the weeds. He delighted in seeing Joe Bob tortured by Lizard. The only time that Spike did not throw bombs into the weeds was the real ORI, which he invariably aced.

Spike, responded after giving his "Spike" smile. "Sure, Dickie, the new Nav and I will go over to the sim [flight simulator] and practice for hours so we shack [direct hit] everything. Then Lizard'll give you a break. Let's go, Nav."

Spike grabbed Graham by the arm, and they left the planning room while Joe Bob was still talking.

THE GOLF OUTING

Spike put his hand on Graham's shoulder as they walked away from Ops. "You a golfer, Jeep?"

"Yes, I enjoy it when I get the time. I played a lot at Mather."

"Good. Go home, and change into golf threads, grab your sticks, and meet me at the course at 1100. We'll have a little lunch and tee off around noon. I'll call Sluggo and Wildman to see if they can play. See you there… do you know where it is?"

"Yes. I found it right after I got here, but what about the sim?"

Spike shook his head in simulated disgust: "You disappoint me, kid. The last thing I need is a sim. I can do this shit blindfolded. You'll quickly learn that. Oh, and don't worry about the crew. They are morons, but we'll get all the ones we don't like moved out pretty soon and bring in guys we like. See you at the course."

One hell of an introduction. It wasn't all bad though; at least I'm not getting shot at every day.

Graham got to the course a few minutes early, but Sluggo was already there. He grabbed a sandwich and joined Sluggo who waved him over.

"You are one lucky navigator, Graham. Did you know that?"

"Why do you say that?"

"Do you know who you're flying with?"

"Yeah. I met the crew this morning at planning."

"I don't mean those dipshits. I mean Spike. Spike is a legend."

"How so?"

"I'm stunned you don't know. Spike is the flat out best bombardier in SAC. He is famous for some of the things he's done, places he's been, rat fucks he's pulled, and the people he knows. But you'll never know it from him. He never ever talks about himself. I heard about some of his feats at various times in Clubs at other bases as well as here, along with his popularity with the local women in various countries. I found out he got shot down on a run over Vinh in '68. He never told me about it, and I'm one of his best friends. I also heard he's very wealthy…

doesn't have to be in the Air Force. He made a fortune in gold from Asia and bought land somewhere back home. He talks about that sometimes but never about what he's done in combat."

"No. I never heard about him. I guess I am lucky. I can learn from the best of the best."

Spike walked through the front door of the clubhouse.

Sluggo: "Here he comes. Don't say anything about what I just told you."

The threesome teed off and played a pretty good round.

The following Wednesday while flying the ORI simulation, Spike gleefully threw two simulated bombs into the weeds. Lizard went berserk and ripped Joe Bob, as usual. Spike started to consider keeping Joe Bob.

"Shit, there's no other redneck pilot in SAC that I know of, and Joe Bob is so much fun to humiliate. If we get another pilot, it might get boring."

THE SUNDAY SURPRISE

In the months that followed, Spike and Graham became a good team and good friends. They aced the ORI for Lizard despite Lizard almost having a nervous breakdown when the actual ORI team showed up. The crew spent one week a month on nuclear alert living at the alert facility. Two or three times a month, the alert horn would go off and the alert crews would race to the aircraft. When they got onboard they would decode a simulated war message and proceed accordingly, usually starting the engines and pulling the chocks. Unlike the "old days," they would never taxi the aircraft with nuclear weapons onboard. If they taxied, they were going to war, or at the very least, to their "failsafe" points to await the go code or a recall.

The alert crews could use trailers next to the alert facility to have "dinner and conversation" with their wives or girlfriends. This broke the monotony for the crews but created more than one unplanned child since nobody ever had dinner. The war seemed to be winding down, and the Vietnamese were back at the peace talks. Graham made first lieutenant, and Spike was turned down for Lt. Colonel, which was no surprise to anyone since Spike was not political and politics were required.

Spike and Graham were out hunting illegally the first Sunday in April '72. Spike was hunting with his 9mm automatic pistol, which made things even more illegal. They were in the woods southeast of the base about twenty miles when a Sky Cop [the base air police] came out of nowhere. Spike was shaken. *How the hell had he found them? Why had he found them? Sky Cops didn't enforce the Washington hunting laws.*

"Major Wilson, sir. You and Lt. Graham are to report immediately to base operations. Do not return to your quarters to change. Go directly there. That is a direct order from Colonel Roberson."

Graham came into the clearing and was shocked to see the Sky Cop. "What's up, Spike?"

"We are. Up shit creek, that is. Whenever they send the Sky Cops to track you down in the woods on Sunday, something is up, and it isn't ever good. I smell a rapid deployment, or we are on the edge of going nuclear with the Ruskies or China… but that's unlikely. Let's go find out."

Base Ops had three crews waiting: Sunny Nagahashi's crew and Leeper's. Spike thought this was unusual as well. Too few crews. Lizard came in the room and the crews stood at attention.

Lizard came in and went behind the podium; he was licking up a storm. Spike was always amazed that he could dart for flies and speak at the same time,

"Be seated, gentlemen. What I am about to tell you is classified top secret. The North Vietnamese have again walked away from the peace table last night our time. The President has ordered a major escalation in bombing as a result. SAC is deploying G models to the war for the first time, which gives you some idea of how serious this is. You will be flying in 24 hours, so go home and pack for an extended stay. I expect two to three months. You will be given your destination at the PTOB (pre-take off briefing). You are to tell your families only that you will be gone TDY for an indeterminate period of time. I will see you back here in 21 hours at 1800 hours local. That is all. You're dismissed."

When they were leaving, Spike was delighted. "You'll love Thailand, RJ. It's close to paradise. The natives love us. Hell, the King went to Harvard. He had to learn his own language when he was 18… he only spoke English. The women are beautiful. The food is great, and booze is cheap. On top of that, the missions are only two or three hours long and we only fly every three days, so it's one on and two off. We can go down to Pataya Beach after we land and stay for two days. That *is* a tropical paradise. Too bad you're a newlywed; I have so many girlfriends there that I can't deal with them all. You should consider a temporary divorce."

Graham went home and broke the news to Priscilla. She was in tears. "You can't go to war. You promised me you wouldn't go to war! This is crazy. The war is almost over! Tell them you don't want to go."

"I don't know that I am going to war, only that I'll be gone for a while, honey. Relax. I'll be back soon."

He hugged his bride, and she buried her head in his chest, sobbing.

"They are trying to get you killed. You're young, brave, and loyal! You do whatever they tell you to… they send you to die, so that… so that they don't have to go!"

She pulled her head away and looked up at him, still sobbing. Her beautiful eyes had turned red, and tears streaked her pretty face.

Still sobbing, she continued: "It's a bunch of pompous old men playing games with the lives of the young. That's what all wars are. Games of death by decrepit old farts! I don't want you to go... Don't go!"

Graham knew now that this was really devastating news to his love. He should have known better. She had grown up hearing stories about her father's friends being shot down in Korea and WWII where her father served. He picked up his bride and carried her to the bedroom.

The Club would wait.

He managed to console Priscilla and promised her dinner later. He left for the Club a little over an hour later.

Spike was in the main bar with Wildman. They were drinking Black Russians. He greeted Graham with a smile. "You're late, Jeep. You nearly missed take-off. Let me guess. You broke the news to your wife that you were in the Air Force and they are flying you non-stop to combat in 24 hours in an attempt to get you shot at and she threw a fit? Now why do I know that? Too many deployments and too many wives, that's why. But don't worry; it gets better later after you're leaving on TDY number six or so. Then she doesn't even hug you. Instead she says, 'be sure not to duck. You're well insured.' 'Course she says that because she thinks you're seeing someone else, which you are."
Spike smiled.

Wildman shook his head: "Don't listen to that asshole, Jeep. He picks bad wives. Or they pick bad husbands. And besides, the SAMs always miss him because his wife wants him shot down, so he's very safe to fly with. He's kind of a SAM shield due to evil spells from bad wives."

Spike waved off Wildman's assessment. " I wish that were true. Grab a stool and sit down, Jeep. Have a Black Russian. This is the SAC combat drink of choice. We only drink these when we are going into a combat theater or we are already there."

Graham could tell they all had a big head start on him with the Russians.

Wildman: "Yeah, but they are combat Russians, which means they are vodka with a splash of Kaluha. Or depending on if we need to stay up, Kaluha with a splash of vodka."

"Whatever. The Wildman and I were talking, and we think that you need a callsign since you are now heading into combat. I won't haul around a Jeep in a combat theater, especially my Nav. So we decided that you are mostly full of bullshit, which is required since we are too, and that you are extremely tenacious."

Wildman, slurring a clarification: "That means you never give up."

"Shut the hell up when I am explaining callsigns, Wildman. Yeah… you never give up on anything until you win, like in 4-5-6, or lose, like in fishing for eight hours and not catching squat. So the appropriate callsign for you, the Wildman and I decided, is Bulldog. You are full of bullshit and, like a real bulldog, will bite until somebody beats you to a pulp, kills you, or you win. Henceforth it is written in the reinforced concrete of The Great Runway in the Sky. If you don't like it, tough shit. We are the purveyors of callsigns and once purveyed, they stay purveyed."

Wildman: "That's true for the most part. Lizard put out a bounty to find out who gave him 'Lizard.' He doesn't like Lizard because he knows he's a Lizard and that's why we gave him Lizard. Even SAC HQ calls Lizard 'Lizard.' It's probably the best callsign we ever did, so far."

"Whad'ya mean 'we gave,' white boy? I gave Lizard his callsign. You get partial credit for Bulldog, but Lizard was mine. Have another Black Russian, dick."

"Yeah, but I'm the one that gave him a box of flies for his birthday last year."

Graham: "Trout flies? I didn't know he was a fisherman."

Spike, smirking: "No. House flies. It was a stroke of genius I must say. Grab a dice cup. We're going to war, and I need some dough."

C.K. McCUSKER

CREW E-05 GETS PROMOTED

The three crews assembled at base ops at 1600 the following day. No wives or family were allowed. Lizard came into the room, and the crews came to attention. He was licking at moderate speed. "Gentlemen, be seated. You will be wheels in the well at 1820 hours local. Your destination is Andersen Air Force Base on Guam."

Spike under his breath: "Shit."

The Lizard went on, with lots of licks. "You will be the first B-52G crews in theater. Other crews will be following you to Guam in the next few days, but I suspect that you will fly the first combat missions in a G. You were chosen for the combat experience in D models that key crewmembers have, specifically the Pilot and Radar Navigator. Colonel Nagahashi and Major Wilson are the most experienced in their respective assignments. By virtue of the performance at the last ORI and the academic performance of Major Wilson and Lieutenant Graham, crew E-05 has been designated a StanBoard crew as FAI S-02, effective immediately. Colonel Nagahashi's crew will be senior, followed by S-02 and S-03. I know you gentlemen will bring great credit to the Wing and perform admirably. Squadron staff has assembled all the mission plans for you and will brief immediately following. Good luck and God speed."

Lizard turned and left the podium. The room came to attention then sat back down.

Spike to Graham quietly: "We're screwed. Guam is a shithole. Rain, heat, humidity, more rain, and Guaps. That's all that's there. A true shithole. It's supposed to be the Japanese honeymoon capital but that's only if you want a bad marriage. This better be a short tour."

"What's a Guap?"

"A Guam native. They're mean, ugly, thieving, little shits that hate the military and there're way too many of them. We will stay away from them and hang out at the Clubs and the beach hotels. Even then, you won't see any good looking women for the duration… oh that's right… you don't care."

"Right, it doesn't sound that bad to me. What do you mean by 'Clubs?'"

"There're two on the island: ours on the north end and the Navy's on the south end. Great steaks at the Navy Club, great view at our Club. We'll go down to the Navy Club after Sluggo gets over there."

"What makes you think that Sluggo will be deployed?"

"He'll be right behind us in days. Trust me. I bet every G in SAC will be on Guam before this ends. And forget about two or three months like Lizard said. We'll be there just short of six months and then rotate back for a short period. Mark my words, kid."

Graham was in shock. "Six months! Why six months?"

"Two reasons. This war isn't going to end until we pound the shit out of the north just like Goldwater said back in '64, and only B-52s can do that. But the President can't risk losing a lot of bombers, so he'll drag his feet. Secondly, if we are in theater for longer than 180 days it counts as a combat tour, and they can't send us back for a year. So after 175 days they send us home for thirty days and then right back for another six months. That will go on until the war ends."

One of Lizard's "Flies" (staff), as they were called, briefed the mission.

Graham was seriously depressed. Spike couldn't be right this time. No way.

CHAPTER V:
LET THE GAMES BEGIN

GUAM, THE FIRST TOUR

On 11 April, 1972, FAI SO-2 landed on Guam. Crew FAI SO-2 were the second B-52G to land in the combat theater. The first thing Graham noticed was that it was *very* hot and *very* humid, and it was raining. Spike was already right.

Colonel Richard Dangle, Director of Operations, 43rd Strategic Wing (Provisional) welcomed S-02 and the other two crews to Guam. "You gentlemen will be flying combat missions every thirty-six hours until further notice. I'm certain that you are professionals and will meet the rigorous standards that this schedule will require. The Officers Club is open for you to utilize when the crew rest schedule allows. I must insist that you gentlemen refrain from drinking alcoholic beverages more than one hour per night, of course observing the "no alcohol 12 hours before flight" regulation, and there is no gambling or foul language allowed at the Club. You will also not make remarks or suggestions to, dance with, touch, or proposition the female patrons of the Club, as they are the wives of officers stationed here and will not welcome your advances. There are two bars and restaurants at the Club. One is in the back near the pool. You may wear flight suits in that location. No flight suits in the main bar as the Officers' Wives Club find them offensive. Again, I welcome you to Guam, and with any luck we will not be here very long as the North Vietnamese will return to the Peace Table and give up. Are there any questions, gentlemen?"

Spike: "Yes, Colonel. Do the Officers' Wives Club members fly combat missions?"

"What's your point, Major?"

"Why don't you tell them that we don't allow dresses in the Club? Except in the back bar, of course."

Joe Bob, whispering: "Spike, you shut your pipes boy."

Spike, almost whispering: "Screw you, fat boy. This is bullshit."

Dangle: "I understand your displeasure Major, but I do not appreciate your tone. The rules are the rules, Major. Live with them."

Spike was pissed: "Stand up for your crews, Colonel. Stand up for the guys doing the job. The ones risking their lives every 36 hours."

Dangle just stared at Spike in disbelief without saying a word. He looked at the nametag on his flight suit.

Wilson…Wilson…I wonder if that's THE Wilson. Spike Wilson. I'll check the files when I get back to the office. If it is, the damn Lizard screwed me. All kinds of crap will start to happen. That son-of a-bitch! Watch, that asshole will send me Sluggo and the other hellraisers next… no maybe not…

"Major Wilson? What's your first name?"

"Gaylord, Colonel."

Dangle was relieved. Dick hadn't sent his crazy crews after all.

Spike smile: "But my friends call me Spike. Colonels just call me names."

THE SMELL POOL

SO-2's first mission was a run into the Central Highlands. It was a long and boring flight, but it gave Spike the opportunity to think up some diversions that would make him some money. He saw an opportunity to make some money and avoid washing his flight suit. Both of these were what one might call "obsessions" of his. Within 24 hours of landing, Spike started a pool at the bar in the O'Club with Nagahashi's crew on who could go the longest wearing the same flight suit without introducing it to detergent and water. The cockpit of a B-52 in Guam is at least 120 F and about 95% humidity when the crew boards for pre-flight. The crew would literally soak their flight suits before they got the outside air running. As other crews arrived at the base, they joined the "wearathon" and were prorated against the guys already in the pool. The first of many contests was on.

GETTING ACQUAINTED

As Spike had said, Guam had two Officer's Clubs, the Andersen AFB Club at the north end, which was gorgeous, and the Navy at the south end of the island which wasn't quite as nice but had the best steaks on the island. Spike's prediction again proved true when Sluggo and Wildman were on Guam within a week. S-O2 had already flown four combat missions, two up north, by the time they got there. After a few weeks, Spike, Sluggo, B-dog, and Wildman would regularly drive the 26 miles south to have dinner at the Navy Club. Not only was the food great, but they very conveniently provided "Captains Only" reserved parking directly outside the door of the Club. A Navy Captain was equivalent to an Air Force full Colonel, which was who the parking was reserved for, but they were Captains, so they decided that the parking was reserved for them too.

"Captains only" parking worked for awhile, then one of the old self important gas-bags couldn't find a parking place one Friday and figured out that the plate on the front of the AF blue sedan didn't have a silver bird on it. They towed Dangle's car.

That really got them in trouble with the Wing DO, Col. Dick "Launch 'em at All Costs" Dangle since it was his staff car. Dangle insisted on being addressed as "Richard" for obvious reasons, but everybody called him "Dick." Except his mother. She called him "Dickie," or so the story went.

Within days of other FAI crews arriving on Guam, Dangle earned his call sign. When he tried to get Sluggo to take an unsafe aircraft in order to meet his sortie [flight] objective for the month, Sluggo refused. Dangle came out to the tarmac and *implied* that it was an order.

They exchanged salutes. "Captain Duggen. There's nothing wrong with this aircraft. You need to fire her up and get going. We don't have a stand-by bird ready yet, and we all know that the sooner we get this war over the sooner we go home."

Dangle didn't know Sluggo yet, although he'd heard of him the first day Sluggo arrived. He heard that he was very good. "Colonel. With all due respect, it's my job as AC [aircraft commander] to ensure my crew that we will only take a bird up that we all feel is mechanically safe. We did the pre-flight, and this one's a mess. It's a notorious mess. Its tail number is 221 as you can see. Ask around. It sucks, sir."

"Now, Captain … don't be unreasonable … [he was scanning a clipboard with Sluggo's 'shit list' attached] … why most of these can be fixed quickly, and others aren't required for the mission. I think that it is quite imperative from, say, perhaps a career standpoint, that we reach an objective compromise on this aircraft and get her airborne right away."

"Colonel. We are not taking this aircraft. Period. If you want it up so badly, take it yourself. And, by the way, never threaten me, Colonel."

"Captain! I wasn't threatening you in any way. I was just asking you to be reasonable about this!"

"You already have my answer, Colonel."

Sluggo saluted and dismissed himself.

Sluggo told his crew to get back on the crew bus and left.

Dangle's reputation with the crewdogs went to shit overnight, which he quickly found out. Desperate after the news, he turned into a kiss ass the next day. That included loaning Sluggo his staff car.

After the tow, with no more car, the guys were forced to use only the Andersen O'Club. SO-2 had just landed from a strike up at the DMZ where they almost got nailed by a SAM that Thump didn't even detect until the last few seconds.

Intel had guaranteed them at the PTOB that the only SAM site up there had been taken out. The old site must have had babies. Spike and Graham were in the back bar heavily celebrating not being dead when a C-141 trash hauler [cargo jet] crew walked in. Spike had celebrated more than most and decided to ask the 141 AC: "Where you been, bub? Dropping toilet paper in Thule? Donuts for Danang? You know if you had to deliver toilet paper to Quang Tri it would be convenient because there's an outside chance you might actually get shot at for the first time ever, and you would have a whole planeload of shit paper to immediately clean your shorts."

The fight started immediately. The trash haulers lost. Badly.

As a result of the fight, Dangle closed the back bar for two weeks. The other crews didn't blame Spike or the other crewdogs since they had been rudely insulted by the trash haulers: they had come into a crewdog bar without an invitation. A *combat* crewdog bar.

THE PILIPEENS

As the mission count climbed past ten, the crew settled into a routine. But Graham and Spike both hated routines, so they started to work on more diversions to break up the monotony. Spike hated the Philippines [known as the "PI"] and Philippinos. No one knew why. Their route of flight would take them out of Guam, west over the PI on exactly the same route outbound and inbound. There was a map coordinate on the western side of the PI where they would turn depending on where the strike was going - North, DMZ, Delta, etc. On the way back, their route would vary again until they got to a different coordinate just south of the outbound. What this all meant was that their route of flight over the PI was always the same. They were on the return leg right over the PI one night, all very tired and Joe Bob asleep, and Spike went on GUARD channel [broadcasts to everybody] with his song:

Oh Pilipeens [pronounced: Pill-e-peens; the song was sung with a bad Philippine accent]

Oh Pilipeens, my Pilipeens!
All time fight but nivir ween!

Joo fight for me! Hai fight for joo!
Joo die for me! Tough sheet for joo!

Oh Pilipeens, my Pilipeens!
All time fight but nivir ween!

SO-2 was flying lead, and the other two birds behind them were in hysterics - at least the ones that were awake. Joe Bob woke up and screamed at Spike to shut the hell up and get off guard. Spike never listened to Joe Bob.

Graham didn't laugh: "Spike, did you know that the PI has a lot of boots on the ground fighting the VC right along with our guys? They are brave and really tough guys according to my Army buddy who fought with them. In fact, if the VC find out they are fighting the Filipinos, they turn around and haul ass. They're our ally, dumb ass."

"I know that. I'm not insulting them now. I'm getting back at them for something that happened thirty years ago."

"What was that?"

Spike didn't answer.

Graham had no idea why Spike hated the Philippines. Graham thought it was a beautiful tropical country with a fascinating culture whose people were very pro-American. He'd gone to college with a Filipino kid who had become a good friend. And besides, Spike didn't "hate" anything. There had to be a very serious reason underlying his feelings. Graham would find out in time.

About the third time Spike gave a concert over the PI, GROUND came on guard: "Snow Flight, joo stay off guard! En do not insult the Pilipeens!" The PI controllers were very aware of the call signs and route of flight. Joe Bob was asleep, and the Co and Graham were flying. Spike was in his seat. On RTB [return to base], word of this encounter spread like wildfire among the crews. Spike's legend grew even more. Joe Bob heard about it and threatened Spike as usual.

After that, nothing happened for a few weeks until they were returning from a mission just north of the DMZ . They got shot at, and Joe Bob was tired. He made the mistake of going to sleep right before they got to the PI. Spike was in Joe Bob's seat, and he and the co were flying. Midway over the PI Spike went up on guard and sang his song. *Twice.*

Ground came up on guard immediately: "Blue Flight!" [codename colors changed with every flight, but they knew Spike's voice and the song] "Joo continue to insult mi country! We are sending up escorts!"

Within ten minutes, Roller chirped up. "We have bogeys 7 o'clock low closing!"

The two PI fighters closed to within about half a mile and escorted them out of PI airspace.

NOW this was an INCIDENT.

The Co woke up Joe Bob after ground said they were sending escorts, and he was beyond pissed. The other crews were in a complete state of hysteria. Joe Bob swore Spike was getting an Article 15, which was a serious letter of reprimand that went on your record.

Dangle was personally waiting for them at postflight and chewed Joe Bob's ass. By now, Joe Bob was contemplating how he could get Spike executed. Dangle ended his tirade by saying that 8th Air Force would handle the incident, and they were not to talk about it again. No action would be taken but "NO MORE SINGING!" That evening Spike couldn't buy a drink at the O'Club. He was now a certified crewdog hero. After the escort, Spike did stop singing. With 17 years in USAF, he had reached the pinnacle of his career as a Major, and he knew it, but Captain's bars no longer had the appeal they once had.

Joe Bob got promoted soon after to Lieutenant Colonel and would be taken off crew duty... maybe. At his promotion party, which almost no one came to and to which Spike wasn't invited, he reluctantly thanked the crew for helping him make L/C. It was his third promotion board, and "three strikes and you're out applied."

RJ and Spike were stunned that an asshole of his magnitude could make L/C.

ROLLER'S LOVE LIFE

Roller was in heaven on Guam. Three weeks after arrival, Roller went to Graham and proudly announced that he was engaged.

"She's a nice Japanese girl whose father is loaded. I'll get out when my enlistment is up, move to Japan, and never work another day. Perfect!"

Graham: "On the contrary, you will be working for the rest of your life at Leavenworth. You'll be court-martialed as a bigamist. That means more than one wife, Yo."

"That doesn't apply because I'm on Guam, not in the States."

Graham: "Guam is a U.S. territory, and it *is* the States. Jail, Yo."

Spike came in, and Graham filled him in on Roller's brilliant plan. Since Spike maintained about the same level of personal hygiene as Roller, they had developed a certain rapport... perhaps based on odor. Spike pounded in the same point.

Spike added: "Frau Eva would find your sorry ass no matter where you are, and that means certain death this time. So break it off, dumbshit."

After a few more weeks of screwing his fiancé and changing his mind back and forth from break-up to marriage, Roller finally agreed and broke off the engagement. The break-up turned out to be just the beginning of the problem.

The father was a very wealthy Japanese *mobster* who had sent his daughter to Guam on extended vacation with the chance she might find a wealthy young Japanese kid that would make a good husband and whose parents might not know daddy's "most wanted" status at home. He was very disappointed when he found that his daughter wanted to marry an older American in the military, but he reluctantly agreed. After all, at least he was a *Colonel...*

When Colonel "Roller" Seeps dumped the girl, she was devastated. Worse. Daddy lost face. Big face. Roller was dead. No. Tortured and then dead.
Spike found out about the situation and went to Joe Bob. "Roller needs an immediate transfer back to the States on a 'family hardship' issue. We have to move fast."

Joe Bob: "I don't care."

Spike thought that meant "OK." He was wrong. It meant he didn't care.

Roller lucked out. Dangle got a letter from a Miyoshi Takagi protesting his daughter's treatment by Colonel Roller and the resulting disgrace of his entire family. He wanted to know what Dangle was going to do about it.

Dangle was befuddled. He pressed his intercom: "Sergeant Lee, I want you to check with base personnel and find out where a Colonel Roller is assigned. Then I want you to have him report to me immediately."

Sergeant Lee knew exactly who "Colonel" Roller was. He had asked her out at least six times. She couldn't stand *Staff Sergeant* "Roller." She pressed the intercom: " Uh…er…Colonel. There is no Colonel Roller, sir."

"Uh.Colonel Roller is actually Sergeant "Roller," er…Sergeant Ron Seeps, a B-52 gunner, sir."

"WHAT TH….", She let go of the intercom key so didn't have to hear "Dangling Dick" complete his standard epithet.

In less than a minute: "Dangling" was screaming over the intercom again: "SERGEANT! FIND OUT WHO THE FU… ER, HELL HIS AC IS AND THEN CALL THE AIR POLICE AND HAVE THEM FIND HIM AND THIS FORMER SERGEANT SEEPS! I WANT THEM IN MY OFFICE WITHIN THE HOUR! DAMN THESE CREWS! ALL THEY DO IS COME HERE AND FLY AND CAUSE TROUBLE!

He didn't wait for a reply. She would do what she was told. He was calming down a bit so that meant he was plotting, which he did often and poorly.

I'd love to screw her, but that might end a career that has already ended… but maybe a Leavenworth ending. What I should do is assign her the task of finding out what the sentence is for a senior officer that's very good in bed, having fantastic relations with an enlisted person of her free will when she accompanies him on a MACV trip to Pataya Beach in Thailand for a week… yeah that's not a proposition… it's an inquiry. I'll make it next week.

But this damn Sergeant…and his AC. What about them? I'll chew the AC's ass and have scheduling give them the worst flight schedule they can devise. Everything North that they have. They can't drink twelve hours before take-off. I wonder if I can schedule them wheels in the well every twelve hours? The gunner… I'll ruin him. I'll bust him and send him back. He'll be an Airman forever. Damn flyers!

Dangle's "plots" this time were especially poor. He couldn't have SO-2 fly all the time, and the states were exactly what Roller wanted - except for Frau Eva.

Dangle set up a peer review board to determine if an Article 15, or worse, was in order. The charges were serious, but the board was populated by some of Roller's buddies who recommend a reduction in rank and that he be sent home on "disciplinary" leave. Roller flew home. Spike got word from Sgt. Garwitz, Roller's best friend on Guam, that Takagi had vowed to find Colonel Roller in the States and "restore his family's honor."

Spike and Graham weren't worried. Frau Eva was there.

THE FLARE GUN WARS

Not long after SO-2 arrived on Guam, the Flare Gun Wars started.

Sluggo and Spike were returning to their third floor "Sweats" at building one at the Monsoon Mansion late one night when a rocket came streaking over and slammed into the upper part of the building. Sparks and flashes went off everywhere.

Sluggo screamed at the rival compound fifty yards away: "That was too close! YOU DICKHEADS! THIS MEANS WAR!" He turned to Spike, still pissed. "That's Patullo's lunatics over in two again, Spike. We're gonna have to take 'em out. Smolensky's got some guns and flares."

There were about fifty yards of grass and some landscaping that had mostly been destroyed between the three barracks buildings that had been converted to crewdog quarters, now known as Monsoon Mansion. Since drinking too much was a major pastime and drinking often led ex-fraternity boys to regress back to college, a rivalry built up between the three buildings that soon led to stunts that were reminiscent, if not exact copies or worse, of stuff pulled off in their fraternity days. The only difference was that now they were four or five years older and had access to things that were far more dangerous than what had been available in school. One of those was flare guns. Sergeant Smolensky, Sluggo's gunner, had been given three flare guns and some flares by some of his buddies in the survival detachment. The guns were normally packed into the kit that was integrated into the ejection seat on the bombers for use in signaling search and rescue in the event of a shootdown.

Sluggo ran down the balcony to his Sweat while Spike walked behind. He came out of the room with two guns and three flares. Spike calmly: "This is not a good idea. Killing Patullo, and or his crew, would be frowned upon. These things are essentially large bullets until they lose the booster. I put a crater the size of a basketball in the wall at the O'Club at U-Tapao."

"Bullshit. We'll aim high and scare the crap out of them." With that Sluggo closed the breach on the gun and fired at building two. It didn't go high. It went low and hit the second floor balcony. They heard another muffled "thump," and a flare went streaking over their building.

Now Spike was irritated. "What did I tell you, shitball? You can't aim those things."

Sluggo had already reloaded. He fired toward the courtyard and this time it went where it was aimed, hit the ground, and exploded.

From Patullo's side came: "YOU GUYS SUCK! SLUGGO MUST BE SHOOTING!"

Sirens.

Spike: "That's an 'oh shit' toad. Now we got the sky cops coming, and they'll start a search for the guns. Ditch 'em."

Sluggo disappeared into his room. By now a small contingent of crewdogs had come out on the balcony. Graham came up to Spike. "You know the flare guns draw too much attention. We should switch to potato cannons. Besides they make a bigger mess and can be loaded with all kinds of shit. I mean literally."

They could hear the sky cops running up the stairs.

Spike: "What are potato cannons?"

"It's really simple. You build cannon out of a two inch pipe with a cap screwed on the end and a small hole drilled into in just past the threads. You put calcium carbonate in the tube and then jam a potato or two down the barrel. You aim, use an eyedropper to put a few drops of water through the fuse hole which forms an explosive gas when it contacts the carbonate, and then hold a match over the hole. It'll fire a potato three hundred yards. We used them in college to harass the nerd house across the street."
The sky cops walked up.

"It figured that you, sirs, would be involved in this. Where are the weapons?"

Sluggo: "I take umbrage to the insinuation, Sergeant. We only came out to assist you in identifying the culprits in this heinous and ruthless attack on our stately quarters. Now I suggest that you go over to Two and nab the real criminals."

"We will go over there, sir, but we are required to search your quarters."

"Feel free."

Spike and Graham went down to Sluggo's hovel and explained the potato cannon. Sluggo yelled over to his gunner: "Smolensky! Come over here." He showed up looking like he just got up.

Sluggo: "We need you to find some stuff first thing tomorrow." He explained the requirements for what would make ten potato cannons. "And just in case the carbonate doesn't work the way Bulldog portrays it, get some good ol' black powder and some fuses."

He turned to Spike: "You guys don't fly tomorrow do you?"

"No, we do fly in spite of the stand down. We're wheels up at 2100 on a one ship."

"You know what that means. Okay, we'll meet at 1600 on Thursday at my house to plan our attack for that night. By the way, I got a new Nav since Pork is grounded for almost ever. He's PCS from Blytheville and a real StanBoard IN, unlike the fake that you drag around. I'll bring him to the party."

Graham: "Sluggo, the guy is doomed flying with you. You will ruin him. Who is he?"

"His name's Bob Foster, and I stole him through a contact Smolensky has."

"I know the guy! We went through flight and survival together. He's a great guy, and he's really good. But you will still ruin him. Almost anyone can be taught to be really bad by you."

"That right? I never had *you* on my crew. Good luck tomorrow, guys."

Graham was curious. Sluggo never said "good luck" about a mission. " Spike, why the good wishes? I thought this mission tomorrow was a high level recon off the coast."
"It may be. But it also may be a low level prop mission which is a hairball [extremely dangerous mission]."

"Prop?"

"Propaganda drop. They load us with 'bluies' which are basically bomb casings that break open after they are released. They are loaded with North Vietnamese counterfeit bills with a propaganda statement on the side. The gooks can pick up the money and cut the statement off the side, and they have a perfect counterfeit bill."

"Why is it a hairball mission?"

"Because we drop the stuff below flight level two zero up north. Not only do we get SAMs, we get triple A. It can get pretty hairy, even with all the fighter support."

SO-2 briefed the next night at 1900. It was a prop mission, but this time they would be flying at 15,000, feet just off the coast of North Vietnam. The triple A might not be as bad as it would be over land. They would fly as Quilt flight. They took off and flew an uneventful mission until they reached the target area, which was two miles off the coast starting east of Vinh. Spike had bad memories of the area.

Spike: "Pilots keep your heads up and out. There's a notorious SAM shooter up here."

Graham: "Pilot descend and maintain 15,000 feet. This is a really dumb ass mission. We have an 80 knot offshore wind. We're going to drop all this shit in the ocean."

Spike: "What a skeptic you are, B-dog. There're at least two gook fishing boats down there. They'll net all this gook money and think that there's a new fish that shits money. This is hardly a waste of time at considerable risk. It's a waste of time at great risk."

Joe Bob: "Crew, we have incoming triple A at nine o'clock."

Thump: "We have threat radar at ten o'clock."

Joe Bob: "Jesus! There's shit going off all over the place! How far are we from TOT!?"

Spike: "Close enough. We're dumping this shit and getting out of here."

Spike could do the bomb release checklist blindfolded. The bombs were gone in less than thirty seconds.

Graham: "Pilot, start climb to flight level three six zero. Turn right to heading one zero five. Max the airspeed."

There was a muffled explosion and the aircraft shuddered.

Joe Bob: "We were hit by triple A, boys. No warning lights. I'm gonna rip those fuckin' planners a new asshole when we get back. They're gonna get a bird shot down and six guys killed with these fucked up missions. We ain't flyin' no more of these, boys."

Spike: "Don't feel like they're picking on us, guys. We have really rotten planning throughout the entire theater. I got a buddy that drives 123s out of Da Nang. The squadron commanders in his outfit are measured by the tonnage of shit that they fly around. He was suspicious, so he put his initials and the date on the inside of a huge tractor tire that he was flying down to Phu Cat. Four months later he picked up the same tire at Chu Lai and flew it back to Da Nang. The Squadron CO was just moving really heavy stuff around and never delivering it to where it was supposed to go."

Graham: "That is completely asinine."

Spike: "This is war, kid. Get used to it. The same guy flew a giant block of ice up to a dirt strip in the jung near the Z one morning. He took a lot of small arms fire going in so he dumped it on the runway and hauled ass. That afternoon he took another block up to the same airstrip. On approach he saw the block that he had dropped that morning on the side of the runway, melting. The fire was even worse, so he did a touch and go and dumped the ice out the rear doors. He had over fifty holes in his bird when he got back to Da Nang."

Graham: "What did he do about it? That could have gotten him and his crew killed for nothing!"

"What the hell do you think we just did? Same thing essentially. He bitched to his Squadron CO, and the CO told him to shut up and gave him an Air Medal for heroism. A month later his CO was promoted to full colonel and sent back to the states as a vice wing CO."

SO-2 touched down just after 0800 on Thursday. They had two large holes in the middle of the fuselage just behind the port wing. They had been lucky. Joe Bob spent an extra thirty minutes yelling at the planning officer that attended the PFB [post flight briefing]. The planning officer maintained that the money would drift ashore which sent Joe Bob into another rage. He filed a written complaint about the mission plan after the rest of the crew left for the Monsoon Mansion. They all knew that no one would ever see the complaint. Joe Bob was an L/C now but still flying. The only thing Spike liked about him was that he was good at ripping brass new assholes.

A GOOD CHANGE IN A BAD PLAN

Everybody left for the Club at 1900 and spent the evening getting in shape for the coming battle, which primarily meant drinking too many Black Russians, singing along with the Pilipeeno band, and bitching about Graham winning at 4-5-6. After number "too many," Spike made a "secutive" decision.

"This whole plan sucks dogs. You can't have a flare gun war with fucking potato cannons! You can only have a flare gun war with flare guns. We're short on flares, and we need what we have in order to attack Coward Quarters soon. Therefore, as senior ranking crewdog, I am calling off the pussy potato gun fight. Anyone that wants to borrow a dress from some broad, if you can find one, is welcome to shoot potatoes at the dicks across the yard, but I ain't showin' up."

Bulldog foolishly protested Spike's mandate.

"Bullshit, Spike. The cannons really work unless we're too drunk to load 'em. Besides, we bought all the pipes and crap to make them. Why not go through with it?"

"Simple, Jeep. Yes, Jeep. You might be demoted back to Jeep for coming up with a pussy plan. Like I said, you can't have a flare gun war with potatoes. Besides the Irish need potatoes, and we'll use the pipes for a different purpose. That's it, B-dog. The decision is written…"

Graham interrupted. "I know, I know, in concrete on the runway. What are we going to do with a dozen pipes? Fix the plumbing?"

Spike was grinning which was unusual. "Hell no. We'll build pipe bombs. BIG pipe bombs."

Sluggo was incredulous. "You really *are* insane. I'm convinced. Do you know what a pipe bomb that big would do? It would make a good sized crater and probably kill whoever lit it."

Spike smiled, "Not if we dropped it."

"From where, Spike? The third floor? We'd kill all the crewdogs on the first floor."

"Nope. We drop it from a BUFF."

Bulldog was fascinated. As drunk as Spike was, there was something up, and it could be big.

"Why would we drop a fused pipe bomb from a B-52 when it's flyshit compared to a 750 pound bomb? You've collaborated with too many Russians."

Spike looked disgusted. "That's the point. We're going to clobber the Russians." Spike smiled the Spike smile.

"What the hell? What Russians?"

There was a Russian "fishing trawler" stationed just outside US waters at the end of the runway. The "fishing trawler" was covered with antennas that couldn't catch fish but they could communicate take-off times and flight structure to the enemy. The enemy would then be able to calculate when the bombers would be over targets in North or South Vietnam. This aided them in manning SAM sites and/or giving them a MIG reception. The Navy and the rescue helicopters from Andersen occasionally harassed them, but it did no good.

Spike was almost wide eyed as he planned the attack while he spoke. "The fisher-spies. The commie BUFF counters just after take-off. We'll do a low altitude test on drag coefficient using a pipe bomb as a marker. If the Spyhauler happens to be under it, tough shitski."

Graham was stunned. "We can't bomb a Russian trawler in international waters! We'll go to Leavenworth forever plus another forever for starting a war!"

Spike looked disgusted again. "Bulldog, my poor student, we're not bombing a Russian trawler, we're testing a drag coefficient measurement device in international waters because it's clearly too dangerous to test too close to our airbase. We can turn the entire area into a drag testing site so the damn fisher spies will have to move too far out to count, unless we accidentally sink the fucks first."

Sluggo had been silent. He finally jumped in, now elated.

"It's brilliant and also fun. We need fun to remember in case we get dead too soon. Why not? We could scare the bastards to death. What are they going to do to us? Send us to war and get us killed? Of course we'll deny everything like we always do, and this attack will be hard to prove."
Spike was delighted. With Sluggo on board, he could get Wildman in and pull Bulldog out of Jeepville. He turned back to Bulldog,

"OK, near Jeep, are you in? I promise you won't go to jail. You and I may get killed before that could happen anyway... well?"

"Alright. I'll go along. But it has to be carefully planned and executed, or we *will* get caught. Also, the Russians will go ballistic. Worse if we sink their Spyhauler."

Spike could tell his good friend was "almost" in, so he'd make him get in.

"You're right. Planning is essential. You're in charge of planning, Bulldog. We need a preliminary plan by tomorrow morning. So pass the dice cup and start thinking."

Spike smiled.

Foster showed up and waited for a seat at the table.

Spike: "Have a seat, Bob. Want a Russian?"

"Sure."

Spike looked Bob in the eye, seeming very serious. "You're Sluggo's new Nav? You're screwed."

Sluggo, turning away from the adjacent table: "I heard that, Spike. Leave my Nav alone. He's sure as shit better than yours. ... and oh yeah ... screw you."

B-dog, turning to Sluggo: "There's no Nav in this Squadron better than me when I'm awake. At least we can get a BUFF in the air intact, dickhead."

Spike smiled. "Ignore them all, Bob. They are all insane. B-dog said you went through Flight and Survival with him and that you're a good aviator and a good guy. With that endorsement you already have two strikes. Where are you from?"

"Georgia, Major."

"You're from the South? Darwin's hanger? The average IQ down there is ten. I hope for Sluggo's sake that you're an aberration. That's two and a half strikes, kid, and never call me Major. I'm Spike unless I don't like you."

"Yes, sir."

"And don't call me 'sir' either."
Bob just nodded with a smirk on his face.

"You've already been in combat with your old crew, so you don't have to be the FNG or a Jeep. In order to be part of this gaggle of crewdogs you have to have an alias, or callsign, depending on who you talk to. You're from Darwin's hanger.... and how old are you? With that red hair and baby face you look like a kid."

"I'm twenty-four. Twenty-five this December."

"You are a kid. Hey Bulldog, how old are you?"

"Twenty-five, but I'm much wiser than my years, unlike an old fart like you."

Spike: "OK. This is easy. You are The Darwin Kid, henceforth and forever. Written in concrete in that great runway in the sky. For short, you are 'D-Kid'. Get it, kid?"

"Got it, Spike. Can I appeal the name?"

Everybody started laughing. D-Kid had asked a dumb question.

"Nope. The concrete is already drying. All of you guys welcome D-Kid. He's going to assist Bulldog in planning Operation Fishmonger."

D-Kid: "What's that? And why me?"

Sluggo, leaning over: "It's double secret stuff. Suffice it to say for now that we're attacking the Russians. I'll brief you on the way back to Monsoon Mansion."

D-Kid wondered if Spike's analysis was right. Maybe these guys were insane. Hell, who cares? He'd go nuts flying off this rock forever anyway. May as well get a head start.

HOME AND BACK TO GUAM

In the fall of 1972, SO-2 returned home for three weeks leave. The crew had been on Guam for 178 days, so they were rushed home because if they hit the magic number -180, SAC couldn't send them back for a year. D-Kid went home to Blytheville to see his new wife and get ready for his move.

When they got home, it turned out that Roller had been assigned to the ·Squadron, but no one knew what he did *and* he was now back to E-4. He was turning into a master at getting promoted through doing nothing.

Most of Lizard's experienced and good crews were rotating to Guam, including StanBoard which were the best of the best and flew lead on the ORI mission simulations. That left Lizard with FNG's and the Defori crews which, while sounding Italian, meant Don't Ever Fly An ORI. Lizard was living in constant fear as usual, so he had taken a new approach. He was sneaking the Defori guys into experienced crews and trying to steal good guys in return. That's how he sent Roller back to S-02. He had analyzed individual records and re-assigned Roller to SO-2 and pulled MSgt. Havermeyer who had replaced Roller on Guam.

Even with Joe Bob, SO-2 had been made a StanBoard crew before their first deployment to Guam, primarily because Spike and Graham had "acquired" all the tests and scored the highest in Wing history on them.

Joe Bob called Spike the day before the return to Guam. "We got us a new gunner agin. A guy by the name of Sgt. Seeps. You go an' tell the rest of the crew."

"He's not new, Dickie. He's our old gunner. He got sent back on a personal and Havermeyer replaced him.'

"Who's Havermeyer?"

"He's now our old new gunner. He was re-assigned stateside."

"I thought you just said we got our old gunner back."

"Never mind, Dickie."

Joe Bob was so oblivious to enlisted people that Spike honestly didn't think he knew who their gunner was at any time. He just called them "guns" if he spoke to them at all. SO-2 returned to Guam with their "new" gunner, Seeps, who Joe Bob did recognize at the PTOB. In a rare moment for Joe Bob, he asked Roller where he'd been. He didn't give a shit, but he asked.

They flew back to the "Rock" in the back of a tanker and froze the whole way. Spike suspected the "Gas Passers" turned the heat down intentionally. The landing on Guam was terrible. The pilot flared too high and had to slam the aircraft down hard. The cockpit was open when they departed, giving Spike an opportunity to thank the pilots for the "popsicle" flight.

"Gee guys, that was a great touch. Where did you guys do your flight training? Wanna Fly U? Are those our flight suits? I guess so... or... did you borrow those? After that landing, I thought for sure that you were Iranian exchange students."

The Tank Co was ready to fight. "Listen, Major, we know..." The pilot stopped him. "Finish post-flight, lieutenant. Sorry for the landing, Spike. I did it."

"OK. Try some heat next time, Captain." He turned and walked out with the lack of response expected. He knew a number of Tank drivers on Guam that were good guys, and they would hear about this dick. *How did he know I was Spike?*

After checking back into the Monsoon Mansion, Spike, Graham, and (unusually) the Co went to the back bar for burgers.

The Co: "I had a neat thing happen when I was going home this time."

Spike: "What's neat about it?

"Well you know how they advised us at PFB when we got home not to wear our uniforms when traveling on leave in civilian aircraft?"

"Yeah. That's bullshit. The country is really fucked up thanks to those bastards at the Communist Broadcasting System and the other shitbird networks lying their asses off. We should draft every son-of-bitch at the networks under 50 and send them to inspect trails up at the Z."

"Well, they're not getting to everybody. I said screw that advice and wore my Class A uniform home to Pittsburgh. I was connecting to an American flight in San Francisco. I boarded the flight and was walking toward the back when this long haired hippie puke spits on my uniform."

Spike was immediately agitated. "I hope you killed him on the spot. You were a linebacker at Penn State, right?"

"Yeah and I turned to take off my jacket, so I wouldn't get blood all over it when I broke the guys face into pieces. Then a fifty-year-old guy that had seen what was going on jumped up and got between me and the hippie shit. He said, 'Excuse me, Lieutenant, but you might get in trouble if you pound the shit out of this scum, so please allow me.' He didn't wait for my answer, and he proceeded to pound the crap out of the guy in a matter of seconds. Then another guy who looked older than the other guy grabbed the guy's shoulder and asked if he might be given the honor of belting the hippie puke and then he gave the guy a few more shots."

Spike: "That's fantastic! Somebody does give a shit!"

"Listen, there's more. The hippie was a mess, blood all over, crying and moaning, saying he was going to sue the fifty-year-old guy, and then the Captain came back with the cops behind him. He asked what was going on and got filled in pretty accurately by the stewardess and another passenger. The Captain had the hippie arrested for assault for spitting and the cops dragged him off the airplane. The Captain said the cops would also 'take care of him.' It turned out that both the guys that jumped to my aid were World War Two vets, as was the Captain who flew B-17s in Europe. The Captain moved all three of us to first class."

Spike: "We're going to make sure every crewdog hears about what happened to Co. It will cheer them up big time. Somebody back home gives a shit about us and what we are doing. It'll make their day. It did mine. We'll get Smolensky after dinner and start right away."

CHAPTER VI:
AN INVITATION TO THE DANCE

JOE BOB AND THE NYT

The first mission back, SO-2 was scheduled to fly a day mission, which meant it would be a milk run and very boring. The crew was in the PTOB when Squadron said that they would have a passenger on the mission. Joe Bob *hated* passengers. If they were white and from the right side of west Texas, he would still hate them because a passenger onboard means that Joe Bob couldn't sleep for 75% of the mission.

Then the briefing officer dropped the bomb. "Your passenger, Colonel Carter, is a *New York Times* reporter."

Joe Bob went ballistic: "What the fuck! Are you fuckin' idiots at Squadron nuts! You're gwan to put a fuckin' pinko commie that writes for the U.S. version of the fuckin' Russian paper on an American combat mission! I'll be hell damned if I will let the son-of-a-bitch on my airplane!"

It got worse.

The other two crews at the PTOB were laughing hysterically along with Spike and Graham. Only Thump remained quiet in his seat, as any good spineless wimp would. The brief officer was an L/C "Kiwi" [kiwi's are birds that can't fly because they don't have wings]. He remained relatively calm listening to Joe Bob's tirade until Joe Bob got to the part about "no fuckin' kiwi Squadron planners" being capable of determining anything related to the safety of combat flight. Then the Colonel got pissed and interrupted Joe Bob, which wasn't easy. "Colonel Carter! Shut up and sit down! This is a directive from 8th Air Force, and *YOU WILL* take this reporter on the mission *AS ORDERED! IS THAT PERFECTLY CLEAR, COLONEL?*" The Colonel had a booming voice when he got pissed, which was unusual for a Kiwi, and Joe Bob actually did shut up and sit down. Everyone was recovering from hysteria when the Colonel dropped a 20 meg bomb.

"Colonel Carter, this is important to 8th AF all the way up to Gen. Andrews, and you will personally be held responsible to see that this reporter is treated with courtesy and respect as if she were a guest in your home."

Did he say SHE?! No he couldn't have said she. Impossible. No…I'm sure he said she!

Joe Bob lost it. He jumped back to his feet and went off.

"YOU FUCKIN' IDIOTS THINK THAT YOU ARE GOING TO PUT A FUCKIN' COMMIE BROAD SPY ON A UNITED STATES AIR FORCE B-52 HEADING INTO COMBAT!! *MY* B-52!!? THERE AIN'T NO PLACE FOR A COMMIE BROAD TO TAKE A PEE ON A B-52! YOU FUCKIN' DOPES! I WANT TO SEE BRACKEN RIGHT THIS FUCKIN' MINUTE!! NO FUCKIN' BROAD IS COMIN' ON MY AIRPLANE FOR NO MISSION!!"

Toward the end of Joe Bob's explosion, the Colonel and Joe Bob were both yelling at each other at the top of their lungs until finally the Colonel said that he would get the squadron commander, Colonel Bracken, out to the aircraft.

Everyone was laughing hysterically. Half had tears running down their face. This would go down in the annals of the United States Air Force.

The crew went out to the aircraft without Joe Bob. He was going to find Dangle. *To hell with Bracken.*

Graham really couldn't understand why, of all people, they would put this person on Joe Bob's aircraft. The only thing that he could figure out was that Gen. Andrews actually hated the *New York Times*. While waiting for Joe Bob, Spike started a pool to bet on how long it would take before she had to pee. Spike told Roller to make twice as much coffee as usual and fill her up.

Joe Bob showed up minutes before their passenger. His neck was bright red as usual, but this time his face was the same color. Graham and Spike later found out that while looking for Dangle, Bracken found Joe Bob. Bracken gave Joe Bob what was apparently an ass chewing on a par with the greatest ass chewings of all time, and it was public in the Wing Ops hallway. By the book, Joe Bob was actually right. The AC of an aircraft is like the Captain of a ship. He is in complete command. Not this time. This was the exception to the rule. He was also right that there was no place for a woman to pee. The "pee" hole was a round tube that was attached to one of the bulkheads.

On the other hand, no one *ever* took a dump on a B-52. There was a bucket provided just in case, but it was *never* used. *If* it was ever used, the Jeep (you automatically reverted to Jeep status if you took an airborne dump) that did it had to wait until everybody exited after landing, take the bucket outside, put it in front of the nose gear, and wait for the crew chief to show up. He then had to formally apologize to the Chief for dumping on his airplane no matter what rank he was in relation to the Chief.

The lady showed up. Joe Bob quietly asked her only one question: "Ma'am, did you attend the safety briefing for this aircraft?"

"Yes, Colonel, I attended the briefing, and I am familiar with the safety requirements."

BOY there must have been a major ass chewing for Joe Bob not to ask her questions that would have DQ'd [disqualified] her for the flight. That was the last time he would speak to her until the PFB. He told the Co to answer any of her commie questions but lie since they would probably end up in Moscow.

The flight was uneventful. The cell dropped eighty-one 750 pound bombs in the Central Highlands. She didn't pee. 12hours, 47 minutes from brake release to touchdown, and she didn't pee. No one won the pool. While she didn't attend the PTOB, she did attend the PFB. She got to the PFB room, and it was very different. Dangle was there. The Public Information Officer was there. Bracken was there and scowling at Joe Bob the minute he came into the room. The de-brief officer was there, as usual.

The beer was not there. The cokes were. No beer. The bitch. The crew went through the normal de-brief – kind of. The language was not normal: "toasted those shitbird zips" was "mission completed," etc. No classified stuff was discussed. They had no beer. They were pissed. And she still hadn't taken a pee!? At the end, the PIO [Public Information Officer], a kiwi Captain, asked the lady if she had any questions of the crew. Graham knew immediately that this was a BIG mistake if she asked Joe Bob.

She did ask Joe Bob. *Uh oh…*

"Yes. Colonel Carter, if you were given the capability, how would you end this war?"

Shit! This is going to be great!

Joe Bob, in his best west Texas accent: "Well, honey, I'd do it this way. I'd round up 50 of the best Vietnamese women, and 50 of the best Vietnamese men. North or south, it don't make no difference, they're all the same fuckin' people."

He said the F word to a female NYT reporter!!

The PIO interrupted. "What the Colonel really means is that Vietnam is populated with a single cultural entity, but the Northern populace has been brainwashed by communist leaders trained in China and Russia."

Bracken's scowl got worse, but no one interrupted.

"An' I'd put all hunert of 'em on a boat in the Gulf uh Tonkin." Joe Bob paused for effect and leaned closer to the reporter. The whole room could still clearly hear what he was saying,

"Then I'd load up 12 B-52s with Mark 28s. Them's 1.5 meg nuke weapons honey. Then I'd fly 'em down to the southern tip of Vietnam and turn North."

The PIO again: "The Colonel is speculating, Ma'am. We have no nuclear weapons in theater at this time." He was sweating profusely in an air conditioned room. Everyone was frozen. With the exception of the PIO, no one said anything. Dangle had a slight smile on his face.

"Then I'd fly due north and melt the whole fuckin' country from the south to the Chink border, and if a couple nukes got let off on the Chink side, what the hell."

Bracken looked as though he was in shock.

Joe Bob again paused for effect and leaned even closer. "Then I'd sink the fuckin' boat!"

The PIO piped in: "I assure you that the Colonel isn't serious!"

"Oh yes I am."

Dangle started laughing. Everybody did except Bracken and Joe Bob. The reporter smiled politely. Dangle then quickly concluded the de-briefing, and Spike and Graham headed for the Club. The PIO grabbed Spike outside of the room and said: "The NYT is going to bury SAC, and Carter is dead meat. Be sure and tell him that."

Spike actually asked Joe Bob to join them, which was very rare, and he did. The article came out about two days later. Inexplicably there was no mention of "Joe Bob's Solution," as it came to be known. In fact, the article was almost complimentary. Very unusual for the *Times*.

Three days after they returned, Joe Bob got his orders to a desk on Guam. The goodbye party was tumultuous.

Joe Bob wasn't invited.

SO-2 got a new AC, Bill Noland. He was a StanBoard Co, so he just moved to the left seat. He seemed like a good guy. He actually looked like Clark Gable, but they needed to evaluate him before he got honored with a callsign. SO-2 got back to the new routine of flying missions every three days, mostly in the south with a few up at the DMZ. For a change, it was pretty safe.

THE BIG RUMOR

Rumor Central had it on the "best authority" that the peace talks were moving rapidly, and the crewdogs would be home by Christmas. The crews were having a picnic and drinkathon on the grass between the Monsoon Mansions on December 16th. The Squadron CO drove up and said that all ACs, Radars, and Navs were to attend a briefing the next day at 1600 hours.

The Go Home briefing! Holy Shit! This is cause for a real party.

Go Home brief at 1600 Hrs on the 17th. This was cause for even more celebration. All crews had stood down for the last two days and no mission schedules were up at ops due to a complete bombing halt in support of the Paris talks. Consequently, the entire Squadron was at the picnic and drinkathon.

Graham was sitting on the grass next to Spike and Wildman. Everyone was getting mellow. The mood was bright.

Spike: "I'm warning you guys. This is no go home mission. Mark my words. The shit is going to hit the fan very soon."

Graham: "Bullshit, Spike. This rumor is too strong this time, and all the signs point toward going home. They want to get some of the troop's home before Christmas. I believe this one."

"B-dog, I told you never to believe rumors. So don't."

Wildman: "Why not believe them, Spike? It takes our mind off of the war."
Spike was quick to answer. "Because I start most of them."

They had opted for daiquiris instead of Russians. The Daiquiris were about 75% rum with a little limeade thrown into a blender with enough ice to thicken it slightly. To say that they were popular was a gross understatement. The Crew Quarters were three story buildings that were ES ("enlisted swine," a Joe Bob term) dorms before the bombers came. Each "suite" (referred to as "sweats,") had three beds divided by a wall that included a bathroom with three beds on each side. The guys on the other side had a bathroom as well. There was a pass through on each end and hurricane shutters on the windows at each end of the quarters. By now most of the Plexiglas windows were damaged or gone as a result of drunken crewdogs trying to get in, Flare Gun Wars, or both. From the outside, the building looked like a Motel 6. The dorms just happened to be perfect for B-52 crews which included five guys and one Nosepick. And yes, to Joe Bob's disgust, the enlisted swine lived in the "suite" but not on his side, of course. Everyone hoped that Joe Bob's replacement didn't have a problem with enlisted. Outside of almost every dorm room door was a blender on an orange crate for the daiquiris. They ran 24/7 depending on the flight schedules. Crews would land at 0800, and the blenders would be buzzing by 0900. Everybody stopped drinking 12 hours before the PTOB. Later in the day (or night) they would head to the Club for some food, and since they were now getting tired, switch to Black Russians.

As time progressed at the picnic, Sluggo was duct taped to a lawn chair, so he couldn't start another Flare Gun war between the dorms. Sluggo's motivation and desire to start the war was in direct proportion to his daq consumption. His legs and arms were heavily duct taped to the respective legs and arms of the aluminum chair, so he was completely immobile. D-Kid and Smolensky had to feed him daqs.

While he consumed more fuel, Sluggo was hatching a plan to start a Flare Gun War with the weenies, kiwis, and jeeps that hid at the "Coward Quarters" on the other side of the base.

Sluggo was lying on his back with his feet in the air. "Listen up, guys. I got it. The CQ is full of non-combatant kiwis that deserve a taste of real war. Plus they will be defenseless. They have no access to the survival kits in the birds where we get our flare guns and flares. They will be too cowardly and sober to fight back, so we can loot their quarters after the initial barrage. They deserve a vicious attack. They have *real* Air Force Officers Quarters with air conditioning and privacy. Some even still have bar refrigerators hidden somewhere. Granted, we have already stolen most of them, but there still is a treasure trove of shit we can steal. Who's in?"

Everybody was ripped. So everybody was in.

The trouble was that they were too ripped to execute Sluggo's new plan, which wasn't new. It was his new old plan. Sluggo wasn't the greatest planner. He didn't need to be. Sluggo and Wildman were the best "sticks" (pilots) in the Squadron. Any one of the crewdogs would have preferred to go into combat with Sluggo or Wildman because there was a very high probability they would come back. But this new old plan had legs. It might go to "The Committee" for consideration in a more sober light.

As it got darker out, it got drunker out. The crewdogs started volleyball games using imaginary nets. The real nets had been destroyed in the Flare Gun Wars before they switched to the tennis nets.

The night wore on. Sluggo ate and then went to sleep since no crewdog ever passed out. He was still taped to the chair but now lying on its side. Spike, Wildman, and B-dog all went to the Club for dinner. Almost all of the picnic burgers had burned to a crisp since no one had paid any attention to them after they were put on. It interfered with their drinking.

The next morning, due to extreme hangovers, the sound of the blenders was almost non-existent. Spike, B-dog, and Jeep headed over to Squadron Ops at 1600. Sluggo and D-Kid followed them in. The mood was light. The crewdogs were happy.

Dangle came in, and his countenance was somber.

Uh-oh. Something not good was up.

"A brief statement, gentlemen. Mission schedules will be posted at 1100hrs tomorrow. Prepare for very long missions. Order two flight lunches. No drinking until further notice. This briefing is concluded."

Graham was delighted. *"Hell. It had to be the go home mission! Only that mission could be that long."*

That evening Spike, D-Kid, and B-dog went to the back bar and got a burger which was pretty bad when sober. Sluggo came in and sat down with them. He had talked to his wife on the phone. Phone calls were a rare occurrence and had to be scheduled weeks in advance.

"My wife said that Cronkite reported that peace talks have broken off. The North Vietnamese walked out, and to quote Cronkite, 'Nixon and Kissinger are very concerned with these actions.' "

They knew immediately that they weren't flying east. They were going west. Spike: "This is it, boys. We're gonna go north in big numbers and blow the crap out of Hanoi and Haiphong. This will end the war. It will also kill a whole lot of crewdogs. I knew this was coming, as did you guys."

At 1100 hours on the 17th, there was a line at Ops. Mission schedules were posted for the next two days. Missions weren't going out as three ship "cells" as usual; they were going as "Waves" which is any number of "cells" flying in close trail formation. The night was divided into three strikes: just after dark, another around mid-night, and one just before dawn. There were a total of 11 cells in each strike. That included both Ds from U-Tapao as well as Gs and Ds from Guam. Callahan's crew out of Loring AFB, Maine was Wave lead on 18 Dec. FAI SO-2 was wave lead on 19 Dec. Nobody knew, but everybody knew. They were going to hit Hanoi, or maybe Haiphong, in a BIG way. Haiphong was the target of choice since you could go "feet wet" (out over water) very quickly if you had the time. Eject over water, and the Navy would save your ass. Hanoi, on the other hand, was the most heavily defended city in the world against air attack. Specifically, it was defended by Russian SA-2s which were originally designed for one purpose: to shoot down B-52s.

One BIG surprise. D-Kid had been subbed to another crew who's Nav had gone DNIF (medical no fly). He was flying the 18 Dec mission. That was the problem that occurred for StanBoard instructors. They wanted very good aviators flying as subs to try to reduce mistakes caused by unfamiliarity with the rest of the crew. Sluggo would get a sub on the 19th. He went ballistic and charged over to Bracken's office.

"Colonel, who in the hell took my Nav when we have to fly a hairball on 19th? I need him! My crew needs him! Why don't you just scratch that other crew entirely and sub the whole damn crew! You can't do this to us. It breaks up our crew integrity. Besides, Foster just turned twenty-five a couple of weeks ago. He's good, but he's a kid. You should put a more experienced IN in as a sub if you can't scratch the crew."

"Captain, no matter who I put in as the sub on Charcoal Three on the 18th, the AC and the Nav are going to raise hell just like you are, so why should I go through that shit more than once. Foster is a StanBoard IN. He's going to fly Charcoal Three – period. You are dismissed."

"BULLSHIT, Colonel! I'm not dismissed! You can't put non-integral crews in that kind of combat! I need my Nav. The Charcoal Three crew should be scratched and an integrated crew subbed!"

"YOU ARE DISMISSED, CAPTAIN! GET OUT!"

The 18 Dec strike launched as a MITO (Minimum Interval Take-Off) at 1700 hours. MITO's were unusual. No one had seen anyone from the crews after they had left for the PTOB. B-52s launching one minute apart was really impressive. Many guys had never seen it before. The crewdogs had all gone out to the runway to watch the launch. It remained unsaid, but in the back of all of their minds they knew that they might be saying goodbye to some crewdog brothers. They didn't know it then, but the first bird from the strike would not touch down until 1030 hours the next day. 17 hours and 30 minutes in the air. Spike was not surprised that there were only three ground aborts. Ground abort happens when something goes wrong after the start of take off roll but before S-2, and the pilot shuts it down, pops the chute, and pulls off the runway. After they pass S-2, which is a certain groundspeed depending on weight, they are "go." They *must* take-off. In a Mito take-off, an abort is extremely dangerous because they have another 488,000 pound bird right behind them.

Three ground aborts told them everything. Only three aborts out of 36 birds was almost impossible. Guys were taking off no matter what unless they absolutely couldn't make it. What this told them was that no one wanted to launch a stand-by manned spare bird. There were four stand-bys for this launch versus one normally. Stand-bys were fully loaded, lit, and ready to taxi the minute a ground abort occurred. No one aborted because no one wanted to be the guy that sent someone in their place on a hairball mission. If the stand-by got nailed, the crew that stayed home would have to live with it forever. The odd part was that two aborts occurred in Charcoal Cell. Charcoal Three was now Charcoal One and would lead the G wave.

D-Kid was now leading the strike.

Three aborts. They were going "Downtown." 216 guys were headed for Hanoi.

A VERY BAD NIGHT

D-Kid didn't like this at all. They had turned into North Vietnam and were now headed south toward Hanoi. Red Crown was making SAM launch calls from the first Wave of Ds from UT that had a TOT just ahead of theirs. He was a sub on a crew that he didn't know very well, and they were about to come under fire from SAMs for about twenty minutes. Very high risk situation. The pilot, Lt. Colonel Russo, a newly named Squadron Commander, was a good stick, he hoped, but he too was on the crew temporarily. They had been ordered at the PTOB not to take evasive action on the actual bomb run.

That's great, just wave a flag at the SAMs when they come up like a bull in a bullfight and dare them to hit us. The pilots would be able to see the SAMs coming at us and just hope. Bullshit. This sucks. Do your job, kid. Trust in God, and get it done. No point in being scared shitless anymore. You're here.

The Co, Bob Williams, who D-Kid had just met at the PTOB, came down to take a pee break. Afterward he tapped D-Kid on the shoulder: "You scared, Nav? I am."

"Why? We're here, and I'm too busy. From this point on, all we can do is concentrate on our jobs, get it done, and get the hell out of here. We're not here to die tonight."

D-Kid almost believed his own advice.

Russo told the EWO, Captain Sampson, not to make any threat calls that would interfere with the bomb run. They couldn't dodge the shit coming up, so why say it was coming?

This is asinine. Why not just take a gun out and shoot yourself. The damn planners should be on this run. Not me. We can hit a target in a forty degree bank dodging a SAM. We can't hit the target if the SAM gets us first.

Charcoal One turned IP (Initial Point) inbound seventy-five miles from the target. Now they were frozen in the sky. No evasive action whatsoever.

D-Kid: "Radar, you see any chaff yet?"

The chaff (aluminum strips to confuse the enemy radar) was to be released by support aircraft to hide the bombers from enemy radar. The radar switched frequencies, and there it was, a very obvious green path headed straight to the target. D-Kid couldn't believe what he saw. "It looks like a highway to show the gooks where we're going! What the hell are they doing?"

Radar: "Looks like they're trying to get us killed. These guys are morons. Why don't they just go man the SAM sites and help them out? Shit."

D-Kid resigned himself to his own advice. Everything on the bomb run became very professional. Put aside fear, get the job done. Charcoal One made the final turn and the target was acquired. The bomb bay doors were opened, and D-Kid started a stopwatch as back-up for release.
Ten seconds prior to release, the SAM went off right in front of the aircraft. The aircraft shuddered and yawed to the left. The electrical system went out, but the intercom still worked.

"They got the pilot! They got the pilot!"

D-Kid couldn't believe what was happening. This couldn't be true. There were electrical shorts and small explosions going off everywhere. It was true. They had been nailed.

Sampson on IC: "The pilots may be dead. The gunner *is* dead."

Russo came on the IC, weakly: "No, the pilot's still alive."

All this had occurred in ten seconds. They were on fire, and the bird was going to go up any second. Normally, there was a bailout sequence. This was not normal. Get out now. OK. You've been trained extensively for this situation. Let's see if it works.

D-Kid reached down and pulled the D-ring between his knees. After what seemed like minutes, everything was moving in slow motion. The hatch fired and he ejected into the freezing cold air. Training took over, and he was amazed at how much he remembered. He stabilized and waited for his chute to deploy. That would take awhile. If it opened at this altitude, it would probably kill him.

The chute opened at fifteen thousand feet, as it was supposed to. He stabilized the chute and looked down. *"Son-of-a-Bitch! I'm headed straight down into the target area. Hell, I'll be burned alive."*

He looked for other chutes. None. *Did those guys get out?* Then concern turned to fear. He was floating into the enemy capital that had just had the shit blown out of it by his fellow crewdogs. *"Look Lord. If I'm going to die, kill me now. I don't want to have those people down there kill me. If they capture me, OK. But if they are going to kill me, please do it now."*

He looked for a safe place to land and begin evasion. There weren't any. No woods, just open fields. *Shit.* The ground came up fast, and he executed the parachute landing well. Nothing broken. He took stock of his situation. He heard voices. *Double shit.* He pulled out his survival radio. "All B-52 aircraft. This is Charcoal One Delta. I'm on the ground, uninjured. I'm surrounded. Will be captured very soon." After the transmission he broke off the antenna of his radio so the zips couldn't use it to track him. The "Delta" meant he was the Nav. He knew that he would be captured. That is if he was very, very lucky.

The Darwin Kid was on the ground in the enemy capital. Ironically, it would soon become survival of the fittest.

THE NEWS

By 0800 on 19 Dec everybody knew. They did go Downtown. And it was bad.

Graham saw the Wing scheduling officer, Colonel Kelly, who was a very good guy and a friend, leaving the Wing headquarters and intercepted him. "How many, Sir?"

"Three. Two from here and a D model out of U-Tapao."

"Who?"

"Colonel Russo and Mad Dog Meyer's crew out of Homestead. Russo was fireballed."

Graham: "Russo was G Wave lead as Charcoal One wasn't he?"

"Yes, Captain, and to answer your next question, Captain Foster was onboard as the Nav. They were hit by one or more SAMs just prior to the target according to Charcoal Two. I know you were close. I'm sorry."

Fireballed meant the SAM had hit, and they had gone up immediately. No chance to eject. They were all gone. They had been Wave lead. The SAM shooters always went after lead. Graham couldn't reply. He couldn't speak. Tears were rolling down his face. He was a kid with a new wife, and now he's gone.

The Colonel continued: "Some of Mad Dog's guys had made it out. The locator beepers fired off."

But Graham knew that today they were POWs, dead, or most feared of all, slaves for the rest of their lives. Mad Dog had been flying for Black Three. He was Stand-by One. The Darwin Kid was probably The Dead Kid. Graham saluted the Colonel without saying a word and left for the Monsoon Mansion. Kelly understood. Graham went to his quarters and found Spike and Hollywood sitting on the beds. Spike looked at him and knew something was terribly wrong,

"What's wrong, B-dog? You look like you had one too many chili dogs."

Graham forced himself to speak. "D-Kid."

"What about him? Those guys will be landing…"

It hit Hollywood. "D-KID WENT DOWN! IS THAT WHAT THIS IS?"

Graham, almost whispering: "Yes. Fireballed."

Spike said nothing. He was crying too. Sluggo walked in by chance and immediately grasped the situation. Only one thing could cause Spike Wilson tears.

"They got D-Kid, didn't they? The miserable bastards got Bob. Oh my God. His wife… I told those bastards not to break crew integrity. I TOLD THEM! NOW THEY GOT BOB KILLED!" Sluggo was also in tears. He left. He didn't want to hear more.

THE CAPTURE

D-Kid pulled off his helmet and ran down a ditch to a culvert he thought might provide some cover. It was too far with so many people around. He laid down on his white helmet and tried to blend into the shadows. Two people were on the top of the bridge but couldn't see him. He decided to disable his S&W 38 that everyone carried by throwing the bullets away and jamming the barrel into the soft dirt in the canal. At least they couldn't kill him with his own gun.

He sensed someone nearby and looked up. There was a woman standing right above him, but she hadn't seen him. She turned to leave and spotted something. She stared right at him.

"BIDI BAO! BIDI BAO! BIDI BAO!"

He knew it was over. Maybe they wouldn't kill him. He was surrounded by civilians who were throwing rocks and screaming at him, so he put his helmet on for protection. He had a strange thought: *If somebody bombed my neighborhood at home, and I caught the guy… what would I do? I wouldn't throw rocks; I'd probably shoot the guy.*

He saw armed soldiers with automatic weapons come up to the ditch.

Ok, I'll know real quickly what my fate is now. They'll either take me prisoner or shoot me right here.

One of the soldiers raised his weapon and pointed it right at him. Another yelled at him in Vietnamese and pushed the weapon aside. He was really close to dead based on that exchange. The guy that had pushed the gun away motioned for him to get out of the ditch. When he came out he was shoved to the ground and stripped down to his underwear. They took everything then tied his hands behind his back and used the remaining rope like a leash. He was forced to walk barefoot on railroad tracks to a nearby village where he was put in a very small brick building. The locals were allowed to come in and stare at him. He was a novelty because of his fair complexion and red hair. One came in and tried to pry his jaw open to look for gold crowns. He braced his jaw tightly. The man left and there was a violent argument outside the hut. D-Kid suspected that it was over whether or not to kill him to get his teeth.

I'm terrified, but I can't show it. Don't be arrogant, and don't talk. Hold your emotion. Resist, but don't get killed doing it. You're still alive.

In about twenty minutes, he was taken back outside. and his elbows and biceps were tied together behind his back and pulled as tight as they could so there were only about four inches between his shoulder blades. His wrists were tied, and a noose was placed around his neck and secured to his wrists. He was again dragged to another village not far away. As he approached the village, he noticed a white sheet on the ground. His captors stopped at the sheet and pulled it up. Under it was Colonel Russo. He had a large wound in his abdomen and was clearly dead.

Go with God, Colonel. May your family grieve in the memory of a great officer and a fine leader. And may their grievances heal them quickly so that they can remember what a great man and father you were.

He was put in another room in the village that was larger than the first. Some women that appeared to be nurses came in and checked him for injuries. They also gave him water and a cigarette. The crowd outside was getting very angry, so the guards used tables to barricade the windows.

Decent treatment? Protection from the natives? What is this? Maybe they won't kill me. Maybe.

He was removed from the hut and blindfolded with gauze, but he could see a little bit by looking down. He was dragged on a much longer walk than the previous two and finally came up on what he thought was a road. On the other side of the road he heard an American speaking. "Hey. Tom Sampson, is that you?" No answer. But he knew it was Tom. He got out.

The bombs started falling again as another B-52 strike came in. God they were scary on this end.

That night D-Kid and his EW were loaded into a flatbed truck, and their journey began. Sampson was injured and had multiple bandages with blood seeping through. But he was alive. Tom started to talk.

"The gunner died in his seat. The pilots got hit pretty bad. What about your radar?"
"Russo's dead. I saw his body in a village. Bobby and Dick must have gotten out."

They stopped at a body of water and were both hauled out of the truck. Two Vietnamese guards came up to D-Kid and beat him pretty severely. They left Sampson alone since he was clearly already beaten up. They got tired of beating D-Kid and put them both in another truck. The truck then drove onto a ferry at the waters edge. D-Kid realized they had to take the ferry because he and the other crewdogs had blown up all the bridges. They were crossing the Red River. They were going Downtown the hard way. When the ferry reached the other side of the river, the truck drove back on to land. After about a thirty minute drive, D-Kid noticed a high wall on his left. The truck slowed and stopped in front of a gate in the wall.

Welcome to the Hanoi Hilton.

CHAPTER VII:
A LONG TRIP DOWNTOWN

19 DEC 72, FAI SO-2 GOES TO THE DANCE

Graham called his wife. It was their second wedding anniversary. They only talked for about 45 seconds. "Hi, sweetheart. Happy anniversary. I can't wait until I get home. I miss you terribly. I love you."

Priscilla asked, "You sound funny. Honey, what's wrong?"

D-Kid's shootdown was controlling his thought process. It was overwhelming, and his voice and demeanor showed it. The call ended immediately as he was cut off. They were monitoring all calls.

All the flight crews were ordered to the mess hall for a mandatory meal of two steaks, minimum, and all kinds of other crap. The reason for the steak was that it would sustain them longer in the event they ended up in a chute that night. Spike and Graham didn't even know where the mess hall was. When they found the mess hall, they heard that Rumor Central had it on absolute authority that they were going after Haiphong since they had hit Hanoi last night. Take it to the bank. Absolutely for sure. A Chief MSgt. had a buddy who knew a guy in planning that said it was positively Haiphong. The same Rumor Central knew for sure that they were going home three days before. Graham wondered how many of them Spike had started. Spike must be Rumor Central.

"Plug" Williams, a Co on a Fairchild sister crew E-06 had gone to the flight surgeon in the morning and gone on DNIF (Duty Not Involving Flying). No one would speak to him again. No one went DNIF when shit like this was coming. Death was an acceptable excuse. Nothing else was. Plug was a "Zoomie," an Air Force Academy grad. He ended his career when he walked into the flight surgeon's office.

At 1430 hours, SO-2 went to the PTOB. It was scary. 108 guys in the briefing room. It was jammed. Crews were set up by rows in the same order they would fly in. As a result SO-2 was in the front row. There was an elevated stage right in front of them. At the back of the stage was the briefing board that was always used. *It was behind drawn curtains.* A first. Never curtains before. If the crews had known they had them, they would have stolen them for the Flare Gun Wars. Things were relatively quiet. None of the usual banter, bullshitting, jokes, and derisive remarks. The quiet was because the room was filled with 108 guys (most of whom were in their twenties) that were all scared to death. As a result of the strike the night before, there were now 18 possible widows and only God knew how many kids were without dads. The room was called to attention and General "Andy" Andrews himself walked up on the podium.

Graham thought, *Holy Shit! Another first! Not a good first. What causes this?*

The General: "Gentlemen, be seated. I am personally attending this briefing to be able to emphasize the importance of this mission. I have tremendous respect for, and confidence in, every man in this room. I'm sure you will execute this mission flawlessly. Now Colonel Lathrop will do the brief."

An O-6 doing the brief. Shit, another bad first.

The Colonel stepped to the podium, and as he did, the curtain opened.

Silence. Some shuffling.

In the center of the large scale map is a large triangle that in USAF means "target." The triangle is in the center of "Downtown."

"The target is the marshalling yards at...

Graham was elsewhere: ... *O Phuc or something. He doesn't remember because it wasn't Oh Phuc. It was in middle of Downtown, and they were going to get there first.*

"..has extreme importance in bringing the North Vietnamese back to ..."

Graham's thoughts wandered to the "parking lot" analogy on SAMs. ...*Remember, unlike the ground where you can hide behind a tree or jump in a ditch and shoot back when the shooting starts, when the SAMs are coming it's like running unarmed and naked across a parking lot for ten minutes or so, with a light on so they see you better, while they shoot at you undeterred, using bullets that only need to get close to kill you ...*

"...and we expect that we will have medium to heavy SAM encounters both before and after the target. However, both the USAF and the Navy have been hitting these sites..."

Graham wasn't listening. He was staring at the map behind the Colonel who didn't know how to brief. *The goddamn planners have us turning west toward Laos into a 130 knot headwind on egress! Our effective groundspeed will be about 300 knots! If we turned east off the target, our effective groundspeed would be 700 knots and we would be feet wet over the Gulf in less than three minutes! The bastards are going to get us killed!*

"…and that concludes this briefing gentleman. Captains Noland and Graham will conduct the lead briefing in this room at 1530."

The room was called to attention, and the REMF idiots left. The crews went to separate rooms and studied all the mission details. It took Graham 15 minutes. They were in deep shit. Their route of flight took them over to the eastern border of Vietnam just below the DMZ. They then turned north and flew on the Laotian side of the border all the way to a point nearly in China and directly North of Hanoi. They then turned South to an IP (Initial Point, the beginning of the bomb run) and then TOT. After bombs away, they took a 90 deg turn to the West directly into the headwind. It left them exposed to SAMs longer than they needed to be. Spike and Graham went to find the O-6 head of 8th AF mission planning. They found him, and Graham launched into him like a guy that was definitely getting out of the service if he lived through the night. He started with:

"The most fucked up plan I have seen in over ninety missions."

…and it got worse from there.

The Colonel listened to B-dog completely and replied: "You're right, Captain. Absolutely right."

Graham was stunned by the response.

"It's nice to see that the Wave's lead Nav knows what he's doing. It's a very tough flight plan, but that's the way it's going to stay, unfortunately. The U-T D's [The Ds flew out of there and Guam] have the same TOT as you do 22 miles east. Plus, the SAM COAs are worse to the east. We tried everything. This is the only plan that will work. Your job is to get everybody there on time, which won't be easy with the winds aloft. G Lead was dead nuts on time last night. And they got him anyway, as you now know, but the others may have survived because he got them there when all the support was ready. Everybody's very tight on fuel. So don't start-stop for timing. Good Luck. And God Bless."

They saluted. He turned and walked down the hall. Spike started laughing. Graham couldn't believe it.

"Bulldog, you were so stunned by his answer you didn't even call him a damn moron. You couldn't. He told you the truth. They screwed us! UT's going feet wet. We turn directly into the 'jaws of death' to avoid them. The UT guys will be swillin' suds in the Club before we even get to La-La Land [Laos]."

They left for the Lead brief. Jeep briefed first and then Graham briefed the route of flight and timing. He concluded with: "I already protested the route of flight and the mission plan to Planning, so don't bother. UT's TOT is the same as ours, and they don't want them running into us on their way to feet wet. Sync watches on my mark." Graham had told the entire room something they already suspected. Now they were sure. They got screwed. But this was a real serious screwing because this one might kill some of them.

General Andrews quietly came into the back of the room.

Intelligence had the last brief. A kiwi 1st Lt. spoke on expected SAM coverage. "Gentlemen, last night there were more than 150 SAM launches. We expect more than that tonight."

HOLY SHIT! Spike couldn't believe it. *They can't have that many to toss up in one night! They had heard from the 18 December guys that the SAMs were coming up from all over the place, but they had no idea it was that many.*

The Lt. went on to say that they could expect to be in SAM COAs [confirmed operating areas] for 14 minutes 34 seconds based on their route of flight.

Damn! A parking lot for a quarter of an hour.

General Andrews told the Lieutenant his information was wrong.

Wow. Strong words from a three star to a white bar.

"Weasels [F-105s whose job was to kill SAM sites] took out that westernmost site this morning, Lieutenant."

"No, Sir. As of two hours ago, the site was still fully operational, and there are no strikes planned against it prior to mission egress."

"Are we talking about the same site, Lieutenant?"

"If you are speaking of the one that's still there, Yes, Sir."

"If you are wrong, it makes a big difference to the men about to leave this room."

"It's there, General."

Spike shook his head in disbelief. *A white bar standing up to a three star in front of 108 guys about to go on the hairball of all hairball missions! This Kiwi must be planning on getting out ASAP just like the Co and B-dog. Maybe even an early out the way he was talking.*

The briefing dismissed, and they headed for the birds at 1605. Shit. They were late already. What the hell? They had 8 hours 03 minutes to be terrified and think about it from wheels in the well to TOT. Everybody would.

Except Roller. Roller was upbeat. He was smiling and joking. Gravitz had told him that they stopped two big Japs at the gate trying to get on base to "visit a relative." Since the base was locked down, no one could get on base. Lucky Roller. The idiot.

Unlike during WWII when each B-17 crew was assigned to their own bird, the crews never knew what they would be flying until they arrived at the plane. When the crew van pulled up, Graham looked up.

Crap! Tail number 221! A known and certified piece of shit!

Graham made sure Jeep knew what they had. "Bill, its POS 221 [POS stood for Piece Of Shit.] Call Charlie tower [Charlie tower was the ramp commander] and tell them we have to have another ride. This one *always* breaks."

Spike concurred immediately as did Co. Roller wasn't there yet even though he was sitting next to Graham. Thump was reading the Bible.

"OK. Let's get the APU fired up, and I'll call Charlie."

Normally they wouldn't care that much. If this weren't a hairball mission, they would have gone through pre-flight until somebody's instruments crapped out and declared the ride a piece of shit. If nothing else was ready, the stand-by crew would take their place, and they would be at the Club in an hour or two. But this was a designated "Press on" mission. The "Press On" designation was a war order mission normally reserved for a nuke strike ... in other words the end of the world. However, this mission was so critical in the view of DOD that it had been deemed PO. "Press On" meant that you were to get to the target or die trying. There was no excuse. A major risk was that they would lose water injection on more than one engine on take-off and be forced to abort because they literally could not fly, at least according to the Boeing tech order. That meant a stand-by bird would launch in their place. While the SB bird would not fly Wave lead, that would fall to the deputy Wave lead crew, and FAI SO-2 would still be responsible for sending six guys in their place on this hairball. That was completely unacceptable to everyone except perhaps Thump who was now in intense prayer.

The bird's crew chief, SSgt. "No Luck" Mazerowski was waiting for them. Unlike the crews, No Luck was assigned to this bird. It was his "baby." Crew Chiefs took great pride in their birds because they reflected their skill set and professionalism. He gave a salute, and Spike and the Captain returned it. Another thing that *never* happens. They normally were pretty casual when boarding.

No Luck: "Major Spike, Captain Noland ... listen gentlemen. We've worked our asses off all night on her. Checked out everything. Replaced everything we could steal parts for. We run her up twice this morning. She's perfect. *She will bring you guys back.* I swear."

Crew Chiefs felt personally responsible to the crews that flew their birds. If *anything* happened to their bird it was *their* fault. If you took a SAM and bought it, it was their fault because the ECM [electronic countermeasures] "didn't work" even though they probably did work. If the pilots screwed up and dinged the bird, it was still their fault. No Luck was giving them his word of honor that his bird would keep them alive. Crew chiefs weren't supposed to know about the mission they would be flying.

Everybody knew.

Spike assured him. "OK Sergeant. We believe you, buddy. We'll run her up and see you tomorrow morning. You will scope us first coming in because we're in lead, pal."

This meant a great deal to No Luck because everybody loved Spike. He was a great guy to everyone. Crew chiefs loved him even if he did stink up their birds during the Flight Suit Wearathon. Spike had just told No Luck that his bird would fly no matter what ... almost. Normally, No Luck would have been directing his plea to Jeep since he was the AC, but No Luck felt it was much more important to get Spike's assurance. Jeep, wisely, said nothing about the break in protocol.

"Wow, Major! My bird is flying lead on this hairball! That's fantastic! She'll do it, Sir!"

Spike smiled and slapped No Luck on the shoulder as he was heading to the hatch. "What hairball, Sergeant?"

No Luck knew enough to shut up and smile back. He didn't know anything, sir.

When Spike told No Luck he would "scope" them first, he was referring to the crew chief ritual of waiting on the end of the runway after the first returning bird was seen on the horizon. All of them had binoculars ("scopes") and would keep the first bird in sight until one of them could call out the tail number of each bird. If they came back in the order they launched (i.e. 1,2,3) the Chiefs were happy. If they came back as 1,3 ... Two might be down. Hell, Two was *probably* down. This morning they had come back: Lead Cell (Charcoal) ... 2,3 ... When

Black Cell was sighted: 1,2 ... The crew chief for Stand-by One was literally in tears. The Chiefs took it so seriously that a chief at U-T earlier in the year had gone back to the barracks, wrote a letter to his parents, and then put a bullet in his head.

SO-2 boarded, as usual, through the hatch just aft of the nose to a "well designed" cockpit. It was well designed for a crew of six dwarf midgets. They climbed up first through the Nav's part of the cockpit "downstairs" and then up top. The Pick and Guns sat abreast facing aft about 20 feet behind the pilots. The guys upstairs ejected up, downstairs ejected down. They did the best job of checking out the seats they had ever done. In other words, they actually *read* and *used* the check lists. These things had better work should the need arise. They all wore survival vests that held all kinds of gear including a Smith & Wesson .38 revolver in a shoulder holster and the locator "beacon" that fired off when their chute opened. They also sat on a survival kit that had more gear, including a raft. The seat kit deployed about twenty feet below them after they separated from the seat and the chute opened. They could inflate the raft using a lanyard before they hit the water, or leave it undeployed if they were coming down on land.

The DCC (Deputy Crew Chief) climbed up to assure them that the seat kits had been "repaired" and told them not to worry. What he meant was that they had replaced the flare guns and the flares stolen for the wars as well as the Dexedrine tabs that were supposed to give them energy during E&E [escape and evasion]. The dex was popular for R&R's [Rest and Recreation] trips where they never rested but recreated a great deal.

They did the checklists and fired up everything. Everything worked! No Shit!! Everything! They were amazed and stunned. They had started pre-flight on POS 221 at least five times before and launched once. Barely. Spike called No Luck on intercom. No Luck was hooked up on an outboard Jack:

Spike: "Hey, No Luck."

"Yes-s-s-sir. What's wrong, Sir?"

Nothing ever went right for No Luck. It was probably something major. Mission critical major. It was always mission critical major. Never minor. Ever. His voice sounded almost as bad as he looked, which was terrible as he had been up all night.

"Nothing, No Luck. Absolutely nothing! You're a genius, No Luck. You stole 556 or 644 (both of which were great birds), painted and re-stenciled the tails overnight, and pulled the ol' switcheroo! You're a certified genius, No Luck. Now tell me which one you switched, buddy. I want to start a pool really quickly on the horn betting on which bird will positively not crap out PTTO [prior to take-off] and everybody will be on 556 or 644 except us! We'll clean up!" Spike was jerking No Luck of course and had no intention of starting a pool for anything because no crewdog would have responded. Not today.

"No, Sir! This is my bird, Sir! 221, Sir! I promised you that she'd bring you back, and she will! She will, Sir!"

"I'm jerkin' ya, No Luck. We might change your name to 'Bust Ass,' buddy. Great job! You guys good upstairs?"

Jeep said he was in good shape. Defense didn't respond.

"Hey Roller, you guys good to go?"

Roller finally replied: "What?"

Thump was praying.

"Never mind, Roller."

What defense. Graham hoped the SAM forecast was wrong, and the MIGS were afraid to fly. He knew that wouldn't be the case, but he could hope.

Jeep piped in: "Good job, Sergeant. Pull the chocks and button the hatch."

"Yes, Sir! Good luck and God bless you all."

Another first. Not good... Maybe D-Kid made it out? Maybe I will.

TAKE-OFF TO DOWNTOWN

Charlie Tower: "Snow One, taxi to runway zero six and hold."

"Roger. Snow One taxi."

Tower: "Snow Two. Taxi to zero six, and hold behind."

"Roger. Snow Two."

... And it went on for 16 more birds.

Tower: "Gentlemen, as you are aware this is a MITO. If you abort, ride the brakes, hit the chute, and get off the active immediately. You are each a great credit to your Country and the United States Air Force. God Bless you all and good luck."

ANOTHER first!

"Snow One. Cleared for take-off runway zero six."

POS 221 pulled onto the active. Jeep: "Here we go, gang. Everyone heads up. Remember, this is not 556..."

Brake release. They were rolling. They were slow which was expected at 488,000 pounds. They were as heavy as you could get a B-52G.

The Co: "Coming up on S-1... S-1... mark."

"No water on four! No water on three!! Lost it on one too!!"

That meant abort now. According to the tech order, 221 was no longer capable of flight.

"Coming up on S-2... S-2... mark!!!

They were committed. They now flew or they ejected. Upstairs had zero delay lanyards and could eject on the ground. Spike and Graham needed 200 feet, in theory, or they died. Jeep knew that very well. At the end of the runway there were about 500 yards of jungle and then a 600 foot cliff falling off into the Pacific. Spike and Graham both gripped their ejection rings and flipped off the safety tabs. Jeep firewalled the throttles.

Jeep, very calmly: "I got it crew. We're good."

Co: "Coming up on unstick."

"Unstick."

They didn't come off the ground. The knot in Graham's stomach was now multiple knots. He was sweating and the cockpit was already cold.

THE DARK SECRET

Colonel Brown, about the only full Colonel on the island that the crewdogs respected and therefore liked, was in his staff car at the end of the runway. God he was proud of these kids. They all knew that they were going into a combat situation that would probably be the worst that they would ever experience in their entire careers. But it was worse than they could possibly imagine. The strike last night had some element of surprise for the North Vietnamese. There would not be any element of surprise tonight. The SAM sites would be fully reloaded and waiting for them. Making matters worse, the G did not have the right counter measures for the SAM sites they would encounter. The Ds, even though they were older than the Gs, had the right blackboxes. The boxes for the Gs were on order and supposed to have arrived weeks ago, but they didn't come in time, and the White House had ordered the strikes anyway. The G crews did not know that they had the wrong equipment. They didn't know that their equipment was useless against these sites. It was top secret, especially from the G crews. He felt a chill with the thought.

What government orders their troops into battle knowing that they are not properly prepared and may suffer horrendous casualties as a result? His government did. He hated the damn politicians. He would not be surprised if they lost six to eight aircraft tonight… or even ten. That's sixty men in one night. Over a fifty percent casualty rate. That's a whole bunch of dead kids and prisoners. He and the General had protested violently to SAC headquarters, and they were told to shut the hell up and proceed with the G strikes. He had done everything that he could possibly do. The only saving grace, if there was one, was that the losses would cause the press to rip the White House like never before and they would be ordered to stop sending Gs north until the boxes were installed. Maybe even better, they would stop sending the Gs north entirely. The press would never know that Nixon had sent these kids even though he knew that they were defenseless. What kind of President would do such a thing? Damn him. Damn Kissinger. He made a conscious decision at that moment. If they incurred the losses they were almost certain to, he would leak the secret to the press himself. He would do it tomorrow to a source he knew he could reach. It would end his career if they found out, and they would find out, but to hell with it. No more kids would be sacrificed after tonight.

THE SLUGGO SWAN

Maybe ten eternally long seconds after unstick, they felt 221 grudgingly leave the runway and start to get airborne. It was very labored and they knew from experience that things were not yet right. Jeep came back on and sounded like he was lifting weights while talking, which he was. It took all of his and the Co's strength to pull back on the yokes and pull the POS's nose up:

"Crew, we're going to lose a little altitude before we start a climb. Hang on."

Spike and Graham looked at each other. They couldn't make eye contact because their visors were down and they were on oxygen. They were ready to eject. But they both held up crossed fingers almost simultaneously. Jeep was going to "Sluggo" the bird.

Some months earlier, Sluggo had been leading a Cell on a routine mission South. It had been raining hard on Guam all day, and it was a late afternoon. The rain had stopped by then, but there were puddles everywhere, including a "pond" in the center of zero six, affectionately called Lake Phuc-U. The problem was that right in the middle of take-off, they would run into Lake Phuc-U, and it would act as a brake and slow them down. Normally, this was not a real problem unless they lost water injection on more than one engine - then it could be a major problem. Sluggo started TO roll and lost water on one in about five seconds. OK. Still good. Then he ran into Lake Phuc-U. Slower. But the speed was coming back up. Then he lost water on another. He was beyond S-2. He had to fly.

He nosed the bird airborne, tucked the gear, got over the jungle at the end of the runway, and then dove over the cliff to gain airspeed. He pulled out of the dive, and the altimeter said they should already be swimming. The Offense didn't eject at 200 feet. This was not so much a vote of confidence that the legendary Sluggo would pull off the impossible as it was that they didn't really believe they could eject at 200 feet and make it. In addition, the ocean below was not just the ocean, it was the Marianas Trench. The Trench was some of the deepest water in the world *and* was so shark infested that when the last crew dinged in, a C-130 trash hauler, the Navy divers were not allowed in the water. Sluggo's Co later swore he had to turn on the windscreen wipers to remove the spray from the ocean. This went down as one of the legendary non-combat Big Balls moves of all time.

Now Jeep was going to do the same thing. But Jeep wasn't Sluggo. He was Jeep...

What the hell ... with their crack Defense team, six SAMs and two MIGs will have nailed them simultaneously in a few hours anyway.

They dove. Co was reading off the airspeed, his voice audibly shaking: "350 ... she's coming up fast."

Graham wondered if he meant the speed or the water. In the middle of this, Spike flipped up his visor, pulled off his mask, turned off the O2, and lit one of his horrid little cigars. At first, Graham couldn't believe it. Then Spike smiled at him with his Spike Smile, and he realized why. If they make water at this weight, full of fuel and bombs, it won't be a "water landing." They will go up like a nuke. Graham started to do the same, but he felt them leveling, airspeed was still climbing, and the altimeter read 50 feet AGL [Above Ground Level].

The Jeep had done it. He Sluggo'd the ride and saved their asses.

The Boeing Tech Order for the B-52G said somewhere in its 2000 pages that the bird can't take off in hot weather, at 488,000 pounds, losing water on three engines, and still fly. It's impossible. It also can't fly at 50 feet AGL.

Boeing was wrong.

Spike intoned in an unemotional monotone: "Nice job, pilots."

Typical Spike. He was dazzled, and Jeep knew it. Two guys had now pulled off what came to be known at SAC and Boeing as the "Sluggo Swan Dive." Coincidentally, Sluggo and Jeep were both B-52 Combat Aircraft Commanders, *and they were both 27 years old...*

Spike, who had his radar on: "We have a bogey at 9000 yards closing. Probably Ivan. We have a surprise planned for him on a later flight."

Jeep responded immediately, still loaded with adrenaline. "Yeah, Spike, we see him. It's Ivan. We'll fly right over the Russian prick and scare the shit out of all of them."

It was a ship.

Spike thought this was good practice for their coming attack on the fisher spies. "Pilot. I'll cycle the bomb bay doors open if you give me the call on range. That'll really scare the little shits."

"Great idea, Spike. Let's do it now. He's coming up fast."

Only Spike could have gone through the procedure to get the doors open that fast with no checklist. In less than ten seconds they heard and felt the doors open.

"Bingo, crew. We went right over them. Co and I could see them dive for cover."

With the doors open, the Russians could see the bombs in the racks clearly from the trawler. They had to think the Americans were done letting them radio mission count and headings to North Vietnam seven or eight hours before they got there. The Navy had harassed them before as had their rescue whup-whups [helicopters]. But this time in was an "Amerikanski" heavy bomber that had "snuck" over the cliff on Guam and attempted to attack an innocent Russian fishing vessel in international waters!

Another INCIDENT!

They didn't give a shit. They can't court-martial dead men. As they climbed to altitude, the terror of what had just occurred was quickly supplanted by the reality of where they were going.

The most heavily defended city in the world against air attack, gentlemen. Specifically against B-52s...

It kept popping into Graham's mind as it must have done with the other 90 guys in the 15 birds behind him.

They passed through 10,000 feet, and Command Post came up on the radio: "Snow One."

"Roger Snow One."

"Charlie Tower said you guys decided to go to the beach on departure. Everything OK now?"

"Roger, CP. The beach was closed. We're going through 15,000, going to three five. We'll rendezvous with the Wave."

"Roger, Snow One. Snow Two and Three plus all of Grape and Copper are ahead of you."

"Good Luck. Nice flying. Keep it up."

Clearly, they didn't yet know about the blatant attack on the unarmed innocent Russian fishing trawler.

Graham: "I got 'em all on radar, pilot. Take up a heading of two niner two and max the airspeed."

"Roger, Nav. Two niner two. Going to the wall again."

Things were somber, serious, and very professional now. They were the best trained aircrews in the world, flying the best aircraft in the world, and they were on their way to prove it. It would stay somber all the way to wheels down and locked tomorrow and for a time after that... It all depended on how many guys bought it.

"Snow One, Snow Two."

"Roger, Snow One. We thought you guys said 'to hell with it' and decided to go on R&R by ditching next to Ivan. Helluva move by the way. Sluggo would be proud, Bill."

"Thanks. Don't try it. Sluggo is nuts, and now I think I am. We're level at flight level 350 coming up on your starboard."

"Got ya. Snow One. You've got the lead."

Lead, pronounced differently, rhymes with dead. Normally lead is kind of an honor. Tonight no one wanted to be lead. Snow Two was a happy guy that Jeep didn't kamikaze Ivan and showed up. Graham had to get to work. They were already late - about 15 minutes - and he had to make that up to meet the Tanks on time. The headwinds were picking up, and they would have to offload more gas from the Tanks than planned if he ramped up airspeed. He put the radar cross hairs on his favorite Westbound islands and updated their position. The cross hairs would tell him how far he was from the island with a bearing.

"Snow One. Two seven one degrees. Now."

The other Navs would turn on Snow's mark when they reached it. Each cell was stacked in trail at base altitude FL350 by 500 feet altitude and one mile separation between each aircraft. So Snow Two was at FL355 (35,500 feet) and Three was at FL360. The second cell was at the same altitudes, and each following cell repeated that. Snow Wave was a seventeen mile long snake with 1,152 seven hundred fifty pound bombs onboard going "Downtown." Hanoi was going to have a very bad wake up call.

"Hey Bulldog-e-ous! You going to get us lost again? How the hell they put you Jeeps in lead defies ... no ... fits with staff logic. Where are we? I dare you!"

Graham flipped the radio. It wouldn't be *that* somber any longer. "WILD-D-D-MAN! How the hell did you get up here!? We thought your whole crew went DNIF! No. No. No. That's right. You paid off Dangle to be Stand-by 10. Sorry for the aspersion on your sorry crew's bravery."

Wildman was one of Graham's closest friends. His "Wildman" version of Latin resulted in the "e-ous" after Graham's callsign. He was actually Stand-by One. He had volunteered, no, insisted, that he get a slot. Once the crew mission assignments were published they stood. The exception was Stand-by. You might be able to trade out of it, but you *would* be flying the next day. No one ever gave up Stand-by. Wildman had pulled a fast one. He was afraid he would miss the "real" war. His crew didn't care. They'd make it back with the Wildman. He was a better stick than Sluggo. Bullshit. He was a strong second.

The Wildman: "Amber Two aborted. Major Standboard lost water on Two after he pulled on the Taxiway. No. Shit. He was almost three feet down the active on TO when he switched it - no - lost it. You know Major Standboard. Everything by the book. His book."

Graham: "Well we'll have to tolerate you and your sorry ass crew then. Try to stay out of our way this time."

"Rog. Bulldog-e-ous. Blackjack will call you up each time you get us lost or we are running more than two hours late. Every hour on the hour so we don't cram the freqs. Have a good one. We'll find you on egress and show you how to get home."

Blackjack was Wildman's Nav. A good one; if he weren't, Graham would be his Nav.

Major Standboard was a flaming asshole who had been head of Standboard at Barksdale. He was universally hated by the crewdogs. Now he was a confirmed chickenshit coward. He would go into hiding now, lest he get the "shit beaten out of him" when they got back. The crewdogs never actually "beat up" a dickhead. They were all officers, so they didn't physically touch anybody. What they did do was cut the person off. They would not acknowledge their presence. They wouldn't make eye contact, salute, or speak to them unless absolutely necessary. If they complained to senior officers about any facet of this treatment, the staff officer would say he'd look into it. They never did. They always knew about the guy too. The guy was screwed. They would almost always request a transfer fairly quickly, but even if they were successful in getting away, their reputation would follow. You had to do something really cowardly to get this treatment. Like abort on a one engine water problem on a Press On hairball mission. Their careers were over.

Spike was out of his seat harness and fiddling with his left leg. He always carried a knife in his right boot but nothing in the left one. Graham yelled at him (off intercom) because of the engine noise, "Spike, what the hell are you doing?"

He did his Spike Smile and pulled up his 9mm automatic.

"I'm making sure it stays with me if we have to punch [eject]. There's only one bullet in it."

"What for? You have the S&W."

"The S&W is for the zips. The nine is for me. I'll nail six of the bastards and then take care of myself. I'm not going to be a slave in Laos until they torture me to death ten years from now."

They stopped yelling and put their masks back on and went on intercom.

"That's a fucked up idea, Spike."

"Everybody has their worst demons, Bulldog. That's mine. I'll deal with it my way."

Thump was alive and was on intercom. "What Demons! Whose Demons?"

"Shit. You're on board, E-Dub? I thought you missed the damn flight. Been snoozin'?"

"Beware of blasphemy, Nav!"

"Sorry, E-Dub. I didn't mean to offend you. I fucking mean it."

Jeep came up. "Cool it guys. We have a long flight."

They didn't like the Pick at all, but Graham was out of line. The Pick was scared shitless too.

Graham kept bumping the airspeed as the headwinds picked up. He had to get them to the Tanks on time for a lot of reasons, not the least of which was that the crews would be nervous as hell if he was late... or early. If he couldn't get them to the Tanks on time before the mission halfway point, how could he get them to the TOT on time? Jeep said he wanted them to get some sleep inbound until they crossed the south coast. Normal rotation. That meant one of the Offense in the bunk (a blanket on the floor upstairs), then a Defense guy, then a pilot, and around again until everyone had some quick shut eye.

Graham was almost amused. *Yeah right. I'm going to sleep when we're late on the hairball of hairballs.*

INBOUND TO THE TANKS

Spike was screwing around with his 9mm, which was against about ten regulations. That didn't matter since he and Graham broke most regs anyway, but it made Graham uncomfortable. They reached altitude and went off IC. At cruise altitude the din of the engines was tolerable, so they could talk off IC without yelling too loudly. The O2 masks were hanging open, attached to their helmets.

"Spike, what the hell are you doing?"

"Cleaning, Bulldog."

"Why are you cleaning a gun that you're only going to kill yourself with anyway? It only needs to work on one bullet. Is that still loaded, dumbshit?"

"I want a clean bullet, B-dog. My family has high standards. It's good breeding that drives me to my obsession with cleanliness. Don't get worried, man. The bullet's right there on the deli counter." He pointed to the brass jacketed bullet which looked brand new. "Besides, you're already scared shitless, so how can you be worried too? There is no room in the human mind for complimentary emotions like that."

This statement was complete bullshit. Spike, the instigator of the "Flight Suit Wearathon," was notorious for being semi-clean at all times. The bullet was rolling around on the "deli counter" which was a small shelf attached to the bulkhead directly in front of them. The radar scopes and instruments were arrayed directly above it. The deli counter was meant more for the Nav than Spike, since he needed it for charts. Its other use was as a lunch counter, hence "deli." There were intentionally no windows in their hovel. They lived in the dark.

"That's bullshit, Spike. I'm rarely scared like I am now, but I worry about you almost all the time. Cleanliness my ass. You remember last week at the 4-5-6 game? You got blasted after losing your ass on an ace n' out and wandered out on the golf course and fell asleep. You know how I found you later, 'Mr. Clean?' By *smell*. I *smelled* you in the sand trap by number 9. I followed my nose and found your sorry filthy ass. If I hadn't saved your ass as usual, General Andrews would have awakened you up with a wedge in the morning, and you'd be a Captain again."

At that moment they hit CAT [clear air turbulence] and everything went flying. Including Spike's bullet. CAT was common over the Pacific, especially when the jet stream was ramped up. The cockpit of a B-52 is one massive array of instruments and "black boxes" that make the instruments work. Sometimes. The place was so crammed that Spike insisted that Boeing designed the bird and at the last minute had a revelation along the lines of "Shit, that's right. We need a crew. Damn. Well, we'll just push this box three inches left and that one two inches forward and this there and that there and" ... and so on.

Spike's bullet was gone.

HERMAN

Herman got it.

The bullet was gone the way God knows how many other things from stopwatches to lighters had disappeared: into the Jaws of Herman. Herman was this "thing" that lived in the bowels of the B-52. He was always the same and his name was universal no matter what bird you were flying. He took every flight.

More importantly, Herman never gave anything back. Ever. The floor of the downstairs cockpit was a porous grate. If you dropped almost any small object, it was gone for good. Herman would smile.

Spike panicked. He couldn't kill himself. He had to get that bullet back. Do the impossible. Wrest it from the Jaws of Herman. He was out of his ejection seat in an instant but still connected to the IC.

"Hey Thump! Thump! I need your help! Thump!?"

Thump must have awakened hearing the name he detested.

"It's against regulations to use nicknames during flight operations, Major. And besides I find that name to be offensive, insulting, and a smear upon my future avocation."

"Ok, Thump. Listen. I need you to say a powerful prayer to the Big Guy to help me get my bullet back from Herman. I need it right away."

Spike was crawling around on the floor of the cockpit. It was gone. Herman never gave anything back.

"Major! I resent being addressed by that name! Now what's this about a bullet? And why do you need a prayer? Did you unload your sidearm!? Are you carrying extra bullets!? Regardless of which it is, both are against Air Force regulations, Major. Are you at all familiar with regulations, Major? Who is this Herman you want me to include in a prayer?"

What a nerd. Super Nerd. Doesn't know who Herman is. They needed to get this asshole off the crew.

"OK, E-Dub. OK listen. Herman is this thing that lives down here and he eats anything that falls on the floor or between black boxes or anywhere where it's not supposed to be. He ate my only bullet. I need you to say a prayer to help me get it back."

Co chimed in: "Herman is just one of the *things* that live down there. Spike and Bulldog do as well." Co was at least smart enough not to ask about the bullet.

Graham responded: "Co, shut the hell up unless you're spoken to by far superior officers. And we aren't talking to you. Spike is in a complete state of panic. He thinks he can get his bullet back from Herman if the Big Guy helps. So shut up and fly."

"Yeah. Sure. You guys know Herman never gives anything back."

Co was trying to be funny! He never tried to amuse anyone ... then Graham suddenly understood.

It was fear.

Humor was a great cloak of fear. With hours before the Dance, he knew too much and had too much to think about for an interminable period of time. Humor was a Band-Aid that might prevent them from flipping out. Thump had his Bible. Roller didn't know where he was. Spike and Graham were reverting to their normal banter. He wondered what Jeep was doing ...

Thump, in his most serious pulpit voice: *"Let* me understand. You want me to say a prayer for your bullet so that some imaginary thing that supposedly lives down there and is sustained by eating things that fall on the floor will return it to you even though you possess this bullet in direct violation of the regulations? You are completely unaware of regulations aren't you? And no, I won't say a prayer for some pagan idol that supposedly ate a vehicle of death."

Spike responded with unusually rapid and ill-conceived chatter. "E-dub, I know all the AFRs. I've broken most 'em. I have to know them to break them. Herman is not a 'pagan' idol. He's a thing, and he eats things, and he ate my bullet, and I need you to say a prayer to the Big Guy to help me get it back, or I can't kill myself if we get nailed, and then I'll be a slave in misery forever instead of dead and happy. Understand!? Now please say the prayer!"

"No, Major. Absolutely not. I will not support your idolatry. Do not bother me again unless it is mission critical. I have some study to do for the mission, and you have already wasted too much of my time."

Graham thought, *Mission my ass. He's trying to speed read the entire Bible in seven hours.*

Spike: "Thump. You're a dork. You really are a dork. But you're lucky because you're such a dork that the zips won't enslave you. They'll shoot your sorry ass. Not because you try to escape, but for preaching your shit to them twenty hours a day, or worse, they'll give you back as a tactical weapon against us. You shit."

Jeep had enough. "OK guys, jam it. We have a mission to fly, and you guys are screwing around instead of flying. Now get to work. Nav, we on time for the Tanks yet?"

THE TANKS

Shit. He was right. Get to work. Graham did a quick wag (wild ass guess) based on his last position. "Pilot. We're 17 minutes out. Still six behind, but we can't pull the Wave any faster than we have. You'll have to top off for sure. Should be in radio contact any minute."

"Roger Nav. Co, see if you can raise Rabbit One."

Rabbit One was the lead Tank. He would be their gas passer. "Rabbit One. Snow One. Do you copy?"

Finally a crackle. They were just coming in range. "Roger Snow One. Rabbit One and all the little Rabbits are holding at the Track (a racetrack shaped holding pattern) for you guys. Hurry up and get here, or we'll all have kids. You know how rabbits are."

They were way too early to be at the Track. That meant they would be burning *their* gas since they only had one supply to feed the birds they re-fueled *and* themselves. The lead Nav on Rabbit was no good. Being that early to the Track was inexcusable.

Jeep: "Roger, Rabbit One. See you at 21 after the hour."

Spike came up seven minutes later.

"Pilot. Bombs. I got the Rabbits. One O'clock. Five-Five miles."

"Roger, Bombs. Co, get Rabbit One. Crew, prepare for re-fueling."

Preparing for re-fueling was the same as if they were going into combat. On oxygen, visors down, strapped in. Ejection handles unpinned. Re-fueling was dangerous. Sometimes very dangerous if there was CAT around. Which there was.

"Rabbit One. Snow One. We hit some bad CAT on the outbound. Be aware."

"Roger Snow One. So did we. Right here, about twenty five minutes ago."

The Tank driver hadn't even bothered to mention the CAT when they first contacted him. There was no point to it. This was a Press On for the rabbits as well. Spike took them in until the pilots got a visual. They were about 300 miles from the Eastern coast of the PI. There was some buffeting but no CAT. It would not be an easy refueling for Jeep. But they had to get the gas or essentially die trying. Press On.

"Rabbit One. Snow One is stabilized."

"Roger Snow One. Rabbit One is stabilized."

"Snow One has Contact. Offloading."

Airborne re-fueling is the hardest flight maneuver a bomber pilot is required to execute. Until later.

Spike had his flashlight out and was scanning the floor from his ejection seat. Graham hit him on the shoulder with the checklist and gave him a thumbs down. Give it up, Spike. Spike flipped Graham the bird and continued his futile search. There's no talking on IC by anybody except the boomer and the pilot during refueling. They were on the Tank almost at nine minutes. They should be done soon. Suddenly, WHUMP! Everything went flying all over the place. There was a loud crack that sounded bad. The boomer, as is his responsibility, calls:

"SNOW ONE! BREAKAWAY! BREAKAWAY! BREAKAWAY!"

As expected they hear other BREAKAWAYS on guard. CAT doesn't play favorites. Jeep retarded the throttles and was in a steep dive. The Tank pilot had his yoke in his lap [going up] and had firewalled his throttles. The birds separate in an instant. Snow One leveled off 2000 ft. lower:

Graham: "Snow One level at flight level 330. Heading two seven nine."

"Flight. This is Snow One. Who else did breakaways? And status."

Both Grape One and Amber One had hit CAT, but they were alright. They would also be short on gas.

"Roger, Snow One. Rabbit One level at flight level 370. Heading two seven six. Bit hairy, Snow One. Nice flying. You almost got all the gas."

Jeep: "Roger Rabbit One. FIGJAM! [Fuck I'm Good, Just Ask Me] You handled your end perfectly. I was so close to the boomer I swear I could read his name tag. Let's close and stabilize for the remainder of the offload."

The Tanker guys had name tags and insignia on. The crewdogs only had insignia and an American flag on their shoulder. No patches or name tags.

"Negative Snow One. You stole our boom nozzle in the breakaway."

Graham thought, *That was the loud crack they heard ... They are lucky. Very lucky...*

Jeep: "Roger Rabbit One. We'll call the CP and have some Tanks airborne on stand-by when we go feet wet outbound. I don't think we'll make it back with this offload. We were tight to begin with. But you did a great job while it lasted."

"Rog. Snow One. Maybe we will see you on the outbound in about five hours. We'll go back and maybe get another bottle of gas. Good Luck and God Bless."

Christ! Everybody knew! The Tank driver never would have guessed that they would be that long unless he knew they were going Downtown.

"Roger Rabbit One. See ya. By the way, what's your name, Tank?

"Scott Keystone ...'Keyman.' Snow One, yours?"

It was Graham's neighbor at Fairchild! Their wives were best friends! Holy Shit!

"Bill Noland. Aren't you a FAI Tank driver, Keyman?"

"Roger that. Bill. I think we've met as well. What's the call?"

"I'm not supposed to know. But it's Jeep."

"Oh. An FNG, huh? You don't fly like one."

Graham jumped in. "Who the hell are you to evaluate a glorious bomber driver's performance, you lowly gas passer!"

"BULLDOG! Small Air Man! How'd you get in lead as the primary Nav? Planning probably wanted to get your flight lost on purpose! You probably have that lunatic Spike with you! I pity you, Jeep. You're screwed. Bulldog won't find the target, but Spike will have dropped them in the ocean or on the 'Pilipeens' beforehand anyway, so it won't matter."

Graham came back. "Do you guys have little white flight suits and squeegees? Screw you. We'd prefer self-serve anyway."

Spike wouldn't let it pass. "Hey, Tank pukes. You got any bullets? I need at least one. Oh. Oh yeah, that's right. You jeeps don't carry side arms. You use the holster for your spray bottles. In that case could you get our windshield please? There's a big tip in it for you... my dick."

Jeep: ""We gotta bi-lao ching ching [Thai for 'hurry hurry go like wind']. Thanks again, Keyman."

"Thanks. Take care guys. Even you, Bulldog. Maybe even Spike. God Bless you guys. We're buyin' when you get back from this one."

No Secrets! Everybody knows the mission plan!

OVER THE PI

Graham brought them back up to FL350 after they cleared the airspace, and the rest of the wave fell in line. They tucked it up. No chatter on the radios.

Graham: "Boost it ten knots, pilot. The headwinds are picking up, and we're still late."

The other guys should be able to handle it, except the guys that had breakaways. They would have to hit a Tank feet wet like them anyway. They had to be on time. People's lives depended on it. Including their own.

"Roger, Nav."

"Flight. Snow One going up ten. Now."

Grape, Copper, Amber, Gold, and Orange all acknowledged. They would start to communicate very cryptically as soon as they got to the PI. Even on "secure" channels. They were monitored by NVA / VC symps [sympathizers] from the PI on. The symps also heard intentional bullshit, which the Commie pricks wouldn't understand anyway. Spike hoped they did understand. Then they would think they were being attacked by complete madmen and surrender.

Spike was on the floor again. He would give up soon. Herman must have been using his toothpick while laughing at the same time.

Graham: "You have to study the bomb offsets, dumb shit. Get off the floor. Herman's laughing at you."

He got up and pulled the offsets out of his flight bag. Offsets were the landmarks showing up on radar in the target area. Spike would put his radar generated crosshairs on the offsets, and the BNS (Bomb Nav System) would calculate the heading, distance, and time to the target based on the airspeed and the prevailing winds. At a point in time after the IP, the pilot would turn over the control of the aircraft to Spike, who would fly the bomber to the TOT point by keeping the crosshairs on his most reliable offset. If the target had a "hard" radar signature, he would put the crosshairs directly on the target and the bird would fly to it. No target worth a shit ever had a hard radar signature, except bridges. Spike was slightly nuts, but he was also a dedicated officer and professional aviator. He was also the best bomb dropper in SAC. But then it suddenly dawned on Graham that he should have known better. Spike had pulled the charts and offsets out so he could get the Combat Kazoo at the bottom of his flight bag.

"Goddammit, Spike! Now is not the time to harass the Pilipeenos! Guys are uptight, and *they* are reviewing mission plans. All the other RN's have already memorized the offsets while you were looking for a damn bullet!"

"Au contraire, B-dog. They need some relief from the tension. A small attack on the Pilipeens will comfort them. Besides, if they shoot at us, I can slam the crosshairs on them and send them 27 'hello-that-was-a-big-mistakes,' which will surely ruin their miserable little night. Plus, then we'll *have to* abort, even with a Press On, on account of being out of bombs."

He was only half bullshitting. Graham hoped he was bullshitting the right half.

"Did your Mom ever tell you that you were from a distinguished family of well bred clean fanatics that were also sane? If she did, she was lying!"

"B-dog. B-dog. You don't understand, kid. We have a National obligation to harass the Pilipeens going back centuries. Besides that, I personally don't like them, and they keep losing wars which sets a bad example."

"Dammit, Spike, study the offsets and forget the PI. You can torture them on the way back. If we get back."

Graham didn't know why he verbalized a thought like that. Maybe because of D-Kid's fate. Maybe Spike's right...

Spike just gave B-dog his Spike Smile, gleefully pulled another Kazoo from his bag and handed it to him. Graham threw it on the deli counter. Spike started humming songs into the Kazoo like an orchestra rehearses. Graham could see the eastern coast of the PI now on radar. He got a radar fix off a peninsula and updated their position.

"Pilot, Nav. Turn to heading 271 on my mark ...

"Mark"

"Roger Nav, 271."

"Flight. Snow One. Two seven one now."

Minutes later they crossed the PI coast. Spike got out of his ejection seat, unzipped his flight suit to the middle of his chest, and pulled a white scarf out which he tossed around his neck. He turned the map light mounted on the bulkhead to shine on his head and shoulders, acting as a spotlight.

Graham thought, *Jesus. He was going to do a stand-up performance ala Sinatra or Elvis or whoever's persona his mind had conjured up! Either he's finally lost it or he's trying to get me to lose it.*

Spike: "You see, Bulldog, you have to get in the right frame of mind to really do a great performance! Now pick up that Kazoo! You are doing the accompaniment!"

Graham left it on the deli counter. He thought he was in shock or just amused to the point of wonder. Spike pulled his mask towards his face and tested the Kazoo on Guard. MI-Mi-Mi-Mi ... Mi-Mi-Mi ... He then went into a full blown and spirited version of the melody to his anthem.

Jeep, very irritated: "Goddamnit, Spike, not now!"

"I'll be finishing the last curtain call momentarily, Jeeper."

At least he responded to the request unlike how he handled Joe Bob. He must have been impressed with the Sluggo Swan Dive.

Spike was literally dancing in the cockpit of a B-52 bomber as he wrapped up his performance. "OH Pilipeens-s-s-s! My Pilipeen-s-s-s-s... ALL TIME FIGHT! BUT NIVIR W-E-E-E-E-N!!!"

"Thank you, ladies and gentlemen! Thank you! You've been no audience. Thank you! And in the words of another great American I SHALL RETURN! Good night! Good night! That's all. Hold the applause!"

He then Kazoo'ed the melody again and faded out.

Unbelievable. Graham was in hysterics after getting over the shock.

This was his greatest performance. Graham actually clapped when he finished.

Jeep didn't clap. "Spike! You shithead! I told you to shut the hell up! We're going to have a discussion when we get back. Now shut up, and study the mission plan!"

Spike responded: "Thank you! Thank you very much! Please hold the applause! Thank you!"

The other crews, many of whom had never heard "Oh Pilipeens," but had heard *of* it, started to give quick accolades on guard. Atta boy, Spike! Way to go, Spikeman! Encore! Encore!"

Then Spike, in a deep baritone: "Ladies and Gentleman! Spike has left the building."

Even the Co responded: "One of your best, Spike!"

HANOI HANA SHOWS UP

Oddly, there was no response from the Pilipeen controllers at all. They were 100 miles north of the outbound track, but that shouldn't have made any difference. Then from nowhere, on guard, they heard a female voice with a slight Asian accent.

"Snow One and your friends. Where are you going tonight? If you are going to Hanoi, all Yankee Air Pirates are going to die. We are waiting for you and your friends. We have many more air missiles tonight. You will all die. You should write letters to your loved ones now and tell them how much you loved them. We will pick the letters from the wreckage and mail them to your widows and orphan children. We are a kind people. Why would you bomb us? You should abort your mission and go back to Guam. If you don't, you will all die and never see your family again. Just think about that. They will all be crying by this time tomorrow. All Yankee Air Pirate die tonight. We will not keep any prisoners. You should go back. We are a kind people. You have been warned. Go home. Remember to write your loved ones. Goodbye."

It was Hanoi Hana. She had never been heard over the PI before. Another first. Hanoi Hana was very common in the North and down by the DMZ, but she had always stayed home. Since they knew the Guam missions always flew over the PI inbound, they must have recruited some PI symp, and taught her the routine. She knew the call signs and the number of cells from the Russian fishing trawler that Snow One had fake bombed.

The crewdogs couldn't help but think about what she said...

"Nav. Pilot. Give me our exact position."

"We're bearing nine two at one eight three nautical off point Kilo."

"Roger, Nav. Nine two at one eight three, Kilo."

"Affirmative."

Jeep would report the New Hana to the CP on Guam. The Pilipeenos would send some of their commandos to the northern villages to try to track her down. Or at least that's what they would tell the U.S. State Department.

INBOUND TO VIETNAM

They reached their turn point on the Western side of the PI and turned to a new heading that would have them reach landfall just below the DMZ.

"Guns. Nav."

"Roller! Nav! Wake up, dammit!"

"Hey, Thump. Reach over and hit Roller will you?"

"I told you men not to refer to me by that name. Cease or you shall face the wrath of God tonight!"

Graham: "Is that right, Thump? Well if we do, you do, Thump. So you better call off your wrath prayer or rescind it if you have already sent it. If you don't you'll be looking up at silk tonight as well. Now wake up Roller, will ya'?"

"No. That is not my responsibility."

Graham unstrapped and climbed the ladder to the upper deck, turned aft, and slapped the back of Roller's helmet which was lying face down on his deli counter. He slowly raised his head, turned, and gave him his brown tooth smile, with a very informal salute.

"Stay awake from here on in!"

Graham climbed back down, took a quick pee break at the pee can, and strapped in. "Guns. Nav."

"Roger, Nav."

He still sounded asleep. Of the 90 guys behind them, Graham was willing to bet Spike's pay that not one had been, or would be, asleep until they went feet wet outbound. Only Roller could do that because he blissfully failed to grasp the gravity of the mission at hand.

That was not always the case. Sluggo had been leading a "Cheese Run" [slightly more dangerous, as in harder, than a 'Milk Run' which were not dangerous at all] back in September when the cell reached the turn point on the Westside of the PI. No one turned.

Sluggo just kept moving on the same heading as did Bronze Two and Three. About seventy miles West of the PI (10 min.) Bronze Three came up on Guard and screamed, "Bronze cell take up a heading of two niner zero now! Bronze One respond. Bronze Three."

Bronze Three watched on his radar as One started turning.

The Nav came up on assigned secure freq and slowly and calmly intoned, "Bronze Cell. Heading two niner eight on my mark ... mark. We were blown off track by a freak wind shear over the Pilipeen cliffs. We're now correcting to intercept the flight plan track. Anticipate intercept and heading correction at one seven past. Bronze One."

Pilipeen wind shear ... bullshit. The *entire Cell* was asleep at the turn. Eighteen crewdogs. They had sailed off over the So Chi and ended up fifty miles south of the mission plan track. The incident, later called the Great PI Wind Shear, became just another Sluggo legend.

Graham made sure that Roller stayed awake. "Guns, we're just past the PI over So Chi [South China Sea]. When we get two hundred nautical from the PI, I'll clear you on exercise."

"Roger, sir."

Sir?

The "exercise" was a guns check. There were four .50 cal machine guns located in the tail that the gunner controlled remotely with his own radar. In the check he would load the weapons and acquire a simulated bogey generated by the black boxes. He would then live fire the weapons for several bursts. They only jammed about 40% of the time. But this was 221, so Graham figured one in ten chances they wouldn't jam...

Then on guard again:

"Snow cell and your friends. You reached your turn point and will be going North. We are waiting for you. We have very many fighters tonight. Their pilots are treated as great heroes if they get you, so they will shoot you down for sure. You Yankee Air Pirates are fools. You should turn back now. You will all die tonight in the North. You will never see your wives and babies again. It is not worth it for you to die. We will win for sure, and you will leave orphans and poor wives for no reason. They will cry all the time. Go back to Guam now.

Then go home to your babies. If you keep going, you will all die. We are waiting for you. We will take no prisoners."

Someone responded, disobeying a serious order.

"Fuck you, bitch. You're the ones that will die tonight!"

She had gotten to him. He just told her that she had succeeded. She had done her job.

Jeep came up secure. "Snow Flight. Snow One. Get that Bozo off air now! I want the AC to meet me at de-brief."

They all acknowledged. Gold Two came on. "It was my guns, Bill. We have him under control. Hana really got to him. He's twenty and just had his first kid."

"Roger Gold Two. Keep him under control."

It was a serious breach. All B-52 crewdogs go through extensive psychological screening, but you can't simulate conditions like they were in now. The kid's a jeep. His flying would be over after touchdown. Now things were somber again, and time was accelerating. They had flown this same route going South dozens of times, but very quickly, it seemed, they were painting landfall at just under 200 miles.

"Pilot. Nav. We are One niner eight from landfall. Three minutes out. We're configured. Turn to heading two six five and add 10 more at my mark."

Jeep did the drill with the wave. Graham was turning them just slightly south of the mission plan track. A little more spacing from the Z [DMZ, The Demilitarized Zone divides North and South Vietnam] since the Z was anything but demilitarized. The zips had at least three SAM sites right on the line. They also had a particularly good shooter unless they had moved him up North for the main event, which Spike was almost sure they had.

Spike was sharpening the knife he kept in his other boot. He had given up on Herman and had actually studied the offsets for about ten minutes.

Graham: "You couldn't have studied those offsets that fast, you shit. It took me 45 minutes for Christ sake. At least you gave up on Herman."

Graham also had to know the offsets in case something happened to Spike before bombs away. The target had six different aiming points, and they had to know all of them. Most missions not controlled by a ground FAC [Forward Air Controller] had three offsets at most. Accuracy on this mission was critical, so they had six. Their target wasn't that far from the Hanoi Hilton where the Brothers were POWs. If someone got off track and slung a load, it could take out their own guys. On the actual bomb run, Spike would acquire the target and then start flipping offsets in and out. If they were exactly on track, the crosshairs would fall on the correct aiming point each time he flipped the offsets. It was like using triangulation with six different lines. The target was under the intersection of all six lines. Graham had to confirm the offsets with him. If they tanked the target, Graham was also responsible.

Spike, almost growling: "Herman's a bullet eating shithead. I will get him someday. I have decided to shoot it out with the shitbirds with my S&W. If they are waiting for me as my chute approaches the dirt I start shooting. They will return fire and kill my ass. I will only shoot at five. Number six goes right here [pointing to his mouth]. If I don't see the little yellow turds as I approach, I will pop the chute, find them, and start a gunfight. Either way, number six is mine."

"You're a complete nut ball, Spike. You eliminate any chance of survival. Give it up. Besides, we're not going to take a SAM, so you don't have to worry about that option."

"Oh yeah, right. We got Leon and Miss Peach on defense upstairs and we're not gonna get nailed. The place is gonna look like the finale at Coney Island on July 4th, and we're going to sail right through. Dream on, B-dog."

"I love your guarded optimism. It's very comforting. You dumb ass. What about the offsets?'"

"Screw you. Number one is a three story building in a field two one miles west of the target that will show up like a light bulb in a dark hole. Two is a river island that could be too low in the water, one two miles southeast and tough to pick up. Three is a bend in the Red [Red River] ..."

He named all six exactly. The guy was the best. A damn unwashed genius.

"Pilot. Nav. You might make sure everybody has everything lit up [equipment staged for combat]. We will be right on the Z. We should make the damn planners fly this plan tomorrow."

"Roger, Nav. Everything ready in this bird as far as I can tell. Shit, even the guns work. For now. No Luck did a pretty good job except of course the ENGINES. I'll poll the flight."

"Pilot. Nav. Landfall. We're in South Vietnam. Heads up crew."

"Flight. Snow One is dry. Heads up, guys. We'll all get home."

AN UNWANTED SURPRISE

They were about five miles dry, and Thump screeched: "Pilot! Uplink!"

Jeep to the flight: "Snow One has uplink!"

Jeep banked hard right. The uplink meant that a SAM was airborne and locked on to Snow One electronically. SAMs are proximity fused. They "sense" when they are close and go off, exploding up and out in a cone shape. If they are close and below them, they're gone. If they are close but have passed above the aircraft, they might get some shrapnel damage, but they could survive. With luck.

There was a bright flash in the cockpit and some vibration. The SAM had detonated.

Jeep came up. "Went off above us crew, but very close. We are very lucky on that one. EW, what the hell happened? No threat radar acquisition? What happened to the uplink jam?"

In order to launch the SAM, the ground site had to know where they were. In order to do that, the site had to "come up" with their targeting radar [threat radar] which the EW was equipped to recognize and jam. The uplink is an electronic "path" generated by the site radar toward a specific aircraft. Once launched, the SAM rides the uplink that takes it to the target at Mach three. When an uplink is detected, the crew literally has seconds to break the uplink electronically or maneuver and hope. Maneuvering the aircraft defeated the electronic defense, but it worked as a last resort. Generally, if they detected an uplink, they were going to get hit.

"Pilot. EW. I saw no threat radar at all. Only the uplink. The rest of Snow cell must have not detected anything either or they would have come up. I don't know why we didn't see it, but it's not a good omen."

"Roger, Dub. Keep your head up. They apparently only launched one, and they were up and down very quickly. We have a huge bounty, so they are motivated. Stay into it."

Any SAM crew that shot down a B52 received a $20,000 bounty. They could earn $10,000 for each crewmember they captured alive and $5,000 for bodies. That kind of money was huge to an NVA soldier that made $500 a year. The crewdogs weren't supposed to know about the bounties.

"Snow One. Snow Two."

"Roger Snow Two."

"That baby went off just above and aft of your starboard wing. Looked like a flash photo, man. I think we took some shrap, but not serious I hope."

Snow Two was 500 feet up and one mile behind Snow One, so he flew into some of the debris.

"Roger, Snow Two. Let's keep heads up, flight. I never heard of a SAM site with one pole. [SAMs looked like flying telephone poles]. We had no warning at all. EW didn't see a thing until uplink. Snow Two and Three, did you guys see anything?"

"Negative until the uplink at the same time you called it. Snow Two."

"Snow Three saw nothing at all until detonation. Our BB's [Black Boxes] may have a problem. Not a good time to find that out. We didn't see shit. We may be TF-BUNDY guys. [Totally fucked - but not dead yet.]"

WEASELS

Ironhand One and Two did see the SAM launch. Two F-105D "Wild Weasels" had been sitting off the Z over the So Chi waiting for the SAMs to take the bait. They had. Very quickly. It must have been too much for them to resist.

"Wild Weasels" had one mission in life: kill SAM sites. It was a very dangerous job. Fifty percent of the Weasel drivers did not come home. The highest attrition rate in the Air Force. They could not buy a drink at any base in SEA or the CONUS [Continental United States]. They were revered. Most had a handful of DFCs [Distinguished Flying Cross. The third highest award for heroism in combat.] A few had the AFC [Air Force Cross. Number two.] And one had the MOH. [Congressional Medal of Honor, the highest honor the Nation awards].

105s: "Thuds," were old, heavy "fighter bombers" that were pretty quick, but they only had one engine in the tail. If that engine took a hit and went out, the 105 had all the aerodynamics of an open safe. They earned their nickname because of that characteristic: engine out, they hit the dirt with a "thud."

"Ironhand Two. One. You got those boys too?"

"Roger One. One niner five at sixty one. They blew it. We got 'em."

"Ironhand One turning to one niner five, going to burner."

"Roger, One. I'm on your wing."

In seconds: "Ironhand One has the target acquired. Lighting off two shitbusters now."

The missiles tracked perfectly. In a few more seconds the ground lit up.

"Ironhand One out of burner going to zero two zero, climbing to flight level 250, now. Man! Look at the secondaries!"

Secondaries are additional explosions on the ground other than the ones caused by the shitbusters. The SAMs and their trailers were going up.

"Roger, One. I'm right behind you. Man! You're right! Look at that sh ..."

There was a bright flash right behind One. The *other* site had nailed Two. Seconds later One heard a beeper go off. Two was in a chute. The beeper automatically went off when the chute opened.

"Red Crown, Red Crown. Ironhand One. Ironhand Two has been hit! I repeat. Ironhand Two has been hit! He's in silk now! We're one eight zero from Lima at six seven. He should make feet wet in two or three minutes. Acknowledge Red Crown. Ironhand One."

Red Crown was the "orchestra conductor." They were the overall combat theater command post on site. They were a large group of Colonels and one General, flying in a C-130 over the Gulf of Tonkin or onboard ships. They would coordinate all air ops at tonight's Dance.

"Roger, Ironhand One. We have a Jolly [Jolly Green Giant search and rescue helicopter] in the area, and he's already on the signal [beeper]. We'll get him, Ironhand One. We'll get him."

"Roger Red Crown. Thanks, guys. I'm nearly bingo. [out of fuel] Ironhand One RTB. Please advise status."

"Wilco [will comply with request] Ironhand One. Red Crown out."

THE FLIGHT

Gold and Orange cells, the last ones in the wave, saw the secondaries and the SAM explosion almost directly North.

"Snow One. Orange One."

"Roger Orange One."

"Looks like Lowboy must have picked up the SAM launch and hosed the site. Spectacular fireworks down there. Also saw another SAM det. Hope they are cool."

"Lowboy" is a massive group of defensive fighters and light bombers that were launched in support of the Linebacker II air strikes. They are positioned at altitudes below the B52s and their primary responsibility is defending the bombers against attack from enemy ground defenses and low flying MIG fighters. "Mig Cap" are USAF and Navy fighters that fly above the bomber waves to protect against MIG attacks at altitude.

"Pilot. Nav. Turn to three zero zero at my mark ... mark. We're now in Laos."

"Snow One to three zero zero now."

The Wave acknowledged. They would hug the border between Laos and North Vietnam almost to China. They would then turn due East just South of the Chinese border until they were almost directly North of Hanoi. Then turn due South to an IP: "Initial Point" which was always seventy-five miles from the target. From the IP inbound they were on the "bomb run." That's when the ground would light up with SAM launches. Lowboy and MIG CAP loved the bomber strikes compared to other ops because the SAM shooters wouldn't shoot at them. They saved the poles for the bombers.

They were half way up the Laos leg.

"Hey Bulldog-e-ous! You personally are a SAM magnet, man! I have not been shot at up by the Z in months!"

Wildman...

"Wildman, you little shit. You haven't been shot at because the gooks don't consider you as a target of any value. In fact, they consider your sorry shit flying an asset to their cause. Why don't you pull up and fly my Wing when we go in-country? We'd feel much safer."

"Pull up next to a SAM magnet? Are you nuts? Besides, if we got that close to you guys, Spike would probably release on top of me given his bomb dropping skills. And by the way, speaking of lost, you seem to be leading them through the *wrong* Country. Weren't you supposed to turn them right at Palm Springs? You turned left man. Not that you'd know that."

"Left is right to you. So we're probably somewhere near where you think we're not. Wake up Blackjack, and see if he knows."

"Pilot. EW. Threat radar at zero four zero. No lock on the range."

"Snow One has TR."

"Roger Snow One. Snow Three saw it too."

"Roger that. Grape One."

"Heads up, Flight. We have stuff up where it's not supposed to be."

Another first...

"Red Crown. Snow One has TR at one seven fiver from Uniform."

"Red Crown copies Snow One. We have Lowboy nearby."

That was it. Nothing came up in the next ten minutes. *They were tracking them. They knew where they were going...*

"Bulldog-e-ous. I told you so. You are a SAM magnet! Charlie's gun must have jammed. When are you going to turn, Ace? Blackjack, The Best, says we're due."

"The best of what, Wildman? The Bimbo of Bangkok said you and Blackjack sucked. Or maybe that was the problem."

The chatter helped everybody to a degree. It took their minds off what they were about to face. Everybody was scared, but they were ready for the Dance. The overriding positive thought was if they got through this one maybe there wouldn't be anymore. Maybe.

"Pilot. Nav turn to zero eight seven on my mark… mark."

"Snow One to zero eight seven now."

"Pilot. Nav. We're still one thirty [1 minute 30 seconds] late but we have a 130 knot tailwind after this turn. Pull back fifteen."

"Rog. Nav. Back fifteen."

They had flown a very long circuitous route that was unnecessary and very tiring. The wave had been airborne for almost seven hours and was still almost an hour out of TOT. The planning made no sense, but the REMF [rear echelon motherfuckers] didn't have to fly it. Only plan it. They were turning them into a 130 knot headwind after the TOT. Damn suicide.

"Pilot. Nav. We're in North Vietnam."

Those words always sent a chill through everybody no matter how many times they had been there… *The most heavily defended city in the world against air attack…*

"Snow One is in Town. Lights off. Radio silence except in emergencies. Good Luck and God Bless. You guys are the best."

All acknowledged. All sounded somber and professional. Most were still kids. The average age of the collective crews was under 29 years old.

Lights off meant that they would turn off the running lights so no one could get an easy visual on them. It was also dangerous because the possibility of a midair collision went up when the shit started to fly.

Wildman: "Bulldog? You sure we know where we are? It looks like Cleveland. What the hell. If we bomb the crap out of Cleveland, we'll all get DFCs. Take care. We'll critique you in Laos outbound if you can find it."

Jeep: "Radio silence. Walt. Cut it."

"Roger Snow One. Amber Two going silent. Good Luck."

"Oh by the way, Snow One… Sorry, but one last thing. We have two bandits at nine o'clock closing. Amber Two silent."

MIGS FROM NOWHERE

The bandits were closing fast on the middle of the Wave, not on lead, which is why Thump wasn't in search behind them. He should have been, but he wasn't. Thump was up serious shit creek with all of them now…

"Red Crown. Snow One. We have bandits closing on the port side. We need Lowboy on site fast. They are one six two at 10 clicks. They are fast burners [fighters], Red Crown."

Spike was pissed. "Hey, Thump! Get your damn head out of your Book and your ass and into your job, dickhead! Roller, you should have been on this shit too. If you're asleep again, I'm comin' up there and kickin' your ass personally! You guys do your job!"

Only Roller responded. "I'm on it, sir! I got 'em. Four thousand and closing on Amber or Gold. Two in tight formation, Boss." Roller was kissing Spike's ass. He had a Doctorate in ass kissing by necessity.

Spike had just done Jeep's job, but Jeep was smart enough to stay out of it. Jeep was the AC, but Spike was the senior officer and experienced well beyond what anyone could even imagine. He could fly in any seat in a B-52 and do the job assigned better than most of the guys that did it as a profession. That included both pilots' seats as well. He could take-off, land, and *refuel.* Graham could do the same, except refuel. Either one of the pilots could also get by doing the offense jobs as well. They intentionally cross trained in case the need arose. It was completely illegal and against a dozen AFRs, but most of the good crews did it anyway. It might save the lives of six guys one day. Screw the AFRs.

Thump was finally in the game. "The MIGs have pulled abreast of Amber Cell. Seemed to have reduced airspeed and are now flying in formation."

Roller came back. "They are just outside the guns range at three thousand yards."

Spike: "Pilot. These guys came from the North, and they know and respect our perimeter. They aren't zips. They are Chinese. This is a different situation. We have to be careful with this, or we start World War Three. These guys are probably purely on a harassment run, or they already would have lit them off."

"Roger, Bombs. I'll advise Red Crown."

"Red Crown, Snow One. We think these boys came from the North. They are sitting out there and just watching. Please advise status of MIG CAP."

"Affirmative, Snow One. We have MIG CAP en route. Do Not engage unless you are engaged first. I repeat. Do not engage."

Roller came up very excited. "Pilot, I have three more at two o'clock low closing! I have lock! Permission to fire, Sir!"

"Negative! Negative, Guns! Positive ID prior! Do not engage!"

Then the "bogies" came up on GUARD. "Red Crown! Red Crown! Gunbarrel One. I have a lock from some nickel dick in the Flight! Get him off me!"

"Snow One copies Red Crown. We are off them."

"Guns! Jack it! You locked on an F-4 flight from Lowboy!"

"Yes, sir! I'm down, sir!"

The F-4s were Navy birds. Snow One would hear about this over and over again whenever they ran into the boys from the ATAs [Airfields That Aren't: carriers]. SO-2 had generated another Legend, but this time it was the wrong end.

Thump was back. "Pilot! The lead MIG broke toward Amber and fired two!"

It was too late to call Amber. Either their defense saw it, or they were gone. Almost instantly, they could see the chaff [aluminum strips blown out of the bomber's bottom to confuse the missile guidance] on their radar. If the chaff went, so did the flares in case the missiles were IR [heat seekers]. Immediately after the attack, the MIGs turned North and hauled ass in burner.

"Amber One. Snow One. You all there?"

"Roger that, Snow One. Not even close. I think they chased the heat. Shit, what causes this? Amber Cell back to silent running."

"What causes this?" was a much used crewdog expression that covered all kinds of issues and agendas. This one concerned the fact that they didn't need this shit. The Navy chased the MIGs to the border and then broke off. Snow thanked the guys through Red Crown.

Back to silence. And worry.

DOWNTOWN

They were really moving on the East heading with what now was a one hundred twenty knot tailwind. What bullshit. They would be turning *into* this wind immediately after bombs away. Planned SAM coverage after TOT had been 14 minutes and 25 seconds. Now it would be more like 16 or 17 minutes. SAM coverage, referred to as the "COA," or Confirmed Operating Area, was carefully calculated based on the confirmed SAM sites and their maximum operating ranges. On the southbound leg to the target, they were in COAs for only six minutes 12 seconds. The westbound egress was the biggest danger.

Spike picked up on the situation too. "B-dog my Nav. Wha'di'say? Look at the wind! Those asshole planners are trying to kill us. When we come off target we might as well be a fucking stationary kite and just let the gooks shoot until they hit us. If we get back, which we won't on this plan, I'm going to find Greenbaum and beat the shit out of him. Literally. I'm going to kick the guy in the head once for every guy that goes down."

Greenbaum was a Lt. Colonel in planning that was also an ex-B-52 Nav. He should have known that this plan sucked.

"Spike, your guarded optimism again overwhelms. Why don't you apply for a job as the new "Hanoi Hank" and scare the shit out of everybody instead of just me? Yeah. I can hear it now, 'Hello Yankee Air Pirates. You are all going die tonight because you are all kites. We can no miss. Say prayers. Children cry. Wife cry. Goodbye.'"

"Snow One. Blackjack. Bulldog, you turnin' us early? With this tail we'll overshoot the TP by miles."

"Yes. Silence!"

Blackjack had broken radio silence in a serious combat situation, and he was good. Really good. It just showed what the stress could do to people. Christ, if the SAMs didn't get them, the stress would.

"Pilot, Nav. Turn to one eight seven on my mark... 45... 30... 15... mark. IP in 15 minutes and 10 seconds. We are over the Red [Red River Valley]. We are Downtown. COA in 2 minutes 58 seconds."

Graham counted the pilot down rather than just saying "mark" like he would in a normal turn because this turn was so crucial to the success of the mission. The other Navs would watch where they turned but use their own radar fixes to confirm start turn. They would count down as well. If they over shot, it would be difficult to get back on the right track for the run. No one would not release if they weren't on a perfect track. The bombs would get blown East because of the wind, but the BNS knew the wind conditions and compensated.

"Time, Nav?"

Graham screwed up. The pilot had to ask.

"Roger, Pilot. We'll be seven seconds early."

Spike couldn't help himself. "Bullshit, B-dog. You'll be three seconds late. That's a ten second swing, which gets a C+, and I win the bet. Damn amateur, Jeep."

Spike was jerking B-dog. His way of a compliment. The bet was +/- 30 seconds either side, and Graham had won. He couldn't lose now unless they got nailed inbound, and then it wouldn't matter... damn... that's where they got D-Kid.

Jeep: "Good job, Nav. Excellent."

"Thanks, pilot."

Graham did it for himself as much as anybody else. Everything was timed to the second. There were hundreds of aircraft in the air. It had to be precise. If they were late, Lowboy and/or MIG CAP may Bingo and RTB (return to base). The last guys in the wave might have much less of a defense, if any defense at all. If they were too early, the cover may not be there yet. Either way it was a bitch flying in the jet stream for nearly eight hours and ending up dead nuts on. Graham had demonstrated that he was pretty good, mostly thanks to Spike's advice over the last two years. He was also lucky.

Graham: "Hey, Spike. Thanks, buddy. You really are the best in spite of yourself."

Spike smiled and gave a nod of acknowledgement.

THE BOMB RUN

Everything was silent. Then Red Crown came up on Guard, in an even voice with no emotion: "SAM launch. Nam Dhin. SAM launch. Nam Dhin."

Jeep: "Hey, Nav. Where's Nam Dhin?"

"Hell if I know. We're not bombing Nam Dhin. I promise when we bomb Nam Dhin to find out where it is."

"Crew, Nav. Heads up. We just crossed into the COA. We'll be in COAs for about 23 minutes on ingress and egress if Intel is right. Check your seats."

Everybody's seat was already configured for combat, but they always double checked them when they entered a COA. Safety pins pulled. Handles unlocked. They could eject in seconds. If a bailout was ordered, a red light would go on in all three crew compartments. The Nav goes first because he's supposed to know where they were when they ejected. The Co went second, then EW, and Gunner. If anybody's seat failed upstairs, they would unstrap and go down to the hole made by the Nav's ejection. The bombardier stayed to help anyone that needed to get out of the Nav's hatch. Then he went. The pilot went after he was sure everyone else was out. The Captain with the ship syndrome. Once on the ground, everybody was supposed to form up on the Nav, and he would know exactly where to go to escape and evade. When Graham was first briefed on that rationale he thought, "*Sure. You take the Hollywood to the Santa Monica, to the Long Beach. Exit at You're Fucked Boulevard and turn left...*"

"SAM launch. Hanoi. SAM launch. Hanoi."

Jeep: "See anything Co?"

"Negative."

"EW?"

"Nothing, Pilot."

Jeep: "I got it. There's some stuff going on way off to the East. The U-T birds are almost inbound IP too."

There was a low overcast at about 3000 ft. Clear above. It was about 2:15 AM local.

"SAM launch. Hanoi. SAM launch. Hanoi."

"SAM launch Haiphong. SAM launch Haiphong."

"SAM launch Hanoi. SAM launch Hanoi."

They were coming up as fast ... or faster ... than Red Crown could call them. The Dance had begun. The band was playing. But not yet for them.

Spike was actually doing his checklist. Well, in a way. He was glancing at it as he performed the bomb release preliminary. Graham flipped to the bomb run checklist. He would call it out. Spike would flip the switches.

Graham came on IC: "One minute to IP."

Spike: "Nothing? Nothing at all? This is spooky. Very spooky."

"Only East, Spike."

Both radar displays went dark. They were blind.

"GODDAMN-SON-OF-A-PIECE-OF-SHIT-BITCH!! WE'RE DARK DOWN HERE, PILOT! OUT! NO RADAR!"

"SAM launch Hanoi. SAM launch Hanoi."

Graham: "Crew. We're IP inbound. Nine minutes to release. I'll DR our track, but no radar means a Withhold. We have maybe five minutes to get this crap working. Pilot turn to heading one eight four."

DR meant "dead reckoning." They took the last known position, estimated the wind effect on the route of flight and corrected accordingly. In other words the

Nav would guess his way over the target. Withhold meant the bombs would not be released. They carried them in, and now they would carry them *out*.

"SAM launch Hanoi. SAM launch Hanoi."

Graham was checking fuses on his side of the cockpit. Fuses were the usual cause of going dark. He turned, and Spike was out of his ejection seat kicking black boxes. This was called "Brogan Maintenance" or the boot approach. Graham couldn't believe it. IP inbound in the middle of the Hairball of Hairballs, in the middle of COA's over Downtown, and Spike was running around kicking boxes. Hard. If they took a SAM, he was gone. He didn't even have a chute.

Then Graham realized he needed to kick three on his side. He was up and out in seconds and kicked the right boxes. Spike turned and hit Graham's helmet hard: "Get the hell back in your seat! And strap! One of us has to complete the run, and I may get this operating late! If that happens it's yours!" He was pissed. Not at Graham. At 221. The situation was unbelievable. Graham jumped back in his seat and strapped quickly. He went on IC: "Pilot. Nav. We're doing everything we can to fix this piece of shit. Spike and I were kicking boxes. He still is. Nothing."

"GODAMMIT! You guys get back in your seats and strap! That's an ORDER, CAPTAIN! I need you guys for another day! GET SPIKE IN HIS SEAT! NOW!

Graham reached up and grabbed Spikes' flight suit: "SEAT NOW! THAT'S AN ORDER!"

Spike had run out of black boxes to kick, or he would have told the Nav what Jeep could do with the order. This was a Press On. He sat. He didn't strap, but he plugged in. He started checking fuses again. So did Graham.

"Spike, Strap man. I need your ass to protect me at the gunfight!" Graham didn't know why he made that statement. He was supporting Spike's bullshit prophecy. Spike buckled up. He hadn't stowed his ejection ring before his rampage which was a major error. He could have blown them both if he kicked the ring or snagged it. "Pilot. Bombs. Offense is back. Still dark."

"Heading and time, Nav."

"We're about four [minutes] out. Maintain heading. Call a withhold on them to the Wave and Crown. Have them work off of Two. We're done."

They were blind. Graham couldn't remember saying "about" before on a time and heading. Spike was still nuts. Playing with fuses. They were all sweating like crazy, and the cockpit temp was about 55F.

Jeep came up. This *was* an emergency. "Snow One is a withhold. We're dark. Work off of Two."

There was no response. They were in checklists and silent.

"Red Crown. Snow One is a withhold. We're dark."

"TOT Crew. Pilot, turn right to heading two five five. Begin climb to flight level three six zero. Now."

"Roger, Nav. Two five five. Flight level three six zero."

"Affirmative."

No mistakes. Confirm everything. They rolled out on two five five and started to climb.

THE WORLD LIGHTS UP

"SAM launch Hanoi."

"SAM launch Hanoi."

"Co, check it your side."

"EW?"

"Nothing. Pilot."

Jeep looked left and low. Under the overcast he saw a bright flash and a ring like a giant smoke ring form. A tiny white light came out of the ring. SAM! Then one - no - *three* more rings!

"Crew, we have four SAMs coming at 10 o'clock. Hang on!"

Jeep counted to ten in his head. That took balls. He was waiting them out. If the tiny bright light moved *across* the windscreen, the SAM was going at another target. If it didn't move, *they* were the target. None of them were moving across. Jeep pitched left and dove right at the inbound missiles. They pulled extreme Gs [the weight of gravity]. It was like the first dive on a rollercoaster... times ten. Graham thought POS was going to break up any second.

Nothing happened. They missed.

Jeep recovered from the move and came back to S&L [straight and level]. The altimeter read 30,500 feet. They had dropped 5,000 feet in seconds.

"SAM launch Hanoi."

"SAM launch Hanoi."

No shit, Red Crown. Their Dance had started.

Jeep: "Two missed us high and two low. Head out of the cockpit, Co. Eyes on the ground!"

Two, then three beepers went off. Guys were in chutes. Three was not a good sign. Everybody had six seats.

Jeep broke radio silence: "Snow flight, OK?"

They all knew what that meant.

"Grape"

"Copper"

"Amber"

"Gold"

"Orange."

Leads had immediately polled their flight when the beepers went off. The guy that didn't answer was down. Everybody answered.

"Pilot! Three at two o'clock! Four! No five!"

Co was wetting his flightsuit. Jeep had climbed back up about 2,000 feet. He dove right. Same move. There was no way that the POS was going to hold up. Spike had his right hand on his D-ring; the left was still messing with fuses. They leveled out at FL272. They had gone down *another* 5,000 feet. Jeep had the throttles firewalled, and they were in a steep climb.

"EW! Any uplinks! Targeting!?"

"Negative, Pilot. They must have gone ballistic!"

No signals meant the SAMs were being fired ballistic. The zips were just throwing up everything they had and hoping that the proximity fusing would get close enough to go off and take them out.

"Shit! Two more at nine o'clock!"

"Pilot! We have three coming from four o'clock!"

Now what? They were coming from both sides. Jeep dove right. Better odds. They heard and felt a strong vibration. Spike thought that any second that red light was going off. Graham had no idea where they were other than somewhere West of Hanoi and very close to You're Screwed Boulevard. He said a prayer for his wife.

Spike was back in the seat still checking fuses furiously. *I've been doing this too long. I lucked out once. Shit! What causes this! It can end it.*

"That was real close, crew. We're OK. We're OK."

He firewalled again back into a climb. This Jeep knew what he was doing...

"Red Crown! Snow One has SAMs all over the place!"

"SAM launch Hanoi."

"SAM launch Hanoi."

"Pilot. Fire warning light on number seven!"

"Shut it down! Shut it down!"

Spike, very calmly: "B-dog, we're doing 220 knots groundspeed. We *are* a fucking kite."

Graham looked over at Spike. He was almost perfectly calm. Then Graham thought, *Shit, so am I.* Neither of them was scared anymore. Not since the first four missed them. They were both pissed instead.

"Pilot! Two at three o'clock!"

Same dive. Right. Sure, these guys were out of SAMs. The radar monitors flickered twice and went on. Spike started pounding on the deli counter. They were at 22,000 feet. No groundspeed worth a damn.

On Guard: "Red Crown! Red Crown! Ivory Two. Ivory One is hit! I repeat. Ivory One is hit! Starboard wing is on fire!"

"Roger, Ivory Two. All aircraft, this is Red Crown. I have an aircraft in trouble. Stay off Guard unless it's an emergency. I repeat stay off Guard!"

Ivory was a cell out of U-T.

"Pilot. Nav. Flight level 260. We have to climb fast."

Two more coming from the left. This time Jeep did a much shallower bank toward the incoming. He probably thought that POS couldn't take anymore.

God, would this ever end?

It did. Eight minutes later. They had been taking SAMs for almost 14 minutes. The site the Intel Lieutenant had told the General about *was* there. No beer for him...

"Pilot, we have radar back. The SAM must have done something. I don't know."

"Roger, Bombs. You and the Nav did everything you could including risking your lives to get that crap to go up. Can't ask for more."

"Guns, you have the rest of the Cell?"

"Yes, sir. I think Two is in *front* of us. Three is about four miles back at seven o'clock. The other guys that I can see are all over the place."

After all that they were on the verge of a mid-air.

"Nav. Is Orange cell out of the COA yet?'

"Should be just about now. Continue climb to FL370. Turn to a heading of two four five. We'll be in Laos in four minutes and thirty five seconds."

"Pilot. Bombs. I have Snow Two at one mile, two o'clock."

"Flight. Snow One. Radio silence is cancelled. Cell leads, poll your cell and report."

Jeep was asking for a loss report. Who went down? Now comes the bad news. Real bad. Most of these guys were their friends. Their brothers... Crewdogs.

"Roger Snow One. Grape is good. All souls good."

"Copper is good."

"Amber is good. Amber Two has one minor."

"Gold is good."

"Orange is good!"

"Snow Flight. Snow One. Thank you Lord. We went through a gauntlet of fire that defies description, and all of us got out. Give thanks and say your prayers. Great job!"

"Red Crown. Snow One."

"Roger, Snow One."

"Snow Flight is outbound. Fully intact. TOT three seconds early."

"Good work. Snow flight. Have a safe return. God speed."

"Snow flight. Snow One. Report battle damage."

"Grape Three has number four shut down."

"Copper is clean as far as we know."

"Roger Snow One. Amber Two took a couple very close. We have shrapnel damage but all systems op."

"Gold is clean."

"Orange is OK."

Amazing. Absolutely amazing. The Big Guy must like them.

"Snow One has number seven shut down. Let's pull together and form up. Bombs and Guns be on top of it. We got birds all over the place."

"Crew. Pilot. Thanks for a great job. God bless you guys. Does anybody have any idea of how many SAMs we took?"

Roller came on: "Yes, sir. I marked them on my radar scope with my grease pen as you called them. Thirty-seven, sir."

Jesus. A Miracle.

C.K. McCUSKER

"Pilot Nav. Turn to heading 165, and begin climb to flight level three seven five on my mark... Mark. Crew we're back in Laos."

The feeling of relief for all of them was overwhelming. They were going to stay alive for now.

IVORY ONE

"Roger, Ivory One. Red Crown copies. The fire is out. Four are shut down."

"Can you make it to U-T?"

Ivory One answered, but they couldn't hear him. Only Red Crown could.

"Negative, Ivory One. Do not go to NKP [Nakom Phnom, another Thai airbase]. The runway is too short. Go to Udorn if you can make it all."

Ivory One had all his starboard engines shut down. He was trying to *glide* to the nearest airfield. Ivory One didn't give a shit if the runway at NKP was too short. If everybody's lives were at stake, he would extend the runway for them.

CHAPTER VIII:
BACK TO THE ROCK

Spike came on IC: "Hey, Jeep, where'd you learn to fly like that?"

"I flew backseat in F-4s over here on my last tour. We always turned into SAMs. It presented the lowest profile for a target. I figured that the same would apply for us."

"What kind of bank? We were in a controlled crash."

"Seventy Five degrees, Spike."

The Boeing Tech Order, as usual, said that was impossible. It could not be done. It also violated all kinds of Air Orders, which pleased Spike enormously.

"Takes balls, buddy. You probably saved our asses. They always throw as much as possible at lead. Good job... Hollywood."

Jeep... Clark Gable... had just been ordained with his call sign, which he earned, by one of the Legends. It was now in reinforced Concrete on the Runway in the Sky. He would be Hollywood from this moment on.

"Thanks, Spike. I thought I was starting to morph into a real Jeep."

Co gave Spike's comments some thought... *Why didn't he have a call sign? He was always just "Co." Even Thump, who is a jerk, has a call sign, although he hates it. But that means it's by design? Maybe. So what, who cares anyway? I don't need a call sign. I need to get out to be with my wife and the baby. I'll go to the airlines and make great money. Move home to Pittsburgh...*

Co *did* have a call sign. It was "Zero." Unlike Jeep, he would never, ever know his call sign. No Point. There was more than one Zero. Unlike Jeep, now Hollywood, he was completely, totally neutral. On everything. He had no opinions. He had no passions. He had no vices. He was a nice guy. He played tennis sometimes. He was a pretty good co-pilot. Occasionally he had a daq with the crewdogs.

He would never know his call sign. That was their responsibility to him.

Spike: "Wildman! Who the hell is the SAM magnet? Seems to me that you said we were, but you guys must have tried to take them all out for us. You guys OK?"

They were climbing through FL 360. Graham didn't like it. The planners *were* idiots.

"Roger, Spike. Guns got something in his arm, but we didn't RD [a rapid decompression]. So I think we must be intact. We had a couple at once that were on both sides. I know we took some shrap, but we seem to be OK. We're watching everything."

Wildman was a pro, but he was nervous. No chatter back to Spike at all. Something didn't sit right with Spike. This was not *the* Wildman.

Spike: "Why don't you call Red Crown and divert to Da Nang, buddy. Couldn't hurt. Might help."

"Negative, Spike. We seem to be OK, or I would divert. Gravytrain is on this side and says we're a go."

Wildman was not Wildman. He was tired and drained.

Andy "Gravytrain" Gravitz was a great co-pilot. He would make AC soon. Wildman's Co's were hand picked and went to the left seat very quickly. Dangle loved it. Gravytrain was from a Mainline family in Philadelphia. He was loaded. No one understood why he was there. Most guys with that much dough were in the Guard in Florida.

"Pilot. Nav. I think we need to alter the mission plan and make the base flight level 340. With them at 370, the tail of the snake is too high if they have damage. We're turning East twenty clicks South of the Z in four minutes. The tanks can meet them over So Chi at that altitude. No problem."

"Good point, Nav."

"Red Crown. Snow flight requests alter to flight level 340 base at Kilo."

"Roger, Snow Flight. Descend and maintain 34 base at Kilo."

Everybody was much more relaxed, including Red Crown. The U-T birds were feet wet to home. Spike and Bulldog didn't understand why Ivory One went inland, but they only heard half of the transmission.

"Pilot. Nav. Turn left to heading zero nine two. My mark ... mark."

"Snow flight zero nine two now. Begin descent to FL340 base on rollout."

Snow Flight acknowledged. They had turned for home.

A VERY UNFRIENDLY WELCOME

D-Kid didn't want to stay at this particular Hilton, but it beat dead. He was pulled off the truck and his ropes were loosened.

Boy, that feels better.

Then they yanked the ropes back so hard that his elbows were touching behind his back. The pain was agonizing.

I bet their room service sucks, too.

Tom Sampson was yanked out of the truck and taken away. D-Kid was pulled into a courtyard and then into a room with a table that was apparently an interrogation room. He had been taught at Survival School to invent a simple cover story in the event he was captured. If it was complex, he would be caught and beaten or killed. He was well aware that no one on the outside knew he had been captured alive, so it would be easy for them to kill him. This was a very dangerous situation. He also had to get word out somehow that he was a POW and alive. Once the world knew you were a prisoner and alive, it was much harder for the enemy to kill you. He had to invent a cover right away on the fly.

A short, mean looking Vietnamese with a four inch scar on the side of his face entered the room. The two guards stayed.

"You are a pig pirate that bomb my people. You will answer my questions or you will not live through the night. I would enjoy killing you. Your B-52s killed my parents. What base did you fly from?"

"Robert Glenn Foster. Captain, United States Air Force. 356-40-7767. 4 December 1947."

"Captain, I want your base, the number of aircraft and what type, the Commanding officers names, how many flights a day you can launch, the names of other crewmembers, and what routes you use to fly here and bomb my country for no reason. I also want to know about your bombing system. You will answer all of these questions truthfully tonight, or you will not leave this room alive. How does the bombing system work?"

"The Geneva Convention states that I must only provide you with my name, rank, serial number, and date of birth. I have done that. Should I repeat it?"

Scarface nodded at the guard, and D-Kid was slammed in the face with a rifle butt that knocked him to the concrete floor. He had no way to break his fall, so the pain was agonizing. He was yanked back up to his feet.

"THE GENEVA CONVENTION DOES NOT APPLY TO PIRATES! YOU ARE A YANKEE AIR PIRATE! WE HAVE THE RIGHT TO KILL YOU, WHICH WE WILL! NOW ANSWER MY QUESTION!"

Wing it fast or this could get really bad.

"I'm a celestial navigator. My job is just to navigate over water. I know nothing about the bombing system. Only radar navigators know about those, and mine is dead."

"Do you have nuclear weapons at your Guam base?"

"I have no idea. I'm a celestial navigator."

Shit. I just told him I was out of Andersen. Well, the Russians would have told him anyway.

It was very cold, and D-Kid was standing barefoot on a concrete floor, in tremendous pain.

"What about Quail? Did you have any on your plane?"

Jesus. How did he know about Quail missiles?

Quail missiles were decoy missiles carried in the bomb bay that could be launched before an attack to confuse the enemy. On radar, they looked like another B-52. The bombers had "babies" in mid-air. Andersen didn't use them.

"No. The Gunner had roast beef. The Co-pilot had chicken. I had a sandwich. I don't think anyone had quail."

"NO! NO! I mean in your bomb bay."

"No. They would die back there. It's not pressurized, and they would freeze to death."

Another nod. Another rifle butt. He hit the floor even harder this time and was yanked back up.

"We know you know. You will tell us tonight, or we will take you out and let your own bombs drop on you. Or we will just kill you here."

Scarface abruptly turned and left the room with the guards. A guard watched D-Kid through the door. He wasn't allowed to lie down or lean against anything. In forty–five minutes, Scarface returned with his goons, and it started all over again. Same questions. Same rifle butt. D-Kid was bleeding from a lot of places. Maybe to protect his sanity, he thought as hard as he could about the wonderful things that he had experienced in his life,

My body can take the abuse. Unless they beat me to death … but I need to take my mind out of this hellhole. Survival said to get your head out of here. Darwin, Darwin, D-Kid, survival of the fittest… Robbie… our wedding…

D-Kid had learned well at Survival. While the Scarface continued to question, beat, and abuse him physically, his mind was no longer there. He envisioned his wedding day with his three best friends to his left and his family standing in front of him. His bride and her father came down the aisle, very slowly.

God that woman is beautiful. I have never seen a face like that before. Maybe angels look like her…

A rifle butt and the floor brought him back from heaven to hell momentarily.

Scarface: "CAN'T YOU HEAR ME? WE TAKE YOU OUT TO DIE! B-52s bomb all time. We take you there!"

They yanked him back to his feet by his neck, as usual.

Screw you, you gook bastard. You bet the B-52s will come back. They will until we are free. I have left your shitbird little country. I'm in Arkansas. I'm getting married. You weren't invited.

D-Kid figured it out in his mind quickly. Weddings last about fifteen minutes. Brutal interrogations last hours and hours. He was going to have to create in his mind the world's longest wedding. He went back to the pastor's study and tried to even remember the smells in the room. He studied the faces of all the wedding guests in detail. He worked to recall each word of the Homily and the vows. He recalled every detail he could and then started over.

Another rifle butt and the concrete floor. Another intermission in the wonderful movie in his mind.

The interrogation continued all night. So did his wedding. They would leave him alone, standing, for about forty-five minutes and then return and ask more questions that they knew he wouldn't answer. More rifle butts to the head. He decided to collapse on the floor to fake exhaustion, which he was close to anyway. They would just pull him back up, using the noose around his neck. Just after dawn, Scarface changed tactics: "Would you like to write a letter home?"

"Yes. That is my Geneva Convention right."

Scarface went crazy again: "YOU HAVE NO RIGHTS! YOU ARE PIRATES! WE WILL JUST KILL YOU! IT IS MUCH EASIER!"

Oh-oh. Maybe I shouldn't have provoked him. I hope it's just good cop, bad cop.

Scarface came back with pen and paper. D-Kid was relieved it wasn't a gun. The ropes were taken off, and he was told to sit at the table on a low stool. Scarface sat on a much higher chair on the other side. "You will put your wife's name and address on the paper and write the letter. You will say that you were flying a B-52 and bombing Hanoi on this date. Then you say you want to send a Christmas message to your wife. When you are done, you will read it over the radio."

"I won't read it over the radio, and I won't give you my home address."

He went off again: "YOU DON'T WANT TO WRITE A LETTER HOME!"

"Yes, I do want to. But I want to use my own words."

"YOU WILL NEVER SEE YOUR FAMILY AGAIN! YOU HAVE NOT COOPERATED WITH US AT ALL. WE WILL PUT THE ROPES BACK ON AND THEN WE WILL KILL YOU SLOWLY AND YOU WILL TELL US EVERYTHING!"

He stormed out again, and D-Kid finally started to cry. He cried for his wife and family. He should be home in her arms. The wedding was over. Now they would kill him for not writing to her. He caught his thoughts and tried to stop crying. He didn't want the enemy to see him. The guards came in immediately and roped him more roughly than ever. He finally passed out from pain and exhaustion. Later, he was awakened by again being yanked to his feet by the noose on his neck.

OK. This is it. I'm going to die, but I won't tell them a damn thing. Robbie, I love you. The Lord is my shepherd…

Then he noticed clothing on the table. It was the "clown suit" and sandals he'd seen in POW photos. They took the ropes off and he was told to put the clothes on. He felt like crying again but this time from relief. Maybe they wouldn't kill him today. Maybe he would see Robbie again.

A SLIGHT DETOUR

Just as Snow One rolled out of the turn, Guard came up.

"RED CROWN. RED CROWN! BATTER ONE. WE HAVE AN EMERGENCY! ACKNOWLEDGE!'

Batter One was a Marine whup-whup.

"Roger, Batter One. Red Crown has you switch to secure three."

Spike smelled something: "Hollywood, put me on Sec three. You stay on two. Something's up."

"Rog. Spike. Here you go."

Spike listened intently to whatever was going on Sec three. His Spike Smile grew as he listened. After about three minutes, he switched to IC.

"Hey Hollywood, we might have a one time, non-reoccurring bombing opportunity... B-dog figure out where these coordinates are... There's a Marine company trapped at a night defensive position in a valley near the Z by an NVA regiment on a ridge overlooking them. The rest of the Jars [Marines] won't get there 'til morning, and there's no air support available because everybody was at the Dance. The problem is the gooks are coming now. The Marines are going to get annihilated. The Marine whup driver called Red Crown in desperation to see if he could help. Red Crown said they were shit out of luck since most have RTB and those that are still en route are clean. Red Crown must have forgotten about us. I got twenty seven 750's that are scheduled to kill fish. I'd rather take out a gook regiment that's going to kill all our guys if we don't. The Whup driver was ballistic. He can't get these guys out, and the gooks are moving down the ridge. What say we take a quick stroll South?"

"Spike... man. You know targets of opportunity in the South are absolutely forbidden. There's no way that Red Crown, or Skyking for that matter, would ever approve it. This is a political issue. Just like this damn war. No way."

"Pilot. Nav. We're one four five clicks out. We better get a decision quickly."

Spike: "Call Crown, Hollywood, or I will."

"Red Crown. Snow One."

"Snow One still has eggs in the basket. Request diversion to assist Marines."

"Negative, Snow One. Targets of Opportunity are not allowed under any circumstance in the South. You are well aware of that, Snow One."

"Negative, Snow One, that is a standing order. Period. Red Crown Out."

They could tell by Red Crown's voice inflection that he was also devastated. Spike told Hollywood that we had to get below FL250 for a strike that would have to be this exact, or they would risk killing the guys they were trying to save. Even at that level, it would be like trying to drop pickles in a jar from fifty feet up.

Hollywood knew that if he pressed this any further, his career might end. If he disobeyed the order, it *would* end.

Spike would not give up: "Red Crown. Snow One requests flight level two five zero to inspect for battle damage. We took some close ones and now have some vibration that is getting worse."

"NEGATIVE, Snow One. You can get clearance after feet wet. Maintain flight level 340."

There was a number of old fart Colonels on board Red Crown on 19 December. One was a former Marine aviator, and with things dying down, he had monitored the transmission.

"Snow One. Red Crown."

"Roger, Crown. Snow One."

"Snow One, you must wait until feet wet for the damage assess. There's traffic below flight level 240 in-country."

It was a different voice. He had told Snow One where *not* to go, and by doing so told them where *to* go. All radio transmissions were recorded. He had just ended his career as well, but what the hell, he was probably close to retirement anyway. Now it was up to Hollywood. He was the only guy onboard who would ruin a promising career. Graham was getting out the first chance that he had. Co was going to go be a pilot in Pittsburgh. Roller didn't know what a career was, and Spike's career was anything but promising.

"Hey Hollywood. Bulldog. We're all in agreement if that matters. We know the risks."

Graham had told him that they wanted to go for it, and they knew that at 240 they might get some triple A. No one cared what Thump thought. He'd be off the crew after they touched down.

There was a long silence.

"Nav. Give me a heading."

SAVE SOME BROTHERS

"One three five. Start descent to flight level two four zero. Target one zero one clicks. Strap it, crew."

Hollywood called the flight: "Snow flight, Snow one. We have to take a slight detour here for about forty minutes. Snow Two, assume lead. We'll rejoin the flight quickly."

"Roger, Snow One. Snow Two up. I'd give anything to go with you guys, but we're all clean. Thanks and God Bless."

"ROGER THAT. Grape cell."

"AFFIRMATIVE. Copper cell."

Wildman: "You're fuckin' nuts. You guys don't know what you're doing, and you'll get lost getting there and Spike will blow up a rice paddy that looks like the Pilipeens... and I would kill to be with you. DON'T MISS this time, Spike. God Bless. Amber out."

"Good Luck and God speed guys. Gold out."

"Orange cell, thanks all of you guys for what you're doing. It's the right thing. Don't miss, Spike."

Spike was wondering when they'd stop busting his balls. *He never missed. Eh. They're all Jeeps.*

Spike and Graham studied the topo maps of the target area, trying to pick out aiming points. This had to be the best release they had ever done. They were technically way too high for such a precise target. They decided to hit the top of the ridge because that's where the command and control of the regiment would be. The General and Colonels would be there. Destroy them, and they have an Army without leadership. Besides, they would destroy the whole damn ridge anyway.

Hollywood on Guard: "Batter One. Batter One. Are you there? This is Snow One."

"Roger, Snow One. I'm almost Bingo. I'm going into an tight perimeter to try to save a few guys from an overrun by the gooks. Who the hell are you anyway, Snow One."

"Switch to sec three, Batter One."

They did.

"Batter One. You up?"

"Roger. Snow. Got any ideas to help me? Got any ordinance on board?"

Batter One sounded terrible. He was tired and beaten. Hopelessness pervaded his voice.

"Roger, Batter One. Twenty-seven seven-fifties and we're IP inbound to your guys. We're a Bee-Hop-Sit-Song, buddy."

Bee-Hop-Sit-Song meant B-52 in Thai.

Batter One was ecstatic. "A FUCKIN' BUFF! A FUCKIN' ARC LIGHT [code name for B-52s in Asia] BUFF! LOADED!"

Using Thai to try to disguise who they were didn't do a whole lot of good....

"WAIT. WAIT. BATTER. Tell him to get his guys as far away from the ridge as he can. Fast. That ridge is going to disappear."

There was a pause in the transmission as Batter One spoke to the Marine commander. "Snow one! Batter. He wilco. He was so happy I think he was crying, for God's sake."

Hollywood: "Nav, Where are we?"

"We're on the BR. Six minutes out. We have the target acquired. Tell Batter One to get the hell out of there now."

Spike and Graham did the bomb checklist...

"Target acquired. Nav Confirms. Pilot center the PDI. We have it."

Spike was now flying the aircraft. If he moved the crosshairs on the aiming point, the plane would follow. The target was a bitch. Hard to find, but they were both sure they had it. The ridge was about a mile and a half long, so they set the bomb interval at one point five miles. That interval meant that a 750 lb. bomb would impact about every sixty-five *yards*. The overlap of the blast radius on each bomb would wipe out everything on the ridge. It would cease to exist.

"Doors."

"Open."

"Release mechanisms."

One set, Two engaged, Three engaged."

"Sixty seconds."

"Thirty"

"Fifteen."

There was a bright flash. Then another. Two more ... It was triple A. The gooks were shooting at them. It would soon be the last time they ever shot at anything.

"Five, four, two, one ... bombs away."

They gained altitude noticeably, as always, when they dumped that much weight.

"We're clean, crew."

"Three, two, one, impact."

"Pilot, turn left to heading zero four five. Start climb to flight level three four zero. Firewall it. We have to catch them quickly."

"Roger, Nav. Good work guys."

Spike was on Thump again: "Thump? What the hell were you doing on the bomb run? Was that triple A radar guided? Goddammit, Thump! Acknowledge!"

Silence. Something was wrong. Thump was always quiet, but now he wasn't doing his job.

Batter One was excited to say the least. "HOLY SHIT! OH MY GOD! IT'S UNBELIEVABLE. I'LL NEVER SEE ANYTHING LIKE THIS AGAIN IN MY LIFETIME!"

His voice calmed some. "You guys walked those things right down that ridge. It looked like noon. Shit was flyin' everywhere, man. And the noise! God the noise alone would kill 'em. Wow! I'll be tellin' my grandkids this story over and over. Thank you! Holy shit, the entire ridge, top to bottom, is gone or on fire. Well thanks forever, guys. We'll find you and thank you properly. The Marine way. I guarantee it. Meantime I'm bingo, gotta crash land at the Marine position. I'll call you guys when I get down so the Company CO can say thanks."

The Marine Company didn't have radios that could get the bomber freqs. If the whup hadn't been there, they would have been dead soon.

"Snow Flight. Snow One. We had breakfast and now we're on a collision course, thanks to Bulldog. We'll see you at four zero past."

Wildman: "Have fun boys?"

Spike: "Yeah. You weren't there. That, plus frying some bad guys and making some Jars very, very happy have made it a nice day after all."

Wildman: "Have I told you guys to bite me in the last half hour? Oh well, bite me to the third power. That will make it up. Good job guys. Took a lot of balls to do that."

"Snow One. Bravo Company. United States Marine Corps."

"Snow One, Bravo."

"You guys saved one hundred and eighteen of us this morning. *Think about that for the rest of your lives.* I'm Captain Cox. Bruce Cox. I'll find you guys."

"Roger, Captain. And thanks for the thought. That really means a great deal to us. Spike Wilson and R.J. Graham did the job. The Co is Bart. I'm Bill Noland. Guns is Ron, and the EW is Don. Give us a call if you ever get to Guam."

"Hell. We'll invade it again to find *you* guys. Thanks much. I have some wounded to look after, so I'm out."

"Roger, Bravo. Snow One out."

Hollywood thought, *yeah, look me up on Guam. I'll be one of the guys in jail.*

BACK TO THE FLOCK

Graham decided that it was time to bust Spike's chops. "Great job. Spiker. You missed that ridgeline by at least ten yards going *only* 350 knots under fire. You're clearly losing it, buddy. Pack it up. Go to the BX, and get a Geezer Kit."

"I missed it by two yards. It was right at least. I don't want to make any liberal mistakes. Such as you."

"Well, Spike the All Seeing, your prophecy of doom was totally screwed, as usual. Even the triple A missed at Bravo. You should get out and get a Masters in

Gloom and Doom. No shit, man. Then you could get a job like Edwards, yeah, a network anchor, and scare the shit out of the whole country every night. They would pay you big bucks to do it, too."

"B-dog, I may have to fire you as my protégé. You can't read through any of my clever ruses, kid. I intentionally scared the shit out of you so that when the SAMs started screamin' at us in waves, you would realize that you might not die if they didn't kill you immediately. They didn't kill you, and then you realized that death was not for sure. I helped you out immensely. You're welcome, you goddamn ingrate."

"You are a lying sack of shit. That will also help you get that TV job. You were convinced we were dead. You were positive. I know how you think even if thinking is a rare exercise in your case… dumbshit."

"B-dog. Not being dead is a good thing… Maybe … But the fact that we're not is a miracle. Like you and the great Yossarian in C22, I have vowed to remain not dead as long as possible. I've never seen so many SAMs launched, and I've been over here since the spring of '68 off and on, as you know. In '68 we went north almost all the time. We're not goin' to be that lucky next time. We used it. You need to get the answer to what causes this."

"Screw you and your 9mm, which you owe me by the way, so hand it over."

The bet had been in two parts. Graham had to get them over the Hanoi target plus or minus 30 seconds and they couldn't get killed. Spike's 9mm against Graham's $200. Spike's logic was that if he did get killed, he wouldn't need his 9mm, and besides there were no bullets. The upside was that he would die $200 richer. If they didn't get killed, it made no difference because of Spike's Rule. The Rule was that Spike did not have to pay any bets that Spike lost. All bets were a win-win situation for him, and everybody knew it, but they all still placed bets with him.

With a tailwind and Snow Flight throttled back waiting for them, Snow One caught up and rejoined very quickly.

Spike was coming back to life: "Hey, Thump. Nice job on the eastbound leg, shitbird. At least Roller tried to shoot down our own Navy 4. You didn't do squat all night."

Spike was patiently waiting for Thump's whining reply. There wasn't one. "Thump, where are you? Are you in the Book again? Asleep? Thanks for not praying for my bullet. If I'd found it, I would've needed it. We're up by the Z again, get your head out of wherever it is and do your job."

No response.

Ironically, on Guard: "Snow One. Snow Two. We had targeting radar up just now! Up and down in less than ten seconds! Didn't you guys pick it up?"

"Snow Three confirms Snow Two."

Spike exploded: "GODDAMNIT, EW, WHAT ARE YOU DOING!"

"Red Crown. Snow flight. We had a hostile paint at one two niner, 15 clicks."

"Roger, Snow Flight. Lowboy's there. They probably made a big mistake. Advise any development."

"Wilco, Snow One."

"Pilot. Nav. I put us on a track south of plan about ten miles. The other Navs know what I'm doing. We should be out of range for anything above the Z. I don't know why they came up. Probably as a range check."

Spike, fuming: "The good shooters will be up North at the Dance. These guys are rookies down here. They'll make mistakes."

WEASELS ONCE MORE

They had.

Ironhand One had RTB to Korat in Thailand, turned around in thirty minutes, and was back in the air as Dragonkiller One. This time he had Dragonkiller Two and Three with him, along with an RB-66. The 66 was essentially a flying electronics warfare station with all the latest black boxes. They could pinpoint almost any threat signal.

They did.

Dragonkiller One took the vector, went to burner, and screamed toward the site. He had his Wingmen, Two and Three, hold. This was personal. These bastards had shot down *his* Wingman. His threat radar warning light went on. The gooks were trying to come up and defend themselves, but it was too late. The rookies had been trying to target the B-52s. Dragonkiller One fired off two shitbusters and banked hard right into a climb. He had probably gone in too close, but he wanted to make sure the shitheads got toasted. The Wingmen saw the ground go up like a small nuke had gone off.

On Guard: "AMF [Adios Motherfuckers]."

His Wingman had been picked up by the Navy without much difficulty and was alright. He'd be back at Korat in the morning and flying by that afternoon.

These guys had balls.

SNOW FLIGHT

On Guard, they heard the call from Dragonkiller One.

Spike: "Another SAM site toasted, thanks to the Weasels. I'm missing the whole war flying around in a POS like 221. You know if I didn't have to hold your hand all the time, B-dog, I'd transfer to TAC [Tactical Air Command] and go into fastburners. But no. No, I'm burdened with Jeeps like you, and I get to hold your sniffle rag while you get us lost. I go make trees into toothpicks half the time, and I don't even get to see them burn anymore. When I get a fun ride like this one, the damn radar craps out, and I can't even melt part of a city. Well, at least we diverted and helped out kids that would have been toast. No shit. I should go to fastburners … maybe after I go to jail."

Spike flew D models before he came to Fairchild. The bombardier could see the ground through an ancient bombsite that the Gs didn't have, so he could see secondary explosions on the ground during a strike. Secondaries meant they hit something other than trees with nobody in them. He could *never* go to TAC. He was too good. SAC would never let him go… although after this detour, maybe they would.

Graham: "You know what, dumb ass? You're a manic depressive. You're a complete nut job. I'm going to get your useless ass committed the next time you don't pay a bet. White coat with straps, buddy. At least the straps will make you feel at home. You need…"

Spike interrupted Graham and went up on IC: "Hey Hollywood… permission to go up and beat the crap out of the E-dub?" He didn't wait for an answer. He just wanted to make Hollywood think he was the AC. He was unstrapped and was out of the seat and upstairs in seconds.

"Negative, Spike. Roller, check on the E-dub. We haven't heard from him since the egress."

Roller was leaning over trying to get Thump's attention. Spike pushed him aside and slapped Thump's helmet hard. Thump was sitting upright in his seat with his visor down and his mask on. He moved, but barely, when Spike whacked his helmet. Spike moved next to him to see what the hell was going on. Christ!

His ejection handles were rotated! The bailout procedure upstairs was "rotate handles and squeeze." *You didn't rotate the handles unless you were going to eject.* When you squeezed the rotated handles your hatch blew, and you were blown out of the aircraft, literally, with rockets on the bottom of your seat.

Thump's hands were *on* the handles. Spike carefully moved Thump's hands from the handles and then stowed and secured them. Thump was almost limp. He didn't resist Spike. He put the safety pins back into position. Something was very, very wrong. He pressed the bayonet clip that holds the oxygen mask on the helmet on each side and raised the dark Plexiglas visor. Spike was stunned. There were tear mark's running down Thump's face. His eyes were a glassy red. His lips were moving slightly, but he wasn't speaking. His Bible was jammed down into the neck of his flight suit. Thump had gone to "Ya-Ya" Land. He was in his seat, but his mind wasn't there. The SAM barrages must have terrified him to the point of a complete breakdown. They no longer had an EW.

Spike slapped Roller's helmet and told him to get up. "We're moving Thump to the bunk."

They unstrapped him; each grabbed one side and lifted him out of his seat between the two seats. They carried him to the bunk which was nothing more than a folded blanket on the tiny walkway between the pilots and the defense stations. They laid him on the blanket, and he curled himself up into the fetal position. Spike jumped down the ladder and put on his helmet.

"Pilot. Bombs. The E-dub is gone. The SAMs must have flipped him. He's conscious but not here. You better alert CP of the situation. We'll need an ambulance at the aircraft at chocks."

There were two casualties from the combat on Snow flight's strike: A Gunner that would be fine and an E-dub that would never fly again, except going home.

Graham: "Pilot, we're feet wet."

"Snow flight. Snow One feet wet. We made it, gentlemen."

CHAPTER IX: BINGO ISN'T A GAME

OUTBOUND TO THE PI

Spike was unusually concerned. Had he contributed to Thump ending up in Ya-Ya Land? Hell, he wasn't sure he wasn't there himself - playing a role on the outside but living something entirely different. Thump's look was imbedded in his mind. Hell. He had to put it aside. It was downstream now. Press On...

"Pilot, Nav. We have the tanks coming up at three seven past the hour on the same track. One hundred twenty out. They need to take care of us and the other two leads that broke. Are we clean at the refuel hole?"

"The doors closed Nav. We should be clear. But we have no choice and no way of checking. If we have a problem, can we get to Da Nang? Co, give him a range based on FOB for three seven past."

They were moving fast track with the tailwind, but they would fight it again if they turned around. The Co gave Graham a range quickly.

"Are you sure about this, Co? Looks really good given we broke ten thousand short."

"Roger, Nav. That's current estimate. I don't understand it myself."

Spike: "Both of you numb nuts remember we have seven shut down? We'll burn twelve percent less gas, kiddies. And with No Luck's POS, the other ones are only operating at who knows what output. The fact that we are still chasing the surly bonds is amazing."

Graham: "Spike, I'd tell you what to go and do to yourself, but I don't want to be redundant. Why don't you take your geezer nap and I'll wake you in time for the court martial after we land."

Hollywood broke in: "Listen, crew. I am the AC of this bird, and I made the decision to divert against orders. I am responsible. You are not. I, and I alone, will take the consequences."

Spike looked up from lunch and spoke into his mask: "Hollywood, you're working your way back to Jeep. Screw the heroics. You couldn't have taken out the target without the crack set of killers downstairs, Hero, so don't try to bite the bullet alone. I assure you that the Board of Inquiry that pre-convicts us in the tradition of the United States Air Force will concur with my assessment. Intervening and saving our own guys in time of war is not a play in the current political playbook, and therefore we are all guilty as a team before we are charged. In any other military, they would give us a nice piece of tin and a two day pass. Not now. The only guys on this crew that will fly clear are Thump, because he left the aircraft before we made the decision, and Roller, because he's never here. So stop worrying about it. We're screwed for doing what we should have done."

Hollywood: "I won't accept that, Major."

"Don't. Facts are facts. Bullshit is bullshit. We are currently governed by bullshit."

Graham couldn't take any more of Spike's philosophizing. "Pilot, Nav. We have the Tanks coming up at one o'clock six zero miles. Turn to zero nine four now."

"Crew, prepare for refueling."

Spike kept eating his lunch. He didn't give a shit. He'd lived through the Hairball of Hairballs. Based on the fact that he'd already been shot out of the sky once before, he should have been dead for sure this time around. No gas passer was going to take them out now.

The refueling was uneventful, smooth and quick despite the fact that Hollywood had been in the seat for over twelve hours. He wanted to take a nap, but Co was already heading down. SO-2 was an amazing group of misfits that had somehow qualified as StanBoard back home. Except for Defense, they were very, very good but did almost nothing by the book. They operated on experience and logic, and there wasn't a checklist for that.

THE WILDMAN'S WILD RIDE

Graham: "Pilot. We're one five zero out. Contact Manila center on sec two."

Suddenly, Wildman came up on guard. "SNOW ONE, AMBER TWO IS DECLARING AN EMERGENCY. WE'RE DIVERTING IMMEDIATELY FOR CLARK."

"Amber Two, nature of the emergency?"

"WE ARE OUT OF GAS."

Gravytrain was desperately flipping his fuel switches. *How the hell did this happen? They had plenty of gas! What the hell? Man, this was bad. Really bad. Three out of four fuel warning lights had come on, all at once! How could he have let this happen? They had plenty...*

Wildman was hand flying and doing the Co's other job, radios, at the same time. He had pulled the throttles back to the "You're going to stall this, you idiot" position and had begun a gradual uncleared glide after Blackjack gave him a "steer clear" heading from Snow flight. Surviving all that had happened tonight only to fall out of the sky because they went bingo... Jesus. "Manila Center. Manila Center. This is USAF Amber Two. We are declaring an emergency and requesting immediate clearance and vectors to Clark Air Force Base for a straight-in immediate approach to runway three one zero."

"Roger, Ambeer Two. Descend and maintain flight livil tree ziro ziro 'en coming to headin of ziro tree ziro. Plis state natir of emergince, fill livils, en souls en bird."

It was Spike's favorite controller! Great. Wildman's screwed.

Wildman: "Manila. I'm already through flight level two four zero, six souls on board, and I have no fuel levels. I'm out of fuel! Now give me a heading for a straight-in to Clark!"

"Ambeer Two! Ambeer Two! My supirvise say thit you air a bee fife two earplan! Combit earplan! No amircan combat earplan me lan en Pilipeens! Pirmisin to lan es deenat! Go eway!"

Amber's engines were still running but they would flame out any minute. Wildman shut down two.

"Blackjack!"

Blackjack was way ahead of Wildman.

"Turn left to zero one zero. Passing through flight level two two zero."

"Co! Get Clark approach on the horn and get a straight-in clearance."

Co was in a daze. He was stunned by his mistake and now only making it worse.

"Clark approach is on sec three."

"Thanks, Blackjack. Don't know what I'd do without you, buddy. Remind me never to free you."

"You better, or I'll marry your sister."

"You're welcome to. She's gorgeous. She may be below your standards."

"Shut up and fly, white boy."

Wildman and Blackjack were like brothers. Only The Wildman would chit chat before a crash.

Wildman: "Clark approach. Clark approach. Amber Two. Declaring an emergency. We need an immediate straight-in approach to runway three one zero. Emergency equipment required. We are bingo on fuel."

"Negative! Negative, Amber Two! Manila Center called us already. Permission denied! You will have to go feet wet, and we will dispatch SAR right now."

SAR was search and rescue. They had just been told to punch out over water.

Wildman was very direct. "Get me the Wing CO, approach. Now! Amber Two is coming in."

"Roger, Amber Two. He's standing next to me."

They had anticipated Wildman's protest.

"This is Colonel Dukwieller. To whom am I speaking?"

"Captain Goldstein, sir. I am the AC of Amber Two, and I don't have time for introductions. I have declared an emergency. I am bingo and I need an immediate straight-in approach to runway three one zero. I have six souls on board. We just left heavy combat, and I have serious battle damage that must have ruptured one or more of my fuel tanks. Please alert the field. We're less than five minutes out."

"Negative, Captain! Your landing is in complete violation of our Philippine agreements, and the runway is too short. You are to go over water and evacuate your crew. I will have my SAR people waiting for your evacuation. That is an order, Captain!"

Blackjack turned them to three zero five. Ten miles. Through five thousand feet. Bombs had the field on his scope and if necessary would use the BNS to assist in landing.

"Listen, Colonel Duckwiener. I'm not risking the lives of six men when I have a perfectly good runway ten miles in front of me. I'm coming in, Colonel, so you better make sure the runway is clear."

"Negative! Negative! You are to abort your approach! Permission to land is de..."

Wildman turned the radio off. The Co came back to life and started the landing checklist.

"I have a visual, crew. Hang on. I'm going to have to lock 'em up on touch down."

Wildman came in perfectly. He landed on the overrun and literally stood on the brakes. Co popped the chute. There were loud explosions as the tires blew. The bird came to a full stop on the overrun at the other end of the runway. The crew was up and out of the aircraft in seconds. The hatch wouldn't fully open because of the blown tires, so they crawled out and ran. Even with no fuel, the bird could still burn. The emergency equipment was arriving and so were the sky cops and the Colonel. The Colonel stopped and leaped out of his staff car and raced toward the crew.

"Which one of you is Captain Goldstein?"

Wildman raised his hand.

"I will have your ass, Captain! You disobeyed a direct order, Captain! You will be court-martialed for this! This is a major incident with the Philippine government!"

"Shut the hell up, Colonel. I want food, water, and first aid for the crew, and I want an immediate patch through to CINC SAC."

The Colonel was in orbit. "What did you say to me, Captain? I will have you thrown in the brig right now! For insubordination! Disobeying a direct order! Gross insubordination!"

Another staff car with a Colonel's plate raced up. A Colonel jumped out and came running toward the assembled group. Colonel "Duckwiener" ordered Wildman cuffed by the sky cops and ran to meet the other Colonel. A loud and animated argument ensued immediately. It went on for five minutes while the crew and Wildman, in cuffs, stood there. They decided to start an immediate pool on which one would throw the first punch. Finally, Colonel "Duckwiener" turned, walked briskly to his car, and left.

Blackjack won the pool. He bet there were no punches. The other Colonel quickly walked toward them. He saluted the Captain in cuffs who obviously couldn't return it.

"Get this man out of handcuffs now, airman!"

The Wildman was free at last and saluted.

"I am Colonel Morrison, Captain. I'm Base Commander here. I must apologize for Colonel Dukwieller's conduct. I understand that you requested a patch through to CINC SAC. I've made arrangements for that. It's in process right now at the CP. If you will join me we can go complete your call now, and I'll have your crew taken to the hospital for a quick check. I have two flight surgeons en route now."

It was dawn at Clark.

"Thank you, Colonel. I appreciate your welcome versus Duckwiener's."

"It's Dukwieller. Richard Dukwieller."

"Whatever, Colonel."

On the way to his car he spelled Duckwiener's name for Wildman. *There might be a motive here.*

Wildman woke up CINC, who took his call. They spoke for twenty minutes. Morrison was anxiously standing outside the CP conference room while Wildman was talking inside. When Wildman emerged, Morrison was quick to ask: "What did John have to say, Captain?"

Yeah right. Like you knew "John" personally Colonel. The only guy on this base that knew John was Wildman. Now.

"He's not happy, Colonel. I think Duckwiener will be even more unhappy a little later today."

Morrison was about to burst with joy.

"Colonel, it's been a long night for us, and we're tired. But in all honesty, we could use a beer before we crash. As Base, could you arrange that?"

"We'll go over right now, and I'll have your crew brought over as soon as the doctors finish with them. The Club will be open before we get there. Now Captain, what did CINC say on your call?"

Wildman now was obliged to answer the Colonel since he was opening the Club for them. "I pretty much listened, sir. Then he said a bunch of expletives. A bunch. How long have you been Base, Colonel?"

Wildman didn't want to elaborate anymore, and besides he had to save some favor with Morrison. He'd need it in a few hours after they destroyed the bar at his club with his promotion party. Yup. Major Goldstein. It sounded good. Four years below the zone, by CINC SAC personally, was worth celebrating a bit. Bulldog would shit. No... he'd salute, only with his middle finger. Spike was the one that would shit. That poor bastard had to *earn* his leaves.

By the time Major Wildman and his crew went to bed later that morning, at two a.m. on the floor of the O'Club, Colonel Duckweiner had received new orders effective immediately. He was the new Snow Removal Officer at Elmendorf Air Force Base, Alaska. They promoted a Second Lieutenant to make the job available.

The CINC PACAF's [Pacific Air Forces] personal jet, at the request of "John," would pick up the new Major and his crew and fly them back to Guam.

Not a bad diversion. Not at all.

THE TV SHOW

After he put on his new pajamas, D-Kid was taken outside where he saw Tom again. They were poorly blinded folded, hand cuffed, and put in the back of a jeep.

Tom: "Pretty bad beatings?"

"A few rifle butts to the head and hard falls to the floor. But I didn't say shit other than Quail is not a dinner entrée on a B-52. They said they were going to kill me for not cooperating."

"Me, too. Maybe that's where we're going. They wouldn't kill us at the Hilton. No one knows we're alive. It would be easy to do."

The guard yelled: "No talk!"

Shit... Tom may be right. We are of no value to them now. God help me.

D-Kid could see pretty well through his blindfold. They were driving through what appeared to be the streets of Hanoi. Finally, they stopped in front of what looked like a real hotel with a swimming pool.

Maybe this is the real Hanoi Hilton and the other was the little known Sheraton Shithole...

More trucks were arriving as they sat in front of the courtyard. The jeep moved into the yard and drove to the back. Both men were removed from the jeep and taken to separate rooms under guard. Minutes later, D-Kid was taken to a large room crammed with people and cameras. He quickly realized it was the international press corps.

This will save my life. I'm now a POW. Thank you, Lord.

D-Kid was led up to a large bank of microphones. The questions from the press exploded around him.

"Why did you bomb innocent people? What plane did you fly? Are you being treated well?"

He didn't hear one question. He wouldn't answer if he did. He looked around the room and knew he was being photographed. That's all that mattered. He didn't say one word. Then his eye caught a familiar face. He stared at her with all the contempt that he could bring after being up for 30 hours. *That's Joan Bass, the folk singer. A little aid and comfort to the enemy, lady? You proud of that? You miserable, stupid, bitch. Go home and marry Jane.*

He was abruptly yanked away from the microphones and pulled roughly back to the jeep. Tom was gone. D-Kid was as happy as he could be, given his condition. He was a POW. His photo would be on the front pages of the newspapers back home by tomorrow morning. They no longer could kill him.

He would go home and see Robbie and his family again. It was now a matter of when.

THE FLOCK HEADS HOME

Spike couldn't believe it. How the hell could a pro like Wildman suddenly run out of gas? The only time that you had too much fuel in an aircraft was when you were on fire. Well, maybe it was Gravytrain… but he was a great Co. Strange things happen to guys in serious combat, especially the first time. Even with the psychological screening that SAC aviators go through, which is extensive because of the nuke assignment, he'd seen it happen before. Thump was the worst ever though. The absolute worst. Had he contributed to that? Shit. All Picks are strange ducks anyway. Music majors. That's what USAF wanted for Nosepicks. PAF's [Probably Are Faggots] in a Bee-hop-sit-song. It was a damn disgrace. LeMay would have hated that profile. Hell, had he found out about it, he would have had all Picks shot for "suspected girly behavior." Then he would have had the guys that wrote the spec shot for "aiding and abetting." He was the General of Generals when it came to the USAF.

Spike had met Curtis LeMay at Castle when he was first assigned to a B-47 as a new white bar. LeMay had come out to the flight line and arbitrarily stopped by *his* bird during pre-flight. Everybody was a nervous wreck. Four Stars, *The Founder and CINC* of the Strategic Air Command.

Shock and surprise. He was charming, encouraging, and open. This guy was a crewdog. He was leaving when he reached into his Jacket and pulled out a cigar while standing under the wing of the bird. He lit it, and a maintenance L/C who was in Lemay's entourage ran over to the General:

"General, sir! General! You shouldn't light that here. The aircraft might blow up, sir!"

Lemay looked at the Colonel and scowled in the more legendary Lemay fashion: "It wouldn't dare, Colonel. It wouldn't dare." He then turned and walked slowly to his staff car, talking to Spike's AC and firing up the stogie.

Now that was SAC. No music majors then. No way.

"B-dog, why the hell do they recruit music majors as Picks? The SAC I joined twelve years ago would have had guys like that guarding the nurses at the base hospital like eunuchs at a king's palace. It makes no sense. It should be against an AFR that I haven't broken yet."

"Ears, Spike. Hearing. A lot of Pick work is *listening* for threat signals. Lots of background noise. They have to find certain noises that are dangerous among many that mean nothing. Hard work as I understand it."

"Yeah, but they're still PAFs."

"No question about it, Spike. Closet dress horses."

"Hell. Screw 'em. They're all spaced."

"I wouldn't. But you can if that's your new preference. I got a PAF sitting on my left? Wonders never cease."

"Screw you, B-dog."

"No. No way. I'm not your type."

"Crew, Pilot. Sounds like Wildman got down OK. I listened to him fighting on approach with everybody from Spike's controller to a tower guy at Clark to no less than the Wing CO on a declared emergency into Clark. What a bunch of assholes. But I heard him call final, gear down and locked, so he must be down. I will guarantee that this will be some sort of incident. They don't know that they are dealing with The Wildman. I pity the bastards."

Spike lit up: "My controller? That little shitbird controller that sent the fighters after us? You sure it was him, Hollywood?"

"The accent is unmistakable. 'Chu' know that. They busted Wildman for trying to land a combat aircraft in the PI. Told him to go 'eway'. But I know what you're thinking already, so stop thinking about it. We're already in enough trouble. I... we don't need any more."

Suddenly, and for no apparent reason, POS shuddered and vibrated like something was out of sync.

"Co, check the fuel and hydraulics. You guys feel that down there?"

Graham: "Yeah. I did. It didn't feel right at all. I've never felt that before at altitude."

Spike came on: "I have, but I don't remember when or how many times since I have a zillion hours in these damn airplanes. Be optimistic, Hollywood. I don't remember crashing after the shudder either."

Graham: "We're one hundred and ten clicks out of the PI. I'll plot a divert heading."

"No, Nav. After what Wildman went through, they would shoot us down if another one of us tried to come in. We'll press on to Guam. I don't want to be late for the party waiting for us. Heads up, everyone, for anything else unusual. Somebody check on Thump."

Hollywood didn't need to specify who. He knew Spike would do it. Spike unstrapped and went up. After all, he may have caused, or at least contributed to, this shit. Thump was still in the fetal position, lying on his right side. The visor was still up, and his eyes were still open.

Spike got down on his knees and tried to make eye contact. "Hey, E-dub. You here, buddy? We're past the PI. Back on that shit island in less than two. You need anything, Dub? Some water?"

No response. Shit. This guy was gone. He had never seen it this bad. Never. He climbed back down. "Hollywood. Dub's still here physically, but he's gone, man. No response. Just stares straight ahead. Whatever got him took him completely. I've never seen anything like it."

"We have Charlie alerted. There will be air meds at the chocks, and they'll come on immediately and take him out. Christ, they'll have an entourage of vehicles waiting. Ambulances, staff cars... prison vans. Hell of a welcome."

THE BLUE STAFF CARS

Robbie Foster was visiting her parents' home in Blytheville, Arkansas, having completed decorations at her home for her husband's imminent return. The mood was light, and Christmas spirit was in the air. She decided to bake some of her husband's favorite cookies because he was due home tomorrow. She was a bit bothered that he hadn't called her en route, but that had happened before. This would be a wonderful Christmas. Robert had basically been gone most of the time since they had been married.

Her father, returning home for lunch, got a call from the Base Commander.

"Yes, Colonel, she is here. Do you wish to speak to her?"

"No, sir. Not right now. But would you please make sure that she stays there for half an hour?"

"Sure. Is there anything you would like me to tell her?"

"No, sir. In fact, it's best you say nothing about my call."

That seemed very odd.

Robbie came out of the kitchen to bring her father a sandwich in the living room. Then by chance she saw the blue staff car pull-up. She dropped the plate and brought her hand to her mouth to stifle a scream.

Every Air Force wife with a husband in combat knew what the blue staff car meant.

She started to cry. The Commander, Colonel Einhardt, the Chaplain, Major Jordan, and the flight surgeon, Captain Swanson, all got out of the car. She knew all of them, and she knew exactly why all three were coming to see her.

Her husband was down.

She became completely hysterical, as any wife would. Dr. Swanson gave her a sedative to calm her down, and the notification team formally read the document to Robbie's parents. It was mandatory, and had to be read word for word:

IT IS WITH DEEP PERSONAL CONCERN THAT I OFFICIALLY INFORM YOU THAT YOUR HUSBAND, CAPTAIN ROBERT G. FOSTER, IS MISSING IN ACTION IN NORTH VIETNAM. ON 18 DEC 1972 HE WAS A CREW MEMBER ON A B-52 AIRCRAFT ON AN OPERATIONAL MISSION OVER NORTH VIETNAM. THE AIRCRAFT

WAS OBSERVED TO CRASH AFTER APPARENTLY BEING HIT BY HOSTILE FIRE. OTHER DETAILS CONCERNING THIS INCIDENT ARE UNKNOWN AT THIS TIME. HOWEVER, NEW INFORMATION RECEIVED WILL BE FURNISHED YOU IMMEDIATELY. PENDING FURTHER INFORMATION HE WILL BE LISTED OFFICIALLY AS MISSING IN ACTION. IF YOU HAVE ANY QUESTIONS YOU MAY CALL MY PERSONAL REPRESENTATIVE TOLL FREE BY DIALING 1-800-521-5101. PLEASE ACCEPT MY SINCERE SYMPATHY DURING THIS PERIOD OF ANXIETY.

MAJOR GENERAL K.M. TILLMEN,
COMMANDER

When Robbie awoke from her sedated nap, the Chaplain was still there. He tried to comfort her, but he had little effect. Within an hour the phone rang. Everyone dreaded calls, because this day had brought nothing but tragedy and great sorrow.

Robbie's father answered the phone and listened intently. Finally, words that brought her hope: "Yes, sir! That's great news! Thank you so much, Colonel." He hung up abruptly.

"Robert has been confirmed as a POW. He's alive!"

Robbie's despair turned immediately to joy. He was alive! He would come home... some day.

SPIKE IN THAILAND

Spike: "I normally pack my mess dress [formal uniform, equivalent to a tuxedo] for such occasions as full-blown court martial's upon landing. Son-of-a-bitch but I left it at the cleaners this time. Piss poor luck."

Graham immediately challenged Spike's bullshit: "Spike, you haven't left anything at the cleaners in years. You don't even know where the cleaners is, you dirtbag. Mess Dress? Shit. You don't even own one."

Graham had opened the door. "B-dog, you're a miserable skeptic. I own two as a matter of fact. One, however, was left in the room at a Pataya Beach hotel suite that was occupied by myself and a Malaysian Princess by the name of Princess Tai Pen. She suffered from enormous tits, Eurasian beauty, and a fairly advanced case of nymphomania. I met her at the Governor's Ball, to which a Colonel Tam had arranged an invitation for me, and was immediately smitten after she grabbed my crotch during the very first dance."

This was another routine Spike-O-Scam story that normally occurred on outbound legs after the PI.

"Since I was at the time staying in accommodations that were not suited for Royalty, specifically in a hammock at Lobster Island, we adjourned after the first dance to her suite at the same hotel as the Ball. This was quite convenient. We ordered the finest champagne, some fois gras, two bottles of Jack Black, and a bottle of Tequila. The Tequila was intended for breakfast, mind you, since I intended to keep my senses about me for this Royal encounter. No sooner had The Princess concluded preparing for the evenings' celebration, which consisted of stripping buck naked not thirty seconds after we walked into the suite, that I came to realize that the suite was not hers alone. Her sister, Princess Lei Pen walked into the living area wearing a beautiful silk robe."

This was going to be a Spike-O-Scam befitting the Hairball of Hairball missions.

"There ensued a small argument between the two sisters in a dialect of which I was mostly unfamiliar, except for an occasional 'fuck' in Thai that I was somewhat familiar with. I was optimistic, if not hopeful, that the 'fuck' was in direct reference to the American War Hero Major in the room who was still clad in his highly decorated Mess Dress uniform save for the trousers and skivvies that now occupied the arm of a chair. The argument continued for about ten tortuous minutes as Rodney was at attention, but I was not. Finally there seemed to be some agreement reached between the sisters that would hopefully not screw up the evening... or rather, would screw up the evening in a positive sense."

Unbelievable, completely unbelievable. But Graham had found some of the Spike-O-Scams to be true in the past, so he was never quite sure what was bullshit and what wasn't.

"I was quickly to learn that it was the latter, when Princess Lei Pen removed her robe, revealing the same condition that her sister enjoyed. Her body was just as spectacular as, if not identical to, her sister's, and they both came over to me and grabbed Rodney. Not to be a party pooper, I excused myself briefly to drain Rodney, which wasn't easy, before an anticipated long workout, and to order yet another bottle of Jack Black to sustain endurance and engender creativity. I returned to find the ladies had gone to the bedroom and were preparing for some activities that would indeed make the evening quite memorable. Just then, room service delivered the refreshments. I quickly put my trousers back on in order not to raise suspicion amongst the help who knew full well who was occupying the suite. I prepared some champagne for the ladies and a second Jack Black for myself and joined the ladies for a very fine and creative evening that pleased Rodney to no end. As it turned out, both sisters seemed to suffer from exactly the same afflictions, and I was beginning to be in need of a brief timeout and a Jack Black refresher course about zero two thirty when there was a loud knock at the door. No, it was more like loud banging at the door, accompanied by some raised voices in the same dialect that the girls had used earlier. The Princesses' eyes got big and their demeanor quite animated as in "you get the hell out of here lao- lao," which I knew to mean hurry, hurry. I retrieved my trousers and a bottle of Jack Black for what I assumed would be a dive out the window, when I realized we were on the fifteenth floor. Just then, one of the gorgeous sisters motioned me toward a different hallway that proved to have exactly what I needed. Another door. As I raced down the hallway away from the yelling, I heard the sisters answer the door and start screaming at whoever had been there in what sounded like a remarkably convincing verbal attack on the intruder which I later found out was their father, The Most exalted Prince of Somethingorother … a Thai name too long to pronounce, as is the custom."

"So, guys, that is where my other mess dress resides to this day. Somewhere in the hotel lost and found after the maids found it in the hall closet when their Highnesses departed. The other one is at the cleaners. I'm almost positive."

Graham thought that this one was too much. Complete absolute bullshit on the order of Magnitude One.

"No way, Spike. That one is a result of your coma after your drunken ass fell out of the hammock on Lobster Island. No way."

"No. You're quite wrong. I'll introduce you to them if we can get up to Chang Mai on our next trip to Thailand."

Chang Mai was a legend in its own right. It was a city in Northern Thailand that was home to the French rubber plantations. The French had married the local Thai natives, and over the years the women had grown to be very beautiful. They had the best of both European and Asian features, with European bodies. They were stunning. But Graham was *sure* it was bullshit this time. In fact he was positive. Almost.

Damn! Hell, don't think about it. We're almost back to the rain center of the Pacific...

"Pilot, Nav. Coming up on two hundred miles out. Notify CP. Estimate touch at two five after. Start descent in eleven minutes."

"Roger, Nav. Snow Flight is two zero zero out. ETA at two five after. Confirm air meds and ambulance at chocks. Guns, you and the Co get the E-dub up and strapped for landing. We can't leave him in the bunk with this POS shuddering and God knows what else."

The Co and Roller got Thump up without much difficulty and ensured that he was strapped. His Bible was lying on the deli counter, and he put his right hand on it when he was back in.

Maybe he would come out of it...

"Pilot, Nav. Contact Andersen approach, and start descent to flight level two five zero."

They were almost home in one piece from the Hairball of Hairballs.

"Snow Flight, Snow One is out of three four zero to two five zero."

BANG! There was a tremendous explosion, and the cockpit filled with fog. They all knew it was a rapid de-compression. Shit was flying everywhere, and it got very cold almost instantly.

"Andersen approach. Snow One in rapid decompression going to 10,000 feet immediately and declaring an emergency!"

"Roger, Snow One. Descend and maintain 10,000 feet. Cleared for straight in approach to runway three zero. Advise fuel status and souls on board."

Roller finally got on. The cockpit was still full of condensation, and they were literally in a dive. "Pilot! Pilot! The EW has ejected! I repeat! The EW has ejected!"

CHAPTER X: BRING IN THE CLOWNS

A SURPRISE WELCOME

Hollywood knew what had happened immediately. He couldn't see the E-dub's seat from his because he was too busy with the emergency. But he knew. *Why did he put him back in the seat? Jesus!*

A beeper went off. It had to be Thump's.

Hollywood's voice was strained. "Command Post, Snow One is in a rapid descent to 10,000 feet. We have declared an emergency and have been cleared for an immediate straight in approach to three zero. Our EW ejected from the aircraft. I repeat. Our EW ejected from the aircraft. We are one one seven at two six five from Alpha. SAR needed on site immediately. Confirm."

"Roger, Snow One. We copy your emergency. SAR en route. All other souls OK?"

"Roger, CP, on souls. Switching to Andersen approach. Snow One out."

"Andersen approach. Snow One."

"Go ahead, Snow One."

"Snow One is level at 10,000 feet with a declared emergency. Understand cleared for straight in approach to six zero immediate. We have fifteen thousand pounds [fuel]. *Five* souls onboard. I repeat. Five souls onboard. A crewmember ejected. CP has SAR on the way."

Everyone but Hollywood was understandably silent. All were on oxygen even though they were now level at 10,000 feet. Standard emergency procedure is to dive to that altitude because if there is also a problem with the oxygen caused by the decompression, the crew can breathe without the onboard oxygen at that altitude.

"Roger, Snow One. We are aware of the nature of the emergency. Will you still need an ambulance and air meds at chocks?"

"Negative, Andersen. The need for that is now floating in the Pacific. We have the runway in sight. Snow One out."

"Crew, I don't know what to say. What just happened is inexplicable. The E-dub must have suffered a major breakdown that we dealt with as best we could. We're home. We can deal with everything."

"Gear down and locked."

"Crew, this place has been busy while we were at the Dance. There're B-52s everywhere. Both Gs and Ds. There has to be well over one hundred birds. This war has gotten really serious."

Snow One touched down at 0837 local. Fifteen hours and thirty seven minutes from wheels in the well. All who were "kids" yesterday were now men.

"Air brakes, six. Pop the chute."

"Six. Chute deployed."

The emergency equipment followed them down the runway on the parallel.

"Charlie Tower. Snow One is down at zero eight three seven local."

"Roger, Snow. Welcome back. We heard it was a real hairball. Taxi to the holding area and shut her down."

The holding area was a large "safe" area away from the other aircraft reserved specifically for emergency or battle damaged aircraft.

Spike came up for the first time since Thump got out early: "Maybe the dumbshit Sky Cops won't be able to find us if we're not in a normal revetment."

Hollywood: "Only thing I see are fire trucks, two ambulances, No Luck in a jeep, and a crew bus."

Spike was delighted: "Great! Let's hijack the crew bus and head for the Navy O'Club. At least we can get a good last meal."

He wasn't kidding.

THUMP'S SWIMMING LESSON

Bravo Victor One Five, the SAR helicopter, was hovering over the splash down site of the B-52 crewman. They had found him quickly by honing in on his beeper. The ejection seat raft had deployed, but the crewman was not in it. He was floating in the ocean about twenty feet from the raft which was tethered to him. The AC and the rescue divers could see him clearly.

They could also see the sharks.

"Skip, he's not moving at all, and his visor's still down. Maybe he got hurt when he punched."

"Roger, Beans. He may also be bleeding as a result. It may be too dangerous for you to go in after him. We can wait for the surface boys to arrive, but I don't think there will be anything left of him by then."

The Mariana Trench off of Guam was world famous for two things: the depth of the ocean and the shark population. For the latter reason, the military inhabitants of the island were under standing orders not to go over the reef at any of the island's beaches. A light Colonel had ignored that order two years earlier and gone over the reef at Agana Beach "for a quick look." The only thing they found was his air tank banging against the coral.

"Beans, I don't want to lose two guys. Those sharks look like a swarm of bees for Christ's sake. Let's wait for surface."

"Negative, Skip. He'll never last. I have Jack on the hoist. I'll be in and out in a matter of a couple of minutes. I'll deploy more dye markers before I'm in. Take us down, Skip."

Staff Sergeant Lawrence Beatty was in the water quickly. He swam to Thump who was alive but limp. Beans struggled to get him in the harness and succeeded after three attempts. They brought him up and sent the harness back down for Beans. It took ten minutes.

DE-BRIEFING

No Luck was waiting for the crew as they exited the aircraft.

Spike got out just before Hollywood. "Great news, Major! The best is that you guys somehow got this piece of shit back here. The next best is that this thing is being pulled off the line for a complete refit by Boeing, compliments of Boeing. They reviewed the records and decided that this was probably the biggest piece of shit in SAC. I got a new bird!"

Spike: "That's great, No Luck. I was going to kill you, but I've had enough for today. Therefore you are no longer No Luck. You are now Some Luck. Sounds gook though, so be careful in public."

They got on the crew bus, and the exhaustion seemed to hit all of them at once. Hollywood actually fell asleep on the short trip to Base Ops. They were so tired that they didn't even dread their coming fate any more. They walked into debrief and found one surprise: there was a cooler of beer on the conference table. The other surprises, that weren't really surprises, were that Dangle was there along with two sky cops, another full Colonel they didn't know at all, the 8th Air Force head of planning, and his idiot assistant, L/C Greenbaum. Spike had sworn he was going to beat Greenbaum to death, but no one got shot down. A miracle.

Dangle: "Gentlemen, please take refreshments and be seated. I know you're tired, but I suspect this will be a long de-briefing."

Hollywood: "No, it won't, Colonel. I request that you have these proceedings recorded so that when my crew and I make our statements - that's right, I said "statements" as if we were on trial - there is no confusion later as to what we said."

"That will be provided."

Dangle told his kiss ass white bar aid to get a tape recorder immediately. "I understand, Captain Noland, that it was pretty bad up there. SAMs were pretty heavy?"

"They launched at least thirty just at *us*. Just at my bird. Not the Cell. It was unbelievable."

Dangle: "How do you know there were thirty, Captain?"

"Guns counted the calls. Remember those are the ones that the Co and I *saw*. I'm certain that there were more than that. "

The kiss ass came into the room with a TEAC recorder. Teac was crewdogs' favorite brand. They would have to remember to steal it the next time they had some down time.

Dangle started the formal de-brief as the Teac was turned on. "This de-briefing is being conducted by myself, Colonel Richard Dangle, Deputy Commander Operations, Forty Third Strategic Wing, Provisional, Colonel John Reinhardt, attached to Eighth Air Force, and Colonel Kaplinsky and Lieutenant Colonel Greenbaum both from Eighth Air Force planning. We are debriefing FAI SO-2, the lead on the 19 December 72 strike on Hanoi out of Andersen Air Force Base, Guam. It is zero nine two one local, 20 December, 1972. Present are the crew: Captain Noland, the AC; Major Wilson, the Bombs; Captain Graham, the Navigator; First Lieutenant Matthews, the co-pilot; and Sergeant Seeps, the gunner. Captain Darden, the EW is not present, which will be discussed first in this de-briefing."

Hollywood: "As I said preceding the formal start of this debriefing, Colonel, it is important that we get this briefing concluded expeditiously. We are tired and, frankly, beat to shit. First, in regard to the EW, it was a nightmare over Hanoi. SAMs were everywhere. We were all over the sky. After egress, we found the EW had apparently freaked, for lack of a better term, as a result of the heavy fire or whatever. We put him in the crew bunk until just prior to landing, whereupon I had him moved back to his seat. Shortly after being placed back in his seat, he rotated the handles of his ejection seat and squeezed both handles, causing his hatch to blow, followed by his immediate ejection. I had no idea that he was apparently suicidal, nor did any of the crewmembers that cared for him after we discovered his condition."

The Nazi from Eighth started to ask a question: "Captain Noland, why didn't..."

"Colonel, with all due respect, please wait with questions until I have finished my statement. The mission started with our very nearly losing the aircraft on take-off. We lost water on a fourth engine after S-2, and I had to dive the bird over the cliff to get enough airspeed to fly her."

Dangle interrupted: "You DOVE the plane off the cliff! I can't believe that you..."

"Believe it, Colonel, and again, please wait until we're finished. The flight was somewhat uneventful after that until we got to the target area; except that we had three breakaways occur during re-fueling due to CAT, and MIGS fired on us up by the ChiCom border. After that, everything was unusually quiet prior to the target area, which was good since the radar went out at the IP, and we were flying blind. Spike and Bulldog unstrapped and tried to fix the radar before the target but the piece of shit wouldn't come up. As a result, we withheld and turned over the target by the Nav using ded reckoning (deductive reckoning). After the turn, the entire world below us opened up like a SAM test range, and shit was coming from everywhere. That went on forever because the idiots in planning turned us into a one hundred plus knot headwind. We got a very close call that took out my seven engine and caused other battle damage that I don't know about yet. We formed up after we all were outside of the last COA and flew south. The crap radar started working again. Right after our turn west, we had a request to save some Marines that were nearby. We did it, knowing that we were in violation of an order that shouldn't exist when you are fighting a war, and saved a bunch of guys. We took triple A over the target area, but we blew their asses up when we took out the ridge the NVA was staging on. We rejoined the flight, resumed lead, and refueled over the So Chi. Wildman left and went into Clark because he was shot to shit and had lost all his gas. We flew back fairly quickly because the headwind that nearly got us killed was now a tailwind.

The EW punched out. We landed, and here we are. Now Spike and Bulldog will de-brief."

Most of the brass in the room were wide-eyed and speechless. Almost.

The Nazi: "Captain Noland, you mean to tell them that..."

Spike cut him off: "Excuse me, Colonel, but I haven't started yet. So shut up, sir."

Reinhardt was writing furiously. Despite the fact that a large reel to reel tape recorder was saving every word. He would have them all executed... like the good ol' days. Shot!

All of them had grabbed three beers each, except for Co. He had one. Spike had finished two and was almost ready to reload.

Spike was ready. "So anyway, your Colonelships. You sent us up in an airplane on the hairball of hairball missions that you knew was a complete piece of shit. So much so that you took it out of service after we landed. What goddamn idiot is running this place! Is *anybody?* The planning was atrocious. It was inexcusable. The Rules of Engagement are idiotic! Do you guys think we could ignore the hundred plus guys, OUR GUYS, that were trapped by an NVA division!? Do you!? WOULD *YOU* HAVE!? Fuck it. I'm done."

Graham: "I have nothing to add to what Spike and Hollywood have said, other than that it's all true, and the guys that planned and approved this mission should be on trial, not us. The maintenance commander should be made to fly the next Linebacker II mission, alone, in POS 221. And I concur with every insult that Spike offered and will add some of my own after my next beer or two. Provided I'm still awake. You want another one, Spike? Hollywood?"

They both took another.

There was stunned silence. They just stared at the crew, seemingly in a state of shock.

Looking at the Co, Dangle asked: "Do you have anything to say, Lieutenant?

"No sir. They've covered it pretty much."

The Nazi, Reinhardt, wanted blood. "Gentlemen, it's your actions that are a disgrace! Not ours! You will be..."

Dangle interrupted the Nazi: "Colonel, these men are under my command. I will lead this de-briefing."

Dangle turned to Spike: "I understand your anger completely, and given the circumstances, I don't take exception with your language since it's borne out of legitimate frustration. You are being brought up on charges for diverting to the target of opportunity which disobeyed a standing direct order that you were fully aware of. It is a serious charge. I personally will go on record to say that, under the circumstances, the order was complete bullshit, and you did exactly what you should have at great personal risk. I will state that at your proceedings as well as here. In addition, you led a flight into an unbelievably hostile environment and emerged with no losses. We *expected* twenty percent, gentlemen. We *expected* to lose three to four aircraft. That was considered *acceptable.*"

The crewdogs just listened. Fuming. But listening.

"In my opinion, you should be nominated for the DFC, if not, the Silver Star for placing yourselves in harm's way voluntarily to save that Marine Company. As your Commander, I will do so, pending the outcome of the proceedings."

A Captain came in the room and spoke to Dangle privately.

"Gentlemen, good news. SAR plucked your EW out of the drink. He's in bad shape, but he'll live. There's no point in visiting him at this point. He's in the ICU, and Dr. Swanson said he is not coherent."

Dangle, turning to the other senior officers, addressing the planners first: "Colonel, your questions will be for information only. They will not be confrontational, and they will be brief. Is that clear?"

Colonel Kaplinsky seemed intimidated, maybe even frightened. He had never seen any officer, let alone numerous officers, so furious. He would be careful. "Captain Noland. You broke formation when the SAMs were launched. The formation as a whole must be maintained for the ECM [electronic countermeasures designed to jam enemy radar] to be effective, and therefore you are under orders not to break formation while under attack. What can you say that justifies your actions?"

Hollywood: "Two things, Colonel. The SAMs had no guidance. First, they were fired ballistic. ECM was useless. Second, we brought everybody back. If we had maintained formation, fifty, not twenty, percent of the flight would have gone down. And that's conservative, Colonel. I will not obey an 'order' that will get me and the crew killed."

Kaplinsky: "I don't agree with your assessment, Captain. We sent yesterday's mission on exactly the same mission plan and they only lost three. Almost all maintained formation."

Graham was stunned. "Colonel, let me understand. You sent yesterday's flight on the same plan, lost three and then sent us on the exact same plan? You caused eighteen guys to get shot down, including one of our closest friends, and you thought that was a good plan? A good outcome? What if you had been on one of those birds, Colonel? Would that have been acceptable?"

Kaplinsky: "Yes, but the SAMs were guided yesterday, and I can no longer fly, or I would have."

Graham: "You're idiots."

Spike: "No *you're* a gaggle of idiots! Are you idiots sending the flight on the same plan again?"

Kaplinsky: "Essentially. Yes. Yes, it is about the same."

Spike stood up. The beer was getting to him. "You guys should be shot. Shot! No, better yet, why don't you fly lead tonight, Colonel!" Graham pulled Spike back into his chair.

The Nazi jumped in: "Your behavior is atrocious. I will personally see that you are court-martialed. You disobeyed orders and..."

Dangle: "Shut up, Reinhardt. You are to leave this de-brief immediately. If you do not, I will have you escorted out by the air police." Reinhart was about to respond. The Sky Cops had moved behind him.

Graham thought, *What a kick! The Sky Cops were here for them, and now they were about to throw this asshole Colonel out on his ass!*

Dangle: "NOW, Colonel!"

The door opened, and an L/C called the room to attention. They reluctantly responded.

General Andrews walked in. "At ease, gentleman. We just received great news and there has been an interesting, but unrelated, development." Everybody was riveted on the three star. Three stars were like fairy godmothers... people had heard about them but never seen them. As they got older, they questioned whether fairy godmothers existed. They had now seen their fairy godmother twice in less than twenty-four hours.

"The news is that Captains Foster and Sampson have been confirmed as POWs. We have no news on the other crewmembers at this point, but as you are all aware, we believed that Charcoal One was fireballed and there was no possibility of survivors. Fortunately, our information was incorrect."

Since he was a three star, the crewdogs waited for him to complete the announcement. Then the room erupted.

Graham: "D-Kid's alive! Thank you, God! Thanks, General! That's unbelievably great news!"

The crewdogs were high fiving everybody, including a smiling General Andrews, like they had just won the World Series. But as drunk as he was, Spike realized that there was a second component to the General's visit, so he told the crew to settle down. They would hit the Club later. They sat back down and waited for the General to proceed. The interesting development was probably related to accelerating Court Martial proceedings.

The General continued: "First of all, Reinhardt, I believe I heard Colonel Dangle ask you to leave this de-briefing as I was coming in. You will honor the Colonel's request and see me in my office at seventeen thirty this afternoon. You are dismissed, Colonel."

Graham thought, *Terrific! The Nazi was toast! Maybe the General* was *their fairy godmother.*

The General: "Gentlemen, I have come here to personally meet and commend this heroic crew for their courageous action last night over Hanoi on a very dangerous mission and for their decisive action in coming to the aid of a Marine company trapped by an NVA Division. The decision to intervene on behalf of the Marines, which was made under duress since there were standing orders not to acquire targets of opportunity..."

Spike picked up the term. *He said* were *orders..!*

" ... has resulted in the literal rescue of over one hundred of their comrades. Among those trapped was Second Lieutenant Tom Thornton, a Platoon Leader with the Company. Lieutenant Thornton's father, Senator Richard Thornton, called me personally, from The Oval Office, I might add, to thank the 8th Air Force and asked that I personally thank the crew that performed such a gallant act. I have brought with me The Distinguished Flying Cross to be awarded to each crewmember that participated in this gallant action."

Spike: "Wanna beer, General?"

"Sure."

THE REAL DE-BRIEF

Spike grabbed a beer and handed it to the General then took it back and opened it. SO-2 was beat to shit and now getting a little blasted... this ought to be interesting. They just got their asses saved by some Senator's kid and lucked out beyond belief. Now with a few more beers, they were liable to step on their dicks with a three star and blow it all.

The General was dressed in a custom made flight suit. "Thanks, Major. You're Spike, aren't you?"

"Yes, sir. I can't deny it any more."

"I've heard about you and Bulldog there. Didn't you guys lead the first strike on the North in Gs?"

Graham answered, fearing Spike's answer given his state of mind. "No, Sir. We lead the second strike in Gs. Lieutenant Colonel Nagahashi led the first. He's also a Fairchild crew and a good friend of ours."

The General: "That's right. We had you guys over here on twenty four hours notice. You did a great job. But last night was incredible."

"Thank you, sir."

The General addressed the room: "Tell you what, gentlemen. This de-brief is concluded for everyone except for myself, Colonel Dangle, the crew, and Lieutenant Colonel Davis [his aide]. Colonel Davis will meet with you subsequent to our meeting and complete the de-brief as necessary. Now you guys go bother another crew, but be brief. That's what these are - brief. Get it, guys?"

There were multiple "yes, sirs," and they bolted out of the room.

Spike was airborne: "General, who the hell is Senator Thornton that he calls from the Oval Office, and how did he find out so quickly about his kid being up shit creek and rescued by the gallant warriors of FAI S-02?"

Spike was only slightly slurring.

The General: "Senator Thornton is Chairman of the Senate Armed Services Committee and a personal friend and confidant of both the President and Secretary Kissinger. That should answer both of your questions, Spike."

"I guess so. I guess we were pretty lucky the kid was there, huh?"

"If he hadn't been, even I couldn't have saved your asses. That's how ridiculous that order is. Off the record, gentlemen, you can't win a war run by politicians. No war in history has ever been won by politicians. This one will not be the exception."

Graham was mystified. "So you're saying the war is already lost, General?"

"Essentially yes, from the standpoint of achieving the outcome that we traditionally define as victory. The Vietnamese will return to the peace table in a matter of days in order to end the bombing that will occur in the heart of their country in the next few days. There will be nothing left for them to defend themselves with, so they will be helpless against further attack. If the politicians weren't running the war, we could land Army and Marines in Hanoi and Haiphong and occupy the cities with little resistance, at least at first. But that will never happen. There will be a complete ceasefire, and they will start to re-arm and rebuild immediately while we start withdrawing troops. Short of a blatant violation of the peace accords, we'll bring everybody out. Then the dust will settle, and in a year or two... or three, they will take over the south completely un-opposed. We won't be able to do a damn thing about it because the media would bury us. Hell, the President would be impeached."

Graham was pissed. "So we have lost fifty thousand of our guys for nothing. That's fucked, sir."

"No Captain... er, Bulldog . Do you mind if I use your call sign?"

Graham: "Are you kidding, sir?"

"No, Bulldog, we didn't. The war did accomplish a very important thing for the future of America in the Post War era. For the first time since the war, we committed the resources to seriously defend our interests on a global position. The world, especially the communist world, thought we were pussies - an easy mark if the going got tough, and I assure you it will get tough downstream. So the value of the war will pay off for future generations that will not end up in a major confrontation that could potentially create casualties that dwarf the terrible losses of Vietnam. The other outcome that may be of even greater importance is that our intervention in Vietnam kept the spread of communism under control. All of Southeast Asia and southern Asia would have collapsed if we hadn't stopped it in Vietnam. I'm certain that history will prove correct in the 'Domino Theory.' Hell, it might have prevented the end of the world as we know it. Could we have won the war? Do you know what Barry Goldwater advocated in 1964?"

Graham: "No, sir."

"He said if we wanted to end the conflict in South East Asia, we should send the B-52s into the North and destroy from the air their ability to make war. It would be over in days. He lost the election because of that position and some others. He was painted as a war monger. And here we are, eight years and over fifty thousand lives later, doing *exactly* what the Senator said we should do. Now he's a politician, but he's also an Air Force General. Vietnam is just the beginning. The day will come, twenty, thirty years from now, that *no one*, and I mean *no one*, will mess with us. Not the communists, not some nickel dick country, no one. Oh, some idiots will try, but they'll get slapped so hard and fast that the other idiots will think twice about following their lead. That's why we *won* the war from the position of future outcome. That is far more important than occupying Hanoi and Haiphong."

They all realized that this guy was one smart man.

"Did I answer your question, Bulldog?"

"Yes, sir. Yes you did."

"Good. You guys are not risking your lives for some bullshit war in Asia. You may well be defending the world from a complete holocaust in the future. Any questions from the rest of you on that subject?"

Uh oh... Spike: "Yes, sir. You mind if I nap, occasionally, in the sand trap on number nine? I find it quite convenient at times."

The General: "You guys haven't figured it out yet?"

Graham had. So had Hollywood. Co didn't care, and Roller was somewhere else as usual.

"You guys are bulletproof. You can do no wrong, gentlemen, short of a serious felony, which you still might beat. Right now you have hundreds of 'get out of jail free cards', guys."

Grinning, the general continued, "Hell, I have to be careful not to piss you off!" He laughed and smiled broadly. "You guys saved a very powerful United States Senator's son from *certain death* by violating dumb ass orders and risking your lives. The Senator asked for, and received, each of your names. Spike, if you like, I'll have a bed put in the sand at number nine. I'll even have them put in a portable toilet next to the trap."

Spike was smiling his Spike Smile. The wheels were turning... slowly after being up twenty three hours and about eight beers. "No, General. The sand is just fine. You can miss a bed. The head would be nice."
"Done. You want a shower set up, too?"

The General was still smiling. He was having fun.

Graham responded for Spike, who had missed the question. "I assure you General, a shower is completely unnecessary. Don't bother."

"OK. You guys are beat. Let's get to the heart of the matter which shouldn't take too long. I need to know what's wrong with these missions and what you think we need to do about it. So be candid. I need to know the real skinny. Hell, you guys are bulletproof, so you know you can say what you think."

They let him have it. No bullshit. The truth. Planning, mission tactics, Rules of Engagement. Everything. It was for them, but just as importantly, it was for the crewdogs that would follow them tonight, the next night, and so on. They couldn't tell a dumb as a brick Colonel anything because they were just crewdogs. Crewdogs didn't know anything. Crewdogs just flew, got shot at, and sometimes got shot down.

As SO-2 got further into it, the General became more and more pissed. They could see it. At the end, he was writing furiously while still listening. Hollywood was outstanding. He filled in any details they missed.

When they concluded, the General was somber. "I'll take care of this today. Right now. Listen, men, if you *ever* have any concerns like this again, I want you to call my office on this line."

He handed a piece of paper with a number on it to Hollywood.

"If I'm not there, you tell them to find me. No matter what time it is. No excuses. Find me. Is that clear?"

"Yes, sir."

"OK. I've heard what I needed to hear. Actually, I heard basically the same thing from General Charles at U-T earlier today. I trust Glenn implicitly, and now you tell me essentially the same thing. And I thank you again, gentlemen. Jack, this is a list of the names of the people on the new planning staff. I want to meet with the old staff at 1500 hours at base Ops, so I can fire their sorry asses personally. Make sure that moron McMoron is there. He's the chief idiot behind these mission plans. Scrub the mission plan for tonight and have a new one ready by PTOB. Get the new guys on it immediately. SAC is going to fight us, but we'll fight them. And find particularly dogshit assignments for McMoron, Reinhart, Kaplinsky, and Greenbaum. Latrine Officer on some remote EWS [early warning station] in the Aleutians might be appealing."

The General turned to the crew again. "At this point, you know how I feel, so I will not belabor it. I have taken the liberty to have new flight suits ordered for you from the same people that did this one [pointing to the one he had on] on a rush basis. You will need them for the interview."

Graham asked: "What interview?"

"I apologize. The one with CBS tomorrow. Your mission plan has changed. You'll launch at 2100 hours tomorrow. You're leading a Cell south."

The General turned to Dangle. "Thank you, Dick. I heard how you defended your crew against my morons. You did as a good officer should. Keep it up. That star is in reach."

The General stood, his aide called the room to attention, and he left.

Dangle was in heaven. He just had the Commander of 8th Air Force tell him he was a shoo-in if he didn't step on his dick.

Spike told Dick they would see him later, and oh, yes, they would need his staff car in a day or two to go get a steak at the Navy O'Club.

On the way out of Ops, they stopped by and got the details on their 21 December mission. They were flying a Cell at 2100 with two other crews that had flown on the 18th. Good guys. Sunny Nagahashi was leading the Hanoi Raid at 1700. The FAI crews were good. There was an Air Order newly posted on the board above the schedules. It was from Reinhardt and said that any crew that broke formation to avoid being hit by a SAM would be court-martialed. Graham took the primary crewdog stamp from his flight bag and gave the new AO the stamp of disapproval:

Bullshit Disapproved!

The order would have at least a dozen more disapprovals before the PTOB this afternoon, since almost every crew had a "BD!" stamp, and no one would obey an order that would get them killed.

Graham: "You know what, Spike? The planning guys should be made to have a drawing before every hairball mission that they did the planning for, and the winner gets to fly the mission in the lead aircraft. Maybe then we wouldn't see dumb ass orders like that get generated."

"B-dog, it will never, ever happen."

"Why not? Why the hell not?"
"Because then the planning guys would stop planning missions and the war would end. That's why. What we need to figure out is what causes this. Once we figure that out, this war will end, and we can all go home. Although, as you know, I personally would much rather go to Thailand. Let's get a chili dog for breakfast."

They stopped at Gilligan's Island for breakfast. It was an old trailer on cinder blocks just down from Ops. Breakfast, lunch, and dinner were always the same: Chili Dogs. Most crewdogs lived on Gilligan's chili dogs, which may have been why so many cockpits smelled so bad if you were a FNG. After a while, you grew used to it, and nothing smelled bad. GI was manned by a "Guap," the crewdog term for a Guamanian, that had two teeth visible, and might have been a man, or might have been a woman, no one could tell for sure, although there was a standing pool on both sexes. They even started a pool that it was neither and got twenty takers. Pools were big. Almost as big as 4-5-6.

THE FNG COLONEL

Spike had just gotten a beer and a chili donut. He had invented chili donuts when Gilligan's had run out of hot dogs one morning. They had subsequently put "chili donuts" on the menu. Other crewdogs actually ordered it at times - a source of great pride for Spike.

A kiwi full Colonel came up to Gilligan's and ordered coffee. Obviously a FNG. Only a FNG would drink Gilligan coffee. He'd probably be dead by the afternoon. Graham noticed the Colonel staring at him while he waited for his coffee, which took time, since they were sure the Guap made it from discarded grounds and iguana piss. Finally, the kiwi couldn't help himself. He was staring at Graham's fake nametag.

"Captain Yossarian!"

The minute Spike heard "Yossarian," he spit the beer he had just started to swallow at least five feet and quickly covered his mouth to avoid hysteria. Graham saw Spike's reaction out of the corner of his eye and almost lost it himself. "Captain Yossarian" was the primary protagonist in Joe Heller's brilliant war novel, *Catch-22*. It was a crewdog's second bible. Everybody in SAC had read it. *Except*, apparently, this Colonel.

The Colonel went on: "Your sideburns exceed the AFR limit, Captain Yossarian! In addition, your hair is unkempt, and you are uncovered (no hat) outside.

It is important in a combat zone that military decorum be maintained. Very important. Consider yourself on report, Captain."

"Yes, sir. I sure do agree with that. I'll get them trimmed right away. I have no idea what possessed me to allow them to get out of hand. My hat is in this bag, sir."

Graham opened the bag he was carrying and pulled out his helmet with the oxygen mask dangling and put it on.

The Colonel was not satisfied. "That is inappropriate, Captain. You should have appropriate head covering, and your hair should be neat when in uniform."

Spike still had his hand over his mouth, but he was audibly whimpering with laughter.

"Sir, my hair is in disarray because my head has been stuffed inside this helmet for the last fifteen hours. Would you like me to write down my name so you get it right on the report?"

"That's unnecessary, Captain Yossarian, I have it memorized. Now take off that helmet."

Graham complied with the order.

Spike was going to wet his pants. He ran, whimpering, toward the waiting crew bus. Graham noticed and bit his lower lip to keep from laughing, but when he responded he was smiling.

"Well, sir, in that case, I need to be going. I'm tired, and I need to get some rest. You can report me to the General if you like. He knows me and said that one more 'bad hair' report, and I would get a note of insubordination put on my permanent record. It's permanent for about eighteen months until I get out."

"Wipe that smile away, Captain. This is a serious matter. It's nothing to laugh about!"

"I would disagree, sir. Sorry, I have to catch that bus."

He turned away and almost jogged to the crew bus while biting his lip to avoid a laughing fit. The kiwi Colonel yelled after him, "Captain Yossarian! I did not dismiss you! You are not dismissed! Come back here immediately! You did not salute either! I am putting you on report for gross disrespect to a superior officer! Yossarian!! COME BACK HERE! YOU ARE INSUB..."

The Colonel's tirade faded as Graham ran on the bus and the bus driver, who had been set up by Spike, slammed the door and took off. There were six other crewdogs on the bus, and Spike had briefed them on the gist of the conversation. They were all laughing almost hysterically.

Spike commented between guffaws, "Can you imagine what will happen to that dufus when he puts one of the most famous characters in the United States Air Force and modern literature on report! I would do anything to be there when Dangle or Bracken read it!"

When Graham told them he recommended that he report him to the General directly, the whole bus went crazy all over again. This incident would become legend.

And it did…

For a long time, all that one of them had to yell at the Club or on the bus, or wherever, was "Captain Yossarian, your fucking hair is out of limits!"

And then everyone would jump in…

"Godammit, Captain Yossarian! Salute me when I'm proving I'm a fucking moron!!"

"Captain Yossarian, can you HEAR me!? Probably not since your hair is over your ears!!"

"I didn't dismiss you, Captain Yossarian! Come back here! You can't dismiss yourself, Yossarian!!'

The drunker the crewdogs got, the more the famous encounter would evolve:

"Captain Yossarian! You are disgusting!! You smell like shit, and you look like crap!! What do you do that gets you so disgusting, Captain!?"

"Dig holes!!? Whcre are you digging holes, Captain!! Are these holes authorized!!?

"SEA? SEA!!? Captain Yossarian, do you think I'm a fucking idiot!! You can't dig holes in the ocean!!"

"Yes what, Yossarian!? Yes, you admit you can't dig holes in the ocean, or yes you think I'm a fucking idiot!!?"

"ANSWER ME, YOSSARIAN!"

C.K. McCUSKER

HEARTBREAK HOTEL

D-Kid was driven back to the Hilton and put in a cell big enough for three or four guys. It was in the Heartbreak Hotel courtyard near the interrogation rooms. The guard brought in a bowl of cabbage soup, a half loaf of French bread, and weak tea. He was starving, so he ate everything.

He inspected his new cell. There was a bed board made of 2X4's covered with a rice mat on the floor. There were two thin cotton blankets, a towel, a mosquito net, some striped shorts, a short sleeved shirt, and another set of black pajamas. He also had an aluminum cup, a bowl, and a gook spoon. He found a tube of toothpaste and a bar of lye soap as well. At first he was surprised he had anything provided, and somewhat relieved, but then it dawned on him.

This doesn't look too good. It looks like they are planning an extended stay.

He was interrogated three more times before he was left to sleep. He had been up for over forty hours.

He was abruptly awakened when the door was swung open and the guards threw another bed board and gear into the cell. A tall black guy in prison garb was shoved into the cell, and they slammed the door behind him.

Bullshit. This is a trick they taught us at survival. This guy was either a turncoat collaborator or a gook ally. Nice try, Ho Chi Minh. Nice touch using a black man, but I'm not talking to this guy.

He moved his stuff in place and got organized on the other side of the cell. Neither spoke. Finally, the large black guy turned and introduced himself.

"I'm Major Alex Alessandro. I was in a B-52 up until awhile ago."

These gooks are good. The plant flies the same bird I did… bullshit.

"Did you fly a G, D, or F?"

Alex looked at him quizzically and his expression changed. "Wait a minute. Who the hell are you? How do I know you're not a plant? The F model is long gone, buddy. You should have done your homework a little better."

He might be real. "I went down in a G on 18."

"I was in a D on 18. Where are you based?"

I haven't told the gooks that yet and don't intend to, even though they already know… what the hell…

"Andersen."

"I'm out of U-Tapao."

Too bad the gooks don't know that I flew my first tour out of UT. Now I got him if he's a plant.

"What could you get at the Roach Coach?"

Alex broke into a smile. He was in prison with a crewdog. "A really bad chili dog."

Alex was an RN out of UT. The gooks had been shuttling between the interrogation rooms working on both Alex and D-Kid.

"They asked me if I was a Mexican, and I said no. Then they had a hard time asking me what I was so I said 'OK, guys, I'll give you one but only one. I'm black. Geniuses.'"

They both cracked up and went on to compare notes on the gook interrogation techniques. They told Alex he was old and not worth much so killing him would be easy. Alex used that against them to say that he couldn't remember anything technical about the bombing system because he was too old. Alex thought that D-Kid's "celestial navigator" bullshit was brilliant. They both settled into a fitful sleep but were awakened with the B-52 strikes coming back. They both smiled at each other and gave a thumbs up. The gooks couldn't take constant BUFF strikes. The population would go nuts.

We're going home sooner than later if this shit keeps up… soon, Robbie, soon… God bless you.

CHAPTER XI: NOT DEAD, YET

SLUGGO SHOWS UP

"Gentlemen! Gentlemen! Or should I say certified, bonerfied, kiss ass, order breaking, fucking war heroes! Time to get up! up! up! We have food to eat, booze to drink, lies to be told, news to relate, women to miss, and in your case, more asses to kiss! Up, boys! Into the Wild Gray Overcast!"

Graham looked at his watch. It was 1830. They had been asleep about six hours. "Sluggo, you little shit. We flew yesterday as opposed to your sorry ass. Go away. Annoy some other crew. Oh… that's right… you're banned from all other crew quarters. Well go up to the Club and talk to yourself in the mirror. At least you might listen. Go away."

Graham rolled over, but he knew it was hopeless. Sluggo would harass them until they got up to beat the shit out of him. Then he would talk them out of it, but they would be up. So why fight it? Graham got up and threw on some shorts and a golf shirt. Spike was getting dressed, and Hollywood came around the corner.

Sluggo continued: "Great news, Gentlemen! Sergeant Smolensky, The Great Rumor Monger in my employ, has related some choice tidbits right off the toilet! Number one, easily confirmed right here, is that you inept aviators, who flew lead by accident yesterday, used my patented take-off maneuver, which was in your case necessitated by poor pilotage; encountered Migs due to Bulldog's traditionally misguided navigation; fucked up the bomb run due to Spike's ineptitude; broke formation in order to avoid becoming deceased; diverted to a target of opportunity which would normally be cause for immediate execution; saved some Senator's kid thereby saving your asses; threw your Bible thumping Nose Pick off the aircraft prior to landing; kissed General Andrews' ass so hard that all your lips are chapped; got Andrews to fire the entire 8th Air Force Moron Staff; and last, but most importantly perhaps, wangled your way into flying a milk run tomorrow and henceforth for the duration because you are the new national treasure! Tell me, boys! Is this or is this not the absolute and accurate truth regarding your exploits of 19 December?!"

Spike was awake. "It's all true. Every last word. Except you missed some. You should fire Smolensky. Now get out. Fuck you very much."

"Missed some, Spike? Oh but I doubt it. You mean about the fake CBS news interview that your new personal Senator arranged for you tomorrow? No, no. In fact, one of my subsidiaries is bidding on the sound contract as I speak. If we win it, everyone that watches Cronkite the night you are on will think they suddenly went deaf."

"Leave, Sluggo. Depart. We'll hide from you at the Club later."

"Ah. But boys that would be aviators, I have additional tidbits that may well be of great value as they relate to the race to become Top Kiss Ass of the Air Force, and I might add at little additional charge, the fate of Ivory One, whom you caused to crash last night in their futile, albeit wise, effort to avoid flying within fifty miles of you guys."

The "charge" he was talking about was of course daqs. Graham went to their new refrigerator that was courtesy of the Coward Quarters and got what he needed. In minutes he would have the crewdog elixir in everybody's hand. Sensing payment, Sluggo went on while Graham was grinding drinks.

"Yes indeed, Gentlemen. Had it not been for the heroics of The Wildman (whom as you will recall, I personally Liza Doolittle'd from a quiet, competent, hard working pilot into the fine example of moral decay that you will see tonight) you might well have fully cornered the Kiss Ass Market and walked away with the USAF Oscar for Biggest Lips."

Spike: "Bite me, Sluggo."

Sluggo went on. "It seems that he executed a controlled crash landing at Clark. Got in a fight with a Colonel That Will Be Cold and through following strict orders that I personally gave him, called CINC SAC directly from their Command Post, woke him up for effect (another tip I gave him), and relayed a tale that was properly embellished to the point of heroics to the Chief Cheese himself. As a result of his controlled whining, the Colonel in question is now slated for a position more suited to reinforce his love of Pilipeen warmth, and The Wildman is, as I speak so eloquently, winging his way back to Guam and a hero's welcome no doubt."

"BFD, Sluggo."

"Oh yes it is a BFD. Did I forget to mention that he is winging in CINC PACAF's personal T-39? What an oversight on my part! It would seem that The Wildman is kissing an ass with four stars tattooed on it, versus yours that has a mere three. I thought I trained you to be more discriminating. Shoot for the top, guys! Or in this case his bottom."

Hollywood: "If we pay for your commercial ride home, will you go?"

"What!? And leave you guys defenseless? Without capable instruction? It would be remiss, if not criminal, for me to accept such a kind, yet unreachable, offer. You know what, my burdens? I almost forgot one last thing about The Wildman. Yes, indeed. Nearly forgot. He's coming back as a *Major*."

Spike seemed to go into shock when the two words Wildman and Major reached his ears. Graham was just stunned, but he knew that if anybody could pull it off, it would be Wildman.

Spike was incredulous. "Sluggo, you are a lying, bullshitting piece of crap. There's no way that crazy little shit could make Major years ahead of his eligibility. No way."

"Spike! I take umbrage at your insinuation that my information is flawed in any way. I assure you that Sergeant Smolensky's information is flawless at least 70% of the time that he's sober, which is about 50% of the time. In this particular case, his source is none other than the senior NCO of the Wing at Clark who is one of his old drinking buddies which, I might add, is a considerable population. The Wing NCO called Smolensky to get his recipe for homemade Kahlua and passed this tidbit along. It is indeed true."

Spike wasn't swayed. "You dwarf midget little turd. How in the hell could Wildman pull that off? I don't even think it's legal for Christ's sake. There's no way that jerkoff gunner of yours has got it right this time. No way."

"But Spike, I assure you it is true. Absolutely true. You just have a hard time accepting such a magnificent job of ass kissing was within the grasp of The Wildman because it took you twelve years and two attempts to reach what will no doubt be the pinnacle of your military achievement. Indeed, it seems that Wildman got into a very big dispute with some asshole Wing Commander upon crashing his bird on his runway in a successful attempt to save his crews' asses, as well as his own. He demanded that he be connected with CINC SAC personally which was accommodated by the Base CO who apparently had no great admiration for the Wing asshole either."

Spike: "CINC SAC? Now I am positive that you are full of shit. Nobody calls CINC SAC directly. Especially a lunatic like the Wildman."

"You just negated your own assumption, Major Minor. It is for that condition precisely that Wildman would call CINC SAC. He is just crazy enough to do it. Add to that he is one of my better protégés, and you have the necessary ingredients that would initiate the call. He apparently woke the CINC up, no less, and described his own incredible heroics, which I'm sure were embellished to the point of Oscar contention. The outcome was that the CINC promoted him on the spot to your mediocre rank. A battlefield promotion, if you will, that is indeed quite legal and binding. The Wing CO, by the way, was removed and re-assigned to someplace very cold."

Graham was curious. "Re-assigned in command of what?"

"The cold, Bulldog. He is Commander of the Cold for as long as it remains cold, which apparently where he's going is forever. His official title is 'Snow Removal Officer' which he understandably attempted to keep quiet but to no avail since his Wing NCO saw the order transmission. It was, indeed, a very long fall from grace."

Spike was still not a believer. "That's horseshit, you little turd, and when I confirm that it's horseshit, I'm going to pound your sorry dwarf ass for spreading horseshit."

Hollywood disagreed. "You know what, Spike? Sluggo's right. If anyone other than Sluggo could pull off a battlefield promotion directly from CINC, it's The Wildman. Besides, it's too bizarre *not* to be true. He's a Major now, so get used to it."

Graham delivered the bad news. "You assholes depleted our entire daq supply in a new record time, so I suggest we adjourn to the Club or risk sobriety. We can hear about Ivory One over there."

THE POST-STRIKE CLUB

Graham's announcement emptied the room very quickly. They took their remaining daqs with them and, as always, flagged a crew bus. This was against AFR something or other, but so was carrying booze around. Now that Thump had gone to Ya-Ya Land, the crew as a whole pretty much subscribed to a policy of breaking as many of the bullshit AFRs as they could manage to encounter. Spike, having a Doctorate in such activity, would guide and mentor their efforts. Besides, if they got caught by some do-gooder that they couldn't intimidate to the point of near hysteria, they were now "bulletproof." They got to the Club, and there was a large corner table open in the main bar, as usual. This was the choicest table in the main bar, if not throughout the Pacific. It should never be open, especially not at 2000 hours. This opportunity always presented itself when they were not flying and would always astound and or irritate subsequent arrivals. Only full Colonels and above could reserve a table in the main bar. No one could figure out how they always ended up with table nine, since whenever they came in ahead of them it was always posted as "reserved."

It *was* reserved.

For them.

MSgt. Roy "Cowboy" Rogers was in charge of both the main dining room and the main bar. He had an addiction to fine Cuban cigars. Amazingly, Sluggo had a fine Cuban cigar supply that was never ending. Spike, Bulldog, and Wildman paid Sluggo a nominal fee each week, and the table remained on permanent reserve on no fly days. On fly days, they let it go so as to not arouse suspicion. They had the same arrangement if they wanted to enjoy fine dining in the main room, but they had to call ahead by an hour or two.

Flight suits were not allowed in the main bar because the local Officer's Wives Club, which was comprised of some powerful kiwi wives, had lobbied to have them banned to the back bar only. The wives didn't like aviators. To them they were rude, crude, obnoxious, and too boisterous. That being true, the crewdogs put on civilian clothes which didn't have name tags so that the wives couldn't complain to their husbands when the crewdogs reminded them that they were fat and ugly. They were officers, if not gentlemen, so they used some degree of restraint in their comments. The OWC really hated crewdogs to the point of trying to get them *and* their flight suits banned from the main bar and dining room entirely. The flight suits passed. The crewdog part didn't. But the crewdogs found out about it and redoubled their efforts to insult the wives to the point of tears. Fat tears. The wives tried to time their meetings and visits to avoid aviators, but that didn't work since crews flew around the clock, and 8 AM could be their cocktail hour if they flew a night strike. The wives really grew to hate aviators with an almost a maniacal passion. The crewdogs enjoyed that enormously.

Besides, all they did was fly. And they smelled bad in flight suits because they perspired. The OWC "hubbies" were in charge of the Base Exchange, or the parts Depot, or the Maintenance Squadron. They *didn't* perspire. Ever. And they never got shot at.

All the crewdogs did was fly and get shot at.

The guys got to their table, and the reserved sign disappeared along with Cowboy. He also had a package under his arm that Sluggo had brought with him. The bartender brought over a large tray full of black Russians, the only thing about Russia that they liked. Russia was the enemy, but Russia wasn't nearly as dangerous as China. They were all fairly expert on certain aspects of each culture. In their "old" jobs, they were "nuclear deterrents," and they had targets in those countries depending on what targets the Wing was assigned. The crews would have to brief their targets to the Wing CO about three times a year. Those briefings included some details on the cultural aspect of the population. Graham never understood why. If they got to the point of getting shot down over their respective countries, there wouldn't be any population left.

Sluggo sipped his Black Russian and said nothing. The little turd was teasing. It was habitual.

Graham pushed. "Ok, Sluggo... what happened to Ivory? Cut the shit, or we'll beat you."

Spike hit Sluggo hard on the shoulder. This was crewdog shit. It was important. Sluggo sensed hostility so he decided to get on with it. "My buddy is the Squadron Ops officer for the F-4 squadron at NKP. That's where they are."

Graham stopped him. "They can't be. The runway's too short."

Sluggo: "They didn't *land* there. They *crashed* there. Let me explain with clarity, Bulldog. Even you will understand this feat of heroic airmanship that you guys caused to happen. They were lead out of U-T and took a SAM right before TOT. They couldn't juke at all since they were seconds away from release. The SAM was a little off track, so they lucked out and didn't get fireballed. The SAM took out the starboard engines and caused all kinds of other problems, but the AC, a guy named Tom "Bozo" Smith was still able to fly it... kinda. He had some hydraulic problems, so it was very hard for him to turn so he can't go feet wet. He's also slowly losing altitude, and he has to go west. The fire goes out, and they decide to try to get to Thailand, for obvious reasons. The Nav gets them pointed to NKP. They get to Thailand, and they are down to 7000. It feels like the bird is starting to break up. They try the gear at 5000 feet and nothing. So they decide their only option is to get as close to NKP as they can and punch. They're down to 3500 and about ten clicks east according to the Nav, so they go. They all punch in order, and they all get out."

Sluggo was amused by his own recreation of the NKP events and gleefully went on.

"The Radar, a Captain Beechamp, came down and landed on a road! No shit! The whole place is jung loaded with two steppers [poisonous snakes so potent that if you are bitten, you take two steps and you are dead], and there's only one road to or even near NKP and this guy landed on it! There was no wind so he got up, pulled in his chute, and rolled it into a ball - don't know why he didn't dump it - and started walking what he thinks is west. The bird went in, and he saw the fire glowing in the jung."

Sluggo paused for effect. "He was not walking five minutes when he saw headlights coming down the road toward him. He started waving at the headlights, and as it came up he recognized it as a damn Baht Bus [a highly decorated Toyota pick-up truck]! No shit! He landed on a road and up comes a baht bus at four in the morning. He got in, there weren't any passengers, and he said 'NKP! NKP! Lao-Lao, go like fucking wind!' The zip drove him right to the front gate! He got out and walked toward the gate, and the sky cop yells at him to halt. He asked for a password! A password! He's standing there in a flight suit and helmet, holding a parachute, and this sky cop wants a password! Obviously

Beechamp doesn't know the NKP password, so he said in a very heavy southern accent something to the effect of, 'Boy, I'm Captain Beechamp of *The* United States Air Force and *The* Strategic Air Command. Don't give me any of that *halt who goes there* crap, boy. I mean shit, do I sound like a damn commie, boy? That fire you see off in the distance is my airplane. It just got shot down. I don't know the gall damn password 'cause my base is U-Tapao. I need the following, son: five baht for the bus, no, make it ten, he's a good ol'boy, six bottles of Jack Daniels, six glasses an' some good ice, and a whole bunch of guys to go look for my crew in the jung. Make sure they bring those survival supplies with them in case one of 'em heard a snake. I need all this shit lao-lao chup ['right away buddy' in Thai]. Now open the gate, and get me some transportation!"

"The sky cop, already a proven idiot, called for some other sky cop who got transport for the crew dog. By mid-morning they found the entire crew, who were OK, except the Co had a broken arm from ejection. That's the no shit truth, directly from my buddy."

Spike: "Sluggo, you're not smart enough to invent a story like that, so this one I believe. Guys, a toast to the Ivory One crew. May they get sober when the war is over!"

They raised their glasses in toast. All of them hoping that they were that lucky when they get nailed. They would always fly lead. They were next.

SUNNY NAGAHASHI

They finished the toast and brought out the dice cup to play a little 4-5-6.

Blackjack and Lt. Colonel Jim "Sunny" Nagahashi walked into the front of the bar.

It was 2030, the main bar was jammed, and Sluggo was on. He yelled across the room, "Hey! Banzai Bob! Good to see your squinty little eyes, man. You boys come on over and take a seat! You can tell Blackjack about minority life in America!"

Sluggo thought the stares from the few non-crewdogs in the bar were wonderful. It was going to be a good night.

Spike saw Blackjack and turned to Sluggo. "Blackjack's back. That means that your bullshit Major is back too, unless he's gone into hiding for fear of blowing his bullshit story. You better get Cowboy over here and have the guys at table eight ejected for excessive consumption. We're going to need the table pretty quick."

"The Wildman will be here, Spike, and you can kiss my ass at sundown. The sundown created by the lights shining off his shiny new Major's leaves."

"Screw you, midget. Ain't gonna happen."

Spike took out one of his horrid little cigars and lit it. There was no pure oxygen available, so Graham grabbed it and put it into a glass of water that somebody who didn't know them had put on the table. Sluggo spotted Cowboy and waved him over. Sunny and Blackjack sat down.

Sunny was a Fairchild AC and a good friend of Graham's. He had two callsigns, which was very unusual. "Sunny" because he cheered everybody up and "Banzai Bob" because that's what he became after a few Black Russians. The gas bag Senior Officers went into cardiac arrest when a Captain called an Asian Lt. Colonel and Command Pilot "Banzai Bob." Sunny loved it.

Crewdogs generally got their callsigns for things they did, an attribute they had (good and bad), a physical characteristic, or even a play on ethnicity. "Blackjack" didn't refer to the game. Wildman's Nav was black and named Jack. It was natural, and Blackjack liked his callsign.

Spike overheard the guys at table eight protesting their ejection from the table, saying they were only drinking cokes. Cowboy flipped the rationale for their removal instantly. "Alcohol consumption is required in the Main Bar. If you gentlemen would like to drink cokes, you're welcome to move to the patio outside the Back Bar. Don't go through the Back Bar to get to the patio, you might get seriously injured. Go outside and around the Club to get there."

One of the guys was foolish enough to protest. "This is bullshit! First you said we have to leave because we drank too much, and then because we didn't drink at all. That's bullshit."

Big mistake. Obviously Jeeps. Maybe kiwi Jeeps.

Cowboy: "I just remembered that the patio is closed for repairs. Some coke drinkers broke the slate tiles with their heads. Sorry. You'll have to leave the Club entirely."

Cowboy waved his arm and from nowhere came two gigantic guys. The former residents at table eight decided to leave quietly.

Graham turned to Sunny: "I haven't seen you in a while, buddy. I assume you heard that they confirmed D-Kid as a POW?"

"Yes I did. Great news. They shouldn't break crew integrity on missions like this, or Bob would still be here. But what the hell should we expect from idiots?"

"You're lead at the Dance tomorrow night, right? Didn't you fly the 18 strike?"

"Yeah, I flew a Cell lead on 18. Bad ass hairball mission. Shit coming up everywhere. I saw Charcoal One take the SAM. I thought that no one got out of that bird. He fireballed in seconds. Bad stuff. Really bad. D-Kid's announcement stunned me. Thank God. I was lucky. I accelerated at the IP out ahead of the rest of my Cell. It seemed to work. I had maybe six after me. But they were just shooting at the walk of elephants and trying to get lucky. Hell, Bulldog, they have got to be running low on SAMs. I heard that you guys took a ton last night, too."

"We did. At least thirty at us alone. Scary shit, man. They may be running out, but don't count on it. Talk to Hollywood or Sluggo. They have tactics that work."

"I will. Can't hurt anyway."

Sunny turned and yelled across the table at Hollywood. Hollywood came over and they went and sat down at the newly reserved table eight.

Jim "Sunny" Nagahashi was a class act. He was a Japanese American who as a little boy had been imprisoned by his own country, along with his father, (a cardiac surgeon), his mother, and his older sister. In the hysteria that followed Pearl Harbor, the government rounded up Japanese Americans whose families in some case had gone back generations, forced them to sell their property at ten cents on the dollar, and moved them to "secure" living areas.

When he joined the Air Force to become a pilot, he took the qualifying tests for flight training and was sent to Navigator flight training instead of pilot training. His assignment was a holdover from WWII when the "most intelligent" were sent to Navigation because it was much more difficult intellectually than pilot training in some kiwi Doctor's opinion. Sunny aced UNT and served as a Navigator in B-47s.

After seven years, there was a pilot shortage because all the pilots were getting out and going to the airlines. Sunny applied for UPT and got in. He graduated number one in his class and could have had anything he wanted: fighters, bombers, trash haulers - anything. His love was SAC, and he chose a new bomber replacing the B-47, the B-52. Sunny was in the left seat (AC) in under a year and moved quickly in rank. He was promoted to Lt. Colonel two years below the zone. He was on a rocket. But he got unlucky.

He was assigned to a Squadron as Ops Officer, which meant that his own Squadron was his next ticket. The Wing CO, however, was an old gas bag Colonel that had flown toilet paper around the Pacific during the war. He *hated* Japs. He wouldn't sign off on any of Sunny's OERs [Officer Evaluation Reports] critical to a career unless the Squadron CO "properly evaluated" Sunny. The CO had no choice but to make Sunny's evals "less than perfect" or *his* evals would be downgraded by the Wing CO. Career survival.

Sunny got smart and volunteered for a crew again, but only at the base of his choice: Fairchild. The Wing CO signed off immediately to get rid of that "dirty Jap bastard." Sunny had actually overheard the CO refer to him as such at the Club. Sunny got his wish and went back to being a crewdog, but he moved fast and was head of StanBoard in four months. But his career was seriously damaged - bad OERs plus a step back. He would never accomplish his dream and pin on Eagles... or maybe, God willing, a Star someday. He was "a great guy and a good stick." If Sunny had a fault, it was his obedience to the "book." That's what kept him from being a "super great" stick.

The Pilipeeno band showed up at 2100. They were great. Only one guy in the band of six, the leader, spoke any English at all, but they sang everything you could think of in perfect English. The Beach Boys, The Beatles, Chicago, The Animals, Three Dog Night, Lovin' Spoonful, and more. They had an extensive repertoire, and they had *memorized* all the words. They opened with Chicago's "You've Made Me So Very Happy," which the crewdogs loved but hated because it reminded them of wives and girlfriends that were sitting back home alone. They followed with "Yellow River" which they mistakenly had memorized as "Yellow Reefer."

Since they were crewdogs, they could easily yell over the band. The band was nothing compared to eight engines. But it drove out most of the kiwis immediately. Spike and Graham ordered chili burgers from the Back Bar for everybody as soon as the spies left.

Hollywood and Sunny finished their strategy session, and Sunny came back and sat down. "Makes sense, Bulldog. If we dive at the SAMs we present a smaller profile, and we're much harder to nail, especially if they go ballistic again. But the new AO says we get CM'd [Court Martial] if we break. It also hurts our ECM [Electronic Counter Measures] if they're guided. I don't know. I'll talk to Sluggo."

Graham felt he needed to provide encouragement. "Are you nuts? What ECM? I have it on good authority, if there is one, that a G's ECM doesn't work worth a damn against SA-2's. The D's does, but we don't have the right black boxes for the Pick, and we aren't going to get them until after this shit is all over. And the AO? Shit. That's already been officially disapproved by the Crewdog Survival

Committee, of which I am a member, as you know. They can look at the radar camera shots after the mission, but what are they going to do? Court martial the entire squadron? Shit no they won't. Besides, the Colonel that issued that AO is on his way to some luxury assignment like Penguin Protection. Forget that stuff, buddy. They can't court martial dead men."

"I'll think about it, Bulldog. I'll discuss it with the crew."

"Suit yourself, Jim. But think it through carefully. It's your ass… and theirs."

Graham knew Jim was screwed. If he asked his crew, they would opt in favor of the book. That's the way it would be. They were *real* StanBoard instructors. They operated "by the book." They hadn't stolen the test. They actually *knew* what the book said. Except for Sunny, they were no good in the air – but they knew the book.

Graham noticed that Sunny seemed unusually introspective, *and* he wasn't drinking or gambling. In a few minutes he excused himself. "Good luck and God Bless, Sunny. See you in about thirty-six."

He waved.

THE FAKE MAJOR SHOWS UP

The band had just finished *Do You Believe in Magic* by the Spoonful when Graham spotted him through the fog of smoke. He was walking slowly toward the corner, no doubt to be seen well before he reached number nine. The Wildman. He was in uniform. A Class B uniform. [Class B was a short sleeve light blue shirt and Air Force blue trousers with rank, nametag, and Wings mandatory. Decorations were optional.] Wildman was wearing his ribbons with his shiny new Major leaves. What a nerd. A kiss ass nerd. Graham elbowed Spike, who was sitting next to him playing 4-5-6, and nodded toward Wildman.

Spike: "Why that little shit. It's true. There is no justice. No goddamn justice. I'm going to beat him senseless if he says a word."

Spike went back to playing.

Sluggo: "Hey, Spikeman! Look who's coming! MAJOR Wildman! Bite me, Spike! Smolensky is always right! Say hello to the Major, Spike!"

Wildman finally came up to table nine. No one acknowledged him. "Hi, guys! It's good to be back! Had a tough time going into the PI. Maybe you've heard. Hey, can I get into the game?"

Spike got up, walked the few feet to Wildman, grabbed the front of his shirt and ripped it open and then off. The Wildman was now standing in his undershirt and Class B trousers. In shock.

Spike: "Now you can. Now you're a crewdog again. Now you're welcome back. Sit down, and tell us about your adventure, punk."

A lot of Spike's reaction was based on his Black Russian intake level. But a lot was also based on his resentment of a system that allowed what had happened. Wildman's entrance with the Class B on, which we never wore, didn't help, even though it was meant as a joke. The Wildman assessed the situation quickly and decided not to continue what would have been a pretty bad fight, which Wildman would have won. Being sober helped that assessment. He sat down in Moondog's seat as Moondog had left to pee. Moondog was a junior Nav, a white bar, and he knew he was always at risk of losing his seat when he peed.

Wildman picked up his shirt, folded it, and put it over on table seven which was vacated when the band turned up the bass. "Spike, you shitbird. It was a joke! When have you even seen me in a Class B? Let alone with decs? You're buying me a new shirt just in case I ever wear it."

Graham added: "He's right, buddy. It was obviously a joke. You lost your sense of humor? The Wildman probably thinks his making Major on the deal was a joke himself. But when the system deals a windfall, our rules are to take it. The system almost never deals a windfall. It's designed to screw us most of the time. After all... we're scum. All we do is fly. Get over it, Spike. If the situation was reversed and you got popped to L/C, would you turn it down?"

Spiked smiled. Not the Spike Smile, a real smile. "I got away with it, didn't I? I ripped The Wildman's shirt right off his back, and he did squat. Those significant opportunities don't present themselves everyday, Bulldog. Congratulations, Wildman. It's not every day that a weenie of your magnitude makes Major. You're on your way, man. A rocket. In no time you'll be a staff full bull, and we'll hate your guts more than we do already."

"Bite me, Spike. When I make my first star, I'll have you executed. Would you please remind me of that? At this rate, I won't get to the star until late next year. Unless CINC wants to move that up. You never know what my good buddy wants to do. Might be sooner."

There was a break in the music. Sluggo stood up and turned toward the bar: "Barkeep! Barkeep! Mas Black Russians por favor! Ching! Ching! Lao-lao! Sawadee chup! [hurry, hurry! Go like wind! Goodbye (hello) buddy!] go like wind! Donde esta la celebracion? Esta aqiui! Lao-lao!"

A mixture of bad Thai and bad Spanish. Sluggo was almost captured by the Russians. He sat down and turned to Moondog. "Hey, Moondog. Since you insist on standing, why don't you go over to el baroso and get our Russians. Put them on Senor Wildman's tab. He's buying since he got promoted to fake Major. While you are there, check out the two guys standing at la baroso in the foreign flight suits, and report upon your return. Ching! Ching! Lao-lao, Lieutenant!"

Moondog hustled away. The Russians had a beachhead on Sluggo. He was now screwing up the gender and inventing the words in his Spanish vocabulary. He did that by just adding "oso" to English words.

Foreign flight suits at the Main Bar. They must be transient and not USAF. Those people were allowed at the bar. They didn't smell as bad as crewdogs, even if all *they* did was fly as well.

The Wildman started to recount his heroics. No one was listening. They had had enough heroics in the last 48 hours. They were there.

Moondog came back with a tray of Russians and put them on the table after he made another Jeep Co get up to make room for the tray. Moondog promptly stole the Jeep's seat. This kid was going places.

Moondog couldn't wait to report, the spotlight on him was rare. "They're Navy – 4 drivers I think. Seem like good guys. They were drinking real drinks and seemed to be insulting the bartender."

Sluggo: "We can't let combat aviators be left standing at the bar when we have a promotion party going on here wherein all drinks are free until all hours. Bluebird, since it is you that now insists on standing, go over and invite the guys to join us. Be quick about it! Lao-lao hasta la vista!"

4 drivers. Damn. They might know about our idiot gunner. If they did, it would no doubt come up at some point. Maybe they are pussies and won't come over.

Spike elbowed Graham. "4 drivers. We're screwed. They will know."

"Don't worry about it. Blame it on Major Wildman."

"Great idea."

Spike hit a 4-5-6, covered, for about two grand. Now everybody else was pissed. Not a good time for their Navy comrades. Bluebird was smart. He knew that Sluggo was beyond S-2, and he was against the wall. Spike and Graham were on the outside. He brought them to Spike.

Graham got up, as did Spike. "Hi, guys. Captain R.J. Graham... Bulldog. This drunken asshole Major or my right is…

Spike interrupted. "Major Spike Wilson. Please join us. You guys or your brethren probably saved our asses last night. We're buying... or rather our new fake Major, Captain Goldstein, is buying. Please take a seat... Get up, Moondog!" Spike was surprisingly sober.

The guy with pilot wings responded first, shaking hands. "Thanks Spike… Bulldog. I'm Paul Denner. We'd love to join you. We've rarely been on an airbase that doesn't float. No booze onboard, so we have a low tolerance, as you might expect. We're here testing how low. Thanks for the hospitality."

The guy wearing Navigator Wings jumped in, also shaking hands. "Bulldog... Spike, Don Hulbert... 'Sparky.' What's that dark stuff you're drinking?"

Graham responded: "Enemy cocktails designed to kill us. But they're good for you until then. It's also a long standing crewdog tradition. Maybe six months now. We're steeped in tradition as you must be fully aware. Please be seated, and enjoy."

Spike: "Lieutenant Denner. No call sign? Like me?"

Sparky responded for him. "It's 'Dinero,' but sometimes he doesn't answer to it. I'll never understand why. He's worth almost a million pesos."

Spike turned to Dinero. "You guys are F-4 drivers, right?"

Dinero: "Yes. We're off the Enterprise. The ship is en route to the Gulf [of Tonkin] at flank speed to support Linebacker II, which I guess you guys are starring in. We were up on some exercises this afternoon when we had a mechanical... a get down as quickly as you can mechanical. Andersen was closer than the ship, so here we are."

"How long are you here? Can they fix your bird?"

"We lucked out. The Depot here just happened to have the part we need. We're driving an F-4E, which is the newest rev, and you guys fly them out of NKP. There was a parts shipment en route to them that just happened to have what we needed. We were loaned a B-52 crew chief, and he assembled the mechanics to put them back in shape. They were still working on her when we left for dinner, but Sergeant Mazerowski said they would have her ready to go by late tomorrow."

Spike choked on his drink when he heard No Luck's name. Graham's eyes got big. The Navy guys noticed.

"Something wrong, Spike? You guys seem a little alarmed at what I just said."

Spike was still gagging. Graham jumped in. "No. No... not alarmed. I'm sure that your bird will be put back together just fine. Our maintenance guys are the best. They have to be... there's not a single B-52 on that ramp that's less than fourteen years old, and they all have way too many hours airborne. No. We know Mazerowski, and he's used to solving problems. Real used to it. Here. Try a Commie Cocktail."

Graham handed both Dinero and Sparky a fresh Russian.

Spike recovered. "Bulldog's absolutely correct. Mazerowski can almost fix anything. He's really something else." Spike wasn't lying to their Navy brethren. No Luck could almost fix anything. When he was done, it was *almost* fixed.

Graham asked Sparky: "Your callsign is fitting, Sparky. You look like a very large spark plug that you best not screw with, and your partner is no little guy either. We won't ever underestimate Naval aviators. Are you guys going to fly MIG CAP or Low Boy? You know yet?"

Sparky had played football at Northwestern and was a very tough guy, but was also very charming. "Both, I think. We'll know more when we get on station." He grinned. "Either way, I hope we don't have to cover for you guys because if we do, as you know I'm sure, the reason is not good."

Graham was concerned that they *knew*. "Yeah, your help means Migs on our ass and my gunner can be a bit inept..."

Dinero: "Can I get one of these Russians with gin?"

"Sure."

Graham turned to Moondog: "Moondog, can you get the Lieutenant a Russian made with gin? Make that three so we don't have to reload in ten minutes. Thanks."

Spike asked Dinero: "You guys want to learn how to play 4-5-6? You'll clean up when you get back onboard. By the way, when is your scheduled TO tomorrow? I assume you're going west?"

"2115 right now and, yes, the ship will be well west of Guam by then... and sure we'll play awhile."

Spike: "Hey, Hollywood! These guys are out at 2115 tomorrow. Let's see if we can hook up after climb-out."

Hollywood gave a thumbs up. They were on a cheese mission anyway.

Spike: "Is that OK with you guys? I should have asked first, but we've never seen a 4 up close and personal while airborne. The forecast is great. High overcast and full moon. Can you guys cover it?"

Sparky: "Sure. We'd like to hook up as well. Never seen a BUFF airborne that close, either. If we're fifteen behind, it might take about two minutes for us to intercept. Will you be at altitude yet?"

Spike, smiling: "Yeah. Screw you too. We'll be there. Don't get lost in your go cart. Now for 4-5-6. A simple game of chance, only the chance is removed to avoid confusion."

They spent the next two hours teaching their new Navy buddies how to lose. But they were clearly learning. Both won a couple of rolls now and then.

The band was really on. The band's lyrics recall started to suffer as the evening wore on and the booze started to take effect, but they would hum as necessary. Toward 0100 they gave their Navy buddies back their $500 or so. They protested, but Spike insisted, adding that play from there on was final. No returns.

The band went into the crewdog anthem: The Animals classic, *We Gotta Get Out of This Place*. All crewdogs always sang along with the chorus:

We gotta get outta this place!
If it's the last thing we ever do!
We gotta get outta this place!
Girl ... there's a better life for me and you ...
Reprise ... about four times depending on how drunk out it was ...

A MINOR SKIRMISH

The Main Bar doors across the room burst open, and a flood of guys in flight suits poured in. They had blue patches on their chests with a safety net over the blue [actually it was a globe patch and the white lines were the longitudes and latitudes].

MAC guys. Military Airlift Command.

Trash Haulers! In flight suits! In their bar! And they were clearly ripped. Shit. The back bar must have been left unguarded by crewdogs. The Trash Haulers outnumbered them by a lot.

The biggest trash hauler led their pack. They walked slowly toward table nine. Sluggo said something to Moondog, and he headed over to talk to Pico (the band leader). The band immediately struck up the lyric to *Oh I Wish I Were an Oscar Meyer Weiner* as the trash haulers approached their tables.

Dinero to Graham, Sparky listening intently: "What the hell is up? Who are those guys? Crewdogs?"

"Hell no. They're trash haulers. They train to leave. They fly in and deliver soap to Saigon and then leave. They are not our type."

Sparky: "You think they want to fight!? Oh, Boy!"

Dinero: "Calm down, Sparky. This is a crewdog fight. Do not interfere unless they interfere with us. It wouldn't be fair." Dinero knew his RIO well, and he could have single handedly beaten the crap out of the entire entourage of Trash Haulers unless they shot him first - then maybe only half of them.

The big trash hauler approached table nine. "You fucks beat up some of our guys a few weeks ago in that shithole bar in the back. We don't think that is appropriate. We think that you should apologize. Oh, I see that you expected this and hired some Navy pukes to protect you."

Dinero turned to Sparky: "Do you think that calling Naval aviators "pukes" would constitute interference?"

"No question about it." Sparky stood up, grinning at the trash haulers.

"Then they just interfered."

Sluggo to the big trash hauler: "Un momento, senoras. You guys know that flight suits are not allowed in the Main Bar. But then, I guess Doctor Dentons are OK. You should vamanos pronto, or you will have to change your diapers, kiddies. Lao-lao Ching Ching. Sawadee Senoritas."

The big trash hauler was brave. He had the crewdogs outnumbered big time. He was also drunk as shit. Disgraceful.

"You guys have been making toothpicks out of trees in the Delta and claim to be combat crews. Hell, you're just bomb disposal units."

The guy had obviously not heard what was happening; even as he was speaking, tonight's flight was inbound. But it was too late.

Sluggo was little, about 5' 6", but he was as fast as lightening and really *nasty* in a fight. He was up and over the table almost immediately and launched himself into the big guy. He knocked him down since he hit him so high and then started pounding on his face.

Sparky was in a state of profound joy. He picked up the next biggest guy and threw him over the bar. Then the whole bar erupted. Spike and Graham high-lowed a guy who went down trying to break a table with his head on the way. Dinero took people out with plain punches. Wildman, like Sluggo very quick, just kicked guys in the balls. Sparky continued to throw people across the room, none of whom got up. The band stopped playing *Oscar Meyer* and tried to protect their equipment.

In less than five minutes, the sky cops came through the doors. They had been tipped off - Cowboy no doubt. But it was over. The trash haulers lost badly. Really badly. Some of them had slipped out, but most were a mess. A few were still trying to fight, but they were basically helpless. The sky cops stopped any remaining activity, and they cuffed Sparky, probably because they saw him throw the last guy. Right after the sky cops subdued everybody, Dangle came in wearing a flight suit and slippers. Major pissed. Major, major pissed. Ambulances started to show up, with sirens blaring. A crowd gathered in spite of the hour. Spike had their two Navy buddies get down behind them, and Sluggo called Cowboy over.

He gave Cowboy instructions. "Getoso mis compardres de la agua outoso aqui … sawadee chup. Lao-lao! Imediatemente! Comprende? Ahora mi amigo!"

"Yes, sir! Right away!"

Cowboy signaled for the guys to quietly follow him. A sky cop saw what was going on and started toward them. Wildman and Graham got in front of him and started listing charges that the trash haulers committed against them, pointing specifically to the "villains" who were conveniently laying on the floor for an easy ID.

Sparky was still in handcuffs, but the fleet sailed.

Spike grabbed a white bar sky cop and then picked on a dazed trash hauler young Lieutenant. "You guys came over here and started this, didn't you! That fat turd on the floor over there was the instigator, wasn't he!"

Spike was yelling. Dangle was yelling at other guys. The sirens were still on. The medics were all over the place. The kid gave in: "Yes, sir. It was Major Lawrence's idea. We planned it in the back bar. I didn't think it was a good idea, but we had to go when the Major and his guys went. The bomber guys had beaten up some of our guys a couple of weeks ago. We just wanted to harass these guys. It didn't work out too well. That Navy guy threw guys across the room!"

Spike was Spike: "Your guys threw the first punch, didn't you! Go on, Lieutenant. Tell them now, and you'll get leniency. Otherwise it's an Article 15 [a reprimand that goes in your record] for you, buddy. If that happens, your career is over... over!"

"I guess that's right. Yes, sir."

Spike to the sky cop, who was taking notes: "There you go, Lieutenant. A full confession. Congratulations."

The Spike Smile.

The sky cop Lieutenant told the trash hauler squealer to sit down, turned, and walked over to Dangle. "Sir, I have a full confession from one of the MAC officers. Their... er, the bomber crews were attacked by the MAC crews. The bomber crews simply defended themselves."

Dangle: "Alright, Lieutenant. If you're satisfied, place the MAC crew members under arrest - at the hospital if necessary. Instruct our crews to return to quarters and remain there until further notice."

Dangle was turning to leave. "Oh, Lieutenant. Except FAI SO-2. They have an appointment at 1300 tomorrow. And any crew scheduled to fly will meet that schedule. I want the names of all the MAC crew Squadron Commanders immediately. Also, MAC crews are banned from our base recreational facilities until further notice."

"But sir, what do we do with them? The brig? Confinement at the VOQ [visiting officers quarters]?"

"When they are well enough, they will personally pay for any damages to the Club, and then they will leave. They are good at that. Thank you, Lieutenant."

As they were leaving, Graham commented to Spike: "Shit, that Sparky guy is one of the toughest guys I've ever seen in a fight. He was *throwin'* guys across the room!"

Spike: "Yeah, B-dog, I'm glad he was on our side. Maybe we try to get him transferred to USAF. What was his name again?"

"Hulbert. Don Hulbert."

"I'll speak to the general after the interview tomorrow. I don't know if it's legal to steal Navy guys but then a lot of what we do is not legal, and traditions are important to maintain."

THE CBS INTERVIEW

Sluggo, Spike, Wildman, Hollywood, and Graham all crammed into a sky cop car and got a ride back to Monsoon Mansion. They hadn't reached mandatory crew rest time yet, but were well beyond S-2 so they stole a bottle of Jack Black for a nightcap from E-05s' house since E-05 were flying and the house was unguarded.

Spike was uncomfortable about the interview. If it aired, some of his ex-wives might find out where he was. Spike could be very charming with the ladies. The problem was that he continued to be charming to any and all ladies, regardless of his marital status at the time. Graham didn't know how many "Ex's" Spike had, but they were numerous.

Spike: "What the hell do we say at this interview today? I don't even like CBS. Whatever we say, they'll edit it to say what they want us to say. The commie pukes."

Sluggo couldn't help but offer his unsolicited opinion. "Spikeman, how about 'Thanks for supporting the NVA. Without your unfair and unbalanced broadcasting they couldn't have done it.' Shit, I can hear Cronkite's broadcast when he breaks the start of Linebacker 2: 'And last night in North Vietnam, over 5000 B-52 bombers attacked an empty warehouse next to an orphanage in defenseless Hanoi. Fortunately, no orphans were seriously injured according to American patriot and peace activist Jane Fuckya. In possibly related news, a couple of American airmen are reported AWOL. And that's the way it is, Tuesday, December 19th, 1972.' The national news organizations are going to run this country in the future. Remember that, gentlemen. Sluggo predicted it."

Hollywood: "The problem with that prediction, Sluggo, is that you may be uncharacteristically correct. Let's bag it, guys. We'll discuss strategy in the morning."

Graham added: "Let's be careful. Both Dangle and Andrews stood up for us. We do a Joe Bob to that TV interview, and we screw them. Keep that in mind. See ya, Sluggo. Good luck at the Dance tomorrow."

"Thanks. You guys see the mission schedule? They've added two more waves. Close to 50 birds including Ds will be out of here and God knows how many out of U-T. The good news is that ups the odds of our not taking a SAM. Bad news is that it ups the odds that *someone* will. Might be a costly night. What the hell, now that you guys are certified, Senator protected, TV star war heroes, you don't need to worry about that anymore. See you on 22. Make sure our table's reserved. I got a feeling we'll need it badly. Good night, heroes."

Sluggo was envious and throwing a shot. A shot they hadn't thought of. They were not only bulletproof in their activities - they were also bulletproof from bullets. May as well go DNIF.

Sluggo left. Graham raised everybody's new concern. "He's right! We're now official war hero pussies! A few more runs Downtown by the guys and we won't be crewdogs anymore. We'll just be scum sucking pussies. Shit. We may as well move to Coward Quarters. Hollywood, you got to get to Dangle fast - Andrews if necessary. If you don't, someone's going Downtown that shouldn't."

Hollywood: "Yeah. I agree. I'll go see Dangle first thing. Spike, you're coming with me."

Spike didn't answer. He didn't need to. He'd be there, even if Hollywood hadn't decided to go.

DANGLE'S OFFICE

Spike and Hollywood walked into Dangle's office at 1000, unannounced, and closed the door. Dangle was on the phone. He didn't look surprised. He finished his conversation, which was clearly with Andrews, with "Yes, sir" and "Good day, General."

"Spike and Captain Noland. What an expected surprise. Don't worry. We had the whole thing last night blamed on the MAC boys. It should all be taken care of, according to my sources - not just the poor Lieutenant that Spike intimidated masterfully. In any event, gentlemen, you're off the hook as usual. Need my keys? No... no, that's right. Tonight, you're flying a cheese run, as you crewdogs call them. It's a little too close to the DMZ, but we'll have Low Boy and MIG CAP up for you guys."

Spike: "What the hell, Colonel!? Low Boy and CAP for a run south? What is going on? Shit! We never have air cover for a run south! We didn't even have cover when we went up against Vinh a few weeks ago and we had MIGS in the air, and the 'SAM shooter of the Year' on site!"

"Spike, Spike. You are a protected commodity! You are "bulletproof" to use the General's term. Bulletproof both on the ground, *and in the air*. If you guys get blown up, it would be a disaster. After the interview this afternoon and the airing in a few days on CBS, you will be National heroes - to the extent that can be possible in the atmosphere back home - so probably for the duration, you are flying - but in a 'safe' environment. You're lucky, guys. You broke an order that should have resulted in all of you being court-martialed and literally sent to prison despite that order being absolutely asinine. So relax, and enjoy it. Hell, you may go home early!"

Hollywood: "No. No, Colonel. That will not happen. None of that will happen. You will schedule us with the rest of the crews. We *will* fly against Downtown, as lead, until this offensive ends. We are crewdogs, and we will always be crewdogs. We fly when they fly. We take the same risks they do. We will not negotiate this."

Dangle was shocked. "Jesus Christ, Captain! Pew and I COMMAND this Wing! You dare to give me an order! Who the hell do you think you are!? I saved your asses, gentlemen! You will do as you are ORDERED! YOU ARE DISMISSED!"

It was getting very heated very fast. Spike intervened calmly: "Hold on. Turn off the burners. Everybody needs to understand the situation... with all due respect, Colonel."

Dangle calmed down too quickly. He was smart enough to be *afraid* of them.

"Please listen carefully to our position. We want to fly with our guys. That's one of the reasons we are here. If we have to fly cheese runs, or worse, milkers, while the rest of the guys get shot to shit... No way, sir. No fuckin' way. Hell, we'll volunteer for a Kama [Kamikaze] mission like the one you gave us dropping leaflets off the coast of the North in October. Shit! We didn't have any cover for that dickweed mission! You can't do this to us. It can't happen. *We have to go back into normal rotation...* please, sir."

"Major, Captain, I'm sorry, but this is way above me. It's above the General. It may even be in the Oval office. I can't do a damn thing, guys. My Wings are clipped."

Spike held the Ace. "We understand, Colonel, so we will take it to a new level ourselves. You tell whoever that needs to know what we are about to tell you. You don't have much time. We have an interview with CBS in about two hours and twenty minutes. If we don't get written confirmation that we will go back into normal rotation at least thirty minutes prior to that interview, we will give them an interview that will make Joe Bob's job on the Times seem like a sermon. That's not a threat, sir. It's a promise. And there's no way that the dicks that are causing this can stop that because the press already knows who we are. When my name hits the paper and I hit the airwaves, if the real Spike isn't there, my ex-wives will blow the whistle. So you can't use kiss ass ringers. We're serious. Bulldog and I will write Joe Bob Two, and the powers that are will go nuts. On the other hand, if we get a written guarantee to go back on rotation, we will be just wonderful."

Dangle: "I interpret that as a threat, Major. No matter what you say."

"No, sir. Don't confuse blackmail with a threat. It insults our portfolio."

"Do you realize that you may be trying to blackmail the President of the United States!? Are you nuts!?"

"Yes. And why not? He's trying to kill us."

Hollywood: "We are all onboard with this, sir. We have to be. Please let them know in time. Thanks. We know you'll do what you can, sir. Rather, what you have to do. Thank you. sir."

They turned to leave.

"Wait a minute, gentlemen. You are not dismissed!'

"Yes we are, sir. We're bulletproof, remember? Besides we have to write two scripts. Please send the guarantee to our quarters. Thank you, sir. We really appreciate your support."

They saluted. Dangle returned the salute, and they started to leave. Spike stopped suddenly and turned back to Dangle. "How many last night, Colonel?"

"You know I can't speak to that."

"How many, sir?"

"Three. Two from here. Preston and Wagner."

Barksdale and Homestead. They didn't know them too well, but Spike had flown with Wagner's guys. Merry Christmas to eighteen families.

"Understand why we feel the way we do, Colonel?"

They didn't wait for an answer. They turned back and walked out.

Neither one looked at each other. They were both crying.

General Andrews's aide, Jack, personally delivered the letter at 1130. It stated that FAI SO-2 would be back in normal rotation effective immediately. However, since the crews were set for 23 Dec, they could not get into queue until 24 Dec. They would fly lead on 24. It was signed by Dangle *and* General Andrews... Holy Shit. This was a high level deal. Hollywood asked if the crew was in agreement. They all agreed. Didn't look like a scam. Lead on Christmas Eve. Good deal. They could take Christmas off... if they came back.

They went to the CBS interview in their custom flight suits which had been waiting for them when they got back from the "MAC Attack" as it had been coined by Sluggo. The suits all fit perfectly. They answered all the questions "correctly," except Spike said "fuck" twice, but that was well below normal. Dangle was all smiles, and Jack was taking notes. The CBS interviewer baited the crew twice:

"Gentlemen, given the loss rate that you must have experienced in the last few days, don't you think, as educated professionals, that we should begin to temper or end this offensive?"

The normal response from Spike, conservatively estimated, *would* have been,

"You asshole faggot commie. I will temper your ass right now." And they would have had to restrain him. As it was, Graham did have to restrain him, whispering, "Milk runs. Milk runs." He did a Spike Smile and didn't answer.

Hollywood answered: "I don't know that the loss rate beyond the first night has been released. I do know that our flight came back intact."

That triggered a bunch of questions on "how," "why," and "is that expected from now on?" All were answered by Jack with one word: "Classified."

Hollywood should not have answered the question.

The second one was "off the cuff" as they were leaving:

"Would you guys fly these missions again if given the choice?"

Graham answered: "We did the first time. What makes you think we wouldn't again? It's our job. We defend our Country at the direction of the President."

Jack was beaming at that one. Spike looked at Graham. Spike smile. Hollywood whispered, "screw you, kiss ass." Graham was going to get serious shit for that one.

On the way out, Hollywood pulled Dangle aside. "Minor detail, boss. We don't have an E-dub. Any ideas?"

"He's moving into that shithole you guys live in as we speak. You will meet him there."

"Thanks, Boss. Don't forget our deal."

"I'm pissed that you asked the question. Have a good flight."

"Yes, sir."

They got back to Monsoon Mansion, and the new Pick was waiting for them. All of Thump's stuff had been removed by the sky cops, so he figured out where to stow his gear. He introduced himself - First Lieutenant [white bar] Jim Patterson, and he was greeted cordially. He had transferred from H models at K.I. Sawyer in Michigan to Fairchild. Smart move on his part. K.I. had more snow annually than any AFB in the world. He seemed a little unusual for a Pick. He was almost normal looking and sounding. He had a mustache that bordered on being too wide for the AFR, so Spike didn't drill him. Maybe a plant.

He did remark on their flight suits: "Where did you get those?"

Graham answered: "From a United States Senator. Want 'em?

"What?"

"Never mind. Welcome aboard."

Hollywood took him out for coffee.

They threw out the flight suits.

CHAPTER XII: PEW! HE STINKS!

Graham, Spike, Hollywood, Sluggo, Blackjack, and the Fake Major were all convened at the Club as usual, but it was unusual in three respects. First, they were dressed fairly well in nice civilian clothes. Second, they were in the main dining room to have dinner, which they very rarely did. Third, they were taking Lieutenant Barry Bronstein to dinner. He was the white bar intelligence officer that had stood up to the General and argued that the SAM site that was "there" was in fact "there" at the 19 Dec PTOB. Since he was right and they almost got killed because he was, they decided to thank him because they were not hit by a SAM site that he said would hit them... Then they decided that taking the kid to dinner was not a smart thing to do and realigned their decision to congratulate the guy on having the balls to stand up to a three star.

Besides, they were having martinis which was also an "almost never" which added to another "almost never" of being polite and courteous to the OWC broads having dinner with their cowardly husbands that never smelled. This courteous behavior took a great degree of control on their part since the OWC broads were staring at them and pointing. They probably suspected that they were those vile people that flew airplanes. And smelled. And insulted their appearance at every opportunity. As far as OWC wives were concerned, flyers shouldn't be allowed on an airbase.

They were all on their second martini when Lieutenant Bronstein showed up, in uniform, and walked up to the table.

He smiled nervously. "Hi, sirs. I'm Lieutenant Bronstein from Intel. I really appreciate the opportunity to have dinner with you gentlemen."

Spike responded by pointing as he made introductions. "Hi, kid. I'm Spike, that's Bulldog, Sluggo, Hollywood, and Blackjack. Oh and wait... that guy's a Fake Major that just got a KAP - that's K-A-P. We never use our real names while on or off duty, because there may be warrants out for us either by USAF or the enemy, so I apologize for the informality."

Graham: "What do you mean 'might be' by the enemy? Of course there are warrants out by the enemy. They can't kill us without a warrant."

The kid was getting visibly more nervous. "Thank you, sir... I understand. What's a KAP, sir?"

"Kiss ass promotion, Lieutenant. You kiss a four star's ass and you're promoted to at least the next rank without any regard to your capability or performance. Captain, er, temporary Major, The Wildman crashed his bird in the Pilipeens because he was tired of flying and his Co wouldn't help. He and the crew got a ride back on a T-39 due to more ass kissing."

The Fake Major had had enough. Smiling, he stood and saluted Spike with his middle finger. "Pay no attention to Major Forever, Lieutenant. He will one day be in charge of licking my boots as my senior, meaning old, aide. Please have a seat. Your martini is already ordered."

Lieutenant Bornstein pulled out the second to last chair at the large round table and sat down. He now seemed even more nervous. "But I don't drink, sir."

Graham intervened. "Well, you have to learn sometime. Isn't Bornstein a Jewish surname? My best friend in college was a Jewish kid."

"Yes, sir. I'm of the Jewish faith."

Spike was irritated by the whole thing. "Who gives a shit what his religion is? It's probably better than ours. He's not getting shot at every other night, so it must be better 'in ours. Co's late so let's order."

Graham didn't pay any attention to Spike. "The reason I asked, Barry, is that military intelligence is an oxymoron. As a smart Jewish kid, how did you end up in intel?"

Barry relaxed a bit, and smiled. "Because I'm a smart Jewish kid, guys. I have yet to be shot at, thank God. Yours and mine." The whole table cracked up. Spike was sitting next to Barry, by design, and he slapped the kid on the back and shook his hand.

Cowboy himself showed up with a tray of martinis for the table.

Sluggo: "Which ones are dry, Cowboy?"

Cowboy was walking away and looked back over his shoulder, smiling. "The ones you spill, white boy!"

The waiter and the Co arrived at the table almost simultaneously. "Gentlemen, how would you like your steaks?"

Spike looked at the waiter, Spike smile: "I'll have mine medium rare and so will everybody else because I bought them from the Navy. They are the best filets, so I won't allow them to be ruined."

Nobody gave a shit because they were looking at Co who was not happy. In fact, he looked grim. He had a sheaf of paper in his hand and handed them to

Hollywood. "You won't believe this shit, dogs. I made seven copies. Read it so you understand why I made the copies. It's unbelievable." Hollywood passed the copies around. They all read carefully:

DEPARTMENT OF THE AIRFORCE
HEADQUARTERS STRATEGIC WING PROVISIONAL, 72ND (SAC)
APO SAN FRANCISCO 96234

Reply to
Attn of: CC
20 Dec 72

Subject: Air Discipline

To: All B-52 Combat crewmembers

1. An analysis of our recent losses on compression missions indicates that cells became split and entered the target area essentially as single aircraft. It may have been, had the airplanes stayed together as a cell, that we would have suffered fewer combat casualties. This is a lesson that the tactical fighter force learns the hard way over North Vietnam. It is imperative on compression missions that we maintain strict air discipline. Members of cells will not, repeat, will not break formation to dodge SAM's. This only highlights a particular aircraft is out of formation. You must maintain cell integrity, even if it means turning into what in your opinion may be a SAM explosion. Our ECM equipment is designed to give a specific miss distance for SAM missiles fired at the aircraft. The miss distance and a SAM hit cannot be judged accurately in the cockpit.

2. The ECM equipment will work only if all three aircraft in the cell are within a specified distance of each other and heading in the same direction.

3. Therefore, any Aircraft Commander who breaks formation to dodge a SAM will be subject to Courts Martial action.

LEON D. PEW, Colonel, USAF
Commander

To: 72SW/ CC

I hereby acknowledge receipt and understanding of the above letter.

(Signature of Aircraft commander and crew number)

The group at the table snickered and guffawed as they read through the letter.

Graham had tears of laughter running down his face as he quoted: "'…you will not break formation to dodge SAM's!' That statement is so asinine that he repeated it so we would be sure that he was a complete idiot."

The Fake Major was more stunned than laughing. "'…maintain cell, even if it means turning into SAM explosion… ECM gives a specific miss distance for SAMs fired at the aircraft…' Our fucking ECM doesn't even work against SAMs! This guy is the commander of another planet!"

Graham was holding his stomach and laughing as he read on. "'The miss distance and a SAM direct hit cannot be judged accurately in the cockpit!!!' Now the whole table was howling with laughter, even the guest Lieutenant. Graham went on: "This asshole says we cannot judge a direct hit in the cockpit! What?! We're on fucking fire and going down and the ECM can't judge the miss distance!! It's zero for God's sake! Zero! There is no 'miss distance,' you dumb shit!"

Sluggo went on: "'…all three aircraft… heading in the same direction.' He's got to be kidding. Seriously. What? Is one of us going to turn and run away?'

More hysterics.

Spike finally spoke up. He had been laughing but not like the others. "'Any AC that breaks formation to dodge a SAM will be court martialed.' That is honestly the dumbest order I have ever read. In fact, this whole order is a complete travesty. It shows that our supposed leaders are absolute morons. They have no clue what is going on in our combat environment. If we had followed this order on 19, we would have lost at least half of the eighteen birds in the Wave. Maybe more. The only reason we lost none was NOBODY was in formation! Nobody was at the altitudes where the SAMs were set to detonate!" Spike had grown serious, and the table had adopted the mood.

Graham would not allow it to ruin their dinner. "Spike, I agree with you, and I'm sure the rest of us do, too. The REMF have proven by this idiot order that we have to ignore them. In this order, our 'leaders' tell us to assess the situation and use whatever action it takes to do our job and remain alive. Let's hope that somebody commanding us will find out about this shit and do something about it."

Spike stood up and turned toward the front of the Club. "He will. He'll hear about it right now." Spike walked away quickly but didn't forget his martini.

Sluggo smiled at the others and yelled after Spike: "Spike, if you tell him, and Pew is not executed for terminal idiocy, he will have us all flying single ships off the North Coast dropping bullshit at 12,000 feet until they kill us all." As Spike went out of earshot, Sluggo turned back to the others. "On second thought, he's going to kill us anyway testing 'miss distance' accuracy of our non-existent counter measures."

Hollywood was not laughing any more. "Guys, I have to sign this. You don't. When they check the radar photos when the shit starts flying, they'll know that I broke formation to avoid dead for all of us. But I'm the one that will get court martialed."

Graham: "They won't be able to tell, Hollywood, so don't worry about it."

Hollywood didn't get it. "How do you think they won't know?'

"Simple - we'll turn the radar off. They'll be analyzing pictures of a blank screen. Remember, almost all of the REMF are idiots, not just Pew. They issued an order that's not only stupid, it's unenforceable."

Blackjack wasn't buying the solution. "Bullshit, the REMF will court martial the bomb team for turning off the radar, Bulldog. The mathematical probability of all of the Wave's radar systems going out in one mission is astronomically low."

Bulldog was animated. "True, but we'll claim that it was caused by flying compressed cells, where our ECM, that doesn't work, actually did work, for the first time ever, but jammed our own radar. As a result, we couldn't turn the ECM off or we would not be able to calculate SAM 'miss distance' because there wouldn't be any 'miss distance.' According to Pew, we'd all be shot down without the ECM that he knows doesn't work. As soon as we exit the COA's, we turn the radar back on after we all get back on track and in formation, because we turned the ECM off so the radar works again. The REMF can't say that the radar going out due to our own ECM jamming is impossible. They're trapped. They can't court martial anybody because they can't prove we broke formation to remain alive, and they can't prove that our ECM didn't jam our own radar because they can't say in court that it's not possible because it doesn't work"

Sluggo, smiling and looking at Graham: "Bulldog, your call sign is perfect. You're so full of shit it is amazing that you're not emitting repulsive odors." Sluggo turned to his Nav: "But Bulldog's right. They can't court martial me or Hollywood if they can't prove we broke formation. The odds of all the radars going out are ridiculously low, but what Bulldog's really saying is that we're sending a message back to the REMF that we refuse to obey an idiotic order that will get us killed. You can't court martial dead men. Besides, his 'our own ECM jammed the radar story' is brilliant. They can't prove us wrong without exposing the truth. One problem though, Bulldog. If we turn the radar off and have no running lights, they won't have to hit us because we'll run into each other."

"I apologize, Slug. I wasn't specific. We won't really turn the radar off because we'll be all over the sky, playing dodgem with 468,000 pounds of airplane. We'll turn the radar *cameras* off. The appearance will be the same to the REMF."

Sluggo was delighted. "That will really work! They won't be able to court martial me until they catch me for trying to save our asses by disobeying the next dumb fuck order they issue."

Graham was smiling again. He slapped Sluggo on the shoulder. "You get it! Nice job, Ollie!"

Sluggo: "Thank you, Stan."

The steaks showed up and so did Spike. He sat down any said nothing.

Graham: "That's a *rare* occurrence. Meaning the steaks and you not saying anything after you called the General."

Spike Smile: "Your puns suck, Bulldog." He was checking his steak. "HEY, COWBOY, THE STEAK'S PERFECT!"

Spike's very loud yell to Cowboy shook the entire dining room and clearly upset the OWC oinkers and their odorless husbands. Spike's yell was intended to do just that since he knew Cowboy couldn't hear his compliment in the bar.

Behind them, the doors into the dining room were opened briskly and held by a *Colonel*. General Andrews entered and immediately spotted the table he was looking for.

They all stood as the General approached the table. The Co darted over and grabbed two chairs to squeeze in.

The General smiled. "Damn, you dogs are polite tonight." He looked down at the table. "What's wrong? Is that only your fifth martini? Please be seated, men. I'm here on a serious matter. Can I see a hard copy of the order that Pew issued?"

The Fake Major was seated next to the General and handed him a copy. The General read through it rapidly. He was expressionless. When he finished, he said nothing for a moment. He just stared at the table. Then he looked up and directed his view toward Sluggo.

"Gentlemen, I apologize for this ridiculous and stupid order. When I was in your boots flying in Korea, we sometimes got orders like this after a moron rotation. It invariably came from a guy that had no idea what the combat environment was like. I often wished they could fly with us and obey the orders they gave us. So I'll have Pew fly as Airborne Commander of the G Wave tomorrow night."

Sluggo responded instantly: "With all due respect, sir, no fuckin' way. No one will fly with him because he'll have to obey his own order and that will get them all killed. No one will fly with a dope."

"Well, Sluggo, you would be right, but the order is rescinded by my command, effective immediately. The cells will remain integral as long as it makes sense, but no one will watch a SAM fly up their ass. The AC is in command, not PEW, so I'll designate Pew as airborne 'observer,' not commander." He turned to his aide: "Glen, please issue the new order over my signature immediately and transmit to the birds inbound now." The General stood, and the table started to follow suit. The General motioned for them to remain seated. "Stay seated, fellas. I would have joined you for a drink… or ten… but I have some pressing issues at hand that need attention - not the least of which is Colonel Pew. As veterans of real combat over Hanoi, rather than Pew's fairytale, how do you suggest I tell him to prepare for the real thing?"

Spike smiled at the General. "Pew? Tell him to wear diapers."

CHAPTER XIII: PLAY IT AGAIN, SAM

THE CHEESE RUN

They went to the PTOB, and it was a major letdown. It was normal. They didn't have the briefing board covered when they came in - no General, just a new Colonel from planning. Since he was also an FNG, they didn't give him any shit. Jim kept his mouth shut but asked the right questions when appropriate, which Spike was watching for.

They opened the mission plans, and they were not too surprised at the flight designation: Snow flight again.

The target was east of Khe Sanh, so they would be up by the Z again. The strike would be ground controlled by FACs, so it was NVA troop concentrations. It was a cheese run. In and out fast. Ironically the target was not far from the divert bomb run they made on 19. Maybe it *was* the same target - just a couple of days late. No one would be surprised. They went to the bird at 2010. The tail was 446. Not a bad bird. They had flown her before. They pulled up in the crew bus, and Some Luck popped out from behind the wheel well! He ran up to the bus and started to help them unload all of their gear. Spike couldn't believe it.

"Goddamn, Some Luck! You following us around ruining airplanes for us or what? Whad'ya do to this one? Flatten the tires?" Spike was giving Some Luck shit, but he was smiling. Even so, Some Luck seemed hurt by Spike's remark. He had taken shit from everybody for so long on 221 that he didn't know when people were just busting his chops.

"Major, sir. I assure you that this is a good bird. We did a detailed run up, and she's a much better aircraft. She will fly great, sir. We guarantee it."

Graham intervened because Spike was messing with his flight bag. "Some Luck, relax. The Major was just kidding you. You had to deal with the POS for so long that no one kidded you because everything was always wrong. You guys would fix one thing and two more would break. You busted your ass on 221. Now you have a good bird, but they'll still give you shit... this time for fun. Get it?"

"Yes, sir. I guess so. Me and my guys really work hard. You will come back in our bird, sir."

"We got to get going, Some Luck. Let's fire the APU [auxiliary power unit] and move it."

"Yes, sir. It will be up in a minute."

Pre-flight was quick. Spike didn't use his checklist since this was a cheese run. He did everything from memory. Hollywood fired her up. Some Luck buttoned the hatch and pulled the chocks at 2045. Hollywood called Charlie: "Charlie, Snow One ready to taxi."

"Snow Two, ready."

"Snow Three, ready."

"Roger, Snow flight. Cleared to taxi runway zero six. Taxi and hold."

"Roger, Charlie. Snow One is rolling. Charlie, do you have a Navy F-4E ready? We will request clearance from CP to rendezvous with them once we reach altitude."

"Uh... Snow One, they are completing pre-flight and should be up early. No cat. [catapult on the carrier - assists the launch of the carrier based planes like a slingshot.] It may take a day or two for them to get airborne."

"Charlie. Batman One. We heard that, champ. Maybe we go wheels in the well and catch your lumbering vultures in about three zero seconds."

It was Dinero.

Graham switched on: "Hey Dinero. Bulldog. Nice escape last night. Thanks for the help, guys. Does Sparky sleep in a cage on your floating monument to improbability?"

"No. We just keep him in chains. No cage... Yet."

Sparky: "Screw you guys. I'm perfectly safe onboard. No temptations or fuel."

Graham was curious: "Sparky, how'd you get out of the handcuffs? You still had 'em on when you guys bolted from the Club."

Dinero responded to the question. "He broke them. He's almost used to it by now."

Hollywood: "Batman One. Snow One. We'll be level at 350 at one five after the hour. Snow Two and three will be above us one mile in trail at 355 and 360. I'll get clearance from their CP now. Stand-by."

Charlie tower: "Batman One, you can't say 'fuck' on the Charlie freq. So jam it until you're fuckin' feet wet and secure. Notify when ready to taxi, Batman."

"Roger. Ready in one five, Charlie."

Spike: "Thanks for the Naval blockade last night, boys. You were a big help. Sparky broke the bar with one of his launches. The MAC boys have to pay for all repairs."

Hollywood came back: "Batman One, our CP has cleared the exercise. See you at one five after. Good luck."

"See you then, Snow One. Maybe we'll meet again under less dangerous circumstances."

Charlie: "Snow One. Cleared for take-off. Runway zero six."

"Roger, Charlie. Snow One rolling." Brake release, power up, S-1, S-2, unstick, wheels in the well.

"Pilot. Nav. Turn to a heading of two seven five. Clearance through flight level one five zero. I'm moving to the IP seat [a flip down seat between the pilots] after we level off at three five and I have us pointed in the right direction."

Spike was bored and bruised. The trash haulers had done a little damage. "B-dog, after your sightseeing trip, I am taking a snooze, so I won't be there to hold your hand. I expect that you can get us to the Z within two to three hundred clicks without my expert assistance. Wake me when you pick up the coast. Hey E-Jeep!"

No answer. "Hey Pick, you there?"

The new E-dub knew what a Pick was. "Sorry, Major. I didn't know I was an 'E-Jeep.' What's that? My new name?"

"Jesus, E-Jeep, you *are* an FNG. A Jeep is an FNG, only it's the polite society term for an FNG. Since you are also a Pick, you are therefore an E-Jeep. You will remain an E-Jeep until you have morally degraded to the point that the Committee deems that you are worthy of crewdog status at which time you may get a call sign to replace whatever derogatory acronym we are then calling you. Keep in mind that very few Picks have ever achieved crewdog status. Now our old Pick was called Thump, but it wasn't a call sign. It was a name designed to drive him crazy, which apparently it did. Is that clear, E-Jeep?"

"Yes, sir. I'm certain I can decipher it with practice."

Spike went on: "And E-Jeep, never call me 'Major' or 'sir.' It's degrading. We don't use rank on a bomber crew, or among other crewdogs, ever. The one exception is a guy you'll meet called the Wildman. He's a Fake Major and should be addressed as such. As in 'I understand that you are going to keynote the National Kiss Ass Convention in Las Vegas this year, Fake Major Wildman, sir!' In fact, E-Jeep, that's exactly what I want you to say to him when we introduce you to him for the first time.

"Now, one other thing, You see Roller... that's the gunner - sitting there in his seat with his head down studying the tech order in his lap?"

"Yes... er, what do I call you?"

"Spike. Well he's not studying shit. He's asleep. The TO is taped to his lap and his intercom is turned off. It's your responsibility to wake him up, violently if you must, in the event that we get into a threat environment

"Yes... Spike. I think so. This is a whole different situation than my old crew at K.I. Entirely different."

"Of course it is, kid. You're at war."

Hollywood came up: "E-dub. Don't get too concerned... yet. Spike is a legendary asshole, known to be insane, and he's also the best bombardier in SAC.

"Thank you, sir... er, Hollywood. I was StanBoard at K.I. if that's any help."

Graham was delighted, "You steal the test too?"

"What?"

"Never mind, E-Jeep."

A real *book* S guy. And a Lieutenant at that. Pretty impressive to everybody but them. He may be hard to break.

They were level at three five. The forecast was unusually correct. There was high level cloud cover directly below them and a full moon. It was almost as bright as daylight and eerily beautiful.

On guard: "Snow One. Batman One. Go to sec two."

Graham was in the IP seat and switched to sec two. "Welcome to our world, Batman. It's always this beautiful when we fly. We thought you might enjoy it. But its classified Top Secret, so don't reveal it to any of your water logged buddies."

Sparky: "Screw you, Bulldog. We traded this in years ago for HOE, and that's not your last date. It means Heaven on Earth. We can't even get bomber guys a guest pass, so don't ask. We're on your seven. Two miles and closing... Fast."

"Roger, Lightweight. Come on."

Hollywood: "Batman One close to comfort off our port wing. Stay outside 500."

Dinero: "Gotcha, Hollywood. We're there just about now…"

He was there... very quickly. Too quickly. He overshot slightly.

Hollywood: "Batman One. You boys a little rusty? Overshot by nearly a mile. You do that with a MIG, and you'll kama the little shit. Check your fuel. You've been in burner so long to catch up, you may be bingo. We can scramble a Tank for you if you like. We've got connections."

Sparky back: "Bullshit, Hollywood. It was a hundred yards. Maybe. In any event, we do have to meet plan, and that means we have to get our photo ops done and get outta here, so click away. Notice I didn't say S-H-O-O-T? We hear that's dangerous around your gunner."

The assholes *did* know.

Graham responded: "The gunner's harmless. Ask the NVAF [North Vietnamese Air Force]. Besides, that wasn't us. It was TOG. [The Other Guy]"

Dinero: "No point in dwelling on it. It's too dangerous around here. Hey, Hollywood! Can you do this?"

Batman One did a snap roll [quick 360 deg. roll], then a slow roll, stopping every forty five degrees in the compass. A B-52 couldn't possibly do that... theoretically.

"We almost did that on 19 while Downtown. Can you do this?"

Graham saw what he was doing and started laughing.

Sparky: "Do what, Hollywood? We didn't see a thing."

Hollywood: "I just shut down two engines."

"Touché, gentlemen."

"Sawadee, Batman One."

Sparky: "What the hell does that mean anyway? I gotta pee in gook?"

"Roger that, Batman. Use it judiciously. See you guys at home. Take care, and stay safe."

"Same to you, Snow. Goodbye, guys."

They hit burner for effect, broke left, and were gone.

Spike had come up to watch the show: "I am going to TAC after we get back. Meantime, don't wake me."

Snow flight ground along in a seventy knot headwind to the TP in the Pilipeens. Soon after they made the turn, she came up: "Yankee Air Pirates must be going to south. Only three ship. You tell we know much. We wait for you there, too, and you will die. We have many missile and planes left. All you friends that go to North a few hour ago are dead. We shoot them all down. We do not take any prisoner. We warn you all time. Many, many wives and babies all cry tomorrow. Your friend all die for nothing. You will die for nothing. Your own people tell you come home. But you not listen. You die because you no listen. You should turn around now and go back to Guam. If you do not, you all will die and make more widows and orphans. Your family to starve. No one like them. They cry and go hungry. You will die. Go back or die."

Spike was instinctively awake because they were near his hated Pilipeens. The war would be over soon. Bulletproof. What the hell? "Hey, Hana, you shithead. This is The Head Yankee Air Pirate. The rich Yankee Air Pirate. When the war ends, we all go home to great big houses full of gold and jewels. You will go home to a burned out village of rice paper shacks that I probably personally bombed. You will have no food. And your children will all die of disease because we have all the medicine that could save them, and we won't give you any. So who wins, gook? We do no matter what. Your country has nothing left. I blew it all up. You go home and rebuild. I will come back and blow it up again. Don't bother to have any little rice eaters because they will all die of disease. So screw you, gook. Have a nice year thinking about that."

Hollywood: "Goddammit, Spike! You're going to get our ass in deep shit. Shut the hell up."

"Bullshit. Bulletproof. Lest you forget. Besides, I was lying to her just like she tries to lie to us. Only we know it's bullshit. What I just said to her sounds true to her because that's what Uncle Ho tells her anyway. She has no idea what will really happen. We will pull out, and within a few years, if not months, we will go in and rebuild everything at taxpayer expense, ours, and we will give them all the medicine they need. We will pay to train their doctors in our medical schools while some poor round eye can't get in and give them all the financial aid they will need forever and kiss their ass if there is an incident involving an American in their country. All because the sniveling left wing Democrat commies want to save the world at our expense. In the meantime, we will go home to a country that couldn't give a shit since the liberal press has carefully taught them not to and live in a shithole little house on base. We'll drive our wives to work when we aren't on alert so that we can use the car that day, and she can work for the next 15 years so we can send our kids to college. In the meantime, we will sit alert for a year or two until the next war, while decent pay raises for the military are turned down by those same Democrats because we can't afford it since they gave all our money to the gooks. Having said all that, some of which I believe, I will continue to serve my Country until such time that they throw me out on my ass. Then I will build a mansion on some of the five hundred acres of land that I bought in the foothills near Fresno using The Four Seasons bracelets I bought in Thailand as collateral and brought back duty free thanks to this rotten damn war that we have not been allowed to win. God Bless capitalism."

Graham: "Goodnight, Chet."

"Goodnight, David."

Hollywood: "E-dub, you need to ignore the guys downstairs. We really aren't like that all the time. They are both nuts. Good. But nuts. If you want to take out a hairball target the first time so you don't have to go back the next day... or someone else doesn't... you want those guys downstairs. Do you want them downstairs at *your house*? Not advisable. Your wife would leave you."

E-Jeep: "Thanks. I already figured that out."

Spike: "You a music major, E-Jeep?"

"No. Accounting."

"You passed one hurdle. Now don't wake me."

Hollywood: "Hold it, Spike. What's this land and Fresno and bracelet shit?"

Spike had turned off his IC and was head down on the deli counter.

Graham answered: "It's not shit. It's absolutely true, and I found out too late. So did you. I'll let him explain it outbound feet wet. That way we won't have to listen to anymore Thai Princess in Pataya bullshit. Which probably isn't bullshit. The prick."

Snow Flight was on a Cheese Run. Sunny and Sluggo were at the Dance. That was in the back of everybody's mind. Except the FNG. And Roller - who didn't have one. Graham knew Spike was wrapped. He *never* slept *inbound* on any mission.

SUNNY AT THE DANCE

"SAM launch Hanoi."

"SAM launch Hanoi."

"SAM launch Haiphong."

"SAM launch Haiphong."

"Red Crown. Bronze Flight IP. Six late."

"Roger, Bronze."

Sunny was optimistic. It had been comparatively quiet inbound. Or at least it seemed that way. Maybe he was more terrified on eighteen than tonight. How could he be less terrified than now? Many of his friends were dead... or POWs, God willing. Hell, he was getting used to the monotonous drone of the SAM calls. Same voice. You would think the guy would get laryngitis from all the SAM calls he must have made in the last three nights. What an odd thought.

"Pilot. Radar. Center the PDI."

"Centered. You have it Radar."

"Roger. I got it."

Same low overcast as they had on the first night. Bulldog said they had the same thing on nineteen... shit!

"EW, Pilot. I have two launches ten o'clock!"

"Negative uplink, Pilot!"

Sunny firewalled the throttles. It worked the first night. Maybe this time. Hell, he couldn't juke on the bomb run anyway.

"UPLINK! UPLINK! UPLIN.."

The impact was horrific. Violent pitch starboard. Power gone, decompression, sparks everywhere.

Sunny reached for the bailout switch and yelled into his mask, "BRONZE ONE! EJECT! EJECT! EJECT!"

CHAPTER XIV: THE CREWDOG GENERAL

Brigadier General Glenn S. Charles, the Air Division Commander at U-Tapao, had essentially spent his entire career in SAC. He was highly respected by the crewdogs, primarily because he was one. Very few General Officers were considered crewdogs. It was 0330 hours, and Charles was up because his crews were in the air returning from the last strike. Things had gone better tonight than last night. Ivory 1 had been hit but made it back to UT. Still, the tactics were idiotic. The crews had been lucky. He was furious. They had to change tactics, or they would get slammed. He picked up his direct line to General Andrews at Andersen.

"Jack, we have to change tactics. The goddamn planners have birds turning into a 120 knot headwind off the target. Their effective airspeed is 250 knots into heavy SAM coverage! On top of that idiocy, we're flying the same flight plans every night to the same targets at the same times! Goddamn idiots! The fact that we only lost Ivory One tonight is a miracle!"

"I know it seems poorly planned, but the facts are the facts. We only lost one bird, and they made it to safety. As a result, SAC headquarters is going to deem their planning brilliant and stick with the same plan. You know that. I've already requested a change based on a crew de-brief I did here. The senior guy on the crew, a Major Spike Wilson, called our planners quote 'fucking idiots' unquote. He's right. I changed the planning staff today, but SAC said the flight plans and target assortment cannot be changed for the strike today. That's an order from a guy that has more stars than I do."

"Bullshit, Jack! You have to get them to change the mission plan. If we don't, we're going to lose a lot of kids. You have to press it with SAC!"

"I'll do what I can, Glenn, but the 20 strike stands as planned. After 19 and only one shootdown, I have no ammunition to use against the planning staff at SAC HQ."

Charles was furious: "Tell you what, Jack. After we follow this plan for 20, YOU write the goddamn letter to all the crewmembers wives and children that says, 'Dear mom and kids, I'm sorry to inform you that because of shit planning your husband and father was shot down over Hanoi and is now a POW or dead. Merry Christmas.'"

"Knock it off, Glenn! I have no control over it at this point."

Charles hung up the secure line without a response.

Captain Elliot Finney, a B-52 pilot, walked into Charles' office unannounced and took a seat in front of his desk. He was in his flight suit and boots. His eyes were red, he looked very tired, and he smelled of sweat. He had just landed from the "Dance." Charles knew him. He knew most of the senior crewdogs at UT.

"Good to see you, Captain Finney. You look like you could use a beer." Charles got up and went to a small refrigerator in the corner of his office and pulled out two Sing Ha beers. They were Thai and the alcohol content was uncontrolled. It could be none to 25%. You didn't know until it was, or wasn't, too late. The General opened both, walked back to his desk, and put one down in front of Finney.

"I can't drink that General. I'm flying tonight."

"You're more than twelve hours from wheels in the well, Captain. Relax and enjoy the beer. It looks like you need one. Now, why did you honor me with your presence at 0400? By the way, I truly appreciate it."

"I've flown both nights, General. The SAMs are like fireflies. I had one go off just above me on 18 and three just miss me tonight... or this morning... or whatever the fuck it is. If one of them had gone off below me, my crew and I would be dead."

"I understand that. It's been really bad. Colonel White has flown with you guys both nights. I'm not allowed to or I would have been with you guys."

Finney interrupted. "We're scheduled up again tonight, General. We can't go again. The flight plans and tactics make no sense. We flew the same plan tonight as we did on the first night. I'm going to lose it. We need a break."

"I understand, Captain. I really do. You don't have to go on tonight's strike."

Finney looked visibly relieved and even mustered a weak smile. "Thank you, sir. Thank you. We really need this little break." He stood up, grabbed his beer, and saluted the General who returned it.

"You're dismissed, Captain. I appreciate your candor."

Finney saluted again and almost stumbled out of the General's office.

He's a good AC. He's the tip of the iceberg that had the balls to walk into my office and tell me the truth at four o'clock in the morning. I have got to get these plans changed.

Charles picked up the secure line and called Andrews again. There was no answer. He picked up the base phone and called flight scheduling. Captain Morrison answered. "Captain, General Charles. You are to schedule a stand-by AC for Captain Finney's crew tonight."

Scheduling officers don't question a General, let alone at 0400. "Yes, sir."

In the late afternoon on 20 Dec, Captain Finney re-appeared at the General's office. This time he knocked on the doorjamb since the General's door was always open. Finney had no idea that the General had less than three hours sleep.

"Come in, Captain."

"Sir, you told me early this morning that we weren't flying today. Why are we still scheduled, sir?"

Charles looked up from the conference table where he and Colonel White were studying the 20 Dec plans with a slight smile on his face: "Captain, I said *you* wouldn't fly. I didn't say your crew wouldn't fly. You're dismissed."

Finney was wise enough not to say anything other than, "yes, sir." He saluted and left quickly.

On 20 Dec, nothing changed. The same marshalling yards, Hanoi radio again, and the petroleum storage area at Gia Thoung. Same flight plans as on the 18th and 19th.

It was a disaster. The SAMs were everywhere. The NVA were waiting for the attack on the same flight plans at the same altitudes, at the same times as the night before. That's how the Americans attacked. General Giap was stunned, but very pleased. They shot down six or seven and crippled many more. They were winning! He ordered the representatives at the Paris talks to depart immediately.

At 0230 on 21 Dec, Colonel White walked into General Charles' office. He gave a cursory salute to his boss, which was returned. He was in his flight suit. He had just led the third mission over Hanoi from U-T.

"Glenn, it was a disaster. There were constant SAM calls. There were beepers going off everywhere. I saw two of our birds nailed. THEY WERE FUCKING WAITING FOR US!"

Bill White slumped into a chair. He almost seemed in tears. "How many, Glenn?"

"Six, maybe seven. You're right. They *were* waiting for us as we both expected. It was a turkey shoot, but it was our guys." Charles seemed close to tears as well. "It's over with. It won't continue. Not while I'm in command."

He handed White a piece of paper. He glanced at the top. It was labeled **TOP SECRET - ESI.** He started to scan down and read the message. The address shocked him,

To: Commander-in-Chief, Strategic Air Command

From: Brigadier General Glenn S. Charles, Commander, 17th Air Div. (Prov), U-Tapao AFB

John:

I have a deep concern over the planning and tactics that have been employed during Linebacker Two. I must intervene at this point on behalf of my aircrews...

White continued to read the message and was visibly shaken. It was copied to General Andrews. It should have been *sent* to Andrews, not copied.

"Glenn, you're not going to send this are you? It will end your career. You know that."

"I already sent it. Now I'm going to call him to make sure he knows I'm serious."

Charles picked up the secure phone and dialed. Colonel McDonald walked into the office. They both listened intently, but it was difficult to pick up everything being said. Charles raised his voice as he apparently got to his key point: "... No, sir, please understand that I will not launch any more B-52s out of U-Tapao until the tactics are changed."

Could he be talking to CINC? He was obviously talking to someone who was very high ranking. White couldn't believe it. *Shit, he's damn determined. God Bless him.*

The conversation continued briefly and at a lower tone. Charles hung up and turned to his senior officers: "The Wing will fly tonight. But we will have an entirely different attack plan. That plan will be transmitted by 1300 today. If we find the plan to be unacceptable, we will stand-down."

White and McDonald were speechless. They both knew what the General had done for the crews. He saved their lives at the expense of his career. White finally said what both he and McDonald were thinking.

"Thank you, Glenn. You saved many of our guys' lives by what you have done."

Out of respect, both men turned and quietly left the room. The fallen star sat down behind his desk.

Minutes later, Captain Finney came in, again unannounced and in flight gear, and plopped down on the General's couch, smiling. "Thanks, General. Thank you so much. You taught me a great lesson. You knew damn well I would never let my crew fly to the Dance without me. It was bad, sir. Really bad. Shit all over the place. But we made it. I had to fly with them, and you knew it."

"If you had let them fly without you, Captain, you would never have flown as a B-52 Aircraft Commander again. Now get us both a couple of beers. You know where they are. You got shot at and God Bless they missed you. I shot myself. But it didn't hurt. In fact it felt great."

Finney knew enough not to ask for an explanation. He appreciated being able to have a beer with a man he was positive was the greatest General Officer he would ever meet.

MORE HEARTBREAK

D-Kid and Alex were lying on their concrete beds in the mid-afternoon. They had no choice since their living room furniture hadn't been delivered. They could hear an aircraft patrolling the city.

Alex: "That's an F-111. The switchblade Edsel. Called that because the wings are like blades and they flip out and back. They kept disappearing on their early missions over here with no communication, no bailouts, just gone. The REMF finally figured out that when the birds were using terrain avoidance radar the gooks were firing chaff into the air in front of them and they would fly straight into the ground."

"I wonder how many guys bought it before they figured that out."

"One's too many."

"Roger that, brother."

Alex, up and smiling at D-Kid: "You callin' me 'brother,' white boy?"

"You bet. You're a crewdog. That automatically makes you a brother. And don't call me 'white boy.' I'm particularly sensitive to that. My skin and hair make me the whitest 'white boy' in SAC, if not USAF. I take a lot of shit about it."

"You nuts? That makes you super white boy!"

They both cracked up. They heard the 111 getting very close. Suddenly, there was an enormous explosion very, very close. The doors of their cell were blown off the hinges from the concussion.

Alex: "Jesus, that was close! You'd think that they would brief the drivers about a place full of POWs!"

They were both shaken by the blast. The last thing they needed after everything was to be killed by their own guys. It had crossed both their minds before.

D-Kid: "They must have taken out that triple A battery on the next block. The gooks must have shot at them one too many times." Guards carrying AK-47s ran into the cell and started yelling at them in gook. They raised their hands and didn't respond.

What the hell do they think we're going to do? Escape? A 5'9" super white guy with bright red hair and a giant black guy walking down the street in downtown Hanoi? C'mon. No one's that stupid.

They were motioned to get up and moved out into the courtyard. Other POWs were there and they had some time together under guard. It seemed as though the guards were really shaken.

One guard came up to D-Kid: "They bomb very near here. Very near."

"Yeah, they did. Remember that."

The POWs in the yard immediately took the time to do what they were trained to do. They all exchanged names and personal information as quickly as they could. Tom Sampson was there, along with three guys from Alex's crew, Captains Hal Nelson, Charlie White, and Hank Burrows. They were taken to the worst part of Heartbreak and put in pairs in cells with two concrete "bunks" and rat droppings all over the floor. Each bunk had leg stocks.

Shit. What does this mean? Can't be good.

That night, D-Kid saved some bread from dinner in case they didn't get any food in the morning. He was awakened by rats eating his bread while standing on his blanket. He froze. If he shooed the rats away and got bitten, the infection might kill him, and the gooks wouldn't care.

Everyday, D-Kid and Alex were taken out separately for daily interrogations. Same old shit.

The interrogator was new: "What do know about the Quail?"

"I already answered that, and you hit me in the head with a rifle butt. So I won't answer it again."

"You know we can take you out to where they will bomb and leave you there. Your own people will kill you while you were trying to escape."

"How are you going to figure out what we are going to blow up tonight?"

The interrogator was really pissed based on his expression.

Rifle butt, dumb ass. Nice thinking. Why don't you let your brain operate before your mouth does?

Nothing happened.

These guys were afraid! Afraid that the bombing preceeded US troops on the ground and the tables would turn. The old American POWs would remember the new Gook POWs who had tortured and beaten them. They were right. If that happened, we'd remember every rifle butt and fall. And, most of all, we'd remember who did it.

CHAPTER XV: THE CHEESE MELTS

Spike: "B-dog, give me the heading planned IP inbound on this FAC drop. I have a sneaking suspicion."

"Two three three. What suspicion? This is a cake walk. Strike out of the northeast, turn left to zero nine two after release, climb to three six, and head for feet wet. Easy and boring. It's FAC strike. Why the headings? They give us everything."

SO-2 would be guided by a team sitting in a portable trailer on the ground. Their only job on this Bomb Run would be to run the BR checklist and release on the FAC call. Their other job was to monitor the terrain by radar and ensure that the target area looked like the target on their charts. The only reason it wasn't a milk run was that we were very close to the Z for a short period.

"Snow flight. Red Crown."

"Roger, Red Crown. Snow One is zero six from Lima. On time."

"Roger, Snow One. Be advised the Low Boy and MIG CAP are on station now."

"Snow flight acknowledges, Red Crown."

They had their air cover. They were either USAF or Navy F4s. No one talked to them unless they saw activity.

Graham came up: "E-Jeep. Nav. We're landfall in four minutes. Make sure that Roller is onboard and heads up for you. We had SAM activity up here two nights ago."

"Rog, Nav. We're on it."

They drove in on track, hit the IP, and turned the run over to the FAC.

"Roadrunner. Snow One. You got it."

"Roger, Snow One. Maintain current heading and airspeed."

The FAC used very sophisticated radar to bring them in on target. It was theoretically far more accurate than their BNS.

Spike: "I KNEW IT! I DAMN KNEW IT! We're bombing the same ridge we blew up on one nine! Look at the topo, B-dog. See that other ridge intersecting what looks like a hill? We're after the same damn thing."

He was pushing the switch that took radar photos to document his suspicion. They would match up against the ones he took on one nine. As Graham looked at it carefully, he could see that Spike was right. Spike *was* a damn genius at his craft. No one but Spike could have figured it out in the terrain that they were painting on radar.

"Snow One. Roadrunner. Three zero seconds to release... fifteen... ten... five... release."

"Bombs away, crew. Pilot. Left to zero nine two. Climb and maintain flight level three six zero."

The other birds would release off their mark. They had just dropped three times the bomb load that totally destroyed the same target two days before.

Spike: "You know what happened? Those idiot planners that Andrews fired on one nine planned this run. The new planning staff was so busy re-doing all of the Dance numbers that they just sent this out as planned and assumed that the FAC would change it if necessary. We are surrounded by morons."

"Snow flight. Snow One level at flight level three six."

"Roger, Snow Two at three six five."

"Snow Three at three seven zero."

Snow Flight headed back to Guam. The entire mission was a waste of time.

OUTBOUND FROM THE WASTE OF TIME

No one said much of anything en route back. The usual spirit wasn't there. They were all still wondering what went on at The Dance.

They cleared the PI and Hollywood came up: "Hey Spike, what's the shit about land in Fresno and the bracelets that you were talking about inbound?

Spike: "I'm sorry, but Mr. Wilson is unavailable at the moment. You'll have to set up an appointment with his lackey, a Mr. B. Dog, who is available on this line."

Graham was on: "Screw you, Mr. Fart Bag. Take the guy's call. He writes your ERs. Not that it makes any difference because you only have one board left for LC and you're universally known and hated by most of the REMF that will influence the decision to turn your ass down for the third time. Face it. You have three DFCs (Distinguished Flying Cross), a zillion Air Medals for combat, all kinds of other decs, been to all the right USAF schools, are the best at what you do in USAF, and you are a capable, if not competent, commander. No one but a complete staff kiss ass will be selected ahead of you. So you're screwed, Major. Forever. Take the man's call any way."

"You should see if I'm available."

"OK Major Pain-in-the-Ass, are you in, sir?"

"Actually, I'm having a meeting with Herman trying to negotiate the release of numerous valuable objects, some of which may be mine. Could he call back? Say in ten to fifteen? You may give him my private line."

"You are nuts, Spike. You really are. You have tipped over the edge, buddy. You heard him, Hollywood. Call back in ten on his private line which is... got a pencil?"

"Yes."

"This one."

Hollywood: "Roger that, B-dog. I'll call in ten."

Hollywood waited about fifteen and tried again: "Spike. What's with the bracelets?"

"Mr. Wilson" had left for the convoluted recesses of Spike's mind: "I started buying Four Seasons bracelets in Bangkok back in '68. They are beautiful hand carved eighteen carat solid gold bracelets that depict the Chinese four seasons in relief. We can buy anything and bring it back with no duty if we have been in a combat zone more than 120 days. I brought them back, and they appraised at more than double what I paid for them. The next time I bought ten. The third time I went in with my buddy E.Z. Mark - no shit that's his real name - and we bought 40 of the things. I've bought maybe 250 total by now.

So anyway, the first two I brought back appraised at double what I paid. The next ones at triple what I paid, and it got better than that as we moved on. Long tale short, we have had them appraised and re-appraised as gold goes up, and we now have over a million bucks in appraised value sitting in a bank vault in Fresno. E.Z. used that as collateral to start buying land adjacent to the park in the foothills outside Fresno. We now have close to a thousand acres of developable land and we're buying more. Gold may hit $800 an ounce in the next few years. Bottom line: I'm a multi-millionaire right now. But I love my hobby, bombing bad guys and breaking things, and as you have correctly observed, I'm nuts. So I stick with you guys to keep you from getting killed. It's that simple."

Hollywood: "I don't believe it. A crewdog gets rich smuggling gold. Brilliant."

"It's not smuggled. Federal law allows us to do it."

Hollywood: "There's still time. I'm volunteering for all the U-T tours I can get and spending all R&Rs there."

Graham: "I'm in."

Everyone else did as well, except Roller, who was always worried about Thai wives.

"E-Jeep. You're up for this?"

"I'm an accountant, remember? You guys are nuts, but logic interfered with your insanity."

They touched down at 0831 local. Eleven hours and thirty one minutes. The Dance attendees were about thirty minutes *behind* them. They went to de-brief. An L/C FNG from planning was there.

Hollywood started: "The bird is great. I had only two write-ups. The mission was a gigantic waste of time and resources. Spike?

"You nickel dicks had us take out a target that we blew to shit alone two days ago! What the hell are you doing? I have radar pics. You compare that to the target we diverted to on one nine. Same ridge. Different angle of attack. You guys are morons. We aren't telling our close and personal friend, The General, about this - this time - because you guys are FNGs, and we want to give you a chance. But not a second time."

"But Major, that's not possible. How could you make the determination? It might have been close but not the *same* target."

Spike: "It is. It wasn't easy. The same."

"Where's our beer?"

A white bar with the Colonel left and came back with a cooler very quickly. The Colonel was really upset: "Our Intel sucks. We confirm all active targets through them twelve hours before PTOB. For you guys to go level a target that was already gone is inexcusable."

Graham: "Colonel, we have been here since April. We have made runs in the south that were FAC runs that we knew were toothpick runs when we had guys on the ground screaming on guard that they needed help immediately. But we can't divert to real targets that would save our guys' asses. We just press on with the toothpick. It's bullshit. Our guys are dying because some REMF decided not to allow diverts. You think you feel bad? How do you think we feel?"

Roller awakened from the dead: "Oh yeah, Colonel, I have a write up the boss doesn't know 'cause I forgot to tell him. The guns don't work."

They all stared in disbelief. Hollywood, stunned: "What the hell do you mean the guns don't work? Why are we hearing this now?"

"Well... I did the regular check west of the PI when the Nav said 'go,' and the guns didn't. I think they're jammed."

Hollywood: "Why didn't we know about this until now? What the hell were you doing?"

"I decided to wait a few minutes and then test them again. If they didn't work then, I was going to tell you guys right away."

Hollywood: "Then what happened? They still didn't work, right?"

"No. I forgot to test them again. So then I forgot to tell you, too. If I'd remembered to test them, I would have remembered to tell you."

"Sergeant. You're restricted to quarters until I decide what to do with you. I'll meet with you tomorrow morning in that regard."

"Fine with me, boss. I ain't leaving the room anyway. There's some Jap guys looking for me."

Hollywood: "We know. We're tempted to put a sign on the door."

They completed debrief and checked the flight schedule on the way out.

They were lead on two four, as promised. An eight cell wave. Twenty four birds and one hundred and forty four guys. There was another wave of D models with twenty four birds scheduled right behind them. Forty eight bombers and two hundred and eighty eight guys from Guam alone. Graham suspected that there would be at least that number out of U-T. Almost one hundred bombers over Downtown at the same time.

They walked out of Ops headed for chili dogs. Sluggo and his crew were getting off the crew bus. They looked like they all did: tired, dirty, and beat to shit.

Sluggo approached, and Graham had to give him some shit: "Sluggo, you and your crew are a disgrace to yourselves and the United States Air Force. You look like shit! Your flight suit isn't pressed. Your hair is out of limits, and you are generally a walking book of AFR violations."

He didn't respond at all. No comeback. No smile. No bird. He just walked up to Graham and stopped: "They got Sunny."

Graham turned ice cold. He felt empty and sick. Sunny's down. God, first D-Kid, now Sunny and his crew.

Sluggo continued: "I talked to dep wave on the ramp. He accelerated at the IP, and they nailed him. He fireballed. Tony didn't see any way the guys could have gotten out. He said they burned for maybe thirty seconds and went up big time."

Sluggo was crying. So was Graham: "What about beepers? Any beepers go off?"

"Yeah we heard beepers, but they got Copper Two at about the same time. Copper wasn't a fireball. They had time to get out."

There was nothing else to say. Sluggo went in to debrief. Graham turned to the crew. Tears. Widows. Kids with no dads.

Spike: "The blue sedans will be out tomorrow morning at home."

Sunny's Radar had five kids. All were under ten years old.

Spike and B-dog no longer wanted any chili dogs. They jumped on the same crew bus that Sluggo got off of and headed to Monsoon Mansion. Overwhelming grief. D-Kid made it alive. Maybe Sunny's crew would.

No one said much. There wasn't anything to say. They all showered and went to bed.

MASK THE THOUGHTS

Just after 1700, who else but Sluggo came through the door with a large bottle of rum and a bag full of limeade and chips.

Graham: "Goddamnit, I thought we were going to put bolts on the doors. E-Jeep! That's your first assignment! Go over to the BX and buy four sets of bolts and a drill. Give Spike the bill. I assure you that he won't pay it."

Graham was the first to acknowledge his presence, which was probably a mistake. "Goddamnit, Sluggo! We're in mourning for Sunny and his crew. Get out! Go home."

"Wrong, Bulldog! I thought about it, and Sunny and his crew would have wanted a party to celebrate their lives! An Irish wake or a celebration of their survival, as it were. Up boys! Bring in the sacrificial virgins! Lao-lao! Ching! Ching! Sawadee chup! Fun, Fun, Fun, 'til her daddy took the T-bird away! Donde esta el blendoroso Torodog!

"It's in the sink in the bathroom. It's a different green than the limeade, and there's a dead gecko in it. Geckos never die from our daqs... they just get drunk. So we have a problem. Wake me when they are done."

"Ah, but guys! I have a wealth of great information straight from my Sergeant Smolensky's semi-accurate library of rumors! Up! Up! Up! Here's a teaser. Two absolutely gorgeous, large breasted, great assed, short skirted ROUND EYE bimbos were spotted near Eighth Air Force headquarters! Granted they had a bodyguard the size of a beer truck with them, but that simply serves to reinforce the other rumor that these fine young ladies have no morals when it comes to decorated war hero aviators!"

They all sat up. Just a *look* at a good looking woman was worthy of a diversion from any other assigned mission.

"Indeed, boys, the rumor is there may well be an entire SQUADRON of these nubile horny young things on this base as I speak! They are en route to Da Nang for a second rate USO show featuring Herman's Hermits and the Majestics, whoever the hell they are. They are traveling on a C-141 that developed engine trouble due, no doubt, to very bad pilotage by those MAC weenies. Since there are no trash hauler mechanics on this *combat* base, their guys managed to get the 141 in the incapable hands of No Luck Mazerowski who will see to it that the vegetable truck will be ready to fly sometime in April!"

Spike corrected the idiot: "Sluggo. You dope. No Luck is now Some Luck, and he is not a bad mechanic. In fact, he is a great mechanic that gets assigned shitbird aircraft because no one else can fix them. He will have that milk truck up and running in a matter of hours, you idiot. You need to get your rumor chief on the case and get Some Luck off that bird, fast."

The blender was running. They all crawled out of bed and started to get dressed. Sluggo didn't know how to make daqs. He always screwed them up.

"Sluggo, what did you put in there."

"The recipe, Bulldog. One can of limeade and three cans of rum. Fill with ice and blend!"

"I knew it. You amaze me. I can't believe that you are considered the fourth best pilot in the squadron! It's TWO to one, not three, shitbird! How many times have we told you that?!"

"Try never. I never make these. You or Spike always do. Go ahead and fix them. By the way, fourth rhymes with screw. As in you. THE rhymes with me. As in THE best pilot on this island is me. At any rate, I will go by the NCO club on the way to ours and tell Smolensky to have Some Luck re-fuck whatever he has de-fucked. So, no problem. We will imprison these fine young things on this island of love. Now this fact, boys, is not a rumor. It is far more important. Intel analyzed the tapes on their strike, and they think there are *more than six* beepers going off at the time immediately after Sunny got nailed. TAC didn't have any shoot downs at that time. So that means that one or more guys on Sunny's crew got out. Maybe not alive, but somebody was in silk."

Sluggo was wrong. Graham was elated: "No. They had to be alive to squeeze the handles. They had to be. One or more of them made it out."

All of their moods brightened. Somebody was alive. Maybe in the hell of the Hilton, but alive. *You could come back if you were alive.*

The blender shorted out just after 1800. Crisis. They went over to permanently borrow E-05's blender, but they had bolted all four doors. Probably in response to Mr. Daniels taking a walk.

Sluggo left to go find the Fake Major and to go by the NCO club on the way to the O'Club. Spike, B-dog, and Hollywood went down and found a crew bus, went to the club, and had burgers in the back bar. Sluggo and Wildman came in just as they were finishing. E-Jeep was with them. The Co had gone bowling. Graham introduced new Pick to the Wildman.

"Wildman, this is Lieutenant Jim Patterson. He's our new Pick. He is E-Jeep until further notice."

Wildman shook E-Jeep's hand: "I would say welcome aboard, but I must provide condolences instead since these idiots will ruin whatever career you may have expected to have."

E-Jeep responded coolly: "It's nice to meet you. I understand that you are going to keynote the National Kiss Ass Convention in Las Vegas this year, Fake Major Wildman... sir."

Spike was beaming. The kid had remembered it verbatim, and his delivery was almost perfect. This kid might make it.

The Wildman: "Jesus! They have ruined you already! This is a new record for these shitbirds. You should go see the flight surgeon immediately and see if they have some sort of antidote. Meantime, put yourself on report for insulting a superior officer."

They all cracked up, including Wildman. Of course Wildman was right. The kid was ruined. He was doomed by association. They all moved to the main bar where the table was reserved, along with number eight. Cowboy must have heard about Sunny and anticipated that it would get pretty drunk out. Sunny had many friends, and they would all show up. The tray of BRs arrived quickly along with a dice cup for both tables. The 4-5-6 game started immediately.

CHAPTER XVI: THANKS FOR THE MEMORY

THE PARTY

The band showed up at 2045. Early. Spike stopped playing long enough to write down a list of songs and send E-Jeep over to Pico.

"4-5-6, boys. Anti-up, gang. Amazing luck. Absolutely amazing."

Graham had the dice and had bet the whole pot, just short of three thousand dollars. He won automatically with 4-5-6 on the first roll. If he had rolled 1-2-3 he would have had to *double* the pot: almost $6000.

Sluggo, who was losing: "Bulldog, you are the luckiest shit I have ever seen. You also have balls the size of cantaloupes, you shitbird. I can't remember when you lost this game. This is turning into a Bulldog charity event. We may change to poker so you don't buy a small city with our money when you get home."

They would never change to poker. It was too slow. 4-5-6 was very fast, very high risk, and high reward. It fit them perfectly. They were aviators. They were all addicted.

"Put in your $20, Sluggo, and stop whining."

Sluggo lasted about another hour and tapped out. It was getting drunk out and they were all very worried about Sunny and his crew. Sluggo and Spike ended up sitting right behind Graham so they could annoy the shit out of him. They were very well Russianed, which added to the problem. Graham was still playing, so to keep them off his case he asked a question.

"If we could end all wars, which we should be able to do with today's technology, all this death and grief on all sides would go away. You guys think that could be done in our lifetimes?

Sluggo: "Impossible. *What* causes this. You have to find that out first."

Spike: "He's right, B-dog. *What* causes all of this."

It was his roll. He glanced at Spike: "What the hell are you assholes talking about? What do you mean 'what' causes this? What is the question, not the answer. I asked what causes this?

"Roll, Bulldog!"

He did.

Spike, slurring slightly: "No. 'What causes this' is a statement, not a question. What causes all wars."

"The point is five."

Graham wasn't paying attention: "You already asked me that! I asked you, for Christ's sake!"

Sluggo: "No, B-dog. You don't get it. 'What' is the cause of all wars."

"What the hell is this? An Abbott and Costello routine? Forget it. I shouldn't have asked you drunken assholes anything."

Spike, very seriously, given his condition: "No, B-dog. It's not a comedy routine. What causes all wars. Nobody knows who what is. They think they do. But no one knows."

Sluggo: "He's right. If you asked a hundred people what causes war, you would get a hundred different answers. Because they don't know what does."

Spike: "Yeah. Nobody really knows who what is. If they did, we could end all wars. Stop killing each other. Stop making widows. Like Sunny and his guys. The wives may all be widows as we speak. Like the guys on the 18th, 19th, 20th... tonight, tomorrow night, and on and on."

"Ace away, Bulldog. Put it in."

"You guys are drunk *and* crazy. People cause wars. Politics cause wars. Incidents cause wars. Borders cause wars... not whatever you call what."

Spike: "That's the point. You don't really know what causes wars because it's really what that causes them, and nobody knows what what is."

Sluggo: "Exactly. Well put, professor."

The band stopped playing and packed up. It was a little after 0100. They had tennis matches scheduled in the morning at 1000, and Graham needed sleep.

Besides, he was starting to lose. He was about to tell the idiots that they were going home when he spotted something out of the corner of his eye coming through the door up front. He focused. It was a guy with three of the most beautiful women he had ever seen. Sluggo and Spike saw Graham's reaction and turned to look.

Sluggo: "Holy shit. We got shot down. We're in heaven."

They were frozen in awe. The women were wearing short, short skirts and had on tight little tops tied above the waist. They had killer bodies. The guy was in a white safari suit and carried a swagger stick. What the hell?

The bar was empty except for about twenty five crewdogs. As they walked toward them, Graham focused further… the swagger stick was a putter.

It was Bob Hope.

THE MEETING OF A LIFETIME

As the crewdogs remaining in the club realized who was there, a large crowd gathered around the Great GI Entertainer. He was absolute class.

"I came by to invite you guys to my show on Christmas Eve. Since I didn't think you would care or even recognize me, I brought along some attention getters. They seem to be working. Don't touch, fellas… they can beat the shit out of you. Believe me, I know."

Unknown crewdog: "What brings you here at one in the morning, Mr. Hope?"

"Love. Boys. The love I have for this country and the love I have for you guys that defend it at the risk of your lives. You heroes, the ones that preceded you, and the ones that will, unfortunately, succeed you are the reason. Coming here and showing our love and appreciation is the least we can do."

He started: "You know, I played golf with your General this afternoon. I made the determination that the wind doesn't blow on Guam, it sucks! And so does your General. Nice guy, but he should stick to bowling. Don't you tell him I said that, or I'll never get out of here."

Crewdog: "You can't anyway, Mr. Hope. The wind will suck you back."

"Stick to bombing, kid. Let me do the jokes… wait a minute, you did stick to bombing. Sorry about that. So did any of your dads ever see my Christmas shows?"

About seven guys raised their hands. They were witnessing history. Something they would never forget. Strangely, as horny as they all were, none of the crewdogs were focused on the girls. They were all riveted to the Legend. "Well, that's good to see. I've been doing this a while. Obviously your dad's didn't tell you about the show, or you would have gone to request an immediate transfer to the front. Oops! This is the front, isn't it? How many of you guys fly those giant green things on the tarmac?"

All but two raised their hands.

"Well the bowler tells me you guys have had a tough time the last few days. God Bless you all, and may he watch over you. I thank you from the bottom of my heart."

Hollywood asked him if he wanted a drink, and he declined. He got all the girls wine. Hope started to circulate and ask individuals what they did, where they were from, et cetera. Nothing political or controversial. After he had chit chatted with almost everybody, he turned around and suddenly approached Spike and Graham. He asked Graham directly: "Where are you from, son?" He stuck out his hand, and Graham shook it.

He was as nervous as if he were meeting the President: "I'm Captain R.J. Graham, sir. Fairchild Air Force Base in Washington, Mr. Hope."

"What do you fly, kid?"

"B-52 bombers. I'm the Navigator."

"Don't tell me you fly with this asshole." He put his arm around Spike's shoulder and shook his hand.

Spike smiled: "How old are you now, Bob? One Hundred? Two Hundred? You entertained Grant didn't you? You old fart. I hope your jokes are better than they were in Da Nang."

Hope: "Spike, you live over here full time? You have ruined most of the shows that I've done in this theater for the last four years or so. You ever go home, buddy?"

Spike: "Hell, I am now, given the company. You're not gonna use that line about the coconut tree and the gecko again are you?"

Hope: "Screw you, Spike. They loved it. But, no. I have some new writers. I'm making you the coconut tree. We have to get going, the girls tire easily. That's why I hired them. They don't have great expectations... at least when it comes to Dickens. I'll see you guys at the show. Spike, you sit in the back and wear a disguise, OK?"

"Screw you. I'm running the lights. Off when you're up. You're the only guy that steals jokes from Henny Youngman. You ever notice you never have to steal any of your own?"

Hope, now serious: "I don't want to see you here next year, Spike. I don't want to see anybody here next year. When you get back, give me a call and come down to see me."

Spike knows Bob Hope on a first name basis!? The guy never ceased to amaze Graham and Hollywood. They had never heard a word about it.

Graham interrupted as he was leaving: "Mr. Hope, we fly on two four, so we'll miss your show. But thanks for coming here tonight. It's unforgettable. God Bless you for all you have done for us."

Hope, smiling with a look in his eyes that was almost parental: "Look at your scheduled PTOB on two four, Captain Kid. It's revised. You have to be there an hour and a half earlier than usual. I'm doing a show just for you guys. Make sure Spike sits in the back, even though you guys are lead."

Graham was certain that his mouth was hanging open. He didn't respond. Hell, Hope even spoke crewdog. The entourage departed, and they went back for a final Russian. They were all so star struck that they didn't notice that there were only two girls leaving with Hope.

Graham: "Spike, you really are a mystery. Poorly written, but a mystery. How in the hell did you get to know Bob Hope? I mean we were all stunned! How in the hell did you get to Da Nang?

"There's lots of things you don't know about me, B-dog. Things you may, or may not, want to know depending on your state of mind. For the record, Bob and I got to know each other in December of 1968. In reality, we met a long time ago. He's a great guy. He shows up at one in the morning to give guys a memory they will carry forever. That's him."

Graham: "Hey, Hollywood! Where the hell did Sluggo go? He was in max Thai-Español stage. Did he meet Hope?"

"I didn't see him after Hope walked in. I assumed that he was just as taken by the moment as we all were, but Sluggo gone for last call? That's impossible. Maybe he's taking a nap in the head."

Cowboy walked in: "Sluggo's fine. Last call, gentlemen. I bet he's a lot finer than you damn autograph seekers. He went through the back bar about twenty minutes ago with two bottles of champagne, an ice bucket, glasses, three large towels, and some chilled caviar, courtesy of me."

Graham: "Bullshit. How'd that drunken dwarf carry all that shit?"

Cowboy: "Well she was carrying the ice bucket and the glasses. And she had the jar of caviar tucked between a magnificent pair of tits. Yes, sirs, I bet Sluggo is just fine, boys."

Now they *were* stunned. That little snake. That rotten little turd. If you don't pay attention in battle, you get killed.

Spike got up and was leaving *without* Graham and Hollywood. Spike smile: "Don't let your imagination drive you nuts, boys. Vicki ain't that good. Debbie's the one. See you tomorrow."

E-Jeep's eyes looked like saucers. This whole evening was a dream... *how do I tell my wife I've fallen in love with my hand?*

Graham, depressed: "Hollywood, we're supposed to be the movie star clones here. We lose out to a dwarf midget and a grungy old fart that is generally offensive to people most of the time. What does that tell us?"

Hollywood: "What causes wars, Bulldog. You need to listen more carefully. Let's go back and be depressed. At least we can take their dough on the court tomorrow. They'll be worn out."

TENNIS, EVERYONE

Spike, Hollywood, Sluggo, and Graham all took a crew bus to the tennis courts at 10 AM. Spike had shown up minutes before they left.

Graham: "You nickel dick asshole, Spike. You could have at least provided some company for the rest of us. You are a selfish greedy turd. Bring your wallet."

"Jealous, B-dog? I may have a nickel dick, but it's been places in the last twelve hours that you only dream about. Besides, you're a newlywed. You couldn't do shit without dying of guilt."

"I'd like a test at this point, but you're probably right. Don't forget your wallet, and leave the money in it."

They went to the gate of the number one court. It was padlocked. The center court was padlocked as well, but there was a small note card taped to the windbreak just to the right of the lock:

ALL COURTS RESERVED FOR GENERAL MEESON AND HIS STAFF FROM 0800 ON 22 DEC UNTIL 2100 ON 23 DEC. DO NOT ENTER EVEN IF COURTS ARE NOT IN USE.

Graham asked Spike: "Who the hell is General Meeson? He can't do this shit."

"He's the new CO of MAC. He's the head trash hauler. The guy came from SAC. He was CO of 15th Air Force. Got his fourth star and was moved to head up milk trucks. C'mon, we're going to the BX."

They walked to the BX, and Spike bought a hacksaw, four large jars of Vaseline, and four plastic spatulas. They were running low on daq ingredients so Graham went to get some rum at the Commissary. There wasn't any. The commissary was out of everything. Something was up. They walked back to the courts and put the stuff in the shade. Spike cut the chain off the court door with their new tennis hacksaw, and they went in and played both singles and doubles for a couple of hours. Everybody hated playing Graham because he didn't know how. He worked on the assumption that the objective was to get the ball over the net inside appropriate lines so that's what he did. He didn't care about form. The other guys did. Graham rarely lost, which drove Hollywood crazy. After more than two hours, the General never showed up. He had reserved the courts *in case* he wanted to play. The Prick. Milk truck driver.

Before they left, they each took a jar of Vaseline and spotted it around the courts using the spatulas. It wasn't easy to see on the court. As they were walking through the parking lot, three staff cars pulled into the lot on the other side of the courts. Suddenly one of the staff cars started up and raced around the parking lot to their side. The car pulled up to them, and some fat guy in tennis clothes that were two sizes too small jumped out: "Were you people playing tennis on these courts!? That is not allowed! These courts are reserved for the General! You may not use them until the General does not anticipate their need! Who in the hell are you that you would violate the reservation! I want your names and ranks immediately! You are on report!"

Fatboy had no idea of whom he had accidentally encountered. What a set-up. This would make their day.

Spike responded to the fat guy: "We just fly airplanes. We don't apologize for using courts that weren't used. But that's not the point. Who the hell are you? You could be a commie spy from the Fat Province of China. We will need to see identification. Now!" The fat guy was suddenly intimidated.

"I-I-I- don't have an ID! It's in the car! I'm Lieutenant Colonel Meeson! General Meeson's aide! I can show you ID. Just let me get it out of the car."

This was getting to be very entertaining. Graham joined the torture session: "You know who you're dealing with, Colonel spy? We think we're in OSIFO. That's the Office of Special Investigation, Flying Operations. It's so secret that we aren't allowed to know we're in it. But assignment to OSIFO gives us a license to kill... Kill anybody, Colonel Fat, if we're in it."

Now Meeson looked totally confused and more terrified. "OSIFO? I never heard of OSIFO. Even my General has never heard of it... I think."

Graham: "Of course you haven't! If you had, we would have to kill you after we find out that we're assigned to it."

Sluggo looked over at the courts. They were all playing. No one gave a shit about the fat guy.

Sluggo: "You guys aren't even good at what you don't do. How did you make it through spy school? Jesus! You have the same name as your commie General! Explain that!"

"I'm... I'm his nephew! Just let me get my ID! I-I-I- didn't know you gentlemen were OSIFO! I apologize! Please let me get my ID!"

Graham, almost yelling: "We're not, and you can't know because then we'd have to kill you when we find out we are!"

Spike, snarling: "Go get your ID, and it better say that you are who you say you are!"

The fat aide went to the car and returned with his wallet and handed it to Spike.

"You see I am who I say I am."

Sluggo was having fun as well: "We need to inspect your car. You stay right here while we do that."

They all jumped in the staff car, drove around the courts and threw the fat guys' wallet in the parking lot. They headed back to the Haven and dropped off the car a block away.

As they were walking up the stairs, Graham thought out loud, "How the hell do dumbshits like that make L/C?"

Spike: "Uncles, B-dog. That's how. Uncles with four stars or Dad's or friends thereof. Ability has nothing to do with it. Bloodlines have everything to do with it. It's the SUMU Principle: Show Up, Move Up."

On the way upstairs, Spike and Graham stopped by the Day Room [a community room in each building] to get ice and check the TV in case the news was on. It was. CBS was misleading America, as usual. They stopped for a minute as the news of the strike on the 18th came on:

"B-52s attacked targets in North Vietnam in a stepped up offensive to bring the North Vietnamese back to the peace talks in Paris." They showed a shot of the remains of a G model tail section surrounded by Vietnamese peasants. It bothered them both, but no one said anything.

"The Air Force declined to release figures on how many of the bombers were lost in the attack, but we obtained these pictures from the French news bureau clearly showing the remains of what appears to be a B-52. In other news..."

The bastards. The wives must have gone nuts. Wildman had a call scheduled back to the base. They had to have his wife reassure the other wives.

Sluggo called Dangle and reserved his car for the evening. Steaks at the Navy Club. On the way upstairs, they ran into Deke Murphy out of Robbins.

Deke said that they lost two more last night. They didn't know the guys personally, but they knew them because they were crewdogs, and now they were dead or POWs. D-Kid had made it. Maybe others did. Maybe.

Sluggo came in with a huge grin on his face: "I have great news, boys. Extraordinary news actually... I'll have margarita, no salt."

Graham, still irritated from the news broadcast: "You little shit, Sluggo. If it is really good news instead of your Smolensky bullshit, and you pull this stall for dramatic effect to crap on us again, I'm going to throw you off the damn third floor. I'm not kidding, you little prick."

"OK. OK. I have it from a very reliable source called Dick Dangle himself that [another dramatic pause] SUNNY AND BENTZ ARE POWs! CONFIRMED! They are alive, guys!"

Everybody cheered and yelled. Except Spike. He was very disturbed with the news. So he made a statement.

"There are six crewdogs on a crew, guys. We have two confirmed. That's not a very good recovery rate. The shitbird gooks murdered the other four, or worse. They probably murdered the guys that D-Kid flew with, too." They all fell silent as quickly as they had cheered, all reflecting on Spike's statement. He was right. This was bad news in a sense. They knew that if the other four were POWs they would have heard that at the same time.

Sluggo, Spike, Hollywood, and Graham all left for the Navy O'Club in Dangle's car. The Wildman's wife had flown in from the CONUS so he was down at the Agana Hilton getting his brains screwed out. Another reason to get depressed. On the way down, Spike made a point that was even more disturbing, "Put it this way, boys. If some gook pilot landed in your front yard after blowing the shit out of your town, what would you do? I know what I'd do. I'd shoot the bastard."

En route, they had to stop for fuel. Sluggo: "We better stop in Agana and buy some rum and shit. We're almost out and we have a long drive ahead of us."

Graham agreed: "Sluggo's right. We got at least another twenty minutes. We better hit a Tank. We'll bingo in another ten."

As much as they drank, which was generally too much by design, they rarely got drunk. But this time Hollywood was well down the runway.

Hollywood: "I'm having a slight difficulty seeing anything. One of you other guys drive."

Spike decided he was fine, took the wheel, and drove over the center divider in the parking lot.

Spike: "They shouldn't have put that damn thing there. It's a hazard. It's probably a Navy plot. We're on their third of the Island you know. "

They all got out to look at the damage and couldn't see any. There was a little when Spike backed into the pole on his next attempt to leave.

They managed to get to the Naval Base without hitting anything else. They were waved through the gate and saluted smartly by the guard. They had broken tradition. The only one left in the car that was sober was Spike, and he was drunk.

When they parked in the "Captains Only" reserved space and got out, Sluggo glanced at the front of the staff car and stopped cold.

"Hey dogs. We took the wrong car, unless Dangle just got three stars."

They all broke into a wave of laughter… nobody gave a shit about general's cars.

After laughing stopped, which took awhile, they had another couple of drinks that no one needed, and decided to eat. Hollywood kept everybody quiet, kind of, and somehow they were seated in the main dining room. Everybody ordered steak and mashed potatoes along with all kinds of other shit on the menu and three bottles of wine. They were going to be civilized and discreet.

They were just finishing their steaks, which were particularly good, but they were fast becoming sober. Suddenly from nowhere, Andrews's aide, Jack, appeared at the table with two sky cops.

Spike, smiling while eating: "Hi, Colonel!" He swallowed slowly. "How ya been, buddy? Sit down and join us. The sky cops can stand behind you and guard your six."

"Major, you know why we're here. Please pay your bill, and join us for a ride back to Andersen."

Sluggo, who was still ripped after having enjoyed an entire bottle of wine with dinner: "No, Colonel, we don't know why you're here… unless maybe you're car shopping. That's it! You're looking for a new car for the General! Well, we beat you to it! We brought that beat up piece of shit that the General has been hauled around in down here to trade it in on a brand new Navy Admiral's car."

The Colonel was clearly intimidated: "C'mon, guys, don't give me any of your shit. We have a bread truck waiting to take you back. Let's go. There's nothing wrong with the General's car. It's in perfect shape.

Graham hinted at the new problem: "Not any more, Colonel. Not any more."

They loaded into the bread truck that was actually a paddy wagon and napped as Jack followed them in the General's car. He noticed it made strange new sounds and didn't drive well at all. By the time they reached the Monsoon Mansion, Jack was even more furious. They had destroyed the General's car. When they pulled in, he met them at the back of the van:

"You guys destroyed the General's car! This is serious, gentlemen! We are also in deep shit with MAC because you guys beat the shit out of a bunch of their guys the other night. The MAC guys started it, so MAC aircrews got banned from *our* Club indefinitely. It seems that whenever you guys are not flying, this shit happens. When you are flying, *nothing* happens. Everything is peaceful. The result of all of this, gentlemen, is that the supplies that MAC flies in, like beef and booze, are drying up. That was *before* Meeson broke his arm. General Andrews is sure that it will get worse now. You guys have screwed things up royally! General Andrews will patch things up with both the Navy and MAC, but he specifically told me to tell you guys that your bulletproof era has drawn to a close. No more passes."

Spike: "Let's bomb the bastards. Cutting off our booze is an Act of War! Wipe out a base or two, and they'll come around."

Graham made a point: "You can't bomb 'em because all they do is leave. Bomb what base? They're all over the Pacific, leaving other bases. They eat at other bases, sleep at other bases, and go to other bases' Clubs. Then they leave. No defined target. We'd have to bomb all the bases in the Pacific and SEA, including our own. No shit. That won't work. We're going to have to think of something else.

Jack: "Goddamnit! You're not listening, men! YOU'RE DONE! NO MORE FIGHTS, ATTACKS, CAR THEFTS, FLARE GUN WARS, OR ANY OTHER DISRUPTIONS! YOU'RE DONE!"

Jack, who had paused and regained his composure: "Like I said, this is serious stuff. The General will see you at 1000 hours tomorrow. Be there on time. Now you are all clearly over fueled, so I suggest you get to bed so you are presentable for the General."

"Yes, sir. See ya, Jack."

Jack turned back toward them as everyone was stumbling off the paddy wagon: "Oh, yes. The General said the uniform of the day are the flight suits he gave you. He'd like to see them."

He turned to his car and left.

Hollywood: "The flight suits... shit. Now what?"

They all stumbled up the stairs and collapsed on their beds.

Graham heard Spike snoring in about thirty seconds. Soon after, he pulled onto the same runway.

GENERAL ANDREWS AGAIN

The next morning, they awoke to heavy rain. Monsoon rain. It would last a while, probably all day. They dressed in regular flight suits and went over to Ops to get a chili dog for breakfast. Sluggo met them at the Roach Coach by accident but came back with them. By the time they got back, their flight suits were soaked.

Spike: "We're saved, guys. We can tell the General we didn't want to ruin our good flight suits in the rain. Besides, Sluggo doesn't have one, so we felt sorry for him. He wouldn't feel right wearing a regular guy flight suit while accompanying guys wearing War Hero flight suits. Poor little dwarf."

Sluggo: "I won't even say it, but you know what you can do. You guys don't even have those pussy suits anymore. I know that because Smolensky found them in the dumpster while making his regular rounds. We already stripped off the name tags and insignia and sold them over at the NCO Club for $30 apiece. That's right guys, $180 for just being alert. Besides, Spike, if it were not for my heroic efforts on your behalf, you would already be court-martialed and in prison for life. And by the way, you assholes are all going to be designated as DNIF Douches since 24 December got scratched this morning. You pussies will miss the entire war!"

Hollywood: "What the hell are you talking about, Sluggo? What's scratched? They aren't going to back-off now. That would be idiotic."

Sluggo: "The REMF *are* idiots. You know that. They announced a thirty-six hour stand down for Christmas. It's posted on the board. Your lead on two four is gone, boys, and you're not scheduled on two six, because it's too late. So you may as well pack up and move over to Coward Quarters so you can take a nap through the rest of the war. Meantime, my heroic crew is scheduled to lead a wave on two six."

Hollywood, incredulous: "If this is your typical bullshit, Sluggo, I'm going to beat the shit out of you, and you're the one that will be DNIF. E-Jeep! Go over to Ops and check this out, and then meet us at 8th headquarters at 0950. They gave us their word that this wouldn't happen."

Sluggo: "Don't be naïve, Hollywood. You know they never keep their promises. In fact, it's against some AFR to keep promises to crewdogs. So believe it, my friend. You guys were screwed."

Hollywood was really pissed. He knew Sluggo wasn't lying. He just hoped he was. They all did.

SO-2 left for 8th at 0945. The mood was glum. E-jeep met them there and confirmed that they were scratched. They waited outside the General's office until his secretary told them to go in. The General was not smiling as they came to attention and saluted.

"At ease and be seated, men. I am not going to repeat what Jack told you last night. Those were my words. You guys are done. No more of your bullshit. Hang it up. I'm dead serious on this, no matter what Senator watches over you. Is that clear?"

Multiple, "Yes, sirs."

You're dismissed, gentlemen.

Hollywood didn't care: "Excuse me, General. We were scheduled to fly lead on two four and that has now been canceled. We were promised that we would not be given preferential treatment, and now we've been screwed. We need to fly on two six."

The General: "You know that schedule is hard, Captain. Washington ordered the stand down. I would not have. It only gives the enemy time to reload the SAM sites and re-group so they will be waiting for us on two six. On the other hand, I don't want to see our crews get hit on Christmas. The tension is already ridiculous. My God, men, every time one of our crews go down it kills me as well. I even asked CINC SAC to let me fly a strike, and he laughed at me. You are dismissed."

"Yes, sir." He was a good guy.

As they were leaving, the General changed his mind: "Captain Noland, I'll tell you what I can do. I can make you Stand-by One on two six. It's a big strike. There's no way at least one G won't crap out. You will be assured of launch. Consider it done."

"Yes, sir. Thank you, sir."

They walked out, both relieved and scared again. Spike filled in Sluggo when they got back.

Sluggo: "Well, you kiss asses lucked out as usual. I may abort just so you're sure to go. On second thought, my heroic crew would go nuts if we aborted. No crew except Plug's and that other asshole StanBoard dork from Chickenshit AFB would ever abort unless they were literally on fire during TO roll. But then the General's right, somebody *will* catch fire and abort. You won't have to move to Coward Quarters yet."

Hollywood: "Yet? Screw you yet. We've done everything we can to get into rotation. In fact, I'm going to see Dangle right now to get us on for the 27th if the Wing is flying. And Sluggo, you are a professional trouble maker. You heard what the General said. No more trick fuck events or we're all screwed. So we are all going to cool it."

Spike: "Absolutely... for a day or two."

Hollywood: "Spike! Goddamnit! I'm serious! You back off! I have a career at stake here. You don't."

Really bad judgment. On both accounts.

Spike used the opening: "Hollywood, I have an obligation to tradition. You have an obligation to Hollywood. Get it, Captain? I need leadership on this crew. If you don't provide it, I will."

A fight was imminent, so Graham intervened: "Why don't both of you just shut-up and start thinking again. That would be novel. And in reality, Sluggo and Wildman are the guilty ones. Let's dump on them instead of ourselves."

Sluggo: "Bulldog, you shitbird. You're the felon and instigator here. I am the mediator, general counsel, and overall Mr. Nice Guy. So bite me."

More arguments ensued, but finally they all agreed. The General was right. The tension was off the wall. Their friends were dying, and they might be next.

DISAPPOINTMENT AND HEARTBREAK

D-Kid and Alex were worried on the night of the 23rd when they were not awakened by the B-52 strikes. Could they have stopped so soon? Was the war over? Or had the REMF pulled back again and decided to screw around for a few more years while they rotted in this hellhole?

Tomorrow was Christmas Eve. Great place to be on Christmas Eve.

"Hey, Alex, does your family open presents on Christmas Eve or Christmas morning?"

D-Kid knew he shouldn't have asked the question the minute he did. He had been thinking about Robbie and their families on Christmas. Kind of a self-inflicted torture.

What a dumbshit question. Make the guy think of Christmas and home out of nowhere.

Alex let it go: "Christmas morning. Always. We'll do that next year, too, only I'll be there with them."

D-Kid didn't respond. He knew he'd been given a pass.

Later in the day they were taken down the hall to a little washroom to empty and scrub their honey buckets and bathe in freezing water with lye soap that didn't lather. At least it was a bath. The FOGs were on the other side of the wall. FOGs were the "Fucking Old Guys." Alex and D-Kid were FNGs: "Fucking New Guys." The FOGs told them to keep the faith and continue to resist. The FNGs were carefully kept away from the FOGs by the gooks. The slip was a serious breach, but the gooks didn't know that they could make contact through the washroom wall.

In the cell next to D-Kid, Tom Sampson had slipped into delirium from a very serious infection. He had been wounded when he ejected, and the wound had gone completely untreated. The gooks would let him die. Why bother to treat it?

CHRISTMAS EVE

December 24th came quickly. Everybody went to the Hope Show and sat in the third row from the front, including Spike, who kept harassing Bob. Bob's years of dealing with such shit kept him from responding.

After a great show, they all headed for the Club dressed in flight suits since uniforms were required at the Hope show. Graham was astounded to find that the Club was jammed and full of the forbidden suits having fun. Fortunately, Cowboy had managed to keep their table reserved, and they settled in quickly. Wildman showed up in civvies. He looked out of place: "Bulldogeous, I decided to come up and have a shooter with you guys since it's Christmas Eve and I thought you would need my guidance in your efforts to shoot down Santa. I can't be here too long but certainly long enough to formulate such a simple plan."

Graham responded: "Fake Major, how un-nice to see you. You look refreshed and relaxed, due no doubt to screwing your eyes out for the last few days. You prick. Who's guarding Gail? If I were you, I'd have an army of eunuchs surrounding her around the clock. Now go away. You're completely out of place here now since you're no longer horny."

Hollywood: "No more cockamamie plans, Wildman. We're not shooting down Santa or anybody else."

He looked at Spike who had his Spike Smile on: "At least for awhile. We had our ass handed to us yesterday by the General. REALLY handed to us. We can't do shit. We get caught doing anything, even minor everyday rat fucks, and we are toast. No shit until further notice."

Wildman: "Come on, guys! We can't break tradition! The entire Squadron would be pissed beyond belief! The entire Wing would be pissed! All the shit that we do gets blamed on us by default. In fact, we get blamed for a ton of shit that other guys do. Send E-Jeep back for the potato cannon and we'll fire off some rounds onto the General's golf course. We can improvise how to get Santa from there."

Hollywood: "NO! We lay low at least through Christmas! Period!"
It was Christmas Eve, and everyone was thinking about two things: their families and their brothers, who were either dead or POWs, and *their* families. D-Kid… Jimmy's crew… No one argued with Hollywood. They ordered BRs and a dice cup and got the game going.

Zero came in and walked back to their table. Very unusual.

"I came over to tell you guys something that is unbelievable. It's…"

Spike: "So get on with it, Co."

"My buddy Toby Sands from Barksdale was up at the pool yesterday. Suddenly a Sky Cop comes into the pool area, and he's followed by Colonel Pew and two other guys."

"Was he sure it was Pew?"

Pew was the "Major Major" of the 43rd. He was named after a character in *Catch-22*. They knew he was the Commander but no one ever saw him.

"Toby saw his name tag. It was Pew. The Sky Cop pointed out a lady that was sitting not far from me. She had her little boy with her. She looked up at Pew, and she knew immediately. Her husband was down. She started crying, and they read her the formal notice. She just kept sobbing and held her little boy close to her knees. He was crying, too, but Toby said he was too little to know why."

Nobody said a word. No senior Air Force officer could be that stupid and callous. It was completely unbelievable.

Finally, Sluggo broke the silence: "It has to be true. No one could think up something that awful. 'Major Major' better hide out after the crewdogs find out about this. We will make sure they all know quickly. Then we hatch a plot on what we're going to do to Major Major. It won't be nice."

"B-Dog, you go tell that table of crewdogs about this incident and tell them to pass it along. Co, go tell that table."

The word spread like lightening, and the mood of the room was not good. The Pilipeen band came in at 2100 and started the normal concert. The Club was jammed with crewdogs. The stand down had allowed most of the guys to take a needed break. Cowboy quietly brought them a tray of cheeseburgers from the back bar. They were playing it very low key.

Spike: "You know what, guys? We are in an environment full of amateur drunks. Look at the bar. They're three deep. This whole place is a powder keg. Every guy up there in a crewdog flight suit has lost friends in the last six days, and now they all know about Major Major's stunt. One trigger and this joint goes bananas. If this place goes up, we all know who will get blamed. Let's finish the burgers and get the hell out of here."

Too late.

The band launched into *We Gotta Get Outta This Place,* and even the rookies joined in the chorus. They pumped up the volume, and the song went on for fifteen minutes. As soon as the song concluded, a fat Kiwi wife in a purple dress with a poinsettia bouquet trudged up on the stage and went to the microphone: "Attention! You men! I am Colonel Pearlwater's wife, and I am also President of the Andersen Officer's Wives Club. Flight suits are not allowed in the Main Bar, nor are they allowed in the Main Dining Room. In addition, the music from the band is way too loud. All of you that are in flight suits must leave immediately or go to the bar we have put in the back for you. The band must turn down the volume and should be restricted to Christmas carols since it is the eve of the celebration of our Savior's birth. Now my husband, Colonel Pearlwater, will be here in less than a half..."

It was incredibly quiet.

WHAP!

She was hit with what looked like a wet napkin.

"SCREW YOU!"

"GET THE HELL OUTTA HERE!"

More napkins. More insults. She waddled off the stage quickly. Sluggo desperately signaled to the band to start playing again, which they did. A bunch of guys grabbed the Christmas tree in the lobby which could be seen from the Main Bar and dragged it toward the back.

Pandemonium.

Furniture was being dragged toward the back, everything was being dragged through the Main Dining Room, out the back, and into the pool. Then the dining room started to go in the pool. They could see into the dining room through another set of doors next to the band. Some LC in a Class A uniform tried to stop one of the guys that was carrying a chair. Someone else decked him.

Hollywood put his head on the table and spoke to it: "We're screwed. I guarantee you guys that we will be blamed for this. Totally screwed."

Wildman: "Bullshit. Pass the dice, Sluggo. Let the games continue."

Some fights broke out between the crewdogs. This would be a Christmas that all of them would remember for a lot of reasons. All bad. At least half of the bar furniture was in the pool, along with about the same from the dining room, and *all* the Christmas decorations. Cowboy came over and sat down next to Sluggo.

"Merry Christmas, boys. What a dumb bitch. I can't believe this."

The Sky Cops charged though the doors. Everybody scattered. The L/C Sky Cop came over to the table: "You men are under arrest. The charge is inciting a riot and disorderly conduct. Get up!"

Cowboy: "Colonel, these men didn't do a thing. They never left the table. They aren't guilty of anything. Now please go and find the person that you should put in jail, Colonel Pearlwater's wife, and leave these men alone."

Sluggo: "Yeah, Colonel. We're completely innocent. This time. Besides, this is an amateur job. We would have burned the place and gang raped the Colonel's wife..."

Sluggo was interrupted by Wildman: "Screw you, Sluggo. I wouldn't touch that pig. Even with *your* dick. We would have drowned her. The point is five. Roll, Bulldogeous."

More Sky Cops. Then Dangle in slippers again. He came straight to their table. They all concentrated on the game and didn't look up. Cowboy stood up and started talking to Dangle. No one could hear what he said despite being the only ones left in the bar except Sky Cops.

Dangle: "The Club is closed until further notice, gentlemen. Return to your quarters. Now."

Dangle turned and left. So did they.

CHAPTER XVII: YOU BETTER WATCH OUT, YOU BETTER NOT CRY

A HEARTBREAK CHRISTMAS

"Merry Christmas, Alex."

"Merry Christmas, Bob."

That was all that either one of the men expected this Christmas morning, but they would be surprised. Christmas would be difficult. But they were alive. They knew a lot of guys that were not. A week ago or less, they were alive. They all had a dream that by some great stroke of luck, they would be home with their families for Christmas. They made it. Their spirit was home.

The first surprise came when the gooks went into Tom's cell and gave him a shot of penicillin. It no doubt saved his life. Merry Christmas, Tom.

The second surprise was real food. Scrambled eggs, BBQ pork and some greens, along with coffee, full of grounds. They also gave them a red liquor that tasted like shit, but they didn't care. They got a little buzz. The gooks even said that they had arranged for a Christmas Mass, but it was cancelled because the B-52s had blown up the church.

D-Kid didn't care. The bread, wine, and lack of a priest reminded him of the Supper of Our Lord, which is central to Christmas. He was at peace. The gooks could control physical things but not his thought and prayer.

As night fell on Christmas, there were again no airstrikes. D-Kid and Alex became even more concerned.

Alex was first to voice his dark concern: "Bob, you think they'd leave us here and then negotiate a release after certain other conditions were met a few months from now?"

Bob was always optimistic, especially on Christmas Day: "Shit no. No way. A primary objective is to get us out and end the war. We knew that when we started Linebacker. Although… I really don't understand why they stopped. It only gives the gooks time to re-arm the SAM sites. When our guys come back to finish the job, it might be really bad, especially the first night."

Alex: "That's what I meant. Why would they stop? That makes no sense."

D-Kid's optimism was fading: "Because the guys doing the planning are idiots…
or Nixon didn't want another half dozen widows created on Christmas Day."

CHRISTMAS ON GUAM

Christmas morning was typical – rain and 95 degrees. Christmas was really
tough. Thoughts of family pervaded the crewdogs' minds. They all wrote letters
home in the morning except Roller who was worried that Frau Eva might start
to like him again. Graham carried the suspicion at this point that Roller was not
a bigamist but rather a polygamist. He spent most of the time on Guam hiding
except when he disappeared with his powerfully ugly, round eyed girlfriend.
Graham couldn't figure out where he disappeared to for his meetings with her.
It had to be off base, but he was too frightened to go off base, given Mr. Tagaki's
search for him.

Sluggo walked in with some rum and limeade: "Gentlemen, Merry Christmas.
I'm sure that you are all as depressed as I am, but hopefully this will be our
last Christmas at war, at least for a year or two. In any event, I have it on good
authority, specifically the ever reliable Smolensky, that Mr. Takagi is now hell
bent on tracking down Colonel Roller because word leaked out to the Japanese
community here on Guam that the good Colonel had dumped his honorable
daughter most dishonorably. Apparently this not only causes the family to lose
face, but the fact that she was harpooned by a round eye makes it doubly worse.
Before the Jap locals found out about it, Roller was maybe just beaten to a pulp,
but now he has to be 'made into a public example' of what crossing 'Don Sushi'
means to the offender. It means dead. According to Smolensky, who you know
is highly reliable, and in fact won my Employee of the Year Award this year."

Hollywood: "It's the 40% chance that your information from that bum
Smolensky might be correct that concerns me. I don't understand why this has
become such an issue that never goes away. If that moron Seeps could keep his
dick under control, none of this shit would ever happen."

Hollywood yelled through the bathroom: "Seeps! Get in here!"

Roller came through the bathroom looking beat to shit, as he almost always did.

"Yeah, Boss. Merry Christmas. What's goin' on?"

"You're really up shitcreek now due to your wandering indiscriminate dick.
According to Smolensky, word of your on and off engagement to Mr. Takagi's
daughter has leaked to the Jap population here on Guam. Apparently that has

made a bad situation even worse for you, since the leak is apparently very serious in Takagi's world. We need to figure out how to hide you for the duration."

Roller had his face in his hands: "Boy-o-boy, boss, this is not good. The word getting to the Japs here is real bad. Real, real bad. I gotta get out of here for good. Right away, boss."

Roller had considerable knowledge of Asian customs and culture due to lectures from the various bimbos he was screwing and or married to throughout Asia. Amazing, considering he was as dumb as he was.

Spike: "You can't get out of here on another emergency domestic leave. So you have only one real choice besides being cut up with sushi knives and fed to the sharks. No, that isn't what they will do. It's not public enough. Your only option at this point is that you're going to get re-engaged."

Everybody stared at Spike in disbelief. He had to be kidding.

"I can see by your looks that you guys think this is a really dumb ass idea. But you should all know me better than that by now. We can intervene on Roller's behalf and mediate a re-engagement. We come up with some logical reason why Roller broke off the engagement the first time and say he wants to get back together with her. His heart was broken, whatever, it doesn't even need to be that good of an excuse. They will accept almost anything."

Graham didn't understand: "Now why would the 'Don' accept that?"

"Different world and a whole different culture, B-dog. They literally don't think like we do, which may serve them well with China later, but that's a different story. The Jap mob hangs out at the bar at the Daichi Hotel in Agana after five. We should go down there and make some overtures this afternoon. It can't hurt."

Hollywood turned to Roller: "You little shit. You go over to tent city and disappear until we send somebody to get you. You are going to get your dick under control after this or you'll be cleaning boots in Elmendorf. Now go hide."

Hollywood left, and so did Roller. Roller was literally skulking down the walkway to the stairs.

The three met downstairs in the Day Room at 1730 and took a cab downtown to the Daichi which was a new, very high class Japanese hotel. The bar was crowded but they found room at the bar. They ordered rum and tonics and grabbed the bar peanuts because they had forgotten to eat after breakfast. The Japanese bartender came back with their drinks.

Spike was blunt with the bartender: "We need to meet with Takagi-san right away. Can you arrange that?"

The bartender averted his eyes and replied: "Takagi-san? I never heard of a Takagi-san, so it would be impossible to arrange meeting."

Spike knew he knew the guys in the booth: "Well, then why don't you go over and ask all of Takagi's guys in that booth if they ever heard of him and say that we have information on colonel Roller."

The bartender didn't respond. He washed some glasses and then went over to the booth that Spike had motioned toward.

The bartender returned after what seemed to be a quick conversation: "Those men may know the guy you look for. They will talk."

They closed the tab and finished their drinks quickly. As the three approached the booth in the corner, the Japanese noticed them coming and there was a bit of commotion.

Graham reached the booth in front of Spike and Sluggo: "Hello, gentleman. I'm Captain Graham, and this is Captain Duggen and..."

Spike interrupted and stepped in front of Graham: "Major Wilson"

He stuck out his hand to the guy in the middle of the five seated in the booth. The guy seated to his left had his right hand stuck inside his coat and looked a bit menacing. The guy in the middle shook Spike's hand and responded: "I am Tatsuri Yashida, Major. We would ask you to take seat but no room. Do you know a Colonel Seeps by chance?"

If anything, the guy was direct.

Spike: "Yes we do, Yashida-san. That's why we're here. We want to talk to Mr. Takagi about Colonel Seeps."

Yoshida spoke in rapid Japanese to the other zips at the table. All but the guy faking the hold on a gun in his coat got up immediately. Yoshida looked at Spike: "Please be seated, gentlemen. My associates have a meeting they must attend."

Sluggo: "Lao, lao. Sawadi chups."

Spike: "Shut the hell up, Sluggo. These guys don't speak Thai, you dipshit."

Yoshida: "Yes we do, Major. Again, please sit."

One of those leaving got up and did a short bow towards Spike. Spike returned a slightly shorter bow. He made sure that Spike was seated directly next to Yoshida by holding Graham back. They all sat, and the others left. The guy kept his hand in his coat and stared at Spike. It was almost comical, right out of a badly made crime movie.

Yoshida, speaking quietly to Spike: "We have interest in speaking to Colonel Seeps. Could you make that meeting quickly?"

Spike: "No. We need to meet with Takagi-san first. Then we will arrange for a meeting if Seeps is back from his secret mission."

"When would you want meeting?"

"How about now?"

"I will see. Please order whatever you like."

A Japanese waitress appeared from nowhere and took orders for three black Russians. Before she left, Yoshida snapped at her in Japanese. She bowed to Yoshida and left.

Yoshida to Spike: "So Colonel sent you to see Takagi-san for him? Very smart. He owes big explanation to Takagi-san. Very big. We try to arrange for meeting right away."

Spike: "Thanks. Now would help. Seeps may leave on another secret mission very soon."

Yoshida signaled, and one of his boys appeared. Yoshida spoke rapidly in Japanese, and the guy disappeared, after many Hai! Hai! Hai!'s

Graham: "What does 'Hai' mean?"

"It means yes. Always pronounced in kind of a staccato, abbreviated way. They have no word for no."

Yoshida turned to Spike, smiling: "Spike-san, we do have word for no. It is 'fuck you.'"

"That must be cultural crossover, Yoshida-san. Amazing what thirty years will do, isn't it?"

"Not good idea to bring up what happened thirty years ago. You especially know that, Spike-san."

The conversation continued for another ten minutes on what appeared to be a much lighter level led mainly by Spike and the Zip, with some bullshit thrown in by Sluggo and Graham. Suddenly, lackey number one appeared in front of the table and spoke to Yoshida. He turned to Spike again: "Takagi-san will see you now. Very unusual. Be careful what you say. Have your friends shut up unless Takagi-san speaks to them directly."

He stood up and they all followed him to the elevator.

The meeting with Takagi-san was abrupt and controlled completely by Takagi, as would be expected. Spike's years of dealing with Asians worked to their advantage, and Takagi agreed to allow "Colonel" Roller to again date his daughter. Of course, he didn't even bother to ask his daughter if she wanted to date Colonel Seeps again.

As they were escorted out of Takagi's suite, Spike was irritated: "Let's just get the hell out of here. Seeps gets his sorry ass up shit creek again, we are going to leave him there."

CHAPTER XVIII:
ANOTHER BOYS' NIGHT OUT

26 DECEMBER 72

SO-2 attended the PTOB. It was going to be a massive attack. Over 120 birds would strike ten different targets, all at the same TOT. The tactics had finally changed big time. They would be attacking in waves, as usual, but coming from all different directions, and the planners had taken great care to get them feet wet after the TOT as quickly as possible. Graham wasn't nearly as terrified as the first strike, but he still had that knot in his stomach.

As Stand-by One, they were virtually assured of launch, which was the plan. The chance of no ground abort in the entire G wave was almost impossible.

Spirits were not that bad. While everybody was nervous about all those people trying to kill them, they knew that this shit couldn't go on much longer or they would literally run out of targets, even if the gooks didn't run out of SAMs, which they were almost certainly about to do for absolutely sure any day now… this time. The SAM assessment was given by a new nerd Intel Major that the crewdogs disliked so much that they openly hissed his briefing. Graham wondered out loud what had happened to the white bar that had taken on General Andrews at the 19 Dec PTOB. Probably what happened to all white bars that piss off three stars.

They got to the bird just after 1600 and were astonished to have none other than Some Luck Mazerowski waiting for them. He smiled and saluted Spike as he got off the bus and helped them drag their shit off.

Some Luck: "This bird is ready, sirs. She checked out great. Only some radar glitches so I borrowed the component from 337. They won't need it since she came back full of holes anyway. She will bring you back. I promise."

The crew chiefs really had a dog shit existence on Guam. They lived in tents that leaked. Packed in like sardines with limited water resources so they all stunk all the time.

On the other hand, they weren't in a foxhole in the Mekong Delta surrounded by VC, and they knew it, so they didn't bitch.

They got done with their pre-flight in record time and kicked back. Now they just wait. Except Spike. He was hooking up a tape recorder to the comm system. This had to be interesting.

Graham: "What the hell are you doing now? This is another one of your cockamamie schemes to cut a deal with Herman?"

"No, B-dog. It's a brilliant plan to drive Hanoi Hanna nuts and confuse the shit out of the gooks. Put on your helmet, and go on IC."

Graham did and heard moo-ooo-ooo. Moo-ooo-ooo. Clang. Clang. Brr-r-r-rip blop. Multiple moos all at the same time. Multiple clangs. Multiple fart sounds. It was a recording of a herd of cows.

"Where in the hell did you get that, and what the hell is the idea?"

"Simple, B-dog. Hana will think, and report back to Hanoi, that the crews on B-52s attacking the north have been replaced by cows. Yes, cows. The gooks won't know what to think. Or they'll think it's a Yankee Air Pirate plot to do something extra awful to them. I have Smolensky's crooks buying bags of cow shit all over the island. I'm going to load a few potato bags full of cow pies in with the bombs so that when the gooks do the post strike inspection, they'll find cow turds among the bomb debris or near the impact area, thereby convincing them that some, if not all, of the B-52s are now being flown by cows. To add to that, I got Smolensky borrowing some of those old helmets at Life Support. We're going to drill them with cow horn holes, and I even got some real cow horns coming back from an R&R. We take half a dozen helmets, fit them with real cow horns, and drop them with the cow turds.

"Now the crown jewel will be the real, no shit, cow that I'm buying in Agana. Smolensky's guys at the chute shop are doing a custom made chute harness for the thing, and the guys at ordinance are going to down load one bomb which weighs just a little more than a cow. We load the cow in the top rack so the bombs don't hit it at release and it goes out last in the chute, actually two, opens after release, and the Yankee Air Cow floats down right in the middle of downtown Hanoi. Then the gooks find a real cow in a chute, complete with patches and wings and a name tag, which we are gluing on the cow.

"The gooks go nuts. They complain to the UN that we are conscripting cows to fly bombers against them. They complain and give photo ops to the commie media, which hopefully will release the story internationally. Told ya. Brilliant, isn't it?"

"No. You're getting crazier. Every day. You have drifted beyond the reef, buddy."

"Oh yeah. We even have a name for the cow: Moojor Malt Milk. Get it? That will be on his nametag when the gooks find the body. If we could pressurize the bomb bay, we could even drop a live cow, but the guys say that's impossible, at least for now."

Charlie Tower: "Brass One, taxi to position and hold for release."

"Roger Charlie, Brass One."

Hollywood: "Crew, with this big a launch, we'd waste too much fuel if we lit them up now. Wing wants us to do a hot start when we are needed. Everybody stay strapped and ready."

Spike: "Some Luck, you still on IC?"

"Yes, sir. What broke?"

"Nothing, buddy. Relax. Did you get those burlap bags loaded on the last rack in the bomb bay?"

"Yes, sir."

Hollywood: "What burlap bags? What the hell are you doing, Spike?"

Spike: "Nothing much, I have a plan to drive the gooks nuts with very little effort. I'll tell you about it at debrief. Trust me. You'll love it. It's not anything that General Andrews will hang our ass for."

Hollywood: "Tell me now."

"Cows. Hollywood. Cows. It's a secret weapon. I can't go into detail now. It's classified."

Hollywood: "Godammit, Spike, don't give me that shit! Have you loaded cows in the bomb bay!?"

"Not yet."

Charlie Tower: "Stand By One, light them up. We're half way through the G launch and no one has gone down. It can't go on. Taxi to primary holding area. Stand By Two, follow one."

"Roger Charlie. Stand By One will taxi and hold."

Graham and Spike couldn't see, but Hollywood kept them apprised of the launch progress. It was unbelievable. No one aborted.

Hollywood: "Crew, the last bird, Bronze Three, just went wheels in the well. The impossible has happened. There are guys that took off with balls the size of basketballs. That I guarantee."

Charlie Tower: "Stand By One, miracles do happen. I've been here two years and what has just happened has never happened before. You are some lucky people. Taxi to the parallel and shut her down."

Spike: "Well, the good news is we lead the strike tomorrow. Meantime we have only a quick aircraft de-brief so we can go straight to the club. The Fake Major should be over there since Gail went home and he's up with us tomorrow. That should drive him nuts since he was lead if we went today, which I will remind him of throughout the evening. Oh yeah. By the way, Roller, you are going DNIF tomorrow. Roller, you there?"

"E-Jeep, hit Roller's helmet and wake him up."

Roller: "Yes, Boss? I was studying the tech order and didn't hear you."

"Yeah, right. Listen, numb nuts. You are going DNIF in the morning. We thought we were flying for sure tonight so we made you a date for tomorrow night. With this scrubbed, you'll have to get a cold and go DNIF."

"A date, Boss? With who? It gotta be on the base 'cause I can't dare go off as you know, Boss."

"Don't worry. It's safe. It's with Takagi's daughter."

"WHAT!? BOSS, THAT'S CERTAIN SUICIDE, AND YOU KNOW THAT! I'M NOT GOING ON NO DATE WITH HER! YOU TRYIN' TO KILL ME FER SURE!"

Spike: "Would you relax? It was a surprise we were going to tell you about after we touched tomorrow. Hell, we couldn't even find you until the PTOB. We got everything straightened out with Takagi himself, at great personal risk I might add. You're engaged again. We even have the ring for you. I'll fill you in on everything after we de-brief the bird."

The aircraft lurched forward as the brakes were set. The engines shut down quickly, and the hatch was opened not long afterward. Spike and Graham were buttoning up their gear when they saw Roller bolt down the ladder and out the hatch. Spike followed quickly only to see Roller disappear into the darkness toward the far revetments.

He was gone.

THE RESPONSE AT HEARTBREAK

There had been no bombing for three days. D-Kid and Alex were now really concerned.

D-Kid, naively: "Maybe the war has ended? Maybe those sorties were enough."

"No way, Bob. We have to bring them to their knees. Right now I think their knees are only slightly bent."

It was late and suddenly the world exploded. The noise was deafening, and the vibrations shook the concrete walls of the prison. This was a huge strike... and very close.

Alex dove into the rat shit under his slab bunk.

"Alex, what are you doing? If our guys take us out by accident, you won't even know it, man."

"The ceiling may fall!"

D-Kid, yelling over the din: "If the ceiling falls on your bunk, you'll be crushed underneath and seriously injured. That means you will die a slow and painful death because you know damn well that the gooks won't treat you. On the other hand, if you're up here with me and the ceiling collapses, we'll be killed. As in dead immediately. You should know by now that death is much more preferable than injury in this shithole. Now get up, chicken little. The sky isn't falling, but you *are* covered in rat shit."

The massive strike only went on about 15 minutes, but it scared even the aviators that knew what was going on. The gooks must be terrified. Indeed, soon after the attack ended, a guard named Moonbeam, whom they didn't hate as much as the others, came bursting into their cell.

"Why they bomb prison!? They bomb prison they kill you! They go crazy! They kill everybody!"

D-Kid offered little consolation: "If they wanted to bomb the prison, it would be gone. They won't bomb the prison, but if the war doesn't end very soon they'll bomb everything else until it does. Every night. So you better move into the prison. It's the only place that will be safe. You can have the lower bunk under Alex. Pay no attention to the rat shit."

D-Kid and Alex and all the other POWs knew that the tactics had changed beginning that night. They had gone from "take out specific targets in planned multifaceted attacks" to "hit very hard all at once and scare the shit out of everybody."

They knew it would work. Home pretty soon… maybe.

27 DEC 1972

Spike sent Roller's buddies out to find him and drag him back to Monsoon Mansion. At 2200 they brought Roller through the other door, thoroughly duct tapped, and threw him on his bunk. Spike, Graham, and Hollywood came back from dinner not long afterward and Spike filled in Roller with the details of the meeting with Takagi and the negotiated outcome. Roller, despite his bindings, seemed to settle down emotionally and accept his fate. "Ok, boss. I'll do it, but if Takagi kills me on the spot when I go to pick her up, it's all your fault. You can't trust Japs. They're sneaky."

Spike: "Takagi is in a bind. If you don't get re-engaged he loses enormous face. If he turns you into sushi, too many people will know that he did it and he'll have to leave the island fast. Everything is cool. You hang out with her until the war ends, and we'll be sent home on 24 hours notice."

No one trusted Roller's fortitude. Sluggo and his guns were not taking him down for his protection. They were taking him down to make sure he showed.

HAIPHONG

At 1705, SO-2 put wheels in the well on their way to a strike on Haiphong. They were lead as Blue One of seven cells, twenty one aircraft in all. There was a much larger D wave right behind them going to Hanoi. Pretty easy strike for Blue flight. Inbound over water, four miles into the target, then a hard turn starboard to feet wet very quickly. Very minimum SAM threat since they would only be in a COA for about seven minutes.

Three birds had gone down on 26, and the SAMs had been really bad, especially over Hanoi. The General had been right. The gooks had used the one day stand down to re-arm and reload. The Intel guy at their PTOB had said there had been dozens of MIGs at altitude, but they were apparently just feeding heading and flight levels of the bombers to the SAM sites. MIG CAP had nailed three of them.

Spike had six potato sacks of cow turds loaded in the bomb bay, and his tape recorder was all set. He had spent more time preparing for his Great Cow Offensive than he had on preflight. Graham was worried that the damn cow turds would screw up the bomb release and cause a "hanger" in the bay. A hanger was when one or more bombs did not release and stayed hung up in the bomb bay. The danger was that the bomb could partially release and be attached by one clip when the BNS showed that all of the bombs were gone. When the bird landed back on Guam, if the bomb had armed itself, the touchdown might cause a release and detonation. A detonation had never happened but hangers were too common.

There was a 60 knot headwind most of the way inbound to the PI, but they were actually about five early, so Graham could relax a little. Unfortunately, the knot was still there so he couldn't really relax. Spike did. He was in the bunk as soon as they got to altitude and slept until they were about 200 miles from the PI.

Hollywood: "Spike, you on yet?"

"I'm always on, buddy. What can I teach you today, Jeep?"

Hollywood: "Kiss my ass, you crazy bastard. Listen, you heard Dangle at the PTOB. The gooks are on their knees, and this shit is very close to ending because there will be nothing left. I don't want to create another 'incident' with the Pilipeen government. Ever since the Fake Major landed at Clark, the relations between the two governments have been strained pretty badly. Dangle told me after the PTOB to keep you under control. No kazoo serenades, choir crap, or outright insults to the PI controllers. I mean it this time."

"You don't honestly think that you can keep me under control, do you? Come on. That statement is like waving a red cape in front of the bull. Speaking of bulls, Bulldog has his kazoo and has been practicing for a duet in C minor since wheels up."

Hollywood: "Godammit, Spike, I mean it!"

Graham: "Would you relax, Hollywood? Spike is full of shit and you should know that by now. I don't even have my kazoo with me. And stop giving us orders. You know we never listen to orders unless they make sense, and most don't."

Hollywood: "C'mon, guys. I'm the AC. You have to listen to me. They hang *my* ass for all the shit that you guys pull."

Graham: "You know what? In the RAF the AC is the senior ranking officer on board, not necessarily the pilot. In fact, in most cases it's the bombardier."

Spike: "Good point, B-dog. Crew, all in favor of adopting the RAF command structure say 'aye'"

Spike and Graham alternated saying aye until they reached five ayes.

Spike: "The crew has decided to adopt the RAF command structure unanimously, excluding you, pilot. I therefore am now in command."

E-Jeep: "I didn't say aye!"

Guns: "I'm just DNIF cover. I'm not even part of this crew. I didn't vote."

Co: "I didn't vote either. You guys are nuts."

Graham: "You guys can't change your vote. Only your first vote counts, and that was clearly an aye."

Spike: "Guns, you are part of the crew on this flight and therefore you have a full and equal vote. Plus B-dog is right. You can't change your vote so shut up or I'll have you court-martialed for insubordination and vote changing. The latter carries the death penalty. Captain Graham is my executive officer and will assume command anytime I'm not on board."

Graham: "Aye aye, sir."

"That's two more votes in my favor, which is a clear majority. I assume command effective immediately. From now on speak only when spoken to."

Hollywood: "You guys are truly and absolutely crazy."

On guard: "Hello, Blue flight. Many Yankee Air Pirate die last night in the north. You go north tonight you die for sure. We have big shipment of new missiles and many more airplane that will shoot you down…"

The minute Hana came up, Spike was fumbling to put his recorder on the deli counter. It was a Teac. It suddenly dawned on Graham where he had seen the recorder before.

Hana: "Your children will be orphans and cry all the time and your wives will cry forever. You can go back to Guam and save your families…"

Hana paused for a second, and Spike was right there: "Moo-o-o-o. Moo-o-o-o Brr-r-r-r-rip blop, blop.. Clang, clang. . Moo-o-o-o. Clang. Moo-o-o, moo-o-o-o-o-o., moo-o-o-o."

Hana: "...turn back now pirates. We take no prisoners. All pirate that been shoot down are dead. Your family will be so sad. You will never see them again if you keep going."

Spike was quick again: "Moo-o-o-o. Clang, clang, blop. Moo-o-o-o, moo-o-o-o-o. Clang. Brr-r-r-rr-rip blop, Moo-o-o-o."

Silence. Hana was gone.

Hollywood: "Godammit, Spike, I know that was you. Get the hell off guard! Spike!?"

Neither Spike nor Graham could answer. They were in tears. They had never laughed so hard.

On guard: "Blue fight! Joo get off guard! Joo obee our rules! Joo stop right now! We send escorts! Joo fart on my countree!"

That put them back in convulsions of laughter.

Hollywood was near hysteria: "Godammit! Now you've done it! We've got interceptors on the way! Another damn incident!"

A few minutes later, Spike regained himself a bit and pulled the power from the deck and put it back on the floor.

Graham, still snickering: "Pilot Nav, left... to 274, back ten."

Hollywood: "Roger, Nav. 274, back ten. Where've you been, Nav?"

"In the land of laughter. It's a great place to go when you think you might get killed in a war your country doesn't want to win."

Spike: "Hey, E-Jeep, can you jam that Pilipeen intercept radar?"

E-jeep: "Shit yes. They're flying F-86s. Flying model T's. I can make the whole wave completely invisible."

Spike unstrapped and climbed upstairs quickly. He would have a private conversation with the Pick off IC.

Hollywood: "Spike, you're not jamming the damn radar! That will just make things worse. You'll get the damn PI over fly privilege revoked for everybody!"

Graham: "Spike's off IC pilot. I'll tell him to call you when he gets back."

On guard: "Blue flight, Gold One."

It was The Fake Major.

Hollywood: "Go ahead Gold One."

"I don't know how Spike came up with that one, but I'll bet the entire wave is still laughing their asses off. A herd of mooing, farting cows. Unbelievable."

Graham: "We'll tell you about it at the club tomorrow. Right now it's top secret."

The Fake major: "Roger that, Bulldogeous. Congratulate Spike for us."

Spike climbed back down and strapped, off IC: "E-Jeep will jam the shit out of those Pilipeen fighters. They'll never be able to find us, and we'll forget to tell Hollywood. If they rescind our over fly we'll just fly anyway and continue to jam them. They can't do shit about it."

Graham: "Hollywood is really pissed this time. I think he's starting to worry about his career."

"He'll get over it. Besides they can't pin something on him they can't prove."

Hollywood: "Keep an eye out for bogeys, Defense. I think we'll be getting company."

Guns: "Roger, sir, I'm painting 360. Nothing yet. Wait a minute… there are four bogeys at seven o'clock low, but they appear to be heading away from the flight."

Spike: "Those Pilipeeno pilots suck pond scum. Altitude, airspeed, and brains. At least two of the three are required to fly and they all lack the latter."

Hollywood: "Between you and E-Jeep I smell a rat. If you guys jammed those guys we are in deep shit."

Spike: "We wouldn't ignore your request even though I'm in command."

The inbound leg continued on a heading to the northwest from the PI. There was a lot of banter between the aircraft over the So Chi. The mood of the crews was much lighter than on 19. Graham didn't understand why. The gooks had still nailed three bombers the night before. Maybe Spike was right. Once they shot a damn arsenal at you and you lived through it, the fear factor was reduced. Blue flight made the IP on time without incident. The target offsets showed up easily against the water in the harbor. Things were going very well. Too well.

Twenty miles from target, E-Jeep: "I've got threat radar dead ahead. Heads up for visuals, pilot."

"Pilot, Guns. We have a bogey at three o'clock at altitude."

Hollywood: "Red Crown, we have threat radar at target and a bogey at three o'clock at altitude. Where's MIGCAP?"

Red Crown: "They are there. Heads up."

Guns, excited: "Pilot, the bogeys changed course and closing. Permission to fire?"

Hollywood: "Roger, but only when in range."

Co: "There's a missile in the air at two o'clock!"

The Co saw a bright flash where the missile had been tracking.

Guns: "The bogey's gone off radar, pilot."

Hollywood: "They got the bastard!"

Spike: "Pilot, center the PDI and give it to me."

Guns: "Another bogey came on and disappeared, then a third. They are heading away from the flight."

Hollywood: "You got it, Bombs."

Spike and Graham finished the checklist.

Graham: "Thirty seconds to TOT….fifteen….ten…"

"SAM launch Haiphong."

"SAM launch Haiphong."

"… two… one, bombs away."

The bomber leaped up as usual.

Spike: "We're clean."

Graham: "Pilot turn right to zero one zero. Climb and maintain flight level three six zero."

E-Jeep: "I HAVE UPLINK!"

Hollywood: "Hang on, crew!"

They went into a steep dive in the turn. There were no visuals so they didn't know which way the SAM was coming from. Hollywood was hoping the missile was coming from starboard. If it wasn't, they would be hit. The aircraft shuddered. They started to level off 5000 feet below the bombing altitude.

Hollywood: "It went off below us. I have no idea why we weren't hit."

Spike: "Because they missed."

Hollywood, laughing: "Heads up and out Co."

This time they saw the launches. Co: "Three coming from starboard! Two o'clock!"

Hollywood dove right again.

E-Jeep: "No uplinks. They're ballistic!"

"SAM launch Haiphong."

"SAM launch Haiphong."

Co: "These are moving across. They're not after us."

On guard: "RED CROWN. BRONZE THREE HAS BEEN HIT! HE'S ON FIRE!"

"RED CROWN ACKNOWLEDGES. BRONZE THREE HIT. ALL AIRCRAFT STAY OFF GUARD. WE HAVE AN AIRCRAFT IN TROUBLE."

Graham: "We're over the harbor, crew. Climb and maintain flight level three six zero, continue right turn to zero nine five."

Beepers went off.

Spike: "Somebody got out. It was Buck Layton's crew."

On guard: "Blue flight leader go to sec two."

Hollywood and offense switched over.

Hollywood: "Blue One up on sec two."

"Hi boys. Dinero and Sparky here. We're flying your CAP in Bolt One. You've had a busy night. We lost our Wingman after he toasted that MIG that was coming after you. The MIG's wing was laying in the weeds low. We nailed him but not before he got Bolt Two. These were not gook pilots. They were Chinese. The gooks aren't that good."

Hollywood: "This is a lousy place and shit circumstances for a reunion, guys. Your wing probably saved our ass. That MIG was inbound on us. Who were the drivers?"

Sparky, very upset: "They were in our squadron on the E, Coleman Evans and Cameron Wilson. They fireballed. No beepers."

Hollywood: "WE KNEW THOSE GUYS! DAMN! We got into a friendly food fight with them at the Navy Club on Guam. Get us their numbers in the CONUS. I want to write their families."

Graham had tears running down his oxygen mask. He couldn't speak. *God I hate war.*

Spike: "I don't know why the MIG in the weed bed went after you guys. He shouldn't have. He should have killed us. Evans and Wilson saved our asses twice. The second time with their own lives."

Dinero came back. He, too, was clearly choked up: "Roger that, Spike. We'll get you the numbers. Maybe we'll see you on Guam on an R&R."

Spike: "We'd come to you, but we can't. Your runway's too short. Maybe we could meet in Bangkok."

Dinero, he had recovered his emotions somewhat: "Good idea if we can coordinate it. Beats Guam. We're almost bingo, and there're heavy swells at the ship. I got to get back so I can scare the shit out of Sparky on landing. Adios and God Bless. Bolt One out."

Spike: "We owe those guys big time. Anybody ever says anything bad about Naval aviators and I'll bomb the bastards. Meantime, the gooks are running out of SAMs. I only counted eight. Unfortunately, one got Bronze Three, but this thing is going to end soon. That I guarantee. We'll be home by Spring so B-dog and I can pick up where we left off, hunting Bambi off season with AK-47s. How sweet it is… or will be."

Graham: "Not me, Spike. I've killed the last living thing that I ever will the day we touch down from our last mission."

Spike: "Oh shit. Another one ruined. The United States Air Force goes and yanks you out of obscurity, trains you to be a professional killer, at great expense I might add, and you go and throw it all away. What a damn shame."

"I'm done, Spike."

NOT QUITE OVER

Blue One landed at 0712 AM local, and Some Luck met the aircraft in front of the assigned revetment. They shut her down and unloaded their gear quickly with Some Luck's help. They were loading it on the crew bus when Spike noticed that Some Luck was unusually quiet: "What the hell's wrong with you, Some Luck? Your dog die? Your bird flew great, man. We dodged a SAM that was dead on, and she held."

Some Luck: "No, sir, it's not that. I'm just tired of this shithole. Tired of living in shit quarters and working eighteen hours a day in this shit heat. I wanna go home and get laid in an air conditioned room."

Spike put his hand on Some Luck's shoulder: "Listen Kid, this shit will end very soon. I promise you that. I have been blowing up gooks since 1966, and they are about all blowed up! Keep up the great work. You're the best, and you'll be home soon."

Some Luck looked better immediately. He smiled and saluted: "Thank you, sir."

Spike returned the salute.

Spike got on the bus, and it headed for Ops. Graham, leaning across toward Spike: "You know what, 'Major Spike?' If enlisted men in the Air Force elected General officers, you'd have four stars. Those guys love you, for Christ's sake. I don't know why other than maybe you smell the same - bad. Yeah, maybe it's an aromatic attraction." Spike didn't respond to the comment other than his Spike Smile. He'd get a ten minute nap on the way to the PFB.

The de-brief officer was a surprise: Lieutenant Colonel Joe Bob!

Joe Bob: "We have already got a formal protest from the Pilipeens that somebiddy had broadcast what sounded like cows mooin' and fartin' en their bells a-clangin' over their territory on guard about the time that Blue flight shudda been there. They launched interceptors but they couldn't find nothin' cuz their shit din work. Now I know perfectly well who it was that did this shit… right, Spike?"

Spike, Spike Smile, popping a beer: "Did what, Dickie? How could I fit a gas filled cow in the cockpit? You know better than that."

Joe Bob: "I know fer sure thet you was behind this thing, Spike. It's got Spike all over it. If we get over flight problems cuz of this the General's gonna hang your ass."

Joe Bob looking at Hollywood: "What do you know 'bout this, Captain?"

"Beats me. I heard the cows, but I have no idea where they came from. Maybe Hanoi Hanna is using psychological warfare that's cow enhanced."

Joe Bob: "I'm gonna nail you guys on this one. Fer sure this time."

Spike: "Can't see how that's possible given your abilities as a dick-tective. By the way, Dickie, how did you become a de-brief officer? I thought you were assigned as Officer in Charge of enlisted morale, which was a travesty. That didn't work out? Can't imagine why."

"Them enlisted swine complained to Dangle thet I was ruinin' their morale, not improvin' it. Them lyin' scum. If I had my way I'd send half of 'em to the DMZ en the other half to be shot. They might have ruint my chances to make Colonel. I'll get 'em back, mind you."

Spike: "But Dickie, you're such a thoughtful and caring guy that I can't imagine that outcome. And don't worry, Dickie. You don't have a snowball's chance on Guam of making Colonel so they didn't ruin anything. It's a terrible miracle that you made L/C, but the Fumu Principle operated in your favor as usual."

Joe Bob: "You watch your mouth, boy! I am senior to you!"

With the "boy" Spike leaped to his feet. Graham grabbed his arm and asked for a definition of the Fumu Principle, just in case Joe Bob didn't know it.

Spike: "Fumu means 'fuck up, move up.' It's unfortunately rampant in the Air Force. The worse an officer is, the more that his commander will do to get rid of him, so some of them even promote idiots like Dickie in order to get rid of them."

Joe Bob's face got as red as his neck. They were seconds from a fight, so Graham got another beer and dragged Spike out of the room. The rest of the crew debriefed quickly after Spike and Graham left. Joe Bob told Hollywood that he was putting Spike on report, and Hollywood told Joe Bob to get screwed. No matter what the General said, they were still bulletproof, and Hollywood knew it.

LIFE GOES ON AT HEARTBREAK

Not long after Christmas, D-Kid and Alex were moved to a new cell in Heartbreak Courtyard near the interrogation area. They were joined by five more POWs. Several from their own crews.

Five of the seven had festering wounds that remained untreated, as usual. Alex and D-Kid were the healthiest, so they worked on the cell to try to keep the cold out. There was no heat, so the wounded huddled together at night when it fell below freezing to use body heat to keep warm. It did little good.

The food actually got worse. The old bakery had been blown up in a raid, so they now got bread from a bakery that was made with flour that was infested with rat dung and insects. Sanitary conditions were still very bad. They could only bathe once a week, in freezing water, but at least they could empty and clean the honey buckets every day. The rats roamed freely in the cell every night looking for dropped bits of food and often woke the men up when they walked across their sleeping bodies.

One of the cellmates, Tony Golonik, a BUFF pilot, had dislocated both shoulders when he ejected. The gooks took him to the hospital and sedated him to kill the pain but also to interrogate him. When he returned, he told Alex about it.

"They kept asking me if the exhaust on the B-52 went straight back or was angled down. I said 'how the hell do I know that.' Why would they want to know something like that anyway? That's a big who cares."

D-Kid looked at Alex and answered for them: "Heat seekers, Tony. That makes a big difference on heat seeking missiles. It's a good thing you were too groggy to answer."

"Oh shit. You're right. If they hadn't drugged me, I would have told them they go straight up."

Their clothes were not enough to keep them warm and they couldn't wash them because they would take too long to dry. The stench inside the cell built up to be awful, but the prisoners didn't notice since it happened over time. Finally, the kitchen boy came in with the soup bucket for lunch. He took one step in, gagged, dropped the soup bucket, and yelled at them.

"You open window! You open door! Place stink!"

A little later, two guards with weapons burst through the doors and opened the windows. They left the doors open when they left and told them not to close them.

Alex: "Shit man. The doors are open. We have an obligation under the Code to try to escape."

"Great idea, except how are we going to get through that concrete wall on the other side of the courtyard before they shoot our asses? Maybe we can stink our way out. We smell so bad we could just go to the gate and the guard would puke and faint."

Alex: "Yeah, that's it. Then this giant black guy and super white guy with a red signal beacon on top of his head just walk down the streets of Hanoi making everybody that notices them and tries to capture them puke and faint."

"Sure. We could make it provided it doesn't rain and clean us up to the point they would only puke but not faint. But the gooks with gas masks that they would eventually send after us could follow the trail of vomit right to us. There's the flaw."

Alex: "No, there's another one too, now that I think of the gooks with the gas masks. The odor coming from our bodies could be classified as a toxic gas, and that violates the Geneva Convention."

The camp commander came in to lecture on hygiene. Surprisingly, he neither puked nor fainted when he entered the room. Maybe he smelled as bad as they did. That blew the "Stink Your Way Out Plan."

The "Stink Out Plan" was bullshit from the beginning, but a key part of survival is humor, and the crewdogs used it as much as possible. The POWs had nothing to lose so they blasted the gook commander. D-Kid: "We haven't been allowed to bathe or wash our clothes in ten days. The guards haven't let us empty the toilet buckets in four days. Some of the guys have serious festering wounds, and your medics refuse to treat them."

Amazingly, after that encounter, they were allowed to clean their toilets, bathe in freezing water, and shave on a more regular basis. D-Kid wondered aloud:

"Why is the camp commander suddenly being Mr. Nice Guy? Maybe it has to do with the massive and terrifying raids every night. He knows this will end soon, and he doesn't want any repercussions for treatment."

Alex responded, though it wasn't necessarily directed at him: "I think you may be right, Bob. But he can't make it up. Some of the FOGs went through inhumane torture. That'll get out. The rifle butts to the head. The falls on concrete while bound. No sleep at all. That shit will get out, too. We're not going to forget that due to the 'kindness' of an ice water bath in December."

THE COW PLOT REVEALED

Hollywood, Spike, and Graham all showered and left for the Club a little after 1800. The Fake Major, Sluggo, and Blackjack were already at the table when they arrived.

Sluggo: "The Fake Major says you guys got shot at by MIGS and SAMs. Must have been a fun night. Sorry to hear you lost one. It's a damn shame this late in the game."

Spike: "We appreciate your sentiment, especially since it's unusual for your callous persona. A Navy 4 got nailed as well after saving our ass. It was flown by two of the guys that we met at the Navy O'club when we stole the General's car, Coolman and Cameraman. Ironically, Dinero nailed the MIG that got them. Coolman was flying Dinero's wing. It was a bad night. Eight guys bad. Speaking of bad nights, any other intel on Sunny's crew?"

Sluggo: "Nothing, and you know what that means. Let's change the subject. You jeeps are flying lead tomorrow, and you're lead again on the 31st. The Fake Major here has kissed the CINC's ass so much he's not scheduled at all in the next five days. They may take your suite at Coward Quarters."

The Wildman flipped the universal salute: "You know I could have you court-martialed for insubordination and being short in front of a superior officer, literally, you little shit. Are you through puberty?" He didn't wait for Sluggo. "BARTENDER! Whiskey for my horses, water for my men! And bring a dice cup! Lao-lao! Ching-ching!"

The Club had been cleaned up and reconditioned pretty well, given the destruction of Christmas Eve. The table at the back corner in the Main Bar was their sanctuary from reality, but the reality of what was happening was starting to overwhelm them all. There was no end in sight even though they kept telling themselves that there was. If the peace talks didn't come together, stay together, and reach conclusion soon, one of the three crews represented at the table was going to dive the wrong way from a SAM, or a MIG would get lucky. Spike, Hollywood, Sluggo, and The Fake Major all arrived at the Club within minutes of each other. Sluggo had Smolensky with him.

Spike: "You dare to bring this rumor monger with you into an officer's conclave? And besides, his rumors are of very low quality."

Sluggo: "This isn't about rumors. It's about your idiot gunner who we escorted to the Daiichi for his mandatory date last night. The Sergeant brings years of educated perspective to the encounter so I brought him along. So shut the hell up and listen."

Smolensky: "Gentlemen. I think Seeps is in deep shit, sirs. We got up to Takagi's suite, and the two goons that you have already met were waiting at the elevator. They picked up Seeps by his elbows and carried him through the double doors. They told us to get back on the elevator and leave. After years of experience with the Japanese, I do not believe that this is a good sign."

Sluggo: "Yeah, like he might be a main entry at the sushi bar as we speak."

Spike: "Where the hell is he now?"

Sluggo: "We don't know. We waited downstairs for almost an hour and he never came through the lobby. Did he come back to quarters last night? Was he there when you guys got back from the mission?"

Spike: "No, but that's not unusual. In fact, if he shows up at all other than to fly is unusual. So I wouldn't read much into that. Smolensky, why don't you go back down to the Daiichi and see Jack, the bartender. See if he can find out anything or if he already knows something. Tell him I'll make it worth the exploration."

Cowboy came up to the table: "Smolensky, what in the hell are you doing here? You know enlisted swine are not allowed in here."

Smolensky: "But *you* are enlisted swine, Cowboy, although we consider you a traitor and a brownnose."

Cowboy: "No, Smolensky, I'm King of the Club. Ask your crew."

Sluggo and the others just nodded their heads and smiled. They weren't about to even have fun with Cowboy's statement because he *was* what he said he was. Cowboy snapped his fingers, and his two giant cohorts appeared as usual. Smolensky got the hint, got up to leave, and turned to Spike. "I'll do as you asked, Major, and let you know as soon as I hear anything. Good evening, sirs."

Sluggo: "He better find out that your moron gunner is OK. We don't need to be implicated as part of a homicide because of your screwed up plan, Spike. Speaking of really screwed up plans, The Fake Major said you have devised a plot to drive the zips nuts by attacking them with cows or something. What's the story?"

"If I hadn't come up with the plan to have Seeps reconcile with Takagi's daughter, he'd already be dead. Relax he's OK. He might be a little dented, but the whole thing had too much visibility for anything really serious to happen to him. Now on to the Great Cow Offensive."

Spike explained his entire plan essentially the same way he had explained it to Graham. Sluggo and the Fake Major were in hysterics, but Hollywood had just grown darker as Spike went on. He didn't interrupt, but by the time Spike got to the dead cow being loaded in the bomb bay he was fuming.

"You mean to tell me you had six bags of cow turds loaded into our aircraft on the last mission? ARE YOU FUCKING NUTS, SPIKE!?" He stood up and was leaning over at Spike: "You could have gotten us all court-martialed, and you endangered the entire crew!"

Spike was intense in his response. The others had stopped laughing but were still snickering.

"Sit down, Jeep. You're embarrassing our corner. All the cow turds were loaded on top of the last bomb string, and they were loaded by the ordinance guys so they were safe. You've got to lighten up, Jeep, and stop playing AC. I've got more than ten times the hours in this bomber than you, and I know more about it than you ever will. AND YOU DAMN WELL KNOW I'd never endanger the crew."

Wildman: "He's right, Hollywood. You've got to lighten up. Everybody reacts to the stress of combat and getting shot at a little differently. You react by getting tense and giving orders that no one listens to unless they agree with them, which makes you even more tense. Spike knows what he's doing, and the crewdogs know what he's doing. His cockamamie stunts lighten the load and reduce the stress for everybody.""

Sluggo: "Yeah, get over it. Spike's the best that there is when it comes to B-52s. No one even comes close. You are damn lucky to be part of his crew. Of course, I personally would never allow him on my *crew*, but you… you are damn lucky."

Hollywood, smiling: "Fuck you, Sluggo."

Sluggo: "Ah yes. The standard U.S. Air Force rejoinder. Someday a good looking girl officer is going to say that to me and I'll say, 'You're on, lady. By that I mean on top, of course.'"

Hollywood, lightening and still smiling: "You guys may be right. I have been getting more up tight I think. Just let me in on what you're doing beforehand so I know what's going on. *That*, I can deal with."

Spike: "I'll consider it. But it breaks tradition. Part of the process is that no one but the B-dog knows what I'm up to in its entirety. It lessens the impact. Plus, back in sixty-eight the Wing CO at U-T heard about the Great Garbage Can Drop and intervened before we could pull it off. He ruined the whole week."

Sluggo: "You best lighten up, Hollywood, or they'll pull the old RAF change of command stunt on you, and you'll lose command of the aircraft to Spike."

Graham: "We already did it. Stand at attention when we are denigrating you, Hollywood."

Hollywood: "The *old* RAF stunt? Hell, it was new to me."

CHAPTER XIX: WE GOTTA GET OUT OF THIS PLACE

MISSION NUMBER 109

On the evening of the 28th, another crew was scratched and Wildman's was added, so the mission on 29 December was unusual in that Hollywood, The Fake Major, and Sluggo would all fly it.

The guys met at the Club and the games began as usual, but would cease twelve hours prior to TO.

Graham finally saw the opportunity he had planned and prepared for, with D-kid's help, to utilize the "Drag Coefficient Measurement Tools."

He was sitting next to Spike, who was rolling.

Graham whispered so Hollywood couldn't hear him: "They're ready, and they're very cool."

Spike was pre-occupied. "What's ready? You finally ready to lose, B-dog?"

"No, the coefficient measurement tools are ready."

Spike rolled a loser and bowed out to go to the head. He nodded at Graham to follow. They went toward the head but stopped at the far end of the bar.

Spike was animated: "You mean the pipe bombs are ready! Where are they?"

Graham was proud of his plan: "Smolensky's got 'em. They'll be delivered to the aircraft tomorrow at pre-flight. Two each for us, Sluggo, and the Fake Major's bird. They are ultra cool. Smo painted them 'Air Force' green and then lettered them in standard yellow. They say 'Drag Coefficient Monitor, Top Secret, Eyes Only.' On the other side, in smaller letters, it says 'Do not light fuse until instructed by the Offensive Team, then dispose of per their instructions.' They have a fake antenna attached and a little gauge attached to the end opposite the fuse. Each one is packed in a custom pine box, again Air Force green, and marked Top Secret." Graham was smiling broadly.

Spike stared almost in disbelief: "You're shittin' me! That gets them onboard, but how do we get them on the Russian Spyhauler?"

"There's only one way. We have the pilots light them and toss them out the window at 3500 feet approaching the spy HQ. The fuses are cut to a length that anticipates the impact time, give or take three seconds"

Spike's expression changed to one of dislike: "Bullshit, B-dog. The only guys that drop bombs from a B-52 are us. Your plan sucks. Pilots can't drop bombs."

Graham was ready for the objection: "No, no, no. WE drop the bombs. They are just human bomb racks. You line up the crosshairs on the Spyhauler, and I'm on IC upstairs in the IP seat between them. As we approach release, you give me a head's up. I tap them both on the shoulder twice, which means light the fuse. Their windows are already open so you call bombs away, and I tap them twice again and the bombs go out the window."

"That's brilliant! THEY dropped the bombs on the spyhauler! They're trapped! When the General throws a shit fit all they can do is keep their mouths shut because they are accomplices! They are the racks! I love it! Hollywood will kill us, but I love it!"

Graham was not done. "Smolensky will have a note delivered to the PTOB that will be read by the briefing officer. This is the note." He handed it to Spike,

Some of you will be given a top secret device prior to take off that will require some action shortly after you are wheels in the well. The Offensive team will instruct the pilots on exactly what needs to be done. Both pilots will need to comply with those instructions exactly.

Spike was delighted. He slapped B-dog on the back and said thanks.

Graham was almost finished: "Sluggo and The Fake don't need the masquerade, They are both fully in on it and fully engaged. We're good to go."

Thay were both still smiling when they returned to their "reserved" seats. Hollywood noticed and was uncomfortable.

Something was up with his bomb team... shit.

Hollywood was the lead of the G wave, so SO-2 would get nothing but shit for fourteen hours. Roller showed up alive the morning of the 29th to mixed reviews, since by now there were those that wouldn't be that upset if Takagi had made him into sushi rolls.

SO-2 entered the briefing room to cat calls and hoots from the other crews that were no doubt orchestrated by Sluggo and The Fake Major.

"Jeep Alert! Jeep Alert!"

"FNG training mission!"

"Can we get real aviators to lead this wave rather than these mud wrestlers, Colonel?"

"Room, aten-sh-s-shun!"

Dangle entered from the back of the room. "At ease, gentlemen, and be seated. I have a few announcements prior to mission brief. First of all, the North Vietnamese lodged a formal protest at the Paris peace accords that we are using inhumane tactics in our bombing missions on their country. Specifically, they say we are using… cows, yes cows, to fly our bombers in order to save our aircrews from their highly effective air defenses."

Dangle was on the verge of laughing out loud. "They claim to have irrefutable evidence in the form of recordings that they intercepted over the Philippines and actual physical evidence that they recovered from what they claim was an orphanage destroyed near Haiphong on the 27th. They would not define what such physical evidence was, but said that they would produce it at the conference no later than the 29th or 30th. Personally, gentlemen, I smell another crewdog psychological warfare scheme…"

Now he was actually cracking up: "…and you know that those are not allowed any more. So, whoever is behind these activities, Spike, is to cease this activity, and no, I'm not kidding. Now, on to another protest by the North Vietnamese at the same meeting. Our Intel learned that a certain American female singer turned traitor, by the name of Joan Bass, that you guys call a PHUC singer (that's p-h-u-c singer when we are in public) was scheduled to leave her meeting aiding and comforting the enemy on 21 December at 1100 hours departing out of Hanoi's Gia Lam airport. As it were, a B-52 out of U-T experienced a BNS malfunction while on a mission north and accidentally dropped one hundred and eight 500 pound bombs on the airfield and blew the crap out of everything, including all the aircraft, at 1050 hours on 21 December. We explained to the North Vietnamese that the incident was unfortunate."

The entire room stood and cheered. Dangle was smiling and clapping.

Graham turned to Spike: "Nice double negative. Is the cow ready?"

Spike: "We'll know when we get to the aircraft. Smolensky said that the cow looks great. They sewed all the patches on, and they are wrapping the helmet with horns in the parachute bundle. Fortunately, cattle rustling is not a hanging offense on Guam."

The Colonel from planning briefed the mission. The target was Hanoi radio again. The mood in the room sobered. This time they would take it out.

Hollywood convened the Lead briefing at 1500. They suspected that they were going to get a raft of shit from Sluggo and the Fake Major. Their suspicions were correct. Both Hollywood and Graham briefed the mission and asked for questions at the conclusion.

Sluggo: "Yes, your Jeepship, I mean Captain Noland, if the lead B-52 left Guam on time tonight, which we doubt, climbed to 350 and maintained a true airspeed of 500 knots, assuming the pilot was capable, which we also doubt, and another B-52 left Kansas five hours earlier, climbed to 360, and maintained a true air speed of 515 knots, and hit two tanks on the way to Oz, which one would Dorothy, given a choice, pick to get to the target on time?"

Hollywood: "Get bent. Next question."

The Fake Major: "Two follow-on questions, Captain... and stand at attention when you're speaking to a superior officer."

Hollywood and Graham sat down on the stage. The Major ignored the insult and continued: "Given that we have been on this island way too long and are all very horny, why wouldn't you scrub the mission and just gang bang Dorothy? And second, with your incompetent Nav team, why would you think that we could even find Vietnam, let alone OZ?"

Hollywood: "Fuck you, too. That's 't-w-o,' dickhead one and the other dickhead. Now, seriously, we have all flown Linebacker, and we know the danger is significant. I don't believe that we should assume that the Vietnamese are out of SAMs at all, so the pilots' heads should be up and out over Downtown. We all believe that the war is close to over. Let's finish it and go home, guys. Now, let's get to the aircraft. This briefing is concluded."

Sluggo, loudly, as the crews were filing out: "But what about Toto? If the zips manage to nail the Kansas bird, won't they *eat* the dog? The poor little pooch."

Spike: "No, dwarf. Tomorrow they'll be eating beef, remember? By the way, you are third in command of the Munchkins by virtue of your physical attributes and singing ability."

SO-2 got to the aircraft and were surprised to see Some Luck.

Spike: "Some Luck, this is 556. What the hell are you doing on this bird?"

Some Luck: "I asked O'Brian if we could switch for this mission. I bring you guys luck, maybe because I don't have much. You always come back with me on the bird, sirs."

Hollywood: "You do, Sergeant. Thanks for the thought. How is she?"

Some Luck: "She's a great bird, sir. You know that. She's got a great reputation."

Some Luck was responding to Hollywood's question, but addressing Spike. Hollywood ignored the affront and went to the hatch. Some Luck saluted Spike after Hollywood passed, and quietly updated him: "There's a few hundred pounds of USDA Guam in rack three, sir."

Spike: "Great work. Thank the ordinance guys for me and tell them I'm buying when we touch down. See ya, my friend."

SO-2 was flying Wave lead as Cobalt One. Sluggo was leading the second cell in the Wave as Copper One, and The Fake Major was behind Copper as Gold One. The mission would be a circus.

Spike managed to convince Hollywood and Co that the "test project" was legitimate, primarily because the boxes and the "drag coefficient" measurement devices looked like "typical USAF official" stuff. Graham carefully went over the drop procedure, explaining that he would be in the IP seat and using the shoulder tap code to let them know when to light the fuses and drop.

Hollywood was suddenly suspicious: "Why the hell do you need to be up here beating on our shoulders when Spike could make the call from downstairs?"

Graham was quick to respond in USAF talk: "Because this mission is so sensitive and important that they want a rated officer in the IP seat to insure mission integrity."

Hollywood was convinced because Bulldog was obviously just mimicking what some Colonel had told him at the PTOB.

"OK, we'll do it that way, but use two taps for the fuse and three for the drop. But why does this thing have a fuse?"

Graham, again pulling shit out of the air: "It ejects a special device that floats as it nears the targ... er... ocean that contains a beeper like our chutes at about 500 feet and the navy can pick it up."

Hollywood's suspicion was back: "You almost said 'target' and then corrected yourself, shitbird. What's going on?"

Dancing again: "The 'target' is imaginary. Spike is using the bomb nav system to calculate the drop point or 'target' per se, so the Navy can locate the floating measurement devices that are ejected at 500 feet."

That made sense to Hollywood so they buttoned up and got ready for take-off. Spike couldn't stop laughing when Bulldog went down and related the "Hollywood Challenge." Graham went upstairs as soon as they pulled the chocks and strapped into the IP seat between the pilots. He plugged into O2 and pulled the visor down on his helmet because he was afraid he would laugh hysterically after the "drop."

Take-off and the "procedure" went flawlessly, except Cobalt Two reported seeing what appeared to be two explosions very close to the Russian trawler.

Hollywood sensed a "Spike in the Air." "Dammit! If you two assholes tricked me into bombing a fucking Russian trawler in international waters, I will have your ass! That could be construed as an act of war! Jesus!"

Spike was quick with a planned response to such an eventuality: "It isn't our fault if the drag coefficient measurement tool's ejection device malfunctioned! Besides I didn't drop the device. You and the Co did." Spike sounded serious but he could barely control himself.

Hollywood didn't bother to respond. He'd been had, and he knew it. He took his helmet off and took a drag on the cigar he'd used to light the fuse.

Why did I fall for that!? You are a complete dumbass! God… I hope they missed… er, I missed!

The Co said nothing at all. He just smiled at Hollywood and gave him thumbs up. He was oblivious to the potential consequences for what they had just been conned into.

The Fake Major came up on guard: "Hey, Bulldogeous! You morons missed! When I came up he was fully underway heading out to sea! I had to chase the Commie bastard for our release! But I think I got him! On the run, no less! I was told that you two were the 'Best of the Best.' I guess whoever told me that was misinformed… Oh Wait… Now I remember who told me! It was you! Son-of-a-bitch! I have to stop listening to a lying prick!"

Spike couldn't help but respond before Bulldog: "Listen, fake-o. Bulldog was right, but remember, to be better than you we could be well below average and still be judged better, so bite me, Captain."

That gave cause to an on air verbal sparring match that the Wave Lead, Hollywood, had to order to stop. After he shut down the debate, he became concerned again.

These maniacs are going to ruin my career. What are they gonna do next? Shit, bombing a Russian trawler in international waters was the end already. Who are you kidding!? Not only did you bomb them, but God knows how many more were dropped? Fuck it. You're already cooked. Just sit back and enjoy whatever these guys do next. Yeah… just enjoy it. The airlines might have jobs after you get out of Leavenworth, if you're not too old. Shit, I'll just ask what's next.

"Okay, Navs, I give. I'm already toast, either figuratively or actually. If we just started WW3, it will actually be toast as we all get toasted in a nuclear holocaust attacking the Russkies. So I'm in. Why not? C'mon, what's next?"

Spike gave a one word reply: "Moo-o-o-.."

Sluggo lost his number four engine at 8000 feet. Gold Two's gear wouldn't retract. Silver Three had a "bomb bay door open" warning light come on, so the Nose Pick had to crawl back along the tiny catwalk to the bomb bay to check it before they passed 10,000 feet. It didn't appear open, but it probably wouldn't open when they got to the target. Amber One had fire warning lights on for all four starboard engines illuminate right before reaching altitude.

Normal for a Press On mission.

Hollywood: "Cobalt Flight, Cobalt One. As you are aware from the brief, we have a typhoon about Long 133 [133 degrees east longitude], and she's pretty worked up. We'll probably be IFR in rough weather until just before we reach the PI. I didn't say anything at the brief, but I want all ACs in their seats until we clear the weather. Acknowledge, flight."

All cells acknowledged. But Hollywood was worried about Rick Seddeler in Gold Three and Mike Ramon in Bronze Three. They were the two worst pilots in the Wing, and in his opinion, as well as most of the other pilots, neither one of them should have ever reached the left seat. Shit, they should have washed out of pilot training. Rumor had it that Seddeler was a queer and that his primary instructor pilot had been his boyfriend, which explained why he got through. Seddeler was particularly bad. He had aborted on 21 with a minor malfunction, and Dangle had ripped him. Seddeler's call sign, which everybody called him to his face, was Pimp. Ironically, Cobalt Flight had the two worst pilots in the Wing and the two best… no… the three best. Hollywood had to include himself. After all, he had pulled off the Swan Dive and led the Wave through hell on 19 with zero losses. Hollywood's thoughts were interrupted by sudden violent turbulence.

Hollywood: "Cobalt One has hit some rough stuff already. Heads up, guys. The tops of this stuff can reach 750 in this part of the world."

The weather was really bad and getting worse. Andersen had been put on a typhoon evacuation warning before they briefed, but the weather officer had said the storm was still far to the west. It wasn't.

Hollywood dialed in the command post at Andersen: "CP, Cobalt One. Be advised that the typhoon that was supposed to be at 133 is much closer, and it's big. We're in heavy turbulence at planned altitude."

Graham: "Pilot, we're 210 at 185 from alpha. Can we get a snow day and stay home?"

Hollywood: "Great idea, Bulldog, but you know this is a press on. Besides if we go back we'll be arrested for bombing the trawler."

"Of course, and I was half kidding. But the problem is that we'll have no place to land if this shit isn't gone by the time we get back, so they can't arrest us. Minor point, I guess."

Spike: "No, if the weather is too bad at a point after we egress, they'll divert us to Da Nang. Da Nang is a shithole. Every zip whore within fifty miles has been screwed about a thousand times, this week, but it beats drowning. But don't worry about it. This shit is moving so fast that it will be long gone by our touchdown."

Pimp, on guard: "COBALT ONE! GOLD THREE IS LOSING AIRSPEED AND MAY BE GOING DOWN! ALL MY INSTRUMENTS ARE SCREWED UP! I CAN'T GET AIRSPEED UP! I CAN'T GET IT UP!"

Spike: "What an incompetent asshole. No wonder he can't get it up. All the guys on his crew must be dressed. Tell him to pull his throttles back, Hollywood."

Hollywood: "Yeah, he is an idiot. GOLD THREE, WE'RE IN TYPHOON CONDITIONS. THROTTLE BACK AND TRUST YOUR INSTRUMENTS."

Gold Two: "COBALT ONE, GOLD TWO, MY GUN SAYS THAT THREE JUST BLEW BY US! DAMN NEAR HIT US! THE GUY'S A FUCKING IDIOT!"

The first beeper went off.

Gold Two: "JESUS CHRIST! GOLD THREE HAS EJECTED! THE BIRD IS GOING IN!"

Hollywood: "CP, COBALT ONE. GOLD THREE HAS APPARENTLY ABANDONED THEIR AIRCRAFT. PLEASE SEND SAR ASAP, AND NO, I DON'T KNOW WHY, OTHER THAN THE PILOT CAN'T FLY."

The other beepers were going off.

CP: "Roger, Cobalt One. SAR cannot deploy at this time. We'll advise."

Spike: "What a fucking asshole. His poor crew will be in forty foot swells. There's no way that SAR can get them in the middle of this shit."

Seddeler was in his chute getting blown all over the dark wet sky. He had no idea why his aircraft had just stopped flying. He had no idea why the engines had flamed out. He had some idea that he might not be a very good pilot. He saw the ocean coming up quickly. He would be drowned if he hit the water with his chute on. He flipped open the releases. The water was coming up fast! He released his chute... 2500 feet above the ocean. He was killed on impact.

Sluggo: "Cobalt One, Copper One. That pimp is truly the worst that has ever been put in the left seat. The fuck may have killed his entire crew. We should have his home base investigate who the hell the StanBoard pilot was that passed the shithead for a left seat qual. Meantime, there's nothing we can do except say the prayer for his crew."

Hollywood: "Roger that, Sluggo... roger that... Damn..."

Thirty minutes later they were still in the fringe of the typhoon. They had been bouncing all over the sky due to turbulence. Normally, they never would have flown into this weather except under a war order [nuclear] or, as now, a conventional Press On.

Graham: "Pilot, turn to 275, bring the airspeed up ten, and when you can, maintain flight level 350... heh-heh-heh..."

Hollywood, sarcastically: "I love your sense of humor, Bulldog. Why don't you write a damn book?"

"I will, Hollywood. I guarantee it. I couldn't pass up relating this wonderful experience to the public. Every parent should know that they have the opportunity to let their sons go get killed. But you know what? It wouldn't make any difference. No matter how much we bitch and moan, we did this on our own. We're all here because we volunteered to be here. No one held a gun to our head. We may be stupid, but we're stupid patriots that love our country. Just good breeding, I guess."

Spike: "That's the smartest observation that you have ever made on your way to your doctorate in Naiveté, B-dog. How far out of the PI?"

"Two twenty. We'll see the east coast on radar pretty quick."

Spike was already setting the Teac up on the deli counter, smiling his Spike smile at Graham.

Spike, off IC: "You'll love this, B-dog. The guys in comm mixed this like you mix a record. I've got multiple cows almost singing and farting in harmony. Great stuff. We may release it as a single when we get back to the CONUS. Then I'll buy airtime on the Pilipeen radio as well and drive them nuts. The flip side will be 'Oh Pilipeens!'"

"You never cease to amaze me. Why in the hell would you put in such a great effort on this stuff? We have a dead cow in the bomb bay, God knows how many more bags of cow turds, and now a customized recording of cows mooing a song. What's the song?"

"It kinda sounds like *Be True to Your School* by the Beach Boys, but the farts are a little out of sync. We didn't have time to re-mix and still make it in time."

Cobalt Flight hit the tanks on plan and were about to cross the eastern end of the PI, when Hana came up on guard: "Yankee Air Pirates will die tonight for sure. We executed many of you yesterday for war crimes. You will all meet the same ending…"

She paused for a second, and Spike jumped in with his new hit: "Moo-moo-moo, blap blap, moo-moo-moo-moo- moo. Clang, moo-moo-moo-moo-moo-moo, blap-p, blap, clang"

Hana was quiet after Spike broke in, and he just about completed an abbreviated version of what he had named "Be True to Your Farm."

The CP came up on sec two, which was unusual.

"Cobalt One, the Navy has sent a sub to try to recover Gold Three's crew. We'll advise you on egress. Good Luck."

Hollywood acknowledged, and thanked CP for the update.

Spike: "I never heard of that before. A sub is pretty clever. Nothing else could get to those guys in the middle of a typhoon. The Navy keeps saving our asses."

CENSORING HANOI RADIO

The mission was relatively uneventful on the inbound. The mission plan had Cobalt flight fly over the GOT and track north of Haiphong to a feet dry entry point north of the Haiphong COA. They would then fly inland to an IP due north of Hanoi and turn southbound to the target. Hanoi radio was heavily defended against air attack with revetments and concrete barriers. It was also deep inside a SAM COA.

When the Wave was inbound over water off the coast, they could be easily seen by the NVA radar, so their approach was not secretive. Besides, the ever-present Russian trawler had long ago communicated the Wave's launch from Guam to the enemy, and they would calculate an approximate time of the strike based on that.

Since they were still off the coast inbound, Spike decided to fire off the Teac and give them a moo serenade on guard, which the NVA monitored constantly.

"Moo-moo-moo, blap blap, moo-moo-moo-moo- moo. Clang, moo-moo-moo-moo-moo-moo, blap- br-r-r-rip, blap, clang. Moo-moooo- moo-moo. Blap, blap, clang."

Hollywood: "Godammit, Spike! We're going into combat! Red Crown will have my ass if they find out where that came from!"

Spike: "FEITCATAJ, Pilot. We need to confuse the enemy. Red Crown only confuse themselves. I need radio traffic to support all of the physical evidence that's loaded in the bomb bay in order to convince the gooks that they are being attacked by the most intelligent cows in history."

FEITCATAJ was the recently coined term for "fuck 'em if they can't take a joke" which had come into broad use during the Navy O'club car theft.

Hollywood: "Shit, I give up. Turn it off and don't even tell me what's loaded in the bomb bay."

"We did tell you what would be loaded in the bomb bay, but you forgot because we told you at the Club when you were well beyond S-2."

Graham: "Turn left to two eight zero. Maintain current airspeed. We're three from the zip ADIZ, so strap it up, everybody."

They all acknowledged.

E-Jeep: "We have radar painting us from the coast, but it doesn't look like threat radar. Very unusual."

Cobalt Flight proceeded to the IP and turned south. The flight was very uneventful. Too much so.

Roller: "We have two bogeys at three o'clock, 4000 yards."

They were MIGs shadowing the flight for altitude and airspeed for the SAMs.

Hollywood: "Red Crown. Cobalt has two bogeys at three o'clock. MIG CAP on station?"

"Roger, Cobalt. They will be on them momentarily."

Roller: "The bogeys just hauled. Red Crown was right."

It was too late. The SAM site already had the information.

Graham: "Crew, we're IP inbound."

Nothing was happening from the ground. It was way too quiet.

Cobalt cell released and turned southeast off the target to get feet wet as fast as possible.

Red Crown: "SAM launch. Hanoi. SAM launch Hanoi."

Hollywood: "Shit, they could only be shooting at us, but that low overcast is gone so it's a bitch to see them. See anything, E-dub?"

"Negative. Must be ballistic or a different freq that only a D model can see."

Sluggo, in Copper One, released and was in his turn when it went off.

Sluggo: "RED CROWN! RED CROWN! COPPER ONE HAS BEEN HIT! WE HAVE FIRE ON THE PORT WING AND HAVE LOST PRESSURE!"

Red Crown: "Roger, Copper One. State souls on board, fuel status, and intentions. Your nearest airfield is Da Nang. All crews stay off guard. We have an aircraft in trouble."

Sluggo, his voice sounding like he was struggling to fly the airplane: "Copper one has six souls and fuel status is good but I'm certain we're losing it. We are going feet wet and will assess after we reach water. SAR should be on station."

Red Crown: "Roger Copper One. Advise after feet wet."

Spike, on IC: "I knew it. I told you guys that we were pushing our luck. One of us was going to get nailed. What I don't get is how they got Sluggo. He's got the second best crew on the island. You saw nothing, E-dub?"

"Nothing at all. I have no idea how they got him. Must have been a ballistic pole proximity fused that got lucky."

The other members of Cobalt flight were off the radios. No one but Red Crown talked to a crippled bird.

Graham: "We're feet wet. Sluggo should be wet in two minutes."

Roller: "I got him. He's four miles and losing altitude."

Sluggo: "Red Crown, Cobalt One has the fire out, but we must have serious battle damage. We are going feet wet and then heading for Da Nang. Request SAR on station at intervals on our route of flight. This thing may go in at any time. We're descending to a lower altitude due to pressure loss."

Sluggo knew that Crown knew they were going to 10,000 feet because of the loss of pressurization, but the gooks wouldn't.

Red Crown: "Roger, Cobalt One. Red Crown will maintain radio contact until you reach Da Nang. Good luck and God speed. You are cleared to the altitude."

Ten minutes later, Sluggo came up on sec two: "Cobalt One, Copper One is turning for run to the south. If you nickel dicks had reached the target on time they would have nailed your ass instead of mine. So fuck you very much."

Graham: "Screw you, Sluggo. We were one minute early, which is why SO-2 always flies lead, even when in the sorry company of you and the Fake Major. But we can discuss that at the Club in a couple of days when you get back from your R&R."

Hollywood: "Copper One, you good to make it to D base [Da Nang]?"

Sluggo: "At this point, I think so. She's flying very stiff, and we are losing fuel."

Hollywood: "Roger that. Good luck and God bless, see you in a few."

Spike: "Sluggo, you and that crew of professional malingerers will not get out of any missions by getting your ass shot out of the sky. Believe me. I know. So don't dilly dally at D-Base, ya puke."

Sluggo: "I appreciate your concern for our welfare. We'll be back on that shithole quickly so that we have time to make sure that we don't fly with you assholes since you get people shot out of the sky."

Spike: "Good luck in spite of yourselves. Don't ding in. I need your money. See ya."

Graham smiled to himself. Spike had just confirmed what everybody suspected: He had been shot down before. "So brother, since you just admitted to it in your conversation with Sluggo, when and where did you go in?"

"Vinh. April, '68. Don't ask me about it again. It's classified Top Secret."

A GREAT DAY FOR CREWDOGS

Cobalt Flight landed at 0837 on 30 December. They were tired, dirty, and depressed as usual. Depressed because in about 48 hours they would get to go do this again. And then again…

Charlie Tower came up right after Cobalt One turned off the active.

"Cobalt One. Charlie. You and the rest of your flight are to postpone de-brief and take your crew bus direct to the Base Ops auditorium. They are holding a briefing for your arrival. Also, the Navy picked up Seddeler's crew. They're all OK, but Seddeler is missing."

Hollywood: "Roger, wilco after we get a chili dog. It'll take that long for the rest of the wave to get in the chocks anyway. Glad Seddeler's crew is OK."

Hollywood on IC: "Seddeler is missing. If he's missing in that stuff he's gone."

Seddeler was not well liked by anyone, so no one really cared. They had many other crewdog buddies that were gone or POWs.

Spike: "We'll go by and get our beer, too. I can't eat a Roach Coach dog without beer. They can start the briefing when we get there, and we'll get there when we are done with our mandatory errands."

Some Luck was waiting at the bottom of the ladder when they came down the hatch. He was in tears: "They got my bird, sirs. I traded to get you guys, and Captain Duggen was flying my bird."

Graham: "Bullshit. This was your bird for this mission, and she flew a perfect mission. Besides, Captain Duggen got blindsided by a SAM turning off the target. It was pure luck on the part of the gooks. So forget it. You did a great job."

Spike: "Bulldog's absolutely right, which is rare for him. This bird flew great. This was your bird today."

SO-2's crew bus had an Airman driver who was new to the island and didn't understand that a crew bus was a personal mode of transportation for crewdogs. He insisted that he could only take them where he was authorized to take them. He was a brave and stupid eighteen year old who hadn't learned that AFRs didn't apply on Guam. Spike had him come off the bus to check what appeared to be a bad tire. Spike then got on the bus and closed the door so the kid couldn't get back on and sat in the driver's seat.

The kid: "Major! What are you doing, sir! You are not authorized to drive this vehicle!"

Spike: "We are at war. We are commandeering this vehicle to serve the needs of the United States Air Force. We'll return it after we complete some mission critical duties."

The kid was running alongside as Spike started driving away: "But where will you return it!? I could get in big trouble for losing a bus!"

"We'll return it to its proper place, which is wherever we park it after we're done with our duties."

They completed their errands and showed up at the Base Ops auditorium about forty minutes later. The last of Cobalt Flight had just arrived. Graham and Spike had the pockets of their flight suits filled with beer. Graham gave a couple to The Fake Major's crew when they entered the room.

Just after they entered, the room was called to attention, and General Andrews came out on the stage. Something big was up again.

Spike whispered to Graham, who was standing next to him: "I don't get it. The gooks are out of SAMs, and we leveled the entire city. Maybe they want us to take out the rest of the majors in the north."

"Be seated, Gentlemen."

"First a few pertinent announcements - Captain Duggen's crew landed at Da Nang after being hit by a new rev of SAM over Hanoi early this morning. They could not get the gear down due to battle damage, so Captain Duggen bellied the bird in. I'm told it was a spectacular feat of airmanship. Second, Cobalt Flight finally managed to take out Hanoi Radio after three other attempts. Hana is off the air."

The room cheered for both announcements.

"Now for the reason you are all here. At 0600 local I received a top-secret communication from CINCSAC. At 1400 Zulu yesterday the North Vietnamese signed a formal cease-fire at the Paris talks that will effectively and immediately end all hostilities of any kind on 28 January 1973.

"Gentlemen, the war is over."

The room erupted into pandemonium. Everybody was standing, cheering, hugging each other, and slapping each other on the back. Spike and Graham handed out some more of their beer.

General Andrews: "Gentleman, I appreciate your elation, but please be seated for a few more moments."

They sat, while whoops of joy still filled the air.

"Most certainly we all know that your efforts of the last eleven days were the key catalyst that brought this announcement and I commend your dedication, professionalism, and bravery in that task."

More cheers.

"We lost fifteen aircraft in the last eleven days in combat. We do not know how many of the 93 men that flew those aircraft have survived as POWs. Part of the accord is that all U.S. POWs will be returned very soon. The dates will be confirmed shortly. Lastly, we will start sending crews home with their aircraft within a day or two. Now if you gentlemen will join me at the Club, I'm buying."

The room exploded again. This was the day and the announcement that they had all dreamed about.

Spike: "Hey Hollywood, fuck the de-brief. Let's go drink on the General's nickel. By the way, did you notice he didn't say one word about the Spyhauler being bombed? Maybe she sank before she could contact Moscow. "

Hollywood: "Great idea for once. I hope the gooks don't rescind the accords when they find the cow. But the Russians are a different story. They must be using formal channels to protest the attack. We're in deep shit either way, but I don't care anymore! Let's drink some Russians in celebration!"

Graham had tears in his eyes as they walked out. Spike noticed: "B-dog, it's over. No time for tears, man."

"Shit, they're tears of joy. We made it. There was a time that I thought we never would. I really thought there was a SAM with our name on it waiting for us, and I would never see my new wife again and never have any kids."

Spike put his arm around his protégé and good friend: "Well, you did, and you will, so cheer up, brother."

The Club was a zoo. It was like the biggest and best fraternity party in history, except without the girls. Cowboy managed to get hold of the Pilipeeno band, and they showed up just after noon.

SO-2 and the Fake Major were at their normal table in the bar. The General and his staff were at the next table, which was normally SO-2's spill over table, but they decided not to take it away from the General.

Suddenly the General, who had been mixing with the crowd at times, was at the head of their table: "Major Spike, Bulldog, Hollywood, and Wildman. I wish that D-Kid was here too, but at least he's alive. Sluggo should be here and will be soon. I had him and the crew put on an aircraft an hour after he crashed that bird on the runway at Da Nang. You guys and Sunny were the first crews to fly Gs into combat. Spike, you and Bulldog flew the second G off this island, behind Sunny as I recall. You guys caused me untold problems with your pranks, fights, and bullshit schemes, but they made this shithole island and shithole war just a bad memory at times. That's why I didn't have you shot for half the stunts you pulled. Now I heard about the cow turds in the bomb damage and the mooing of cows on guard from the Pentagon. The North Vietnamese raised hell, complete with photos and recordings. Of course I understand that you guys had nothing to do with that or the Flare gun battles, or the tennis court greasing, or the theft of a General's car, specifically mine. And of course, baiting the Philippines with song to the point that they launched an intercept."

The General paused, and his expression turned serious.

"But the coup de gras was bombing a Russian ship in international waters. Now that REALLY took balls! And careful planning! Two of the six bombs reportedly almost hit the ship! I smell the Yankee Air Pirates, meaning you guys, all over this incident. One BUFF could not have dropped all six."

The newly named Yankee Air Pirates were frozen. Their expressions were neutral to somber.

The General smiled again: "Fortunately for you Pirates the dumbass Russian Captain decided that they were 'warning shots' because he must have drifted into U.S. waters. We actually got a formal apology from the Kremlin for their vessel violating our sovereign waters! No shit! You guys are incredibly lucky! If the other obvious response had occurred, you Pirates would have already walked the plank!

"But all that was 'The Other Guy' or 'TOG' as you call him every time I'm going to hang your asses. TOG has done a whole lot of shit, hasn't he? Well, since you never did that shit, you'll be happy to know that the crews that got here first will go home first. You'll be wheels in the well at 1400 hours on Thursday."

Thursday was two days away.

Graham: "That's great news, sir! Thank you. And we heard about that stuff, too. Now it's only fair to warn you that we heard a rumor that the same guys that dropped the cow turds may have dropped an actual cow, complete with a cow helmet, rank, wings, and name tag sewn right on the carcass. It's clearly a rebel crew or crews that are out of hand."

The General, looking directly at Spike: "An actual cow? In uniform? You must be kidding. You guys bombed a Russian trawler and dropped a cow on Hanoi all in one day? If you guys weren't going home as first off, I'd change it just to protect the Wing and Air Division! The sooner I get you guys' outta here, the safer we will be!"

The General was now smiling broadly.

Spike smile: "Thank you, sir. We'll use our connections and get to TOG and tell him to keep it low key until he departs. But we can't guarantee that TOG will listen to us, sir."

The General was still at ease and smiling slightly.

"I think that you Pirates will be able to control TOG. If you can't, I'll have to send you to find him instead of going home. We'll start with Da Nang, then U-Tapao, and then every other shithole that I can think of. It might take weeks. Got it, Spike?"

"We'll control him for sure, General. I personally guarantee it. TOG listens to me, sir."

Spike smile.

The General, again smiling, gave a loose salute to the table, which was immediately returned by all, and as he turned to walk away:

"Thanks, Captain TOG."

SLUGGO RETURNS

The General had Sky Cops at the Club's entrances with instructions that only crewdogs, Wing, and Squadron staff officers were allowed entrance into the Club on this particular day. A major argument between a Sky Cop Major and the President of the Officer's Wives Club ensued when she was denied entrance for her "bridge club and eating large amounts of donuts" meeting. When she persisted, one of General Andrew's staff ended up calling her husband and told him to remove his wife from the main entrance immediately or risk re-assignment the next day. A car pulled up within minutes and the supply Colonel aided his wife into the car. Spike and the others witnessed the whole incident from their table. This was truly a wonderful day.

At 1300, Sluggo and Blackjack walked into the Club, still in flight suits like everyone else that had flown the last combat mission for B-52s in the Vietnam war. It had dawned on SO-2 that they had led the last mission, but The Fake Major analyzing their observation said it didn't mean anything. Spike pointed out to the Fake Major that leading it did, but Wildman's gold leaves didn't mean anything. Sluggo and Blackjack came right over and sat down after getting sincere handshakes and greetings from everybody at the table - the only time that had ever occurred in Graham's recollection.

After sitting, Sluggo started in: "What the hell is the big party for? At 1300? What did they do? Order another stand down so the gooks could re-arm the north and shoot the shit out of us all over again?"

It dawned on Spike that the General had said that the SAC communication was Top Secret and that the only people that may know were the crewdogs briefed and the air staff officers. Sluggo and Blackjack didn't know.

Sluggo continued: "Charlie Tower told the AC that brought us back that we were invited to the Club, but the rest of my crew are too beat and went to the Mansion."

He looked over at the other table and saw the General's back to him. The General was never in the Club with crewdogs.

"Oh I got it. General Andrews got his fourth star. OK that explains it. Well, you guys want to hear about our heroic crash landing at D Base? Boeing was there on the spot and said the bird could not fly. We had hundreds of shrap holes from the SAM."

Spike: "Who cares? No big deal. And your assessment of the situation is completely incorrect as usual, you dwarf midget. General Andrews is celebrating because he's going to get rid of SO-2, The Fake Major, and your crew so the base will return to some semblance of military decorum."

Sluggo: "U-Tapao, right? The bastard transferred us all to U-T."

Spike couldn't play with them any longer: "Wrong again, Captain America. The war is over, guys. We're going home."

Sluggo jumped up on his seat, then on to the top of the table, knocking over a bunch of drinks and stepping on Graham's hamburger: "THANK YOU, LORD! GOD BLESS AMERICA!"

He jumped back down and hugged Blackjack, who was tearing up.

Sluggo's outburst caused the General to get up and come over. He shook Blackjack and Sluggo's hands: "I heard about your crash landing at Da Nang. Nice job, Captains. I also heard that all the crew came out OK except for bumps and bruises. Correct?"

Sluggo: "Yes, sir. They're all fine. Hell, we'd fly a go-home mission in a full body cast if necessary."

General Andrews: "Well, you shouldn't have to, barring an unforeseen outcome from one of your bullshit schemes, because you guys are wheels in the well in two days. Meantime, celebrate and then get some sleep."

Sluggo: "FAN-FUCKING-TASTIC! Uh-oh… sorry, sir."

"No need for apology. It is fan-fucking-tastic, Captain! Have fun."

Blackjack was sitting at the end of the booth. He grabbed an unguarded Black Russian (which they had switched to for the caffeine) and got up: "I'm going back to the Mansion to wake up the crew and drag their sorry asses over here. I'll be right back."

The band played at least ten renditions of the revised crewdog anthem. Everybody sang along to the new chorus:

"We're gonna get out of this place! It won't be the last thing we ever do! We're getting outta this place! Girl, there's a better life… for me and you!"

By 1700, Graham was asleep on the table. Hollywood was sleeping on the floor next to the booth, The Fake Major had disappeared and Sluggo was sleeping in the dining room. The rest of the crew were sleeping in various places unknown.

THE FAIRCHILD CREWS GO HOME

Three Fairchild crews that were first on the island would go home first. That was Hollywood, Sluggo, and The Fake Major. D-Kid and Sunny would have been with them, and this crossed all of their minds. They would fly three Fairchild bombers home with a stop at Hickam AFB in Hawaii en route for crew rest. They would then fly straight to Fairchild and go through customs at the base after landing. Sluggo had been waiting to fly his own bird home. He could carry a lot of "stuff."

The crews started packing their things into the bomb bay of their respective aircraft six hours before PTOB. All three Fairchild bombers that were going home were parked next to each other on the ramp. Each crew had commandeered their own crew bus for the trips back and forth between the Mansion and the aircraft. B-52s had a three foot catwalk on each side of the bomb bay that would serve as the luggage rack for each crew.

Sluggo made more trips back and forth than anybody, and Graham noticed it: "Spike, what the hell is Sluggo's crew taking back? Part of the island?"

"No, he's taking back everything that he's stored for when he got to take a bird straight into the Base. The customs guy at the Base is a retired Air Force L/C, so he is far more forgiving than the traditional customs guys."

"What would he need a guy like that for? Has he been growing some funny weed on the back forty?"

"Shit no. You know better. We can't fly and 'fly.' Sluggo's no doper, but he's got friends on the ground in Nam, so I suspect he has a few war souvenirs that regular customs might frown on."

"What do you mean by 'regular' customs? Customs are customs aren't they? I don't get it."

"Customs are slightly different at home. The customs guy is a retired SAC L/C that has a better understanding of what should be allowed to enter the country from a war zone. If Sluggo gets him instead of TOG, he will have a memorable return. If he gets TOG, he'll probably have a very bad day."

"Who is this L/C? I've never heard of him or anything about him until now."

"His call sign is Scratch. He's a good guy. He's a crewdog. C'mon, we have wheels in the well at 55, and we have more stuff to get in the bomb bay."

Some Luck was working SO-2's bird as a trade off again. Most aircrews didn't grow very close to any individual crew chief because the crews didn't always fly the same airplane, but Some Luck had been through a great deal with SO-2 in the last two weeks.

Spike got off the crew bus, and Some Luck ran out from under the cowling: "Major Spike, this bird took some battle damage that wasn't picked up. The normal chief on this bird ain't what I'd call the best. Me and Milligan have been checking her over pretty carefully, but I'm not sure that she shouldn't go in for a close inspection. You never know where that SAM shrapnel might have done some damage."

Hollywood overheard the conversation that should have been directed to him in the first place.

"Are there any major hydraulic or oil leaks?"

"No, sir. 'Bout the same as is usual. Couple quarts here and there."

All the aircraft were very old and leaked constantly. Years earlier a thimbleful of oil or hydraulic would have grounded the aircraft until the source was found and corrected.

A jeep pulled up, and Spike and Graham saw the brown tooth smile. It was Roller who they were going to leave behind if he didn't show up for the PTOB.

Roller: "Hi, bosses! Sorry I'm late. I had to go down to Agana real quick."

Spike: "What the hell for, Yo? You best let that sleeping dog lie until you can sneak off this island safely."

"What dog? She ain't that good lookin' but she ain't no dog. I resent that, boss. Som' the other ones are close to dogs, but she's further away than most'em."

Spike: "You are a certified dumbshit. Why in the hell did you do something like that without first talking to me or Bulldog? What did she say?"

Roller: "Well you might be right, boss. She might not believed me much this time. She started crying, and then she got kinda mad and started yelling at me in what I think mighta been Jap swear words. Her Jap bodyguard started givin' me dirty looks. I tried to give her a hug, but she pushed me away and went to the elevator with her guard guy. I decided to get outta there before she got to her old man. I figure we'll be long gone before her old man's guys can get to me so it should be OK."

Hollywood had walked up behind Roller and had listened to the last part of the conversation.

"Roller, Godammit, Spike is right. You are an idiot. Get on the crew bus until we're done. Then you're going back to pack your gear and get dressed in flight gear. Load your shit in the bay, and then go over to ops and stay there until the PTOB. Got it?

Roller: "Yes, boss. I'll do that fer sure, boss. But I'm safe on base, boss."

Hollywood: "No you're not, dumbshit. The base is no longer on lockdown because the war is theoretically over, so the Japs could think up some reason to get on base."

Roller: "Uh-oh. I din know that the base had opened back up, boss. I mighta fucked up a little again, boss. Sorry, boss."

Spike: "You are a career fuck-up, Roller. You'll learn to use what little brains you have and change your ways or one of these days you're going to get yourself killed. Now get on the bus and wait for us.

"Yes, boss."

SO-2 took another twenty minutes to load their gear and went back to the Mansion for the last time to get the last of their gear and change into flight suits. They were leaving with the last of the gear 45 minutes later and walking on the balcony toward the stairs. Roller was walking in front of Spike and Graham when they heard the two gunshots in rapid succession. Simultaneously with the shots, the stucco wall popped two large holes right behind Roller and just in front of Spike and Graham.

Spike: "GET DOWN! THOSE WERE SHOTS AT US!"

They all hit the concrete floor of the balcony. Since there was a solid partition on the balcony railing from the banister to the floor, they were now out of sight of anybody from the ground. One more shot hit the partition just in front of Roller. Suddenly there was a lot of yelling coming from the other Mansion and from the yard. Spike crawled 50 feet and peaked up over the railing. He saw two guys in work uniforms running toward a Guap vegetable truck that was parked in the lot. Both guys threw objects into the bed of the truck and jumped into the cab. They started to back out when the elite Sky Cop special forces armored vehicle blocked their path. Four sky cops with machine guns jumped out and took cover behind the armored doors of the truck.

"PUT YOUR HANDS ON YOUR HEAD AND GET OUT OF THE TRUCK! IF YOU DO NOT COMPLY IMMEDIATELY YOU WILL BE SHOT WITHOUT FURTHER WARNING!

Spike watched intently and spoke to no one in particular: "These are the same special cops that guard the aircraft on nuclear alert. They will not screw around. Those guys have about fifteen seconds to get out of that truck."

Spike and Graham were now standing and watching the live TV show. Roller was still groveling on the balcony floor. The two "vegetable" delivery guys complied and came out with their hands on their heads. Hollywood and E-Jeep came out with the Co just as the Japs were being cuffed very roughly. Hollywood came up to Spike.

"What the fuck is going on!?"

Spike pointed to the bullet holes in the stucco and gave a quick rundown of what had occurred.

Hollywood was furious: "Roller, you miserable piece of shit. Get up! You nearly got one or more of the crew killed with your dumb ass actions. I think you are overdue for an Article 15. Consider yourself under house arrest and proceed as I had ordered you to do earlier!"

Roller, looking terrified, spoke softly: "Yes, sir, boss."

The sky cops wanted to keep the entire Go Home flight for at least a day to be de-briefed on what caused the attack, but Spike made a call to General Andrews, and the sky cop Colonel got a call in thirty minutes.

The Colonel was visibly shaken when he got off the phone with the General. "You men are free to leave… immediately."

Spike: "Thanks, Colonel. We have a plane to catch! You have a great day. We'll miss you… uh… oh… no we won't. Bye."

When the crew left the Sky Cop HQ for the bus, Hollywood slapped Roller on the back of the head. "You're not causing this crew any more trouble, dumb shit. When we get back to the CONUS, I'm taking you off flight status." Roller didn't care, but he said nothing.

CHAPTER XX: IF IT'S THE LAST THING WE EVER DO

THE GO HOME BRIEF

The Fairchild crews all assembled in the briefing room two hours late at 1700 for the much dreamed about Go Home PTOB. The mood of the crews was understandably very upbeat. The tension and overwhelming fear that pervaded the PTOBs of the days immediately preceding this brief only served to amplify the elation that the crews felt. They all came in without the usual notebooks for the brief because they could fly the mission with their eyes closed.

Sluggo was waiting for the assemblage: "We are all here today two hours late thanks to SO-2's usual fuck ups. This time it would appear that a detachment from their myriad of enemies attempted to shoot their asses while they were planning their final escape from this shithole. As we all know, this delayed all of us in returning to our family and loved ones, which is a crime so egregious that I haven't even thought up the penalty as yet."

Graham: "You know what, Sluggo? This is a rare case where the penalty has already been served preceding the so-called crime. That penalty was having to baby-sit you and your semi-capable crew for the last eight months and being trapped on this shithole so we couldn't even get away from you guys."

Hollywood intervened, even though everything had been said tongue in cheek: "We do apologize for the delay, guys. It was beyond our control by the time it came down to it. Fact is, we'll be wheels in the well headed east very soon, so let's dwell on that and perhaps torturing the briefing officer so that our final departure makes his day as well."

"Room, atten-n-shun!"

The crewdogs were stunned when General Andrews, Dangle, *and the never seen Major Major, Colonel Pew*, came in from the back. General Andrews took the podium: "Be seated men. First of all…"

Spike interrupted a three star General: "Excuse me, sir, but there's a very important issue here that must be cleared up before we continue. I apologize, sir.

"What's the issue that is so pressing, Major?"

"I have a question that must be answered by Colonel Pew before we continue. It's imperative, sir."

Pew was just staring at Spike. He didn't know he was the best bombardier on the island. He didn't know him at all. He didn't know any crewdogs, but he was their Wing Commander.

"Go ahead and ask it, Major."

"Yes, sir. Thank you... Colonel, it is our understanding from somebody that was there and witnessed it, that you and your staff informed a crew member's wife and her little boy that her husband was missing in action over Vietnam. This notification took place at the Officer's Club swimming pool when you and your staff walked up to her. She was seated in a chair by the pool wearing a bathing suit. Is that correct, sir?"

General Andrews was visibly shaken by the question. Pew turned very red and stumbled: "Major... I... have the misfortune of having to notify... many, many... wives and relatives... of crew members that have gone missing... whose people are here on the island."

Spike, fuming: "You didn't answer the question, Colonel. Did you, or did you not, inform a crew member's wife and child, at the Officer's Club swimming pool in front of a number of strangers, that her husband had been shot down!?"

Pew was now almost near panic: "I do recall that we were forced to inform her for fear that word would get... back in some other fashion... we didn't want... to... wait any longer so... we made the notification... almost as you describe it... we had no choice... at the time."

Spike, erupting: "NO CHOICE! WHAT THE FUCK, COLONEL!? Why couldn't you send the Sky Cops out and have them politely ask her to join them and take her to a place that was more private so that she wouldn't have to share her overwhelming grief with everybody at the Officer's Club pool!? In front of her little boy! For God's Sake! Your action was despicable!"

Spike remained standing, staring at Pew.

General Andrews was swift: "Colonel, that kind of insensitivity, and frankly stupidity, has no place in not only 8th Air Force but in any other Command or branch of the United States Military. You are dismissed from this briefing, and you are to wait outside my office until I return."

Pew wheeled around and left very quickly. A dead man walking.

The crewdogs stood and cheered his departure with "fuck you," "enjoy the cold," and "nice move with a mommy and her child, dickface."

Spike was very relieved. The good officers outnumbered the bad by a great deal, but some were absolutely terrible. That dick shouldn't have even been commissioned.

General Andrews: "Let's settle down. This is supposed to be a good briefing… and now, I suppose it will be since another moron was exposed. So… to get on with it, cheer up. As you probably know, I only participate in combat briefs. No, we have not re-engaged the enemy. You *are* going home. No in fact, I'm here to welcome your departure, since the sooner we can get you boys off the island and out of the theater, the sooner we can begin to repair the relationships that your antics have destroyed. The damaged parties are too many to enumerate so I won't. Worse, I suspect that there are relationships out there that have been damaged or destroyed that I don't even know about… yet. A perfect example of such unbridled behavior may be exemplary in the post-talk formal complaint by the North Vietnamese that we had enslaved and tortured helpless cows into flying our 'vehicles of death' against their 'innocent cities'. They sent photographs of a deceased cow… still in a parachute harness with USAF insignia sewn on the hide, and a custom altered helmet with cow horn holes to prove their allegations. They released the photos to the international press last night, and I had to explain them personally to Dr. Kissinger this morning. I said that it was an experiment in psychological warfare. Dr. K laughed and said that it was clearly successful."

The General was smiling and occasionally laughing as he made his opening remarks and the crewdogs were roaring, especially when it came to the cow. Nobody gave a shit what anybody thought anymore, including generals. This place was history.

The General continued, but the smile went away: "On a more serious note, you men have been through a great deal in the past months. Certainly that's an understatement in the last eleven days, but you all survived while too many of your brothers were not so fortunate. I thank you all personally for your sacrifice and professionalism under fire. You made me, the United States Air Force, and the Nation thankful that men of your abilities serve this Country. This is no time to be long winded, so with that I will say goodbye and good luck. Have a smooth flight home."

The room stood and applauded the general. He was a good guy, they thought, for a staff weenie. What they didn't know was that he didn't have the balls to do what General Charles did at U-T. Many in the room would never know that he nearly killed them with lack of leadership. Some would find out years later.

Dangle came to the podium: "I get to brief the Go Home flight, men. Rank has its privileges, as you know. Oh excuse me, you apparently don't know. [laughter] So anyway, the Navs have the charts. You take-off and turn starboard over the Russian spy ship instead of port. Please do not bomb the ship. That concludes the briefing. I can't say with complete honesty that it was a pleasure serving with you, but it certainly was entertaining… at times. Good luck and God speed."

The room was called to attention again, and the Colonel followed the General to the back of the room. They stood by the door and shook the hand of each crewdog as they left. When Spike and Graham came through the door, the General grabbed Spike's hand with both of his and Dangle did the same to Graham.

The General, smiling broadly: "We know who did the cow stunt, Spike. It's got your 'hoof prints' all over it. I personally loved the 'Moojer Milk' name tag. And bombing the Russian Spyhauler, as you Pirates call it. That was unbelievable. So all I can say is nice job, Colonel. That's right, you crazy bastard. At the next board you'll pin 'em on. Your outstanding performance has been overlooked by the 'REMF' for too long. Yes I know who the REMF are, and what it means. It's a fitting tag. Congratulations in advance."

Spike, stunned by the surprise: "Thank you, sir. I am truly speechless. Thank you, sir."

Spike, smiling ear to ear, after he and Graham had gone through the door: "A three star standing in a doorway shaking hands with crewdogs; I've never even heard of that, let alone seen it, and I finally make light Colonel in the same doorway. We should have done more shit, B-dog."

"Bullshit. Now we got a Fake Colonel to commiserate with The Fake Major."

Graham yelled at Wildman who was about ten yards ahead, walking toward Gilligan's: "Hey, Wildman! I got a Fake Colonel now who outranks your Fakeness, so get behind us in line at the Gilligan's!"

Wildman responded quizzically: "What fake Colonel? No one in your entourage of losers will ever have the capability or connections to be able to make O-5."

Spike walked up to Wildman still smiling: "Well it took awhile, but I certainly deserve it, contrary to other kiss ass fake Majors that we all know of. I pin 'em on at the next board, which is less than sixty days in my recollection. That's according to my General, Captain… er, Major."

Wildman knew that Spike really did deserve the promotion and shook Spike's hand: "I never even dreamed that dropping a dead cow on downtown Hanoi and bombing a Russian ship would get a guy promoted. My sincere congratulations, Colonel."

TAKE-OFF FOR HOME

The guys all chowed down on chili dogs for, hopefully, the last time, took the crew buses to the aircraft, completed pre-flight, and fired up the engines.

Charlie Tower: "Homerun One, taxi and hold. Two follow one, Three follow two. You guys have a good flight back. You did a great job and we all are very proud of you guys and the other crewdogs. You helped end a war that could have gone on much longer."

Hollywood: "Thanks, Charlie. At least we get to go home. There are a hundred guys that will not be going home. God bless them.

Sluggo: "Some of them will make it back, Hollywood. Don't forget that."

Hollywood: "Roger that, Sluggo. Homerun One's in position and holding."

"Homerun Two"

"Homerun Three"

Charlie: "Homerun One cleared for take-off. I hope the next time I see you guys will be stateside."

All three had a normal take-off and turned eastbound, which was a strange but welcome feeling. They climbed out and leveled off quickly because they were so light without a bomb load.

Sluggo was bored already: "Homerun flight, Homerun Two has a pool going on how many miles Bulldogeous misses Hawaii by. Five bucks a square, eighteen squares total. The range is fifty to a thousand miles. Get in now. They will all go quickly."

Graham: "Screw you, Sluggo. I'm in your pool, dickhead, and I'll miss it by exactly the number I have. So if I get a thousand we'll all run out of gas in the middle of nowhere."

Sluggo: "No way, Bulldogeous. You were automatically disqualified due to poor judgment and poorer navigation skills."

Homerun One shuddered violently.

Hollywood: "What the hell was that? It would be just our luck to get a pig for the Go Home flight. Andersen CP, Andersen CP. Homerun One"

"Homerun One. This is Andersen."

Hollywood: "Andersen, Homerun One had severe vibrations at flight level 350. No other unusual instrument readings."

"Roger, Homerun One. We'll get maintenance up here. Stand-by."

The maintenance staff got on the horn with Homerun One and went through as many scenarios as they could think of. Nothing was abnormal.

Hollywood: "Crew, I think that the vibration was an aberration. But if any of you are uncomfortable, I'll turn the bird back. Respond."

Graham woke Spike who was asleep even before they had reached altitude and filled him in on what had occurred. No one would respond until they heard what Spike had to say.

Spike: "Pilot, we still got both wings? Seems like it. This is a press on mission if there ever was one. Wake me again if we lose more than four engines. G' night."

The others responded immediately that they were all in, except Roller who was someplace else, as usual.

"Andersen CP, Homerun One will press on barring no further incidents. We'll advise prior to reaching TBP."

The TBP was the point at which they could not turn back to Guam and make it with a fuel reserve at touchdown.

The Fake Major: "Christ, you guys break more airplanes than anybody in the Pacific Theater, and you've never even been in a really tough spot like we were coming back from Downtown. If you would like, I can give a quick primer on aerial execution while we have the time flying to Hickam."

Graham: "Shut up, Fake Major."

Spike: "Shut up, Captain."

Hollywood: "Shut up, Jeep Major."

Co: "Shut up, Major."

E-Jeep: "Bite me, Major."

The Fake Major: "Who the hell was that? I didn't even know you guys had that many people on your crew!"

No one responded.

The sleep rotation started with all three crews, but most couldn't sleep in anticipation of seeing their wives and children again. There was more than one occasion in the last two weeks when they didn't think that would ever happen again.

A NEW ZOO

In early January, D-Kid, Alex, and the rest of the FNGs that appeared healthy were told they would be moved to "Cu Loc" (Zoo) Prison. The weaker injured would stay behind at the Hilton. They were loaded on trucks in the middle of the night and transported to the Zoo. The Zoo was a known POW camp, so it had not been bombed, but the SAM sites and triple A batteries that surrounded it had been surgically removed by F4s flying at extremely low level. As a result, the Zoo was a mess from bomb concussions, not from direct hits. The healthy crewdogs methodically started to clean the cells.

Camp regulations were posted in every cell by the gooks.

This was going to be way too much fun.

D-Kid: "You know SO-2 had a stamp that they used to stamp on unacceptable Air Orders and other dumb ass directives. It said "Bullshit Disapproved." That's all. But it made the point. I wish I had that stamp now."

Alex: "We do. Just in a different form."

He picked up a piece of charcoal from the corner of the cell and carefully wrote "bullshit disapproved" across the face of the camp regulations. Things were lightening a bit. Spirits were coming back and so was the open resistance to their captors. The POWs were allowed to mingle much more than had been so at the Hilton, and the command structure was immediately established the first morning with the SRO [Senior Ranking Officer] taking command and establishing a command structure with specific responsibilities for each man.

One of the biggest problems that the POWs had was eliminating boredom. They would make playing cards out of scraps of paper and chess pieces out of the rat dung bread. When they were bored they constantly thought of home, and it was painful at times beyond the abuse and torture they had suffered at the hands of the enemy. The SRO knew this very well, so he hatched a plan with his staff to relieve the boredom, resist the enemy (which they were sworn to do), and have fun at the same time. They would systematically break almost every one of the posted gook rules. One a day, every day. They would not be blatant to the point of causing serious repercussions, but they would be close. The word went out and quickly passed through the command structure.

There were two guards in the Zoo. One was "Tank," a large nasty guard who clearly didn't like Americans or anyone else. He would go out of his way to be nasty to any of the prisoners. The other guard was Radio. He was actually very pleasant to the POWs and talked about his family in the south. He spent his time trying to cultivate a citrus tree in the harsh conditions.

Tank would be the first victim.

1. Detainees must strictly obey orders and follow instructions given them by Vietnamese officers and Army men on duty in the camp.

D-Kid was walking across the yard with Alex, and Tank told them to stop. They walked right past him and didn't even acknowledge his presence,

"You stop! YOU STOP! YOU STOP!"

They finally stopped and turned slowly, both cupping their hands around their ears.

Alex: "Twat did you say? We cunt hear you! Me and Bob here used to fly jets, you know, and we cunt hear nothin' anymore 'cause of the noise. CAN YOU HEAR ME? I can't even hear myself!"

Tank actually seemed intimidated by the large black man yelling at him.

"You go now. You go."

D-Kid, cupping his ear again: "TWAT!"

"YOU GO!"

All the POWs that witnessed the exchange were doing everything they could do to keep from laughing. It was an old playground joke, but it worked. More importantly, they had broken rule number one. Everybody else disobeyed instructions and orders all day, with Tank in particular. Tank had a very bad day. They left Radio alone.

The Camp Commander called in the SRO. Even though the gooks didn't recognize rank, they knew who he was.

"Are *all* your men deaf?"

HAWAII INBOUND

Spike woke up about three hours after take-off and lit up one of his dogshit cigars, causing everyone to go on O2. Graham headed upstairs to sleep in the "bunk." Spike was responsible for navigation when Bulldog was on a sleep break because he could navigate as easily as he could do a bomb run. Sluggo filled him in on the pool after Bulldog went up. Spike knew damn well that B-dog would hit Hawaii right on, but a plot hatched that was too tempting to pass up. He pulled the circuit breakers on the key navigation instruments and pulled out a chart of the central Pacific. He started to manually determine their course through "dead reckoning" (normally called DED reckoning, but they had a different name for obvious reasons) which entailed an educated guess that took into account the course and wind conditions. "DR" dated to World War II and was an acquired skill that required the wind conditions to be carefully plotted. A key element in that was called "drift" which related to which direction the winds at altitude were pushing the aircraft off course. The Navigator corrected for the effects of the wind by making course corrections that compensated. Spike plotted the "drift" backwards on the chart so that it would appear that he was making course corrections that doubled their distance off course. With high winds, which they had tonight, the error could drive the entire cell off course by hundreds of miles. Spike brought the other Navigators into the scam. After three hours, B-dog came back down the ladder.

Graham, still not awake: "Well, how bad did you fuck things up, Colonel? Now that you're a potential REMF, I was awakened in a sweat thinking that you would lose all your acquired skill sets due to REMF-itis."

"Relax. The Nav systems went out soon after you began slacking, but my exceptional skills at DR have us on course and on time. The systems just came back up, but there's no land mass out here, as you're supposed to know, so the radar is useless."

Graham: "What!? Why the hell didn't you wake me, you old fart!? This is the most dangerous part of the Pacific! Christ!"

Spike lit another one of his puke cigars to amplify B-dog's panic: "Are you questioning my ability to perform plebian navigation tasks? How dare you, Captain. As soon as I pin on the leaves, I have a good mind to have you shot."

"Give me the damn chart! I have to work backwards to see if you fucked us up."

Graham got on the horn to the other Navs: "Homerun Two and Three, confirm present position and ETA to Hickam."

The other two Navs were required to back-up lead, but they were ready for the transmission.

Blackjack: "What are you talking about? I've been asleep. I left the navigation to lead, which is perfect, I'm sure, in your more than capable hands. I have no idea where we are although we seem to be over the Pacific and headed east, which is a good sign."

The Fake Major's Nav came up right after Blackjack: "I have us somewhere over the Pacific. Don't bother me again."

Hollywood: "What's up, Nav? Spike get us lost? Why in the hell you would ever expect him to know how to navigate any more defies logic."

Sluggo: "Hey Bulldogeous! Blackjack just took a look and said he has no idea where you have taken us. I hope it's not more than seven hundred miles off or I lose the pool to the Fake Major, and… oh… by the way, we'll all end up punching out after we run out of fuel."

Graham grabbed the chart and started to backtrack Spike's DR. He quickly realized that Spike had plotted all the drift corrections backwards. That meant that instead of turning the cell into an eighty knot crosswind to remain on course, he had turned them away from the course, effectively doubling the error as if they had made no correction at all.

Graham, yelling at Spike off IC: "You idiot! You plotted the drift backwards! We're at least seven hundred miles south of track!"

Spike smile: "You can't call a Colonel an idiot because of your dereliction. I will have you shot if we land on land, but at this point, seems like I'll have to have you drowned. That's too bad since I much prefer the firing squad. Drowning is just too Navy."

Graham unstrapped and grabbed the sextant which was in a hardened case behind him. He opened it and checked it out quickly. There wasn't any eyepiece, so he couldn't take any celestial readings to find out how badly they were lost.

Spike had taken the eyepiece while B-dog was asleep.

Graham was now on the verge of panic: "Blackjack, we're way off course. Shoot some celestial for me. My sextant's broken."

Sluggo: "LOST! The SO-2 Nav got a three ship of B-52s LOST on the Go Home flight! Despicable!"

Blackjack came in: "Absolutely despicable! You should be shot!"

Hollywood, in a much quieter tone over IC: "It truly is despicable. We may well have to have you shot."

The Fake Major blew it: "He-he-haw-he… Certainly one of the most despicable [starting to laugh harder] acts ever committed in the history of aviation. The shooting should be with large caliber bullets… maybe even a bazooka."

Now everybody came up on guard laughing like crazy. Graham finally realized he had been gooned big time.

Very suddenly, Homerun One vibrated violently and yawed hard to the right into a steep dive. Hollywood, the strain in his voice evident as he fought to control the aircraft: "Everybody strap fast. I don't know if I can handle this. Homerun flight, Homerun One is declaring an emergency. Something is seriously wrong with the aircraft. I can barely control it."

They were in a steep dive at a severe degree of bank. Spike was completely strapped in a combat mode which told Graham everything he needed to know. He quickly followed suit.

Spike: "E-Jeep, make sure that Roller is awake and strapped."

Very slowly, the aircraft started to return to level flight.

Hollywood: "Goddamn nearly inverted us. It was all the Co and I could do to keep that from happening. Co, get Guam on the horn."

Co: "We're out of range. I'll try to raise Hickam."

Hollywood: "Nav, can we reach Hickam on UHF?"

"Not yet. Try Skyking."

Hollywood dialed in SAC HQ and squawked emergency on the IF at the same time.

"Skyking, Skyking, this is Homerun One bound for Hickam declaring an emergency. Do you copy?"

Almost immediately given the war frequency, Skyking responded: "Roger, Homerun One. State nature of emergency, souls on board, and fuel."

Hollywood: "Severe vibration and hard starboard yaw causing extreme difficulty in maintaining control of the aircraft. Six souls, thirty six thousand five hundred pounds."

Skyking: "Switch to secure two, Homerun One."

There was a five minute pause as Hollywood communicated with Skyking, then he came back on with the crew: "OK, guys. We have a hydraulic problem… at the very least. Must have been caused by the battle damage that Some Luck found. Skyking gave us some action items that we have already completed but with no guarantees. We're climbing back to altitude to save fuel and so that we have a margin of error in case this shit happens again. If the hydraulics start to fail completely, we're screwed, so I want everybody strapped and ready to go. We may even go inverted in a worst case, so I will want everybody out before that happens. Right now, we can make it to Hickam and land… I think. Bulldog, give me a range and ETA based on existing airspeed."

Graham gave him the information instantly since he knew he would be asked. They were climbing, but they could all tell the bird was straining.

Spike: "Christ. We go through over a hundred missions, including two of the worst I've ever been on, and the fucking airplane itself tries to shoot us down after the war ends. I'm gonna go fly fastburners. Screw this."

Graham: "Forget it, Colonel. You're never going to get out of SAC. You try to go to TAC, and SAC will promote you to a REMF job, and we'll all send you hate letters. You're screwed either way."

Hollywood, chuckling: "Bulldog's right, you know. Just pin on the silver oak leafs and shut up, or you'll be a REMF immediately. With your war record and reputation, you'll be at Castle commanding the training squadron and hating every minute, along with hiding from ex-wives."

"How did you know about my central California ex-wives?"

Hollywood: "Who else but Smolensky. The guy is an Air Force Almanac. He knows almost everything about everybody he's ever met in USAF and a lot about guys he hasn't met."

"That damn Smolensky, I'm going to kick his ass… or better yet… break his jaw so that they wire it shut. That'll force him to keep his big mouth shut. The prick."

"Relax, Spike. It's nothing that everybody doesn't suspect or know about before Smolensky. Remember that you had other buddies in USAF that knew your wives. Don't concern yourself because then you start to believe that anyone really gives a shit, which they don't."

Graham, off IC: "How many wives have you had, champ? A dozen? Two dozen? You ever marry a gun?"

Spike: "I told you never to ask me personal information, B-dog, so don't. Besides, they are really beautiful women, as you might expect. They're just too demanding. Especially when they found out I had some dough. Never get a divorce, B-dog. It's too expensive in the long run. The two most expensive words in a community property state are 'I do' and 'you're done.' Never forget that. Just shoot them like you would a horse with a broken leg."

"Sometimes I can't tell when you're bullshitting me. Then again, Hollywood's right. Don't mistake me for someone who gives a shit. It's none of my business, but it fills in the soap opera that is Spike."

The aircraft vibrated again and pitched to the right.

Hollywood: "Crew, stand-by. If this bird pitches too much more we're out of here. Wait for the horn and light."

Spike and Graham had their visors down and masks on and were ready to go. They were losing altitude again in a steep dive. In about 30 seconds, the yaw started to decrease and the aircraft began to return to level. Hollywood was on the horn to SAC again and explained the reoccurrence. He came up on IC: "Crew, if this problem occurs on approach, which we can't discount, we would have a major problem. Skyking is evaluating options for us, but it's ultimately up to us. My feeling is that we get as close to Hickam as we can and then offense and defense abandon the aircraft. The Co and I will try to put the bird on the ground. We have zero delay, as you know, so we can get out if the bird goes hard right on approach. Spike, your thoughts?"

"Forget it. Skyking wouldn't let you do that for all kinds of reasons: too much risk for you and the Co, you'd make a mess of the runway at Hickam which might close it for a period of time and screw up a few Generals' tee times, and you might kill a few people on the ground. Skyking is going to order us to abandon the bird after the next incident or when we are as close to Hickam as we can get. Then they'll tell us to descend to 10,000 feet, turn the bird away from the islands, and go for a swim."

Hollywood was going to agree when Skyking came up. They laid out almost exactly what Spike had just described, but it made no difference because the aircraft shuddered violently and again pitched hard to starboard. This time Hollywood and the Co could barely control the aircraft from inverting. When they passed through 60 degrees of bank, Hollywood and the Co managed to yank the aircraft back.

The safety cover on the bailout switch was open.

After Hollywood got back to level, all the vibration stopped, and the aircraft appeared to fly normally. No one could understand it. Hollywood went through an impromptu checklist with Wildman and Sluggo to see if they could figure out what was going on. Now everything looked normal.

Sluggo: "I know what Skyking told you, but I would just press on at this point. She came in with battle damage before, and she should make it again. It beats ejecting since you never know when a seat will malfunction. Just get close into Hickam and have Bulldog and Spike eject since they don't have zero delay seats and they are of no value anyway. They can use their rafts and surf into the beach."

Spike: "You are truly a disgrace to yourself and the United States Air Force, Sluggo. I think that I qualify for a bootlicker when I pin on my new rank, and I'm requesting you personally through the Senator when the time comes. You will sit beneath the Deli Counter and keep Herman company."

Sluggo: "On a more realistic note, boys, when we get into Hickam they are going to ground that pig that you are attempting to fly and that means you and all your stuff in the bomb bay gets grounded with her. We need to get SAC to agree to have you guys fly the leg into home with The Fake Major and my elite crew. I will propose that each one of you fly an instructor seat in my bird and Wildman's. I don't know if they will go along with it though since they have this new risk assessment project, and they won't want SB crews flying with each other."

Spike: "Good point, you dwarf midget. I think we'll wait until we get into Hickam and then I'll get a patch back to General Andrews on Guam and plead our case. If we try to go through Skyking, they'll make us wait for a trash hauler or tank to get back."

Sluggo: "Sounds like the right plan even though you thought of it. Let us know if you have any more barrel rolls, boys."

The rest of the flight to Hickam was amazingly normal. No one could believe it. SO-2 became exhausted because they couldn't risk going to the bunk and had to remain strapped for the entire flight. Prior to approach, Homerun One assumed the number three position so the runway would be clear for Sluggo and Wildman if something did happen.

Hollywood touched down, uneventfully, at 0716 local. A school bus sized crew bus met the crews. Graham was asleep before the chatter started.

Wildman: "You know, Spike, that we have a ton of stuff in our B Bay. You will probably have to leave all your crap here and hope that it reaches Fairchild."

Spike could barely stay awake: "Listen, MAJOR, we're taking our stuff even if we have to throw your shit on the ramp. The way we do it is to open one of the B bay doors and pile everything on the door that's closed. If we stack it all to the ceiling, it should fit in your two planes."

Wildman: "We can't do it that way. It will screw up the weight and balance."

Spike: "Screw you, Mr. Weight and Balance. I put a cow in there and successfully dropped it on Hanoi. It'll work. Trust me."

Hollywood was dropped off at the Hickam Command Post to patch to General Andrews. The others went to de-brief, and Hollywood caught up halfway through. He came in and grabbed a beer from the cooler: "Blackjack, please wake up Spike and Bulldog… General Andrews said it's a go. He'll handle it with CINC so we don't have anyone question or abort the plan."

All three crews debriefed and then crashed. Sluggo and Spike went by the Club for a few Mai Thais to honor the tradition and then crashed as well. The next morning, they all agreed that if they gave the REMF any time to think about it, someone would try to change the decision, so they headed to the birds and started loading SO-2's gear in the respective aircraft that the crew would join for the flight. They buttoned up the bomb bays on both remaining birds by 1300 and were ready to launch within an hour.

Unfortunately, a TAC REMF Major had pulled some documents that would change the flight plan. He had a TAC two star intervene on a "safety and possible damage to the facility" premise. It took the REMF Major "Toady" most of the day to assemble the paperwork, but he had the time since he really didn't know what his assignment was. He needed the work and attention from Senior REMF in order to get selected on the next L/C board. The next ride these "war heroes" could get back to the states was in five days. Everything was full up until then… and maybe even longer.

C.K. McCUSKER

A NEW STRATEGY

A staff car pulled up to the aircraft as the crews were waiting for the crew bus. A master sergeant got out and asked for Captain Noland. Hollywood didn't like the staff car or the fact that the NCO had driven out to the ramp. He was uneasy as he walked over to the sergeant who had purposely distanced himself from the rest of the crews.

The sergeant saluted as Hollywood approached: "Captain, Major General Leland has ordered that you gentlemen stand down until such time that the safety and airworthiness of the two aircraft can be determined."

He handed Hollywood the official order. Hollywood didn't even bother to read it. He knew that the REMF had beaten them, but this was only round one. Round two would start immediately.

"OK, sergeant. You know you're the bearer of bad news, but you didn't create it. I need you to drive me to the Command Post so I can patch a call to Guam."

"Yes, sir."

At Base Ops, Hollywood placed a direct call to General Andrews. To his astonishment, the General answered. Hollywood explained their dilemma carefully. The General was silent momentarily when Hollywood finished his recap, then he responded in a tone that indicated that he was really pissed off: "Captain, you return to your aircraft and complete the pre-flight on the two birds that can fly. You will be airborne within two hours, so sit tight. If you are not, I want you to call me back on this line at 1500 hours."

Hollywood was overjoyed: "Yes, sir. Thank you, sir."

The Sergeant took Hollywood back to the ramp and briefed the guys on what Andrews had said. Less than an hour after he returned, a staff car with two stars on the plate pulled up on the ramp. The driver, a Master Sergeant, got out and approached Bulldog who was sitting on a B-4 bag and closest to the car. He saluted while Bulldog was still sitting down.

"Sir, would you assemble the crews? General Leland would like to speak to them."

Bulldog returned the salute and stood up. "Sure, Sergeant. This is a bit unprecedented. I suspect that your General is in deep sushi."

"What, sir?"

Graham smiled: "Sushi, Sergeant. That's 'shit' in crewdog language."

Graham yelled: "Hey, guys! The General wants to talk to us!" and startled the Sergeant. Everyone except Roller appeared quickly. As soon as the gaggle was assembled on the ramp, the General opened the rear door of the car and walked over. The men came to semi-attention as he approached.

The General spoke quietly: "Gentlemen, I…"

Sluggo, from the back: "We generally can't hear you, sir!"

Hollywood cringed. *Godamnit, he's going to piss him off!*

The General spoke up: "GENTLEMEN, I AM HERE TO PERSONALLY APOLOGIZE FOR YOUR DELAY… here at Hickam. I understand that you just completed some serious combat missions that brought on the conclusion of the Peace Accords ending the Vietnam conflict. You are cleared for immediate take-off as soon as you are ready and you contact the Command Post. Again, I apologize for the inconsiderate delay." He saluted the men, and they returned it. He turned and almost ran back to his car.

They were all stunned by the scene and seriously happy. Spike turned to Graham: "*Inconsiderate delay*! Wow! That guy just got the ass whupping of his career, for what it's worth, and I suspect not much anymore. Whoever ordered him to do that is in the stratosphere. He may even be above the stars."

At 14:05, Homerun One went wheels in the well. Homerun Two followed in one minute. They made as much noise as possible, which is very easy to do in a B-52.

They were going home. Next stop, Fairchild AFB, Spokane, Washington. USA.

Thirty minutes after they were airborne, a secretary came in and handed a note to her boss who was in a late night meeting. It simply read, "The B-52s that were at Hickam are airborne and headed home."

The President nodded his approval, and she left.

THE ANIMALS GET RESTLESS

The POWs knew that the war must be winding down. The bombing had stopped, and they believed that it would start again immediately if things were not progressing quickly. As a result, they became even more impatient and defiant of their captors.

9. *In the detention rooms, all detainees are equal with each other. Anyone does have the right to free thinking, feeling, praying, etc. and no one is permitted to coerce any other into following his own opinion.*

This was a direct attempt to break down military order and was blatantly disobeyed by the men in all of their actions. Everybody referred to one another by rank whenever the gooks were within earshot, and the men lined up in formation in the morning. There was an SRO in each cell as well as the camp, and the gooks finally gave up and started to use them to disseminate information.

Dick James, a B-52 RN, was stocky and had a quick wit. He also did a great imitation of Sergeant Schulz on Hogan's Heroes, using a good German accent that the gooks didn't understand at all,

"Vhere is Co-lo-nel Hogan, boys? Ve know dat you hid him sominvhere. Ya vol! Ve vill find him soon. C'mon boys… der Co-lo-nel Klink said I haf gut to find Hogan or it's ein Laotian Front! Ya vol! Vhere is he… please…."

D-Kid played straight man: "Sergeant, there's no POW named Hogan, let alone a Colonel. You're looking for a guy that doesn't exist."

James, breaking a smile: "Do nut lie to me, Lebeau. Ve know Hogan es here."

"serGEANT schULZ!"

One of the other POWs across the courtyard was playing along, and James picked it up right away.

"Ya vol! Mine commandant! I am comink!"

Sergeant Schulz waddled over to the "commandant."

"Did you find Hogan yet, Schulz?"

"Nine, mine commandant. He es nut here, mine fuehrer!"

"Then he must have escaped. Correct, Schulz?"

"He cut nut haf, mine Co-lo-nel, ef he vas nut here. A person cannot eskept from sominvhere he has nut been. Mine Oberfuehrer!"

"But you are here, Schulz. Would you like to escape from here?"

"YA VOL, MINE REICHSMARSHAL GRUPEN FUEHRER! On the first C-141 that they let me on."

The POWs that witnessed the exchange were in hysterics. The Vietnamese didn't understand anything. Tank was completely confused, and he had had enough.

"NO TALKING! NO NOISE! YOU STOP NOW!"

The Vietnamese were still giving "quizzes" to the senior officers, Lieutenant Colonels and above, on a daily basis, but D-Kid and the others were no longer bothered. Spirits continued to improve, as did the food, mostly Russian. When D-Kid saw the Russian writing on the can of beans, his thoughts drifted back to the "Black Russians" at the Club with the guys. He wondered for a moment what they were doing now.

They were on final approach to Fairchild Air Force Base.

FAI SO-2 was home.

CHAPTER XXI: THE HOMECOMING DANCE

THE HOMERUNS GET HOME

Spike, sitting in the Instructor pilot's seat on Sluggo's bird: "Sluggo, you really ought to let me land, buddy. You're going to fuck it up and catch a nose gear and porpoise down the runway like Shamu in front of all the wives and families no less. C'mon give it up, and let Spike take the stick and grease it for you. I won't tell anybody. I swear."

"Spike, the only thing that you grease is your hair. Would you please shut the hell up? We're trying to complete the checklist. Oh, that's right, you don't know what a checklist is. It's this blue plastic covered book in my lap."

Co: "Gear."

Sluggo: "Down and locked."

Spike: "You still have time, Jeep. I can get in the seat in time to make you a hero. Lizard will be watching, too. If he sees you catch a nose gear, you'll be in the simulator for weeks."

Sluggo brought it down so smoothly that they barely noticed they were on the ground.

Co: "Air brakes."

Sluggo: "Six."

Co: "Chute"

Sluggo: "Deployed."

Sluggo laid on the brakes and called the tower.

"Fairchild Tower. Homerun One is home. God Bless America."

"Roger that, One! Welcome home, men! Great to have you back! Homerun One, take the parallel to number 22 and shut her down. Customs is there, and the families are in hanger four waiting."

"Roger, parallel to 22, Homerun One."

Spike: "That was the luckiest landing in the history of the Strategic Air Command. It had nose gear written all over it, and at the very last second a gust of wind raised the nose just a touch which allowed the best landing I've ever experienced in a B-52. You have incredible luck, you dwarf midget aviator. By the way, how do you reach the pedals? Do you have blocks on your flight boots?"

Sluggo understood the backhanded compliment hidden in Spike's meaningless commentary. "You know I thank God that it is an extreme rarity when I have to fly with you because I wouldn't want Linda to have to visit me in prison."

"Homerun Two is on the ground at 26 after the hour."

"Welcome Home! Great to have you back! Homerun Two, take the parallel to number 23 and shut it down. The families are in hanger four."

Homerun One set the brakes, and the ground crews put the chocks in place. The RN opened the bomb bay. Once set, Sluggo shut down the engines. The ground crew had thought ahead and brought lights, so the crews could see while unloading. The crew deplaned and started to unload their gear.

Sluggo came out of the hatch and almost immediately saw good old Scratch: "Colonel! Good to see you, buddy! How've you been?"

"Welcome back, Captain. You guys did great work. I followed it every single day. You guys ended the war in eleven days. We could have done that many years and many lives ago, but I won't get into that… OK, Sluggo, what have you got? I don't want to go through every damn B-4 bag."

"Nothing this trip, Scratch. Didn't have time to go anywhere. We were too busy winning the war, man."

"Yeah, bullshit. OK, let's look at 'em all."

At just that moment, Smolensky threw a B-4 bag down to the tarmac.

It clanked. It shouldn't have.

Scratch: "Sluggo, why don't you just show me what you got, so you guys can get to the wives and kids a lot quicker."

"OK, OK. Hey Smo, throw the rest of the special shit down."

"You sure, boss? Some of this stuff might explode."

"Help him, Blackjack."

They laid out all the "stuff" from the B-4 bags. There were seven AK-47s, 1,000 rounds of tracer ammunition, three rocket launchers, and twelve rockets.

Scratch: "This is it, Sluggo? You swear?"

"Yeah, Scratch. This is it. Can we go now?"

Scratch stared in amazement at the equipment laid out in front of him. "Sluggo, you got to be kidding this time."

"What kidding? These are war souvenirs that were taken away from a vicious enemy. We deserve these as such."

"I can't let you keep the rocket launchers, Sluggo. I mean give me a break will 'ya?"

Sluggo signaled Blackjack and Smo to pack up the AKs and ammo quickly.

"Thanks, Scratch. We're having a welcome back party for ourselves in a week or so. Will you and Dolores come?"

"Sure. Again welcome back, and bless you."

The guys loaded the crew bus quickly, but they waited for Homerun Two to get their gear on board their bus. They wanted to all be there when they met the families. A cold rain started to fall. Graham got on the bus and sat alone. This was a very emotional time. More than once, he believed he would never see Priscilla again. Then he thought how incredibly lucky he was. D-Kid was still in some shithole in Hanoi, and Robbie was waiting and praying that he was coming home soon. Other guys would never come home.

HANGER FOUR

The families and the band were all inside the hanger due to the rain and cold. The crew buses pulled up in trail, and the band started.

"Off we go into the wild yonder…"

When he heard the band, Spike was surprised.

Lizard brought the band out? There must be a visiting dignitary he wants to impress. We've been back twice since April and never got a band. Hell, we didn't even get a Lizard.

The guys started to get off the bus, and the wives started to jump up and down and clap in the little way that wives do when they are excited. The wives and kids finally broke for the buses. They couldn't wait any longer. There were tears and screams of joy as the crews got off the buses one by one. Wives hugged and kissed their husbands, and children hugged their dads' legs. It was a great joy for all.

The band wrapped up *God Bless America,* and the Lizard stepped up to the microphone.

"I want to take a moment to welcome you men home, and believe me I will be brief. You have served your country well in this conflict and come out of it as victors. For that, we owe you a great debt of gratitude. We will not forget your sacrifices or those of your comrades, some of whom gave the ultimate sacrifice. You are all a credit to yourselves, the United States Air Force, and this Nation. Thank you."

Somebody clapped, but no one could tell who. Mrs. Lizard?

Priscilla was all over Graham to the point that he had to gently push her away.

"Honey, let's get out of here and get home."

She almost dragged him out of the hanger. As he was leaving, he saw Spike out of the corner of his eye and turned. He had two gorgeous women hanging onto him kissing him from both sides. They sure as hell weren't his daughters. Spike noticed Graham and gave his Spike smile and a thumbs up.

How does he do it? He smells terrible half the time. He's not that great looking. How?

None of the crewdogs said goodbye to one another. This was a night of hellos. They would find their loved ones and get away from Hanger Four as fast as they could. The crews had ten days of "crew rest" upon their return. Most of that time would be spent in bed, but they would neither be asleep, nor alone.

ROLLER ALMOST KILLS HIMSELF WITH STUPID

Roller didn't go home. Frau Eva, tipping the scales at 230, was at home, and he had neglected to tell her that the war was over and that he was coming home. Sergeant Gravitz, his best friend, was home already because he was a boom operator on tankers. He met Gravitz at the NCO Club at 2300. It would close at midnight. They started pounding beer and tequila, as was their custom.

Gravitz: "You can't stay at my house, man. Sheila would call Eva the minute she saw you and Eva would be there in two minutes and beat the shit out of you for sneaking home."

They continued to evaluate alternatives between shots of tequila until the bartender told them the Club was closing. By then they were incapable of evaluating anything.

Roller: "I'm going to just go home and surprise the fat Nazi bitch. I'll say I was sent home on a secret mission so I couldn't tell her I was coming."

"That's a great idea. Why didn't I think of it? I'll go with you in case she tries to kill you."

They got in Grav's car and weaved their way to Roller's house without hitting anything, which was miraculous.

Roller: "You know what, Grav?"

"What?"

"If the Sky Cops had pulled you over, they would have put you in jail forever. Yup. Forever."

"You're correct. Remind me to walk home... or you drive me and then walk back."

"I can't walk. How could I drive?"

They stumbled to the front door, which was bolted, as usual. Frau Eva had always believed there was a rapist out there that was after all 230 pounds of her. They banged on the door until the lights came on. The Frau stared at them through the small pane and unbolted the door.

"Vas is los? Haf you been demoted again? Vie are you home?"

"I was sent home on a secret mission on a secret airplane, and we landed at a secret base so it took a long time to get here on account of we had to use secret roads on a secret route. Ain't that right, Grav?"

"That's the absolute truth, Eva. It was so secret I didn't even know we were here until I met him at the Club."

Eva grabbed Roller by his flight suit collar and yanked him into the house. "Das is vat I thought, you miserable little shvine. You haf been drinking mit your friends at the Club, and leave Eva here to be alone."

"No! No! We only had two beers, and then I forced Grav to drive me home right away to my loving wife! Ain't that right, Grav?"

"That's the absolute truth, Eva. We had two beers, and they ran out of tequila, and then they closed anyway."

"Ya, das is vat I thought, shvine. Ach! Come in anyvey, and I vill take ein bag. You may haf a beer mit your friend."

"Thanks, Honey!" He went to kiss her but missed completely and kissed her shoulder. She grabbed his collar again and kissed him full on the lips.

"Velcome home, shvine. I unpack for you. You haf und beer."

Grav was already in the kitchen. "Where's that tequila we bought last time?"

"I think we drank it last time."

"Oh… here's some bourbon. Ain't that kind of like a southern tequila?"

"Who cares? Pour it in them coffee cups so's Eva thinks it's "ein beerin"… the kraut bitch."

There was a loud shriek from the other end of the house.

Eva.

Roller and Grav hurriedly stumbled their way toward the bedroom. Eva came out into the hallway and started yelling at Roller in German. She charged at him and smacked him hard but didn't knock him down. She was still yelling in German. She walked past him toward the kitchen.

Roller, rubbing his face: "Boy. She's really pissed this time. Maybe I shouldn'ta come home after all."

The two managed their way into the bedroom to see what caused the blow up. Lying on the bed next to Roller's B-4 bag was a large bundle of black hair. Next to the hair was Roller's wedding picture with his Thai wife. Thai wives traditionally cut their hair off and gave it to their husbands on their wedding day.

"Ooh-ooh."

"Boy-o-boy. You are one dumb son-nufa-bitch."

Eva appeared in the doorway with a butcher knife and renewed her screaming in German. Grav stupidly got between her and Roller. Eva charged, and Grav dodged the blade and pushed her aside.

Grav: "Listen, Eva! Listen! It ain't what it looks like, Eva! I was with him in Thailand! He was honored by the King 'cause of his hero stuff. The King asked him to be best man fer his daughter which is what they does in Thailand, Eva. So he had to take that picture with her an' she gave him her hair, which is also what they does in Thailand, an' then she went off with her husband on her honeymoon on an elephant. It was a real nice wedding, and the King was real happy. That's the absolute truth, Eva."

Eva had calmed down listening to Grav's greatest performance, but she was still muttering to herself in German.

Roller, who was drunker than Grav: "He's right. It's the absolute truth. I was there. It was a great honor by Her Majesty, and she is real, real pretty."

Roller picked up the picture of him and his Thai wife and showed it to Eva.

"See?"

Eva exploded again, but she threw the knife down, which Grav quickly retrieved. She grabbed the picture and threw it at Roller. It hit him in the head, but he didn't even try to duck. He was unfazed if he was there at all.

Roller, blood running down his forehead: "Let's go finish our beers, Grav, now that this here is explained. Good night, Eva. I'll be in later, dear."

Eva followed them out to the kitchen, still ranting in German, but the tone started sounding like a lecture. Roller knew she would calm down soon, eat, eat some more, and then go to bed.

That was a close one. If Grav weren't here, I could be dead now.

CHAPTER XXII: LET THE CELEBRATIONS BEGIN

GREAT NEWS AT THE ZOO

The Navs at the Zoo had gotten together and figured out a calendar so the POWs had a good idea of the dates. It was getting toward late January, and they had heard nothing. But the gook guards, except for Tank, had really backed off. Given the opportunity, they would do something about Tank.

The Rules stated that if the "detainees" required something from the guards that they should address the guards with the words "Bao Cao." If no one spoke English, they would then find a guard that did. The POWs suspected that "Bao Cao" which was said to mean "report" meant something demeaning instead. So they had a terrible time with mispronunciation: "Bow Cow," "Butt Cow," "Boo Coo," and "Bomb Cow" (they didn't know that Spike had). The gook guards would constantly correct the pronunciation. They had many more mispronunciations that drove the gooks crazy. A favorite was for the leader of their Chinese ally: Mousy Dung. The gooks thought that was close enough and didn't correct them.

In late January, they were told to bathe and shave and put on clean clothes. They were led to a large auditorium under guard. D-Kid was walking into the room when he heard a guy behind him. The voice was familiar.

"Hi Bob"

He turned around and it was Tom Sampson, his capture mate. He hadn't seen him for weeks.

"Hey! You look great! They fixed your arm and the mustache is gone. I barely recognized you."

"Where have you been held?"

"Well, currently I'm at a penthouse in the Hilton, but the service is less than I would expect at the rate I'm paying. The rats are quite slow. So I'm thinking I might find a penthouse at the Zoo. Have you been there? I hear the rats are much faster."

"Naw. The rats are gone. We ate 'em."

"That's a shame. It hard to find good help these days. Oh well."

They both cracked up. Clearly the mood was changing.

The gook Camp Commander came onstage.

"This is to inform you that the Paris Peace Accords have been signed. As part of those Accords, all prisoners on both sides will be released within sixty days…"

The room erupted with cheers. Linebacker Two had succeeded! They would all be free in sixty days or less! They had a GHD! 29 Mar 73!

Within a few days of the announcement, they saw C-130s - trash haulers on approach to Jane Fonda International (Gia Lam), which was about five miles away from the Zoo. Wow, trash haulers in Hanoi! They'd probably claim to be River Rats (an exclusive club for guys that had flown combat over the Red River Valley, Hanoi). Speculation as to why they were there ran wild. Picking up wounded? Repairing the runway for our jets? Donuts? Toilet paper? The crewdogs wondered if JFI had a back bar.

The POWs figured that they had less than 60 days, and spirits soared. They had all missed Christmas, but they would be home for Easter. That was great consolation to all of the Christians.

The gooks continued to try to interrogate some prisoners, but now no one gave a shit, so they didn't even answer with their usual bullshit.

They verbally tortured the Tank. He was the victim now, and he knew it.

D-Kid confided in Alex: "You know what? I've given something a great deal of thought both before and after I was shot down. I feel a strong spiritual calling, and that has done nothing but grow since I was captured. When I get back, I'm going to the Seminary. I want to become an Episcopal Priest."

Alex, smiling: "Oh great. Another professional killer down the tubes. How can I possibly retire if all you up and coming bomb droppers bail for some placid profession? They'll never let me out! I'll be sitting alert when I'm 75! On another note… I think that's wonderful. Do it man! If the spirit moves you, let it! Why don't you conduct our services on Sundays? It would be kinda like Flight Training for the pulpit."

"Thanks, Alex. I will do it. I will."

THE PEACE ACCORDS PARTY

Sluggo was mixing 101 proof vodka with grape juice in a plastic garbage can in the kitchen. This would let the women have a great time at the "Piece is Here Party." They would never even taste the vodka - inhibitions out the door. With any luck there would be more than one "piece" celebrated tonight. He had been home for three weeks and he was still horny, even though Linda had been going non-stop. He would just watch the festivities. If his eye wandered, Linda would deck him.

Priscilla Graham was adamant: "I am not going to one of Patrick's insane parties! I told you last time when that bimbo with nothing on ran through the living room that I was done! You go if you like, but I'm not."

"Why not just drop by, and we'll split right away. This is the Peace Accords party. It's important."

"No RJ. You pulled that on me last time and we stayed until the bimbo run. I'm not going."

Graham weighed the consequences of going to Sluggo's alone. He'd been home for three weeks. Things had been great. Maybe it was a good night to stay home. Sluggo's parties always got him in trouble.

Graham always slept with the window cracked in the bedroom no matter what the outside temperature. They had just gone to bed after midnight when he heard the unmistakable sound of an AK-47 on full automatic going off. He jumped up and looked out his bedroom window, toward Sluggo's house.

Those drunken idiots are shooting at the moon with tracers. I can't believe it. The Sky Cops and the OSI will go completely ballistic on this one.

Graham reached under his bed and grabbed his AK.

Priscilla was awake: "What's the matter? What's that noise? What are you doing?"

"Lots, gunshots, and hiding this gun. In that order."

"What?"

"I'll explain later, honey. I have to put this some place safe tonight and then get rid of it tomorrow."

As he was running to the basement, he heard the sirens.

I knew that would be quick. And those guys must be completely blasted. I have got to get over there right now. The crewdogs are in deep sushi.

Graham hid the AK in the basement, dressed, and drove over to Sluggo's house. The sight alone was intimidating. There were seven or eight Sky Cop cars with lights flashing, unmarked government cars, and the armored alert security vehicle.

Sluggo and Spike were standing on the front lawn surrounded by Sky Cops *and* guys in suits. Graham parked and quickly joined the circle gathered on the front lawn.

Spike, to a Sky Cop L/C, slurring slightly, which was rare: "We didn't see him, officer. We only heard him. The lil' fucker must have been a commie… a real fast commie because we came outside to shoot him for shooting, but he had already snuck away real fast."

"Major Wilson, don't give me that CRAP! Somebody here at the party was doing the shooting with an AUTOMATIC WEAPON! Now where is the weapon, and who did the shooting!?"

A Sky Cop in fatigues approached the Colonel: "Sir, we found the shell casings over there. They are 7.65mm tracer ammunition. The markings indicate Russian."

Sluggo, standing next to Spike and just as drunk: "SEE!? We told you they were Commies! The little bastards. Can't you keep Commies with machine guns off this base Colonel? Why we're lucky that an entire Russian division didn't sneak on and attack us at our Peace Party! It would ruin the party! You should go check the fences for tracers of Commies."

Spike, snickering, looking at Sluggo: "He means *traces* not tracers… you dumb shit. But that's a good idea. You want a drink before you go, Colonel?"

"We're not going, and we don't drink on duty. We're searching your residence right now, Captain Duggen. We will find the weapon."

"Oh no you won't, Colonel. That I assure you."

"What?"

"You'll never, ever, find it."

"What are you saying, Captain?"

Spike, irritated: "You can't find what was never here. Now we're going in for a drink. The war is over, Colonel. Did you get to go?"

Spike didn't wait for an answer. He and Sluggo turned and walked toward the house.

The Colonel, clearly flustered with the two drunks: "Gentlemen, get back here. We are not done."

Sluggo turned around: "Want some grape juice? You can drink grape juice on duty…" He continued to walk into the house.

Graham intervened: "Colonel, these are my crewmates, and they are clearly too blasted to answer any questions tonight. They're celebrating the end of the war, which is effective today. They deserve to celebrate, Colonel. Major Wilson has four DFCs. Captain Duggen has two. Between them, they probably have thirty Air Medals. They deserve to celebrate. They not only lived through it, they ended it."

The Colonel: "Who are you?"

"I'm Captain Graham. I'm a crewdog too. I only have one DFC and six Air Medals, Colonel."

"I don't give a damn who anybody is. War heroes or not, we're going to get to the bottom of this tonight."

Coming from behind the Sky Cop: "No you're not, Colonel. These are residential quarters, and these men are entitled to celebrate the end of a war that they fought valiantly in. Your men may finish searching the house and then you will all leave and continue the investigation tomorrow. Make sure your men do not disturb their personal belongings in any way."

Graham was stunned. It was Lizard! His tongue was going like he was at a fly convention, but Lizard had just ordered the Sky Cops and everybody else to leave the party alone.

Graham: "Thanks, Colonel. Want to join us?"

"No, Bulldog. Thanks. But I'm going to make sure these assholes leave and then take off. It's too late for old Colonels to be up. Have fun."

Graham went inside and he could tell immediately that it was very drunk out. *American Pie* was blasting on the stereo system. One couple was making out in the corner. Another was wrapped together on the floor just inside the door. He stepped over them and walked into the kitchen to get a drink. Linda Aaron was sitting on the counter. She was a sexy blond and the wife of a good friend of Graham's,

"Hi RJ! Happy war over! C'mere and give me a kiss!

He walked over and kissed Linda on the cheek, and she grabbed him and *really* kissed him. He gently pushed back.

"Bulldog, don't you ever try to kiss me on the cheek. You know I love you."

That's when he noticed that Linda was wearing a tee shirt… and nothing else. Her legs were straddling the counter, and home base was clearly in view. He got some Sluggo punch out of the can with a plastic cup.

"Linda, I love you too, sweetheart. Where's Shell?"

Shelly Aarons walked into the kitchen: "Right here, Bulldog. My wife proposition you again, or just blatantly grab your dick?"

He turned to his wife: "Linda, Jesus Christ. That's a little too much. Go put some panties on please."

She seemed to debate her husband's direction and then jumped off the counter. Her great tits bounced as she did so. Graham decided he was way too late for this one. It was way too drunk out, and he didn't want to try to catch up. Linda kissed him again on the way by. Hard. Shell didn't care.

Graham walked to his car. The music was still just as loud, and it was late. He could hear many inside singing along. Always the same song over and over. It was the new crewdog anthem.

"Them good ol' boys were drinkin' whiskey and rye sayin'
This will be the day that I die…
This will be the day that I die…
And they were singin'…
Bye, bye Miss American Pie,
Drove my Chevy…"

BACK TO CAMP HO-HO-HO-CHI-MINH

All the wives sent letters and packages to their husbands every day. A few packages made it to the men, and they shared them with their cellmates. Almost no letters made it through. In early February, they gave the POWs paper and pen and said they could write home. They could say anything they wanted to this time. D-Kid didn't believe that at all, so he attempted to get out information about his crew:

Dear Robbie,

Please call my godson and tell him that I was sorry to hear that the head of the family had died. We hope the two brothers are OK.

The two others from my crew are really looking forward to getting home. We're supposed to leave on the 29ᵗʰ of March. I can't wait to see you.

He continued on until he filled the page. What he told his wife was that the "head of the family" (pilot) was dead, and that the two "brothers" (both the Co and the gunner were black) were missing in action. He didn't have a godson so that meant she should go to the Wing Commander with the letter. The chance of the letter being sent was very low, but he had to try to get the word out. All the POWs tried. They were trained to do that.

The food got worse. Not only was the bread full of crap from the new bakery but they found shards of broken glass in it. That started an immediate hunger strike. The SRO went to the Camp Commandant,

"My men have found glass and rat shit imbedded in the bread. You know what that equals? Bullshit! That's what. You poison one of my men, and the B-52 bombers will come back and blow up everything. I want decent food for my men!"

"Must have been big accident. You blow up good bakery, so now we use not so good bakery. You know? I will fix."

They next day there were shards of glass in the *soup*. Alex found some first. It appeared to be from a light bulb: "What the hell is this? General Electric Soup? If I eat it will I glow in the dark? Guys, don't eat the soup. David, go over to the Stable and warn those guys."

The SRO went completely ballistic with the Commandant. The Commandant was at first accommodating, but he then became frightened and had the guards throw the SRO out. The next day, they got tofu soup - flavorless bean curd.

David: "Hey, where's the glass? White chunks of shit floating in horse pee? I want some good glass instead. You screwed us, Alex."

D-Kid, who was very hungry: "You got to be kidding. This stuff tastes like a Goodyear reject. The bastards aren't going to poison us - they're going to starve us to death by feeding us rubber. I bet that this shit is indigestible."

Alex: "Relax, Bob, and enjoy the cuisine of a fine Vietnamese restaurant. Close your eyes and see the elegance of no fine tapestry and really large rats. Relish the smell of really bad food and enjoy some fine Vietnamese wine aged over two weeks on the table. Then imagine that you have to excuse yourself to take a shit. Then open your eyes, look at your bowl, and realize you don't have to take a shit! You already did!"

They all laughed, but they were all hungry. They were always hungry.

The next day they heard the distinctive whine of C-141 engines in the distance. They all went to the windows or walls and looked toward JFI. There it was. A beautiful gray and white plane with a red cross on the tail.

It was the first "Go Home Bird"!

It was really going to happen!

They watched as the 141 came into the JFI on final approach and as the gear came "down and locked." They could feel the aircraft flying in on final. Some were quietly crying with joy. At the last second, the 141 did a "missed approach." The pilot slammed the throttles forward, climbed a bit, and banked hard right. He flew right over the Zoo and "waggled" his wings, a salute from an aircraft. Then he turned back to land.

The Zoo erupted in cheers and shouts of joy. The guards tried to quiet the prisoners down, but no one listened.

D-Kid smiled and thanked God.

One day soon, one of those would come for them.

SKY COP ATTACK

Lizard was pacing in front of his desk formulating an answer for the 15th Air Force head of Sky Police, who was also a full Colonel, and sitting at the conference table in Lizard's office. It had been two weeks since the "machine gun" incident, and the head Cop had come in from HQ to ruin Lizard's day.

"Sam, to be honest, I have no idea how that alleged weapon came on the base and was allegedly fired into the night sky. You're going to have to have your guys get into a serious investigation of how that could happen, because it certainly presents a threat to our Alert capability."

Sam jumped to his feet: "ALLEGED!? What the HELL alleged!? Your damn sky pilots brought back some AKs from Nam in their personal private jets. Then they got drunk off their ass and started shooting in the air on your goddamned base, Colonel! You personally intervened for *your boys* and refused to let my investigators gather the evidence necessary to hang the perpetrators by their balls! That means that there are now felony gun runners flying your B52s, Colonel!"

"Colonel, don't blame your inept organization's inability to keep this base secure from outside incursions by armed lunatics on my valiant aircrews. I know that it is difficult to get capable, intelligent, and motivated people to join your organization given the assignment, but their inability to solve what is clearly a serious security breach is alarming to me and to my aircrews."

Now Sam was nearly apoplectic: "WHAT THE HELL!? THE ONLY OUTSIDE LUNATICS THAT MY GUYS EVER ALLOWED ON THIS BASE LANDED HERE IN A B-52!! You got that, Richard!? I know that your guys were 100% responsible for this, and I will get them! And when I get them, Richard, I'll get you with them!"

"Sam, don't ever threaten me, or DENIGRATE MY AIRCREWS! They just won a war for this Nation while your bozos allow armed outsiders on base with impunity. Now your boys need two things to prove your case. The first is evidence. Simple, we all know that. The second is the IQ to find the first. They currently lack both and since your people need the second to get to get the first, you're screwed. That is all we need to talk about now. Let me or my staff know if we can help you in any way."

"Are you dismissing me, Richard? You have the balls to dismiss a full Colonel?"

"Sure. I fly airplanes. The name on the door is United States Air Force, NOT United States Air Police. Now I have things to do, Sam. Call me if you need a ride home… by air."

THE ZOO TURNS INTO A ZOO

They were "short."

"Short" meant in "airspeak" that all of this misery would soon be over, and they didn't give a shit anymore. They awaited the second 141 with great anticipation. It was due on Saturday, 24 Feb. It didn't arrive.

Near panic.

D-Kid: "What's going on, David? Would they risk the Peace at this time? I can't take this shit anymore. I had no time with my bride. What if nothing happens? We just sit here?"

"Relax, Bob. They know they are done. They couldn't risk an all out attack if this thing collapsed. On top of that, the world would not be behind them anymore if they violated the Accords, and they know it."

David was right. But he didn't know how right. Earlier in the day a conversation had occurred in the Oval Office:

A senior aide was admitted to the Oval Office and approached the President.

"Mr. President, the North Vietnamese have informed us that four of the prisoners that they are holding will not be released under the Accords because they were captured in Laos. They say that the prisoners are therefore prisoners of the Laotians and must be turned over to them."

"Oh? Well, you tell the North Vietnamese that if they want to violate the agreement with bullshit, we will blow the crap out of every city they have with B-52s in 24 hours. What's left of Haiphong will be gone. Hanoi, Vinh… all of 'em. It will make Linebacker Two look like a warm-up. You tell 'em that right away, Tim, and on the way out tell Audrey to get me General Kimball (the new CINCSAC). Thanks, Tim."

D-Kid was not convinced. His luck had not been that great. The last minute move onto the Charcoal Three crew that had a bull's-eye on its fuselage; his marriage having to be moved up because of the deployment; his friend's deaths, the torture, the isolation… but then think. Think.

Everything that you learned before you were captured was a divine composition that defied explanation. God has a plan for you that will unfold over the decades that will follow. You will get home to your bride, and you will make something of your life and time on this earth. God's will was not the tragedies that you have witnessed and experienced. God is working to bring good out of the tragedies that surround all of you, or you wouldn't be here. You would already be gone, like so many others. God Bless them and their families. Your time will come…

Alex had come up and noticed that Bob was deep in thought. He waited a bit and then interrupted in case it was not good thought. None of them needed anymore fear.

"Hey Bob. Want to play a little volleyball? We need to use you and Petrewski's heads as back markers on the court." Petrewski had blond, almost white hair.

D-Kid was at peace with his thought.

D-Kid, now laughing: "Bite me, Alex. Are we going to use you as the net? Most volleyball nets are black, you know."

"No, that's badminton, white boy, which no black man will play because if our wives or ladies ever saw us playing it they would all leave us. Did you ever play badminton? We can try to make some of those little girl rackets and kill the next pigeon we see for feathers. How 'bout it, kid? I'll be the net, and I promise I won't laugh too hard."

"Don't call me white boy, Alex. You know I'm sensitive to that. I prefer your original, 'Super White Boy.' I mean let's call a spade a spade."

David had overheard the exchange, smiling: "You sure you guys like each other?"

They both cracked up.

"Shit no. Do you love your brother?"

Then they heard it. The distinct whine. It was Go Home Two on approach. Then the camp heard it. Everyone rushed to the wall facing JFI. They erupted in cheers when they saw the bird. The guards went crazy. They thought that the PWs would jump the wall. The guards started screaming in both English and gook. No one paid any attention. Again at the last minute the 141 jammed the throttles to the wall and did a missed approach, banking hard right and flying directly over the Zoo. He saluted the POWs by waggling his wings and turned to land. They knew where everybody was and when they would go home.

They were short.

STAY ALERT

Lizard was pacing, and licking, as usual in the Command Post. He had ordered all those assholes back on alert immediately after the confrontation with 15th. They were due in five minutes to brief the War Order (Nuclear) Mission assignment.

If these guys weren't really good, I wouldn't have chased off the Air Police on the night of the incident. That was right, wasn't it? Maybe I should have had them arrested... but then some of the guys at the party were close to real war heroe,s and CINC SAC would have gone ballistic, and my star would be gone. They also know too much...

about me. Best be careful, Dick. One more ORI and you probably get out of here and away from 'The Wild Bunch' to a star far, far away. Boy! I bet Tinkerbelle would be a great piece of ass if I could get small enough.

The Wing Chief Master Sergeant, quietly: "Sir. SO-2, 3, and 4 are approaching. Would you like to greet them here or come in from the rear?"

Lizard raced to the back.

The crews assembled.

The CMSgt.: "Room! Ah-aa-ten-shun!"

Lizard walked in from the back for effect. No effect. He didn't have three stars on his collar like their good buddy General Andrews. He walked to the podium and looked down at his notes, which weren't there. "Gentlemen, as I addressed you upon your immediate return with your families present, I am proud of your efforts. Now to another issue - I know you guys are responsible for the machine gun fire at Sluggo's party. I, personally, have been taking a great deal of heat over this incident, and we need to find the perpetrators immediately. I know you guys did it. I know it. Now, if the guilty parties would just raise their hands at the end of this request, we can be done with this quickly and move on to matters of greater importance. Please raise now."

All eighteen crewdogs in the room raised their hands. Most not really knowing what Lizard was talking about, but no one pulled this shit on a crewdog for a little celebration.

Lizard, fuming: "The old all for one shit, huh? Captain Tobias, I know that you weren't even here on the 29th! OK, gentlemen. I know who did it. There could only be five guys on this base that would do something like that, right Spike?"

Lizard didn't wait for an answer: "Right, Sluggo? Wildman? Bulldog? You appeared out of nowhere. Well planned men! Hollywood? C'mon? And, of course, Blackjack. You know nothing, I suppose?"

"No, sir. I know a great deal. Just nothing about what you're talking about."

Spike, soon to be L/C: "Colonel, this is horseshit. D-Kid did it remotely. We're in a public forum with our peers, and you have exercised extremely bad judgment in bringing up this issue. In fact, it is now a non-issue. We came here for a WO brief to you and your staff. Would you like us to do so? My recollection is that is required for certification and you can't assign us alert lines until that is complete... sir."

Lizard would never make a star. Impossible.

Each crewmember of every crew was required to brief their responsibilities in the event of a War Order mission, better known as The End of the World Mission.

"OK, SO-2 is first. Make it perfect, gentlemen, or you will spend a month in the sims versus the shacks outside the alert facility. Captain Noland. You're up."

Spike couldn't believe Lizard's animosity. What are a few hundred shots into a field across the runways loaded with fortified bunkers? This wasn't the good ol' days.

Hollywood briefed perfectly despite tough questions from Lizard and his "Fly" staff as the crewdogs dis-affectionately called them. The Co did a great job as well, and then E-Jeep and Roller did OK but weren't challenged.

Bulldog was next on route of flight. *Would they nail him?*

"Failsafe to point Echo, left turn to 289, descend, and maintain FL 240 for 8.5 minutes then accelerated descent to 2000 feet, turn left to 205, and another accelerated descent to 200 feet wet AGL for feet dry penetration at Delta. At point Juliet, climb and maintain 500 feet AGL as we approach mountainous terrain. TA [Terrain avoidance] flight through the mountains…. "

Lizard was turned talking to his staff behind him. He knew that Graham knew this stuff. Graham noticed that Lizard wasn't paying attention, so he changed the route of flight.

"So Colonel, after we get over the mountains and through the woods here at point 'Pig,' we release a 1.5 megaton device on Grandmother's House and turn right immediately to 299 for a run on the Straw House, The Stick House, and the very famous Brick House. The Brick House has never been taken out. All three of these commie strongholds will be hit with Mark 28 1.5 meg devices even though they are only about 100 yards apart. That sir, as you know, will level most of that part of the Earth. I might add that a release that quick is a tough task for Major Wilson. The Brick House is probably the most heavily defended…provided the Wolf survived the attack on Grandma's house." The crews were holding their mouths and doing everything they could not to go into hysterics.

"Questions so far, Colonel?"

Lizard turned around quickly: "No, Captain. Continue please."

One crewdog lost it and had to be grabbed and muffled. That *almost* caused the rest to go.

Lizard immediately turned back to his Flies.

"So moving to mission egress, sir. We bank hard right, line up wherever we want since everywhere is now a flat runway, descend on an estimated final, gear, touch, brakes six, chute, and pull off on the parallel which happens to be next to targets C, B, and D, code named "The Pig House Complex." We join our collaborator, a knockout broad by the name of 'Big Tits' Riding Hood for barbecued pork and warm beer. Then we draw straws to see who gets to guard "Red" from vagrant, semi-melted commies, and I win because I have the only short straw, along with all the long straws, due to brilliant planning. Are there any questions, sirs?"

From the back of the room: "Bullshit, Bulldog! We draw cards. High man guards Red!"

"No way, Trout. I got those too. Aces removed. I have two, and Red has two. Besides, your targets are hundreds of miles away."

Trout: "Not anymore."

The room had been struggling to contain themselves through the performance. Now they lost it. They were holding their stomachs, laughing, crying,

"Bravo! Great brief!!"

Lizard and the Flies figured out that something that Graham had said at the close of his brief had been amusing, but they couldn't let the crews know they hadn't been listening so they just all chuckled on Lizard's prompt.

Lizard: "Very funny, Captain, but the Command Post is no place for jokes."

"No. No, sir. It certainly isn't."

Most in the room didn't pick up Graham's double entendre. Spike did and gave him a high five.

THE ANIMALS GET CLOSER TO RELEASE

The Gooks were worried that they would be criticized for poisoning the PWs, so they started feeding them hot peppers with their food to clear intestinal parasites from their systems.

Food became a little better (canned Russian grease was better than rat shit bread). Packages from home started to get through, and they would distribute them equally. The medicines drove the gooks nuts. They could not figure out how to open the childproof caps.

David, with Tank, who was menacing him over inspecting the medication: "See this? All you do is twist the cap left just like you do with your commie medicines and it opens. Then, to close it, you replace the cap, think of America, and turn right. Simple. Here try it." D-Kid was watching the encounter. He could barely control himself. The hated Tank would spin the cap furiously without pressing down and could not get the bottle to open.

Tank: "Medicine not allowed!"

Radio saw what was happening and asked Tank for the bottle in Vietnamese. He handed it back to David. Tank just walked away. They were clearly under orders to now be careful with the PWs.

With the medicine came cigarettes. About half of the PWs smoked. The gooks had no concept of color in branding since there were only two brands of gook cigarettes: really bad and really, really bad. Consequently, they gave all green cigarettes to one cellblock, all red ones to another, and all gold ones to another. The PWs threw packs back and forth between cellblocks to accommodate different preferences. The guards were convinced the Americans had gone crazy in captivity. Besides, American cigarettes were terrible.

They started to let packages from home get through. But the gooks would intentionally give the package to the wrong person to try to start a fight. It didn't work at all. The guy that got stuff that wasn't his simply waited until he could give it to the man that it was addressed to. Invariably, that PW would then share the contents with everybody else.

D-Kid: "Tom, besides what we all want first when we get home, what's the second thing you want?"

"Black bottom pie. It's the best thing in the world. All I want is a piece of black bottom pie."

Alex had overheard the exchange: "Me too. Now *ask me* what I want second."

They all roared with laughter. Shorter.

The whine.

C.K. McCUSKER

It was 17 March. The 141 was on final and right on time. That meant that they were right on schedule. The animals went nuts as usual, but the guards didn't seem to care anymore.

They knew. The next 141 would be *their* 141.

CHAPTER XXIII: WINDING UP AND DOWN

REAL ALERT

It was late March, and SO-2 was on its fourth alert tour since getting home. The one week semi-isolations from their wives and families were a grinding bore. At least they could get laid in the trailers… when they could get one. The trailers had beds, a kitchen, and a small living area that was only used after the beds. The wives got smart, and they brought their own sheets.

Spike and Graham were at the Base Exchange buying essentials.

The horn went off.

The horn went off all over the base, both indoors and outdoors, and it was very loud. It meant that Alert Crews were to get to the alert aircraft (the ones carrying real nuclear weapons) immediately. Spike dropped everything and raced to the truck outside. Graham was already there. They jumped in and took off for the Alert Facility. They only had eight minutes until they had to be onboard the bomber and ready to taxi.

Spike: "You know what, B-Dog? This shit gets really old. I was in the middle of getting laid in the back of the commissary at Dyess about ten years ago when the damn horn went off before I did. Now we'll get to the bird and get the same shit we always do: 'This is Sky King with traffic. GREEN FLAG ONE. REPEAT GREEN FLAG ONE.' You know how many times I've heard that?"

Green Flag was the code name for a simulated War Order. The real War Orders were Yellow Flag for China, and Pink Flag for Russia. They came in orders of magnitude one through three. A Pink Flag One was all out war with Russia; a Yellow Flag One was all out war with China. Either one meant launch immediately and attack your targets. The end of the world. Pink or Yellow Flag Two was start your engines, pull the chocks, and taxi to the end of the runway. A "Flag Three" was start your engines, pull the chocks, and be ready to taxi.

Only the guys in B-47s in the early sixties had ever heard the real thing. They got a Pink Flag Three once during the Cuban Missile crisis.

Graham: "Your oldness, excuse me, Colonel your oldness, I can't imagine how many times you have heard that, so I won't try to guess. I will only hear that stuff for about another year. You could do the same Colonel, 'Soon.' Why not pin 'em on and fly the coop? No way will you ever make Full Colonel, since you're far too capable. By the way, was she cute?"

Spike was racing to the pad and ran a red light (as he should have). They almost hit the car coming into the intersection. The car shouldn't have been moving at all. When the horn went off on base, everybody was supposed to pull over and stop so the alert vehicles had a clear path to the aircraft.

Spike: "Dumb bitch! Is it getting dangerous to drive to work at seventy miles an hour? She was a knockout. Why do you ask dumb questions?"

"That barker in that car? You kidding?"

"No, B-Dog, the commissary girl at Dyess."

"I'll never ask again."

The guards waved them through security, and they pulled into the ramp area and raced to the aircraft. The whole crew, except Roller, seemed to have been away from the facility and arrived at the aircraft at the same time. RJ and Spike followed Hollywood through the hatch, and they jumped into their ejection seats and put on their helmets.

They heard the warbling sound that meant that there was an incoming message.

"This is Sky King. Sky King. With traffic. Yellow Flag Two. I repeat. This is Sky King. Sky King. Yellow Flag Two."

Hollywood: "Spike, you copy the Yellow Flag Two? Bulldog, affirm?"

Spike: "That's affirmative. Yellow Flag Two, pilot. War Order checklist, Nav. I can't believe this! We are going to the biggest Dance of them all! The end of the world."

Everything became serious. They went through explosive engine start, which was used to start the alert airplane's engines immediately.

Hollywood: "Ground, pull the chocks, and get out of the way - fast. We are taxi! NAV! Confirm Yellow Flag Two!"

Graham was about to wet his flight suit.

"Nav confirms Yellow Flag Two. Taxi to the end of the runway and hold. The co-pilot is to unlock the box and remove the authentication code cards. DO NOT break open the cards at this time. I repeat. DO NOT break open the cards." Hollywood, "Roger. Nav confirms Yellow Flag Two as well as Radar Navigator. Co-pilot will open the box at brakes set on the end of the runway. We DO NOT break the cards at this time. Confirm, Co-Pilot.

"Crew, prepare for take-off."

Co, almost in a whisper: "Co-pilot confirms… unlock the box and remove the authentication codes. They are not to be broken at this time."

Everybody was scared shitless. This made the Hanoi raids seem like nothing. They were one transmission and dual authentication from nuclear war with China. That would lead to all out nuclear war. If they took off, they would leave their homes and loved ones for the last time. There would be nothing left to come back to.

They didn't taxi normally. They sped to the end of the runway.

"Tower, this is Cobalt One. We are brakes set at the runway. We are ready for take-off."

The tower controller was clearly shaken by the tone of his voice: "Roger, Cobalt One. Cobalt One is ready for take-off at one four past the hour. Hold until Sky King release. Please acknowledge, Cobalt One."

"Cobalt One acknowledges. Hold launch until Sky King release. Cobalt One out."

"Co-pilot! Get to the box and get the cards! Give one to me and one to the Radar Navigator. Bombs, do not break open the authentication code card. Confirm."

They heard all five of the other alert aircraft check in for take-off behind them. The voices on the radio were terrified.

Spike: "Bombs confirms the card to remain intact. Boys, I have never taxied with Mark 28s in the belly of the bird. This is really serious."

They waited…

C.K. McCUSKER

GETTING READY TO GET OUT OF THE ZOO

On 25 March, the POWs were measured for real clothes and shoes. On 28 March, they were told that the international press corps and the Four Power Commission were coming into the camp so that they could understand how well they had been treated as "detainees."
Screw them.

The gooks hated it when the POWs addressed each other by rank. The key for them was to break down military discipline and order. The SRO, a B-52 bombardier Lieutenant Colonel, spread the orders through the communication system that they had set up from the first day at the Zoo.

The POWs stood in the courtyard of the prison in their typical random fashion when they were allowed to do so, which was seldom.

The press arrived through the front gate, and the POWs immediately formed ranks by cell with the SRO of each cell standing in front. They stood at rigid attention. The Camp Commandant was furious.

One of the Commission members, an Air Force Colonel who was a towering and handsome man, dwarfed the gook Commandant, but accepted his salute. The camp SRO was told by the Colonel to dismiss his men, which he did immediately. They broke ranks and marched in single file back to their cells. They knew the press was coming, so they stood at the end of their bed boards in a parade rest position. The press swarmed in asking questions. Nobody answered any. Nobody said a word.

After the press left, the POWs went back to the courtyard.

D-Kid, laughing: "The gooks were ripshit when we went into formation. I looked at Tank, and he was swearing at me in gook so I mouthed 'fuck you' to him. But, of course, I mouthed it with the "ph" Phuc pronunciation instead of our pronunciation. I didn't want him to misinterpret my compliment due to a language barrier."

Tom was laughing harder and harder: "The little bastards were beside themselves when we showed the press military decorum. They were totally surprised and we…"

A press photographer had stayed in the shadows after everybody else had left.

"Messier, may I get a photo please?"

Alex turned toward her. "Sure."

Then he turned back around and dropped his pants and mooned her. She smiled and took the picture.

Tom was almost in tears: "Alex, that wasn't fair. The lady would have probably preferred a picture of one of those legendary black dicks rather than your fat ass. Call her back here and give her the opportunity."

Alex: "Fuck her."

Tom: "That's what I just said."

The camp commandant ordered the guards to break up the happiness and laughter. They did very quickly and forcefully now that the press was gone.

Nobody gave a shit. Tomorrow their 141 would be here.

Tomorrow they would *go home.*

YELLOW FLAG TWO

Cobalt One sat in the number one slot at the end of the runway, resting on the verge of nuclear war. There wasn't any chatter. The crew reviewed the War Order checklist for all positions over the IC. This could be the big game. But no one wins. Not a very good game to play, or worse, create for real. Tensions were very high. Thoughts were intense.

Graham: *God, I love her. Please keep her safe. Protect my family in Connecticut, and may they… shit, who I am I kidding? If we launch, the world ends. We never had a chance to have our babies… we never had any real time together. From one war to the one that ends the world, but would God allow this? Would He? Maybe… maybe not. God, please help us.*

Spike: *The rotten bastards are going to kill everybody on earth. If we launch, everything we know and love will be gone within minutes of wheels in the well. Remember that press interview where they asked you if you would really carry out a nuclear attack on another country if it really came to it? You said 'absolutely.' There will be nothing to come home to. Nothing. Home would be gone. When we see the bright white flash go off on climbout, everything we know and love will be gone. We will make sure the enemy has less than nothing to come home to. We will melt the bastards.*

Hollywood: *I'm not certain that I can do this. I've been trained to do it. I know how to do it. I can do it. I flew through all the shit over Hanoi. I can get us to our targets unless they get really lucky. They're dead, but why, God? Why would this ever, ever happen? Please stop it, Lord. Please.*

Co: *The Lord is my Shepherd, I shall not want. He maketh me...*

E-Jeep: *Their stuff couldn't be that good. I can get us through it and we can recover to Point Bravo. Their nukes may misfire, and we could still come home. Home might, it might, still be here. Maybe.*

Roller had his head on the deli counter. Asleep.

After almost forty-five minutes, the warbling sound started again...

SHIT! THIS WAS IT!

"This is Sky King with traffic. Repeat Sky King with traffic. All aircrews will stand down immediately. I repeat. All aircrews will stand down immediately. Taxi to your slots and shut them down. Again, taxi to your slots and shut down. This is Sky King, out."

Spike: "YIPPE-AY-KAI-AY-A MEN! WE AREN'T GOING TO END THE WORLD TODAY! THANK WHOEVER YOU PRAY TO BIG TIME, BOYS!"

Graham: "Yipee what huh? What the hell are you? Cowboy Bob? How can..."

Graham covered his eyes and choked up before he could finish busting Spike. He quietly shed tears.

Thank You, Lord. Thank You. Priscilla and I might have a chance at life. The world won't end today. Thank you.

THE BEGINNING OF "THE DAY"

29 March 73. The last release day for American POWs. It was sixty days to the day that the Paris Peace Accords had been signed. Everybody was nervous. Something would go wrong. The 141 would have a mechanical and not take off to pick them up. It would take a week to fix. Then break again.

(What they didn't know was there were three 141s waiting to launch in case one, or two, aborted on the "Hanoi Taxi" mission. The first time 141s were prepared for a "stand-by" launch. Something the B-52s did on every combat mission.)

The war would flare up in the South. Something would go wrong. The men were carrying on nervous conversations about nothing to avoid the thought of delay. Bad stuff wouldn't happen, would it? They got on the buses. This might really happen. The buses started moving. This was happening! Maybe. They weren't there yet. They weren't home yet.

On the way to JFI, they crossed a temporary bridge that had been put over a marshalling yard for rail cars. On either side of the yard were villages. The villages had fences to separate the village from the yard.

D-Kid was sitting next to Alex as he looked out the window.

"Alex, look."

Both villages' fences were completely untouched. The marshalling yard in between them was *gone*. Really *gone*. The bombs had blown everything to nothing. It might as well have been a soccer field covered with pieces of twisted metal rail ties.

Alex: "Shit. I'm good, aren't I? That rail yard was my target. I released right before they got us. You know what? I missed a little tiny siding over there [pointing]. Oh well, back to the Sim next week."

D-Kid couldn't believe his balls: "Your target, huh? What's the address, bucko?"

Alex, smiling: "One Twenty Rail Yard Lane. Hanoi, North Vietnam, Baby Bucko."

"Oh, is that right? See that sign at the end of this ditch? It says it's Thirty Five Marshall Yard. If you did this, you hit the wrong target, BUCKO!"

"Bullshit. You can't read gook! This is my yard. I remember it vividly. I turned slightly left at the IP and just right before release then hard right into a 120 knot headwind and a SAM. Then, as I was floating down to the east at about 70 knots, I went right over One Twenty Rail Yard Lane, which was brightly lit by fires that I started, so I could read the street signs, and this is it."

"It's Thirty Five Marshall. You're delirious. Why don't you stay over a few extra days and get one of those fine gook doctors that never treated you to treat you? That way you can go home even more delirious."

They got to JFI and pulled in behind the hangers because there were spectators and press outside the terminal. They would wait there until the 141, now dubbed The Hanoi Taxi, was on the ground and ready for them. The other POWs on the bus had started a very vocal betting camp about who won the Super Bowl in January. Theoretical money was changing hands rapidly.

D-Kid looked out the window and saw Walter Cronkite walking up from the rear buses. He leaned out the window: "Hey, Walter! Who won the Super Bowl?"

He just kept walking toward the bus, looking straight ahead.

"Why hell, everybody knows that…"

A very famous news broadcaster had just stopped himself in mid-sentence. He looked up directly at D-Kid: "What's your name, son?"

"Foster, Mr. Cronkite. Robert Foster. Captain, United Sates Air Force, sir."

"Well, Captain, you're going to go home today. And we can't wait to get you, and all the men on these buses, home to a very thankful Nation. God Bless you all for your service, bravery, and sacrifice."

The betting pool had stopped. Everybody that could was listening to The Voice. Cronkite looked down for a moment to gather his emotions: "To answer your question, Captain…"

He paused again momentarily and then looked directly at D-Kid. His voice cracked: "Miami, Captain. Miami won it."

The cheers and "Ah shits!" went up throughout the bus when The Voice announced the winner. Walter Cronkite raised his right hand and saluted the boy Captain. D-Kid smiled and returned the salute. Cronkite continued his walk past the buses with his head bowed slightly. He didn't want anybody to see the tears. It was unprofessional.

Then somebody yelled: "Bird in the air! Listen!"

Everybody went silent and listened. The whine. A C-141 whine. *THE Whine!!*

The Taxi, THEIR TAXI was on final! THE GO HOME BIRD!

THE EXPLANATION

The crews taxied back to their parking spots at the Alert facility. Everyone was still so shaken that there was no chatter. They all were now very aware of something that they had always known was their responsibility, but never as they had understood it before. Their job was to end the world as they and their families knew it but only if somebody else tried to end it first. Either way, it was insanity.

The crews assembled in the Alert facility. There were a lot of private and serious conversations going on. Many boys that were not at the Hanoi Dance Pavilion were now men. Suddenly, the Lizard and his staff walked into the facility and the room was called to attention.

Lizard, tongue breaking his own fly snapping record: "At ease. Are… are all six crews present?"

His Vice-Fly answered: "Yes, sir. All thirty-six are present."

Bad fly. He was wrong. Roller wasn't there. But no one cared.

Lizard: "Be seated where you can and if you can. I'm here to explain a Top Secret incident. I said Top Secret. This is not to be repeated any more than your War Orders would be, gentlemen. The incident that we all experienced one hour ago was not an exercise, as you well know. The Chinese launched thirty-six missiles simultaneously from their southeastern missile complexes at 0913 Zulu [Greenwich Mean Time]. NORAD [North American Air Defense Command] computers immediately picked up the missile launches and they determined the missile tracks as targeting the western United States. We went to Yellow Dot Two globally. We were very close to launch, but the authentication code would not have been confirmed until failsafe, as you are aware. Literally with one to two minutes to go before we released you all on a MITO War Order Mission, the Chinese turned all of their missiles downrange to dump into the Pacific. When they impacted, Sky King stood us down. Again men, this is Top Secret. I do not want wives chattering about it at the commissary. Hopefully, in our lifetimes, our children's, and grandchildren's, this will never happen again. God Willing. Dismissed."

Lizard and his staff turned and left the room.

Graham, to Hollywood: "You know what? He actually acted like a Full Colonel. He actually acted like a SAC Bomb Wing Commander. No shit. I'm impressed."

"He didn't get the job without having the capability. Believe it or not, when the times get serious, he *is* a SAC Bomb Wing Commander that is fully capable. He could fly any War Order mission himself. All six are committed to his memory. That's how good these guys are."

He turned to Graham and smiled: "That's how good *we* are too, RJ."

CHAPTER XXIV: TIME TO GO HOME, KIDS

WHEELS IN THE WELL!

The buses sat. They heard the Hanoi Taxi pull in and shut down. They all had similar thoughts.

Something would go wrong. The engines wouldn't start. The gooks would change their minds. They would find an excuse to screw up the last Hanoi Taxi departure. The last Go Home. That's how they thought.

The buses started and moved! They went around the hangers and emerged to the view of a very large group of people gathered in front of the Terminal. Many of the people were press. Some were gooks, but the predominant visual was some large U.S. Air Force and Naval Officers dressed in Class A uniforms towering over the gook captors. It was clearly meant to be intimidating to the North Vietnamese.

D-Kid: "Alex, this is scary. We might get out of here, God willing."

"Don't worry, kid. We're out of here. Look around. Given the audience we could win a good ol' bar room brawl in maybe... uh... thirty, no, maybe forty seconds. It would only take *that* long because we haven't had anything to eat in four months."

The buses stopped in front of the terminal, and the POWs got off. The SRO instructed them to form into two lines based on shoot down dates. The oldest date was at the front of the line. Everybody was nervous. The cameras were flashing. They were all silent. There was an Air Force Colonel standing at a long table. An Air Force Captain started to call the POWs' names in perfect order.

D-Kid: "Hey, Alex, I'm going to get a window seat. Even though you'll get onboard late since you malingered a day, maybe you can get one across the aisle. On the way out, I want to see what we missed in case we have to come back. Most of it will doubtless be your former targets, so if you do get a window, note them on a napkin for me. Will ya? Please?"

Alex, pretending not to smile: "You look like an alien, man. No real American could possibly have hair that red and skin that white. I'm sorry, but I'm turning you in. You're probably an IRA terrorist."

Tom was right behind D-Kid in line: "Bob, when did you actually go boots down on NV soil?"

D-Kid, puzzled: "I don't remember exactly. Let's see, I ejected at 1313 Zulu, the bird hit the ground at 1317 Zulu while I was in silk… oh, I guess around 1325 Zulu. I had to guide the chute hard in order to land safely into one of Alex's target areas. I knew they would be open fields in the middle of nowhere with no gooks within 20 miles."

Alex, now smiling: "You little shit. I missed nothing. Nothing! Plus, I didn't break anything until the next night. So you were lucky I wasn't behind you on 18."

Tom, stepping in front of D-Kid in line: "Just as I thought. I raced to the ground in order to evade and escape and went boots down at 1322 Zulu. Therefore my shoot down minute dates yours."

"You guys are both complete assholes, but unfortunately, I love you like brothers, so I can't kill you."

"CAPTAIN ROBERT FOSTER."

This was it. D-Kid had a chill. A good chill. D-Kid snapped back around and started to walk quickly toward the tall Colonel. He walked up to the man and saluted: "Captain Robert Foster, reporting for duty, sir."

The Colonel returned the salute and then grabbed D-Kid's hand: "Welcome back, Captain. You're going home now."

D-Kid turned and started walking toward the back of the 141. The ramp was down, so they could walk on easily. He glanced to his left. Cronkite was on the tarmac and waved welcome back. The Air Force personnel got thick as he approached the bird. It was an impressive group - CMsgt's, Colonels, and L/Cs wearing Class A uniforms or Class B with decorations. Everyone smiled and tried to shake D-Kid's hand. He did all he could to accept the handshakes, but they became overwhelming.

These people really care about us. God I'm thankful and proud to be an American.

He walked up the ramp into the back of the aircraft. Doctors and nurses immediately greeted him: "Captain Foster, are you alright? Any pain or injuries right now?"

"No, sir. I'm OK. The bruises, cuts, and rope burns healed for the most part a month or so ago."

The doctor pulled him aside as other POWs boarded. The other POWs were cornered by doctors or nurses as well.

"How's your head, Captain. Are you all here? You feel OK? You know what I mean."

"At about 1313 Zulu on 18 December I was almost certain I was going to die, either from mid-air explosion, fire, ejection, or more likely when the gooks murdered me when I landed. In the following days after capture, there were numerous occasions that I was again almost positive that I would be killed. I literally said goodbye to my wife twice. When I was finally photographed, I knew then that it would be harder for them to kill me. I was relieved, but I still knew they could kill me if they wanted to, and a number of them would like to kill any one of us. Now I just walked onboard American property, Doc. American property that flies, and it's going to fly me out of here in a very short time. To answer your question, Doc, my head is on Cloud Three. As soon as we get to altitude, it will go up to Cloud Nine."

The Doc, smiling broadly: "Welcome home, Captain. Your head's just fine."

They finished loading the men and buttoned quickly. The 141 pilots fired the engines and started a fast taxi. Everybody was buckled and quiet.

Something would go wrong.

They heard the throttles advance and then firewall as they rolled. The plane was full of aviators. They all knew what to listen for, and that's exactly what they were doing as they whispered to one and another. They weren't out yet. The gooks could have one last SAM left and be waiting for them. After all, they were the last Hanoi Taxi, and the gooks knew exactly what the flight route was because they had mandated it.

The nose came up. Airborne! The wheels went in the well! A spontaneous cheer arose. Some cheers sounded as though they were over tears.

The crews on the Go Home birds were not allowed to know any of the POWs they were taking out. But they were clearly the best that MAC had. The Major flying this bird knew exactly when to speak and what to say. He had said welcome aboard and good to have you back just prior to taxi. He said nothing on climb out. In about twenty minutes, when they were at altitude, he came back up.

"We just went feet wet, gentlemen."

Now another spontaneous cheer. But no one left their seat. They knew what to listen for, they knew exactly. It came minutes later.

"Gentlemen… WE JUST CLEARED NORTH VIETNAMESE AIRSPACE. WELCOME BACK!"

With that, they really erupted in cheers. The seat belts came off. The cigars were lit. Spirits soared. Moments later, the AC came back on. "Gentlemen, there're some guys that waited to greet their brothers. They have now come in to welcome you guys home. If you look out on both the port and starboard sides of the aircraft, we have six fully armed Air Force Phantom F-4E's flying formation with us. They've been 'hanging out' for the last two hours or so in case the gooks tried to make a statement at the end. There're about twenty more support aircraft in the air in addition to these guys. Chief, when the guys get to the windows, please let me know, the lead on this flight wants to make a statement to our passengers."

"Roger, Wilco."

The ex-POWs crowded the few windows that were available. A number went to the cockpit. The 4s were on either side of the Go Home bird. Three on each side - and very close.

The Chief called the AC: "OK, boss. As good as we can get."

"Roger, Chief, thanks."

"Gunbarrel One, we have the guys in the seats. You're on."

"Roger that. Give them our best. Gunbarrel One movin' now."

Each F4 in trail on either side of the Go Home bird responded. The first two on either side waggled their wings, hit afterburner, banked hard away and up above the 141, and disappeared. The next two pulled up abreast with the cockpit and executed the exact same salute. Finally, the last two came abreast and waggled their wings, but this time they hit burner, turned vertical, and went out of sight in seconds.

The passengers were cheering and crying. *They were on their way home for sure! They were free. Thank you, Lord!*

D-Kid sat back down in his seat with tears welling in his eyes and thoughts of home racing through his mind.

THE PI HOMECOMING

The pilot of the 141 touched down so smoothly that he even impressed the plane full of Aviators. Another cheer arose.

The 141 AC: "Gentlemen, welcome to Clark Air Force Base in the Philippine Islands. You are on American soil. [more cheers] We own Clark by irrevocable treaty. We'll be taxiing for about two minutes and then I'll shut this old bird down in front of the Clark Terminal. By the way, you just flew out of North Vietnam on the first One Four One ever built. Again, welcome out, guys. You're free."

The aircraft was immaculate. It couldn't be that old. It couldn't be tail number 001.

They taxied to the terminal and shut down in front of it. D-Kid looked out the window and saw a sea of blue and suits waiting. It was a bit intimidating.

Shit. All I want is a shower, clean clothes, three... no... four cheeseburgers, a good beer, and then a phone direct to my bride for a couple of hours. I don't need any damn speeches.

The passenger door opened, and an Air Force full Colonel came onboard. "Gentlemen, welcome back and God Bless you all. This is the first stop on your trip home to your families and a very grateful Nation. Yes, the Nation is grateful for your service despite what you may have been led to believe by the media. Now, there's a large number of brass and press outside. Don't be overwhelmed. Just walk straight to the two Flag [General] Officers, one Air Force and one Navy, at the end of the red carpet, salute, shake their hands, and turn immediately starboard. The next guy you see in uniform will be a guy that is the same rank as you and the same branch of service. In many cases, they are the same specialty. They are your escort officers. They will know you immediately by sight since they have studied your photographs. They will accompany you here and on your trip home. Anything you need that isn't there already, just ask them. Please de-plane as you boarded, by shoot down dates." The Colonel saluted the cabin full of officers that he outranked. "Again, God Bless you guys and welcome back."

The now free POWs lined up and slowly de-planed. They were all still a bit anxious and desperately hungry.

They could hear the band.

D-Kid walked off the 141, and cameras flashed everywhere. He walked straight to the Flag Officers and performed the necessary salutations and greetings and then turned right and was met within ten paces by his new guide to America.

"Welcome back, Captain. I'm Captain Jim Kibby, and I will assist you on your trip home."

Kibby was in a Class One uniform. He had Nav Wings. He also had a DFC on his chest and many other decorations.

D-Kid smiled broadly and shook Kibby's hand. "Great to meet you, Jim. Really great."

They started to walk toward the waiting buses. "I'm starving, as you might expect. I also need a phone line to the States as soon as I can get one. If you can help me with that, I would greatly appreciate it."

Kibby, smiling: "Your wish is my command, Captain D-Kid. Robbie can't wait to hear your voice. By the way, Spike, Bulldog, Sluggo, Blackjack, Hollywood, E-Jeep, and The Fake Major Wildman all send their regards and a collective welcome back. They said they were going to 'drop in' to Scott to welcome you home once you get there."

D-Kid, sitting down in the bus next to Kibby, was astounded, "Boy, Jim. You have done your homework. Wow, man. I'm impressed."

"It's considered a great honor to be in this job. Almost every guy in my Squadron at Nellis applied the day the notice went up. I lucked out and got a slot. Of course I did my homework. I'm a crewdog, Captain."

"Gs or Ds?"

"Neither. F4E Wild Weasels. Two tours in the backseat. I thought that we killed the SAM site that got you. The little bastards had rolled in a new one. We killed that one on 23. Sorry we were late."

"I thought you said you were a crewdog."

"I did. I was. I am. There is a crew of *two* in an F4, as you know."

D-Kid looked more closely at Kibby's decorations after the bus started moving. The DFC on his chest had three "Oak Leaf" clusters on it. The guy had *four* Distinguished Flying Crosses. This guy was a major league hero.

Jesus. This guy was one hell of an escort.

But D-kid had his foremost priority on his mind. "Jim, put the cheeseburgers second. I need to get to a phone."

Kibby interrupted him before he concluded his request: "You need to get to a phone to call Robbie. There's a phone waiting for you at our next stop."

"You are on top of everything, Jim. Thanks so much."

"You're very welcome. It's easy to think through it because I can empathize. It's the old saying: *there but for the grace of God go I.*"

The bus pulled up in front of the Visiting Officer's Quarters, which had been vacated entirely to make room for the POWs. Kibby led the way off the bus and then turned and gently grabbed Bob's elbow. "Follow me. You're already checked in, so to speak. I have a phone waiting for you in an office, literally being guarded by a giant Airman I 'recruited.' You can talk as long as you like, and I'll bring you half a dozen cheeseburgers, a beer, and some ice cream."

The 'giant' Airman standing in front of the door really was a giant. He had to be 6'5" or more. As they approached, he came to attention and saluted. "Welcome home, sir. May I shake your hand, sir?"

Bob shook his hand after returning the salute and thanked him. He was left in the office alone and made *the call.*

Despite the hour at home, he knew Robbie would be waiting. The phone answered:

"Hello?"

D-kid was choking up: "Hi, Honey. It's me... I love you so much! I'm free!"

The Pirates had all assembled at Bulldog's house at 0200 to watch, in real time on his new Zenith TV, D-Kid and their other brothers land at Clark. Sluggo was convinced he had purchased the TV for Bulldog with his 4-5-6 donations. Priscilla had made an elegant buffet for the guys, most of which was saved from devastation after a pre-event sneak attack by their yellow "semi-lab" Yankee.

They cheered every POW that was announced as they exited the aircraft and were announced, but roared when D-kid finally got off. Their plans to welcome home D-kid properly were in place.

Throughout the celebration, Spike had cheered for the brothers, but otherwise seemed unusually introspective and quiet. After the last man had exited and been announced, the gathering was wrapping up.

Bulldog went over to Spike as the others thanked Priscilla for being a great hostess: "What's up with you? You're a bit quiet for being in a Spike suit. Is the real Spike really here?

Spike took out one of his horrible little cigars and headed for the door. "Yeah, he's here. I was just thinking too much."

"What about? This is a time for real celebration and thanks. The war was over officially when the last POW walked off the 141. You survived over 400 missions. You, especially, should be really thankful that all this shit is over with."

As he walked to the door with his Nav and good friend, he decided to reveal his thoughts so the shock wouldn't be so devastating later. "Bulldog, I would have been jumping for joy... but it isn't over. It's in "pause." It's going to continue on a covert basis, and I have this sneaking suspicion... that we're gonna be there. Sorry, my friend, but that's what I really believe. It's unfinished."

Spike thanked Priscilla, and Graham followed him out into the cold. As they shook hands, Graham disagreed. "You're wrong this time. You're finally wrong."

"I hope so, Bulldog. I really do."

Walking back inside his real thoughts pervaded the bullshit. *He's right, and you know it. He's always right! Damn!* **What** *causes this!* **What** *is starting to piss me off.*

EPILOGUE: THE FORTUNATE SONS

SACRAMENTO, CALIFORNIA, APRIL, 1982

After four moves in his eight years at GE, Graham had been lucky and gotten a transfer to his wife's hometown. It was a Sunday morning, and Graham was sitting in his second favorite chair in the den sharing the Sunday paper with Bob Foster. Bob was in Graham's favorite chair, but he was a guest in his home and a crewdog, so he would never know.

Bob and Robbie Foster were visiting for the weekend with their children. RJ had been filled in the night before on some of the horrors that Bob had experienced at the Hanoi Hilton. He could relate to that experience perhaps better than anybody that hadn't been there as a POW. It was enlightening, but he never wanted to hear it again.

The sun shone brightly through the eastern wall of the den, which was two stories of floor to ceiling glass. The men's serenity was broken, not unexpectedly, when the three little boys, ages four, five, and six, came charging into the room. Stephen Foster and Graham's two boys were dressed in their "pirate" costumes, which they had put together the night before after watching *Long John Silver* on television.

Graham: "Boys! Boys! Slow down, and stop running around with those swords."

Bob: "Stephen! Come over here please."

Too late.

They stopped and Stephen "stabbed" the younger Graham with his sword, which was, fortunately, soft plastic. He started crying and hit Stephen in the head with his sword. He started crying as well and ran to his father.

Graham: "Cameron! That was not nice. You give me that sword. Coleman, you give me yours too."

Graham had named his sons after the two Naval Aviators that had given their lives saving his. The boys would know of their namesake's heroics when they were old enough. The boys came over and gave their father the swords. He pulled both onto his lap to comfort them as Bob did the same with his son.

"Boys, stop crying, or you'll wake your baby sister. Now calm down, and we'll read the funnies."

Cameron, the youngest: "I don't want to read the funnies. I want to go get a parrot like Long John's."

Graham, gently hugging his sons: "Maybe we'll go to town after breakfast and church and look for some parrots."

That immediately stopped the crying.

Bob: "That's good, Bulldog. Do have any idea what parrots cost?"

"No, but I'm almost positive that they have limited availability such that we'll have to get s-t-u-f-f-e-d ones."

Bob smiling: "Roger, got it, Nav."

Stephen: "Can I get a parrot too, Dad?"

"Sure. We'll look after church."

Cameron: "Let's go now. Brebus later." He tried to get off his father's lap to head for the garage and was gently pulled back. "The stores aren't even open yet, son. Relax, and read the funnies with Daddy."

Priscilla came into the room. The kitchen opened into the den: "Good morning all! You listen to your fathers, boys, and enjoy the funnies. I'll make pancakes."

Graham: "Gee boys, mommy's going to make her special pancakes. The ones with the burned side down."

Priscilla playfully threw a kitchen towel at her husband: "Don't listen to him, Bob. That was just that once, and I didn't have any more batter."

Bob, laughing: "Yeah I understand. I get those now and then as well. It's always the 'ran out of batter' ploy."

Robbie and Mary, their eight year old daughter, came in the room: "I heard that, Robert. Now you'll get them for sure. Good morning, everyone!"

"Good Morning."

Coleman: "Daddy, did you ever know any pirates?"

Graham was taken aback by the unexpected question from his son. Memories flooded into his mind: "Yes. Yes I did. Air Pirates… Yankee Air Pirates."

Stephen: "Daddy, do you know any Air pirates too?"

"I sure did. I knew lots of them."

The wives had overheard the conversation between their husbands and the boys. They knew what had crossed their husbands' minds the minute Coleman had asked the question. They looked at each other as if to debate intervention and then remained quiet. Mary was busy with the pancake batter.

Coleman: "Are those pirates that fly? Did they have big flying pirate ships?"

"Yes, son. They were good pirates that had to fly in a war. They flew in very big pirate ships."

Cameron, squirming to face his father and get details: "How many of the Yankee Air Pirates did you know, daddy? DID YOU KNOW LONG JOHN!?"

He turned to Bob, almost laughing: "No. But I knew Captain Kid… that is… Captain D-Kid."

D-Kid laughed: "Your puns still suck, Bulldog."

The wives seemed more relaxed and amused.

Stephen: "Daddy, did you know Captain Kid too!?"

Graham quickly answered the question: "You're sitting on his lap."

Stephen looked up at his father: "What?"

"I'll explain later, son. It takes a while." Bob just smiled and then scowled at Graham.

Graham was gentle in his tone: "We knew many of the Air Pirates, boys. Not Long John, but we knew ones called Spike… and Sluggo… and Wildman… and Blackjack… and Hollywood… and Alex." He paused momentarily: "Your daddy and Uncle Bob were Yankee Air Pirates, boys."

Stephen looked up at his father again: "When were you a Yankee Pirate, daddy?"

"I came home a little less than 10 years ago, son."

The women didn't like the direction of the conversation again. Priscilla intervened: "Does anyone want bacon?"

No one answered. Little boys, all five of them, were talking about pirate stuff.

Graham, almost laughing: "Uncle Bob's ship sank in a big battle, and he kinda had to jump overboard really fast, and the horrible squinty eyed enemy pirates, called gooks, captured him."

Priscilla: "RJ! You stop that! Right now!"

Bob cracked up. "Yes, boys. I jumped overboard at about 500 miles an hour because the ship was on fire."

Stephen: "Daddy, when the enemy pirates captured you, did they make you a prisoner?"

"Yes, they did. Fortunately for your daddy."

Robbie didn't like the pirate talk now either: "Stephen, wash up for breakfast, please."

Cameron, swiveling around in his father's lap and looking at him: "You was a pirate! Boy! Did you have a parrot? Did you have a s-sward?"

"No son, we didn't. We had things far more important than parrots and swords."

Cameron: "What's more important than a s-sward for a pirate? How did you fight bad guys?"

Graham, reflecting: "With great skill, courage, faith, and camaraderie. That's how we fought and survived, son. Those were our swords."

Priscilla, noticing the faint hint of tears in her husband's eyes, intervened: "You boys go wash up for breakfast. Hurry up. The pancakes will be done soon." Graham gently nudged his boys off his lap to follow their mother's directions. Stephen jumped down as well after hugging his father.

Coleman, turning back to his father: "Can we be Yankee Air Pirates when we grow up, Daddy?"

Graham looked at Bob, and he could tell that both of them shared the same thought: "God, we hope not, boys. We were Pirates so you would never have to be."

LEST WE FORGET....

"What we still don't understand is why you Americans stopped the bombing of Hanoi. You had us on the ropes. If you had pressed us a little harder, just for another day or two, we were ready to surrender! But we were elated to notice your media was definitely helping us. They were causing more disruption in America than we could in the battlefields. We were ready to surrender. You had won!"

-General Võ Nguyên Giáp,
Commander of all North Vietnamese forces, in his memoir

"Experience proves that the man who obstructs a war in which his nation is engaged, no matter whether right or wrong, occupies no enviable place in life or history. Better for him, individually, to advocate 'war, pestilence, and famine' than to act as obstructionist to a war already begun. The most favorable posthumous history the stay-at-home traitor can hope for is oblivion."

-General Ulysses S. Grant

FACT AND FICTION

"GLENN 'THE CREWDOG GENERAL' CHARLES" IS ACTUALLY BRIGADIER GENERAL GLENN SULLIVAN.

The portrayal of General Sullivan's sacrifice for his crews is true. He was never promoted and left SAC as a direct result of the actions he took on behalf of his men. In 1974, he left the Air Force and spent the remainder of his life in community service.

General Sullivan, went 'wheels up' for the last time and touched down on "The Great Concrete Runway in the Sky" in 1998.

"BOB 'D-KID' FOSTER" IS ROBERT CERTAIN.

Robert's (now The Reverend, Dr. Colonel (Chaplain), USAF, Ret.) experiences as a POW were portrayed in the novel as they actually occurred. He was a key contributor to the novel as well as an invaluable sounding board for the author. Colonel Certain was honored to conduct President Gerald Ford's funeral.

After repatriation, Robert enrolled in the Seminary and became an Episcopal Priest, while still on active duty in the Air Force. He then served as a chaplain in the USAF reserves, rising to the rank of Colonel. He later led the Episcopal parish in Palm Desert, California, the largest parish in the San Diego Diocese. Robert is currently Rector of an Episcopal parish in Marietta, back home in Georgia. Robert's memoir *Unchained Eagle* currently in publication (and available at www.deedspublishing.com) recounts the time from his shootdown and imprisonment though his Seminary and Priesthood. Perhaps most importantly for those that have been in combat, and for their loved ones, it recounts his years of struggling with PTSD [Post Traumatic Stress Disorder], its terrible effects, and how to recognize and overcome it. Unfortunately, many veterans of the Iraq and Afghanistan Wars will suffer from PTSD and not even realize it.

"SPIKE WILSON" IS GF 'SPIKE' ANDERSON.

Spike flew over 400 combat missions on tours that began in 1966 and ended in 1972 after "The Dance" ended the war. Over 100 of those missions were spent sitting in an ejection seat next to the author, and he still remained sane. He was passed over for Lt Col, undoubtedly as a result of some of his antics.

Spike retired from the Air Force eight years after Linebacker II, and began a new career in the nuclear engineering and construction field. He currently consults in Nuclear Quality Assurance and has apparently changed his behavior since no cows have yet to be found in our nuclear facilities… emphasis *yet*.

"RJ 'BULLDOG' GRAHAM" IS THE AUTHOR, C.K. MCCUSKER.

Like Robert, he was an instructor StanBoard navigator and led the wave the *second night* of Linebacker II on the same flight plan that Robert had been shot down on the night before. Robert and CK met by pure chance over 30 years after they had flown the Hanoi raids. The introduction led to a great friendship and inspired CK to finish *Pirates* while intertwining and novelizing Robert's experiences as a counterpoint to the wild antics the Pirates pulled whenever they had a chance. Those antics were a diversion to keep them from thinking of Robert's, and the rest of the POWs, fate, who they might join on their next mission… if… they lived through the shootdown and the capture.

Most of the other characters portrayed actually did exist but their names were changed to protect the author and publisher.

As stated earlier, the majority of the events described really happened. I will leave it to the reader to determine what was based on fact versus fiction. You will probably guess incorrectly.

ALSO AVAILABLE FROM DEEDS PUBLISHING